VIRTUOUS WANTON

"What do you want, Ian? It is very late, and I am not in the mood for your recriminations." Ariel sat up in bed, clutching the bed linens around her.

"I have respected your virtuous rebuffs long enough, madam," he sneered, his voice harsh and cruel as he raked her with a sensual stare. "You wanted a marriage of convenience. Well, it is convenient for me to make it a reality."

He turned her face toward him and kissed her brutally, his hand roaming down the neck of her nightgown.

Trying desperately to elude his touch and seeking mouth, Ariel fought ineffectually against him as he forced her back upon the pillows.

Despite herself, she felt herself responding to the urgency of his desire, her limbs leaden and her flailing hands stilled under his skilled handling.

He chuckled bitterly. "What a little wanton you are, Ariel, under that starched facade."

THE BEST IN REGENCIES FROM ZEBRA

PASSION'S LADY   (1545, $2.95)
by Sara Blayne

She was a charming rogue, an impish child—and a maddeningly alluring woman. If the Earl of Shayle knew little else about her, he knew she was going to marry him. As a bride, Marie found a temporary hiding place from her past, but could not escape from the Earl's shrewd questions—or the spark of passion in his eyes.

AN ELIGIBLE BRIDE   (2020, $3.95)
by Janice Bennett

The duke of Halliford was in the country for one reason—to fulfill a promise to look after Captain Carstairs' children. This was as distasteful as finding a suitable wife. But his problems were answered when he saw the beautiful Helena Carstairs. The duke was not above resorting to some very persuasive means to get what he wanted . . .

RECKLESS HEART   (1679, $2.50)
by Lois Arvin Walker

Rebecca had met her match in the notorious Earl of Compton. Not only did he decline the invitation to her soiree, but he found it amusing when her horse landed her in the middle of Compton Creek. If this was another female scheme to lure him into marriage the Earl swore Rebecca would soon learn she had the wrong man, a man with a blackened reputation.

BELOVED AVENGER   (2192, $3.95)
by Mary Brendan

Emily shivered at the sight of the thin scar on the sardonically handsome features of Sir Clifford Moore. She knew then that he would never forget what her family had done to him . . . and that he would take his revenge any way he could. This time it was Moore that held the power—and Emily was in no position to defy his wishes, whatever they might be . . .

SWEET TEMPEST   (2143, $3.95)
by Lauren Giddings

Despite his reputation as an unscrupulous rake, Amberson was not a man likely to shoot a woman—even if she *was* dressed like a ragamuffin and intent on robbing his coach. So his remorse was considerable when he discovered that the highwayman he'd wounded was actually a beauty named Tempest. Letting her out of his sight would be unbearable, turning her over to the authorities, unthinkable. So the cynical lord did the only thing possible . . . he took her to his bed.

Available wherever paperbacks are sold, or order direct from the Publisher. Send cover price plus 50¢ per copy for mailing and handling to Zebra Books, Dept. 2239, 475 Park Avenue South, New York, N.Y. 10016. Residents of New York, New Jersey and Pennsylvania must include sales tax. DO NOT SEND CASH.

An Officer's Alliance

VIOLET HAMILTON

ZEBRA BOOKS
KENSINGTON PUBLISHING CORP.

ZEBRA BOOKS

are published by

Kensington Publishing Corp.
475 Park Avenue South
New York, NY 10016

First printing: December 1987

Printed in the United States of America

Chapter One

Ariel felt the first damp flakes of snow borne by the cold wind blowing off the Danube to her right settle on her pelisse as she hurried down the Kärntner Strasse. Her cloak, a serviceable though unflattering brown wool, did not protect her adequately from the late October flurries, and she felt the wet begin to soak through her thin boots. Dusk was creeping over the regal stones of the Hofburg ahead, casting strange shadows over the baroque palaces and churches as the weak autumn sun set over Vienna. As she turned into the Herren Gasse, few passersby noticed the tall girl hurrying on her way, intent as they were on reaching the warmth of cafés and homes in the growing twilight. A few barouches rattled on the wide avenue, and Ariel gave a rueful thought to the comfort of traveling in such style.

She had been dispatched to change the ribbons on a new bonnet, by her cousin and employer, Fiona, Lady Mackenzie, a cool elegant beauty who had been roused to a rare burst of indignation when the offending piece of millinery had been delivered that morning to the mansion Fiona's husband, Sir Robert, had rented near the Lobkowitz Palace, where Beethoven's first compositions were played. This errand was just the latest in a long list of petty humiliations Fiona had imposed on her cousin, and it was all Ariel could do to accept without protest the orders Fiona so negligently gave to her indigent relative.

Shivering with cold and irritation, Ariel scurried up the broad marble steps of the Mackenzies' temporary home and waited impatiently for the butler to admit her. After long moments Franz, the Austrian butler, opened the door, his impassive face showing none of the distaste he felt at being summoned by this lowly member of the household. Handing Franz her sodden pelisse, which he accepted gingerly, Ariel wondered if she would be fortunate enough to secure a cup of tea or even some hot chocolate to ward off the chill. This was not one of Fiona's "at home" days, so probably the mistress of the establishment was tucked up in her boudoir reading the latest French novel, heedless of Ariel's exposure to the elements. Little chance of tea if that was the case, Ariel concluded ruefully.

"Lady Mackenzie is having tea in the salon," Franz offered a bit spitefully, knowing his mistress would not welcome the interruption. But Ariel greeted his news with relief. Perhaps she would get her hot drink after all. Smoothing her dark hair, which was severely confined in a huge chignon, she wiped her feet surreptitiously on the Aubusson carpet and decided to take a chance. Ignoring the butler, whom she suspected believed she should be having her refreshment below-stairs, if at all, she crossed to the huge mahogany doors of the salon and entered without ceremony.

The couple standing before the fireplace, whose blaze brightened the somber imposing room, started and turned at the opening of the door, interrupted in what might have been an intimate embrace. For a moment the woman's blue eyes shone with anger and then she greeted Ariel smoothly.

"Oh, Ariel, there you are. Were you able to insist on the new ribbons?" she asked languidly, making clear the intruder's proper position in this household. A tall blonde in the fashionable mode of the popular English beauty, the woman appeared to be in her late twenties, although it was difficult to tell her real age so skillfully was her pale complexion, now slightly flushed, powdered. She was dressed in the latest stare in an azure blue Levantine silk, bordered across the extremely low décolletage with alençon lace. Sapphires gleamed at her throat and altogether she made Ariel feel the veriest dowd in her plain garnet wool gown. None of the dislike and insecurity Lady Mackenzie inspired showed on Ariel's face as she faced the couple, waiting for the introduction Fiona seemed reluctant to give.

"I do not believe you have met Captain Ian Montague, of the King's Dragoon Guards. Ian, this is my husband's cousin, Ariel Frazier, who is

7

making her home with us for the moment," Lady Mackenzie explained casually, determined to make Ariel's position clear.

Ariel looked straight into the hot smoldering dark eyes of the tall officer, who straightened from his casual pose against the mantel to bow briefly. A rake of the first water, Ariel decided, her glance passing coldly over the tall well-muscled figure of the officer dressed in the green uniform of the famous regiment. So this was the latest of Fiona's conquests, but a bit more unmanageable than most, she concluded. His gaze met hers briefly, then the lids dropped over the disturbing eyes, and he dismissed her as of no account. He saw a tall dark-haired girl, younger than his hostess but in no way her rival for beauty, noticing her closed face and rigid stance. A poor and undeserving relation, no doubt, was his obvious assessment. He need not bother being more than casually polite. Infuriated by his drawled, "Your servant, Miss Frazier," Ariel barely nodded in his direction and turned away from the couple to seek the tea table.

"Yes, Fiona, I changed the ribbons, and the bonnet will be delivered tomorrow. It is perishing on the boulevards and I would like some tea," she said, ignoring the officer and taking up the silver pot standing on a nearby table. She cared little how Fiona conducted herself, but she pitied Sir Robert, so occupied with the business of the Congress which had brought them to Vienna that he had little time to spare for his beautiful wife. Not that Fiona seemed at all interested in her

dedicated husband and his governmental responsibilities, being more than content with the
adulation she inspired in the crowds of young
officers who surrounded her at every ball and
reception. This was obviously her latest beau, a
cavalry officer who would be better employed in
the field than playing lapdog to a society beauty,
Ariel conceded scornfully. But then Ariel, the
orphaned daughter of one of Wellington's veterans, had little use for the military attachés
desporting themselves in Vienna's drawing rooms,
fawning after the idle matrons who encouraged
their attentions. The officers ostensibly were here
to assist Lord Castlereagh, the British Foreign
Secretary, and his staff in the delicate peace
negotiations, but they seemed to have plenty of
leisure for dalliance. They would be better off
spending their time on maneuvers, although now
that Napoleon had been incarcerated in Elba,
there was little military action to test their mettle.
How her father, the late Major Ronald Frazier,
had despised these poodle fakers, and she agreed
completely. For all his address and fine uniform,
Ariel doubted this one had ever faced a French
battalion on the ramparts. Staring at him beneath eyelashes which veiled her hazely green
eyes, she saw now that he was not handsome in the
accepted mode, but he had an air of lazy
magnetism, an experienced virility which appeared out of place in a lady's drawing room, but
no doubt served him well in a boudoir. His black
hair, brushed into a style now favored by the
fashionable regiments, framed a high-boned

9

tanned face which testified to his Celtic heritage. The sensual mouth, although drawn tight as he frowned in displeasure at her scrutiny, was evidence of his nature. There was little of gentleness or courtesy in the glance he raked over her. She flushed a bit at his mocking stare and turned away, aware that she held little attraction for him.

"We will be attending Count Metternich's ball this evening and Robert insists that you accompany us, Ariel. Do you have an adequate gown?" Fiona asked, her manner implying doubt at the prospect.

"I think I might find something, but it is not at all necessary, you know. I would be quite content to remain here," Ariel said, embarrassed at having her position so insultingly defined before this disturbing officer.

"No, Robert was quite definite," Fiona answered, and turning to Captain Montague with an artificial laugh explained, "Robert thinks I need a chaperone, I can't think why, and Ariel has become my watchdog."

"I am sure Sir Robert realizes what a jewel he has found and fears to have you wrested away, not at all surprising," Ian replied smoothly, looking at Fiona with what Ariel considered a speculative lascivious stare. Well, whatever his plans for a liaison, Ariel did not intend to interfere. She knew that Robert had taken her into his household to watch Fiona and see to it that she behaved herself, but Ariel found the role of spy not to her liking. If the amorous Fiona wanted to tempt fate by taking this hot-blooded Celt to her bed, Ariel felt that was her business, but Ariel believed that Fiona was not one to throw her cap over the windmill no matter what the provocation. She flirted and teased but Fiona cared too much for her life-style and Robert's well-filled pockets to endanger her position. Still, she just might take a chance, for she was obviously mesmerized by the disturbing officer, far different from her usual tame cisce-boes. Captain Montague would not be put off by a few kisses or innocent clandestine trysts, Ariel vowed. A dangerous animal, and Fiona had best beware. Still, it did not concern her if Fiona chanced her fate with the man. They were welcome to enjoy the delights of the bedroom if that was what they intended. She finished her tea and excused herself, yearning for a hot bath and a few minute's respite from her cousin's company. Bidding the pair a curt farewell, she left them to their tête-à-tête.

Upstairs in the bedroom, which had now been her refuge for several weeks, Ariel thought bitterly of her situation. Even this luxurious retreat had been secured only by Sir Robert's efforts. Fiona, no doubt, would have preferred to banish her to the servants' cold quarters. From the beginning, when Robert had rescued her after her father's death in one of Wellington's last battles, at Toulouse, she had found her place in her cousin's household one of humiliation and resentment. Accustomed to the brusque kindness

11

of the serving officers, she found the studied gallantries and foppish manners of the military delegation in Vienna disgusting. Not that she was the recipient of their attentions. A penniless orphan did not attract these experienced philanderers, nor would she welcome their pursuit. Peeling off her damp wool dress, she wrapped herself in her shabby dressing gown and rang for a maid. Most of the servants were aware of her anomolous position in Sir Robert's household and served her grudgingly, but today she was fortunate, and toasting her toes before the fire after her bath, she felt a bit more comfortable. She dismissed the chambermaid, indicating she would need no assistance in dressing for the evening's gala. Certainly she had little choice of gowns. Her wardrobe was not equipped for the lavish life the Mackenzies led in Vienna. She thought the society of the city frivolous and uncaring of the serious business which had brought the British, Germans, French, Italians, and Russians to Vienna to settle the fate of Europe. The Congress was making little progress in carving up Napoleon's conquests and paid little heed to the needs of the poor people who had to live under the iron hand of the new rulers. When she had protested to Sir Robert about the slow progress of the negotiations and the lack of interest in the needs of the people, he had reproved her, but he had admitted that the Congressional delegates seemed to spend more time dancing and dallying than deciding the peace of Europe. Had her father given his life for these popinjays to parade their power? The thought of his sacrifice made her angry and her fine green eyes flashed with indignation. How she missed him, much more than her gentle French mother, whom she barely remembered, having been just seven when Anne-Marie had succumbed to a virulent fever and slipped from a life to which she was not at all suited. Ariel had enjoyed following the drum when her father removed her from the strict convent in the Devon countryside in which she had spent her early years. The rugged privations of the Peninsular campaign had not daunted her spirit, although many a time she had gone hungry and dirty on those long forced marches. Now those carefree days were behind her and she was forced to temper her rebellious spirits to the rigid proprieties which Fiona so hypocritically imposed. Oh well, once back in England, after this Vienna visit, Ariel could look about for suitable employment, which would at least enable her to claim a little independence and remove her from Fiona's orbit.

Looking over her scanty wardrobe, in preparation for the evening's ball, Ariel shook her head ruefully. Finally she removed an emerald silk of a fashionable cut, not her usual style but a reject of Fiona's, who had decided it did not compliment her fair beauty. The plain material, with little adornment, accented her creamy white skin and matched her eyes. She shrugged as she tried to

13

confine the deep black straight hair into a fashionable coiffure, and then abandoned her efforts, returning to the style she found easiest, a severe heavy chignon, which brought her high cheekbones into prominence and showed her long elegant neck to best advantage. Ariel saw little in the cheval mirror which pleased her and, as she had little vanity, did not realize that her uncommon beauty had an attraction all its own. She had, before her father's death, little interest in the impecunious officers who had crossed her path, and had never considered marriage as an option to the dreary life which now stretched before her. Frowning, she realized that even the occasional invitation to balls and routs which now came her way would disappear once she found employment as a governess or companion, situations which would, no doubt, become irksome but would at least spare her Fiona's condescension. She should never have consented to joining Sir Robert's household, but numb with grief at her beloved father's death, she had acquiesced tamely to her cousin's demands. Still, this respite, unhappy as it was, had given her time to recover and plan for the future. Sir Robert would be returning to London with Castlereagh in a few weeks when the Duke of Wellington succeeded him, and then she could settle her future. She spared a thought for the doughty general and wondered how he would adapt to the frivolity and inanities of Vienna life. She admired him extravagantly and hoped he might move Metternich, Talleyrand, and the arrogant Tsar of all the Russias into some sort of

14

compromise, but she doubted even Wellington could force those intransigent, jealous gentlemen into agreement. Giving a last dissatisfied glance in the mirror, she took up her reticule and closed the door on her bedroom and her troubled thoughts.

Chapter Two

The Metternich ball heralded the official opening of the Congress, which had been delayed some
weeks by the intransigence of the four powers
who would determine the peace of Europe. Prince
Clemens von Metternich, Austria's Chancellor,
besieged by France's Charles Talleyrand, had
already agreed to several postponements in order
to allow the delegates of the various countries to
make their preliminary depositions. Now, in the
waning days of October, it seemed the Congress
would never get down to business. Instead the
ministers, crowned heads, and their various
entourages preferred to dance and drink away
the hours, indulging in a hectic round of pleasures, rather than settle the suzerainty of the
various peoples who had been despoiled by
Napoleon. Tonight's ball was just another lavish
display, intended to distract and soothe the
restive members who had been sent to the
negotiations by their governments. However

frustrated the Austrian Chancellor was by the annoying delays, no sign of his discomfort was evident as he greeted his guests at the head of the grand staircase which graced his sumptuous palace on Ballhausplatz off the north end of the Hofburg.

Ariel had to admit that Prince Metternich was a man of considerable address and charm, and she could quite understand that the rumors of his various amours had to have some foundation in fact. Tall, with clear blue eyes, a broad brow, an aquiline nose, and a gentle mocking smile, he completely dominated his dowdy, dumpy wife, Eleanore Kaunitz, whom he had married for her money and position. The Princess's only assets were her wealth and a certain shrewd cleverness, which was spent in furthering her husband's ambitions. She ignored the tales of his various affaires with Caroline Murat, Queen of Naples; Napoleon's sister, a tempestuous beauty; and Laure, Duchesse d'Abrantes, a Portuguese belle. A dynastic marriage based on ambition and power, Ariel decided, but she could not deny the Chancellor's charm as he greeted her with all the courtesy he extended to nobler guests. Fiona had tried her best to lure Metternich to her side, but he treated her with a cool politeness, and accorded Sir Robert a more enthusiastic welcome. Once in the huge ballroom, Ariel was left to her own devices, for Fiona, looking ravishing in a gown of silver tissue over a white silk underdress and the Mackenzie diamonds, was soon surrounded by suitors. Sir Robert, mindful of his duty, introduced Ariel to some of the Austrian and Russian officers who asked her to dance. She exchanged commonplaces with the stiff young men who led her through the steps of the mazurka, and the waltz, still considered shocking by members of England's haut ton but eagerly embraced by the more sophisticated Viennese society. While she answered the polite questions of her dancing partners, she was far more fascinated by glimpses of the Congressional luminaries, all of whom were attending the Metternich ball.

Cynosure of all eyes, his tall figure standing out amongst the crowd of dancers, was Tsar Alexander I, dressed in his white military uniform emblazoned with orders. A strange mixture of Western notions of tolerance, liberty, and fraternity and the autocratic will which distinguished all the Romanovs, he possessed a striking magnetism. Weird tales were told of his sexual exploits. At sixteen, he had married Elizabeth Alexeyevna, a fourteen-year-old German princess who at first admired her impressive husband but soon became a victim of his exotic fancies. Rumor had it that he had insisted she take as a lover Adam Czartoryski, of the Imperial Guards, while the Tsar entertained himself with his official mistress, Madame Naryskin, who bore him several children. Ariel had learned from Fiona that the Tsar, who had brought his Tsarina with him to Vienna, also kept a new love, a pale graceful woman, Julie de Krudener, in a villa outside the city, where he spent most of his evenings. The Tsarina had accompanied him this evening and

Ariel wondered how she endured the public humiliation her husband inflicted upon her. Then there was Prince Talleyrand, with his monkey face and conniving ways, who used occasions such as these to further his machinations with the Tsar's evil genius Count Araktcheef, the Minister of War, a spiteful man who enjoyed flogging his serfs, and Baron Hager, the Austrian King Francis's chief of the secret police, whose spies were everywhere. Sir Robert had told her ruefully that to thwart Hager the contents of the wastebaskets at the British Embassy were burned every evening because Castlereagh distrusted Hager's minions. Even the chivalrous and attractive Metternich was not above petty spying for his master, King Francis, and he, too, was notorious for his mistresses. Ariel despised them all, seeing little hope for the peace of Europe in the hands of such libertines and self-seekers. Only Castlereagh remained sacrosanct, a man of unusual probity and domestic fidelity. He was dancing now with his wife, who was covered in diamonds and wore his Order of the Garter in her hair. In Castlereagh lay the only hope for the successful resolution of the Congressional negotiations.

Eating supper with a taciturn British aide de camp in the grove of orange trees later that evening, Ariel noticed Fiona whispering coyly to Captain Montague under the eyes of Sir Robert. Poor Sir Robert, so harried and so helpless to curb his wife's extravagances and flirtations. Ariel felt little genuine affection for her cousin. He was not a man who encouraged it, but she respected his devotion to his country and his duty. Of middling height, with thinning brown hair and cold blue eyes, he was not a figure to inspire warmer feelings, but Ariel naively believed Fiona owed him loyalty if not love. She could not accept these marriages for wealth and security, untouched by genuine emotion. Her father had loved her mother devotedly, and even after her tragic early death, had never eased his loneliness with casual affaires.

At nineteen Ariel still believed in romantic love, although she feared she would never experience it. Her austere manner and what Fiona called her "missish" ways did not allow her to indulge in the dalliance which other young women found so attractive. How she hated the hypocrisy, the pretense, and the philandering which engaged this motley crew, more intent on satisfying their desires than in attending to the grave matters which had brought them together. What would the great Duke of Wellington think when he arrived to take over Castlereagh's responsibilities? Would he, too, be content to waste his time with these careless pleasure seekers? Ariel sighed and chided herself for her puritanical reactions. She should be more grateful to her cousin, to the home he offered even if she disapproved of the world to which he had introduced her.

Shaking off her disgust and uneasiness, she turned to the aide de camp and tried to engage him in unexceptional conversation. The young man, a former artillery officer seconded to the

British embassy, had found her heavy going, and was somewhat surprised at her sudden attempt to respond to his polite overtures. Really she was a quite good sort, and strangely attractive under that subdued manner with a certain elegance of face and form. And she danced divinely, the young man conceded. He was quite annoyed to have their tête-à-tête interrupted by Ian Montague, who appeared before them and, bowing correctly, requested a waltz.

Ariel, looking into the hot mocking eyes of the Scots officer, intended to refuse, but would not give him the satisfaction of thinking she cared one way or the other about his approval. She acceded with a certain stiff graciousness, and they took the floor, now crowded with hectic dancers, twirling to the music of the spirited orchestra.

"I suppose you disapprove of all this gaiety, Miss Frazier," Ian Montague suggested, his tone sardonic as he skillfully steered her through the crowd, his grasp firm and provocative. Surely it was not necessary to hold her so close.

"Not at all, Captain Montague. Although I wish the Congressional delegates took their duties a bit more seriously," she replied, unwilling to meet his jeering eyes. She concentrated on staring at his epaulettes on the dashing green dress uniform. Obviously Fiona had told him her husband's cousin was a prim dowd who held high moral views. She would not apologize for her beliefs to this womanizing libertine.

He laughed somewhat bitterly. "But the delegates prefer to do their negotiating among the distractions of the scented bejeweled lovelies at grand affaires such as this, and who can blame them. So much more pleasant than confining themselves in some stuffy chamber to argue out the demands of warring nations," he taunted, reversing her cleverly through the sea of dancers.

Refusing to rise to his bait, Ariel conceded that perhaps some progress could be made in the relaxing environment of such entertainments. She could not help but wonder at his own role in all of this. "Were you in the field, Captain Montague?" she asked.

"Oh, yes, I fought all through the Peninsula, up to Toulouse with the Iron Duke," he offered reluctantly. "I would much rather face a French battalion than suffer through these frivolous affaires, although you may find that surprising. Lady Mackenzie tells me that your father fell at Toulouse. Please accept my sympathy. But perhaps he was the fortunate one," he concluded wryly, looking about the lavish ballroom.

"Yes, he would agree. But I miss him dreadfully, and I quite enjoyed following him through the campaigns, for all their horrors. Life seemed much simpler then," she confided almost despite herself, for she could not scorn an officer who had shared those tragic struggles.

"Quite a change from sordid bivouacs to this glittering throng. But you must learn to accept your changed fortunes, I am afraid," he replied, his tone gentle and understanding.

Ariel looked up into his eyes, from which all the mockery had fled, and for a moment was struck

23

by his sincerity, but then she remembered Fiona and his reckless pursuit of that languid beauty. Whatever his gallantry on the battlefield, he seemed quite content to pursue a different foe now.

"You disapprove of me, Miss Frazier. This assignment was not of my choosing, you know. But a serving officer goes where he is sent. Orders cannot be disobeyed, you know," he reproved, as if he cared what she thought.

"Of course, you are quite right. It is none of my business how you conduct your life, Captain Montague," she answered tartly, annoyed that for a moment she had felt in charity with him, forgetting his allegiance to Fiona.

They finished the dance in silence, and once it was over, he escorted her punctiliously to the gilt chairs lining the ballroom, where she waited for her next partner. He did not ask her to dance again and she saw him later squiring Fiona and bending an attentive ear to that beauty's avid gaze. Obviously Fiona was smitten with the gallant captain, but she should beware. He was no tame cat to bow to her imperious demands, and she might find herself enmeshed in a situation she could not handle if she was not careful. Dismissing the pair from her mind, Ariel sighed. How tedious this all was, and the beginnings of a headache throbbed as she endeavored to act the delighted guest. The evening stretched monotonously before her, a kaleidoscope of color, motion, and the hard beat of the music. She was relieved when Sir Robert appeared to escort her home, informing her that Fiona was not yet ready to leave the festivities. He would send the carriage back for her if Ariel wanted to accompany him now. He looked tired and disgruntled. Obviously he had had enough of the ball. Ariel could only agree.

The Metternich ball proved to be but a passing interlude in Ariel's restricted life in the Mackenzie household. Fiona did not encourage her companionship at the various receptions, routs, and balls that followed in the ensuing days, and Sir Robert was too preoccupied to worry about his relative and her duties. Ariel suspected that Fiona was seeing quite a bit of the reckless Captain Montague, but as she never mentioned him, Ariel could only surmise that the affair was marching on as Fiona appeared to be in a complacent humor, always a sign that the current amour was progressing satisfactorily. The Congress opened officially on November 2, and Sir Robert was very occupied with the various preliminary conferences, a demanding task since Talleyrand had forced his presence on the delegates dividing up Europe. Ariel found it difficult to contain her impatience about her own plans, and felt reluctant to disturb her cousin with her request to return to England. While she had traveled in the train of the army during the war, she had lived day to day, never worrying about the future, but now she wanted to settle her life away from the patronizing and frivolous company Fiona enjoyed. She doubted that her cousin's wife would miss her presence in the household. Still she must contain herself for a few weeks, at least until affairs became more settled.

Her days were spent in doing small commissions for Fiona, in walking through Vienna's avenues and parks, and trying to efface herself as much as possible. On Fiona's at home days, she was required to be present, to pour tea and chocolate and murmur inane pleasantries to the company, who paid her little heed. Rarely did the fashionable throng notice the tall quiet girl whose position in the Mackenzies' splendid abode seemed little more than that of a paid domestic. Ariel's pride was affronted, but after all, she did not want to be welcomed into such an ephemeral society. She was annoyed that her dissatisfaction made her so irritable and ungrateful, but she could not deny her feelings.

Preparing to retire one evening, she came to grips with her problem, and determined to put a better face on her situation. Soon the Iron Duke would be arriving to replace Castlereagh, whose absence from London sorely tried Lord Liverpool's government. Wellington was expected within the month, and by the new year, she would be in London with the Mackenzies. As she brushed her long black hair she wondered whether Fiona would continue her reckless liaison with the dashing captain once they had all returned to England. Lately her cousin's wife had appeared more distraught and hectic in her pursuit of pleasures. Perhaps the affair was not proceeding to her tastes, or perhaps Sir Robert suspected the pair. Well, it was not her concern. She put down her hairbrush and took up her novel, prepared to woo elusive sleep by reading in bed, a luxury not often available to her.

Settling beneath the covers, she soon became engrossed in Jane Austen's *Pride and Prejudice*, which had come out in London the year before. She found the story engrossing, the author's sardonic description of the Bennet girls' efforts to find husbands amusing if not completely to her understanding. Suddenly she was interrupted by her door crashing open, and Captain Montague entered her room without ceremony, dressed in his breeches and shirt, carrying his uniform jacket and his boots.

"Good evening, Miss Frazier," he greeted her wryly as he deposited the boots on the floor and sank down on the bed, eyeing her boldly. "I must apologize for this sudden intrusion, but I am afraid I had no choice."

Before she could protest, he had taken her in his arms and begun to kiss her with a thoroughness which spoke of vast experience. Struggling to wrest herself from his arms, she had barely begun to fight when the door opened again and Sir Robert entered her room.

Her cousin, still dressed in his greatcoat and obviously in the grip of a terrible anger, raised his eyebrows in disgust at the sight of the pair, Ariel with her unbound hair flowing over her cambric nightdress, and Captain Montague in an equally disheveled state.

"What is the meaning of this, Ariel? Why is this mountebank in your boudoir at this time of

27

night?" Sir Robert sputtered, his usual composure overset, as he was obviously subduing a terrifying emotion, so foreign to his usual dignified aloof mien.

"As you can see, Sir Robert, you interrupted us while I was making love to your cousin. Rather embarrassing to have an audience, and I quite realize the impropriety of the occasion, so what excuse can I offer?" the officer explained audaciously, tightening his grip on Ariel's shoulders brutally and warning her with a glance from his smoldering dark eyes.

"What you are doing is quite apparent, Captain, but I think you forget yourself. My cousin could not welcome your disgusting advances, I am sure. You are a cad, sir, to force yourself on an innocent girl. But she is not unprotected," Sir Robert raged, his anger not abated by the officer's insolent manner.

Ariel, stunned by the events, started to deny the obvious construction Sir Robert was putting on the incredible scene, but before she could open her mouth, Ian Montague covered it with his own, his whole attitude one of a conqueror who expected little resistance.

Raising an eyebrow at her shocked attempts to disengage herself, he turned to Sir Robert, not relinquishing his hard grip, and explained, "I suppose you feel obligated to make a demur, Sir Robert, acting in loco parentis to your cousin, but I can only plead an overriding passion, which fortunately, I believe the lady returns," he offered as if in understandable mitigation of his daring.

"Ariel, I cannot believe you are acquiescing in

28

this disgraceful scene," Sir Robert replied, his tone skeptical and unbelieving.

"Of course not, Robert. I had no idea that—" she began, but was interrupted by the captain.

"I have become quite overcome by my feelings for your cousin, Sir Robert, and I have every reason to think she returns my emotions. But could we not discuss this in the morning? I have become most fatigued by all this excitement, and somehow your appearance has quite dampened my ardor for the moment," he said smoothly, ignoring Ariel's sputtering denials.

Sir Robert faced with the unbelievable did not know what to reply. He had expected quite a different outcome from his sudden return to the household. He had thought it was Fiona the captain was pursuing, and had expected to surprise them in a compromising position, but he had never suspected that it was Ariel who was involved with the cavalry officer.

He hesitated as Captain Montague rose leisurely from the bedside and retrieved his boots, tugging them on with an unconcern which infuriated both spectators to his insouciance. If the captain was indeed Ariel's lover, Sir Robert must see to it that the rogue did the honorable thing, but he feared that would not be so easily accomplished.

Frowning in distaste at the pair, he struggled to regain command of events. Ariel, beside herself with humiliation and anger, struggled to extricate herself from this damning situation. "Robert, please let me explain," she began, flushing and stammering in her mortification.

"I must agree with the captain. I think explanations must await a more auspicious time. In the morning tempers will have cooled and we can resolve this affair. I am sure the captain intends to fulfill his obligation to you. I will see you in my study after breakfast tomorrow," he said repressively, raking her with a disgusted glance.

"Not to worry, sweet, we will come about," the captain, whose toilet had now been completed, reassured her, ignoring her indignation. "I will come around to lend you countenance. For now, I must bid you both good evening." And bowing briefly, he sauntered past Sir Robert and left the room without more ado.

"I am really very disappointed in you, Ariel, but I think it best to sleep on the matter," Sir Robert reproved, now that the disturbing officer had left them, a certain relief evident in his manner.

Ariel, aghast at what had happened, tried weakly to explain matters, but her cousin, obviously tired of the whole embroglio, bid her a curt good night and left her to muse over her transgression.

Alone, she sputtered with anger and dismay. How could this have happened? She had little doubt that the captain had no intention of claiming an undying passion for her. He must have fled Fiona's boudoir at the unexpected arrival of Sir Robert. She knew her cousin had expected to spend several days at the Tsar's villa on the outskirts of Vienna. What had impelled him to return so suddenly in the middle of the night? It was obvious he had feared to find Fiona in a compromising position, and instead had discovered his prim cousin was the recipient of the captain's favors. Had Fiona sent the officer into her bedroom to escape her husband's wrath? She was perfectly capable of extricating herself from danger in such a fashion, but Ariel would have thought the captain might have faced out Sir Robert, if he really loved Fiona. Oh, what a terrible coil. Her reputation ruined, her cousin insisting on the graceless cad making the honorable amend, and she had sat by like a witless ninny and allowed herself to be used in such a fashion. Remembering Ian Montague's practiced advances, she flushed and trembled. Why had she not fought harder? She could not excuse herself with the thought that the whole affair had taken her by surprise, astounded her by the hot-blooded demand of his lips and arms. For a moment she had almost responded to his impassioned caresses. What a charlatan he was, able to evidence such convincing ardor on demand. Obviously he cared little what humiliation his actions had caused her. How could she possibly tell Robert the real reason he had found the captain in her bedroom? Tossing and turning for the rest of the troubled night, Ariel could see no way out of the impasse, the dilemma of which she was the innocent victim. Finally toward dawn she fell into a restless sleep, exhausted by her emotions and contemplation of what the morning might bring.

Chapter Three

Ian Montague awoke in his rooms the next morning with an aching head and a gloomy remembrance of the disastrous events of the previous evening. His affair with Fiona had just progressed to an interesting stage when she suddenly started with dismay, hearing the arrival of her husband, whom she had told Ian was safely away for the night. Befuddled with passion and brandy, he had surrendered to her tearful pleas and rushed headlong into Ariel's bedroom, not counting the cost if he was discovered. He had attempted to argue with Fiona that he must face up to her cuckolded husband, but she became quite hysterical, pushing him into the corridor and indicating he must save them both by compromising Ariel. Sober he would not have heeded her remonstrances, but his head had been far from clear. Damn Fiona for pushing him into this mess. Curse her and all women who made seductive approaches and then backed off when their

33

security was threatened. He should have learned by now. He had experienced narrow escapes from irate husbands before, but she had been most alluring and most persuasive. And he was bored with the endless round of pleasure seeking in Vienna. He excused his pursuit of Fiona by that ennui. But he had never intended to jeopardize his career by tangling with Sir Robert. And he regretted using Miss Frazier as a scapegoat. He had no recourse now but to offer for her. How had he come to such a pass? Light flirtations, even sensual liaisons, were considered the prerogative of the officers posted to Vienna, but neither participant in these affairs expected to be called to account. Decent reticence and a certain established set of rules surrounded the conduct of these transient amours, but in his case passion had overridden judgment. He had been fairly caught out, and by a man whom he knew would not allow him to evade the consequences of his rash entrance into Ariel's boudoir. Naturally she was appalled at his behavior and an innocent victim of his stupidity. By pretending the colorless companion was the object of his lovemaking, he had embroiled them both in an untenable situation. He could discover no way out of the coil but to offer her marriage, a truly damnable outcome, and certainly Fiona had not been worth this disastrous conclusion to their infatuation. He should have resisted her lures, for certainly, cad though he was to admit it, she had made the first overtures.

Still he was as guilty as she. He could have

34

rebuffed her, but it seemed such an easy conquest. He had been involved in sticky romantic tangles before, since most women found his dark Celtic looks and his smoldering eyes irresistible. Heedless of the havoc he wrought when he became tired of the fleeting object of his lovemaking, he had gone his way, intent on his military duties, the flirtations nothing but an idle relaxation from the heat of battle. Few could deny him when he was determined on bedding them but he had made it a rule to steer clear of proper young virgins. Marriage was not a condition he had anticipated for many years, if ever. He had cleverly avoided being pushed into the parson's mousetrap before, and now he was embroiled in the very situation he had scorned, with a girl who cared no more for him than he did for her. As he tried to bring his befuddled wits to bear on the problem, he barked at his batman, causing that genial fellow to step cautiously. As he dressed, and ate his breakfast beefsteak gingerly, he racked his brains to think of some way out of the situation but to no avail. Sighing, he donned his jacket in preparation for the visit to Sir Robert's house, but before he could leave, his man interrupted his dark musings to inform him that he had an unexpected visitor. Half relieved to postpone the dreaded interview, he would have welcomed any delay, but not the one which now promised even more trouble.

"Good day to you, Ian. I suspect I am far from being welcome, but our father insisted I make this tedious journey. Your recent dissipations have reached his ears and he has sent me to insist on some accounting. You can no longer rely on excusing your shocking behavior by the excitement of the battlefield. The war is over and Father believes it is time you settled down and behaved in a manner more suited to your position," Viscount Arnold Montague greeted his young brother with a disapproving glance, assuming his usual air of superiority.

"This is a surprise, Arnold. How did Father ever prevail upon you to make the journey? I thought you had both washed your hands of me. I am sure you are disappointed to hear that I did not fall at the barricades and thus spare you further embarrassment," Ian replied cynically, having little affection for his brother, the pattern card of respectability and probity. Arnold Montague, the heir and eldest son of the Earl of Strathcairn, had never caused their parent one moment of disquiet. Slightly above average height he had none of the dashing charm of his brother. He dressed soberly and suited his actions to his apparel. His coat of black superfine was unfashionably cut and his linen unexceptional. He wore no jewelry and the most mundane of waistcoats. His pale gray eyes, over the high-bridged Strathcairn nose, looked at life grudgingly, condemning most of what he saw, and his younger brother most of all. They had never been friends, even in their youth, as six years separated them, and their tastes were dissimilar. Arnold was his father's favorite, a dutiful son who punctiliously fulfilled his duties as heir to the Strathcairn estate and pursued an unexceptional job in the War Office. He despised

Ian's rakish style, and refused to credit his bravery in battle. He made no allowance for their disparate temperaments and, Ian suspected, encouraged their father's disdain of his younger son.

"I have brought a letter from the governor and a warning that unless you comply with his wishes, he will stop your overgenerous allowance. You can defy him, of course, you have a lot of experience in going your own way, no matter how embarrassing this is, but I think you will find it difficult to live on your pay. No doubt you are in debt again," Arnold criticized, his tone repressive, his lip curling at the contemplation of Ian's libertine ways. "You can no longer plead the danger of war to excuse your excesses," Arnold sniffed, looking at his brother with some satisfaction as he contemplated the demands their father had made. He handed Ian the letter which was the reason for this irritating journey across Europe.

Subduing the angry words which rose to his lips, Ian smiled sardonically at his brother, refusing to rise to his baiting. He read the letter quickly. The Earl of Strathcairn wasted few words. Unless Ian married, preferably the daughter of their neighbor, Lord Atherton, a demure miss barely out of the schoolroom, and mended his actions, he would be cut off without a penny. He tempered his demand somewhat by congratulating Ian on his recent exploits with Wellington, but stated he was no longer prepared to excuse his son's careless philandering, gambling debts, and other transgressions. It was marriage or he would not supply the money

37

necessary to purchase Ian's next promotion in rank. He preferred that his son resign from the army now that Napoleon had been defeated and returned to the ancestral acres. If not that, then at least marriage to a suitable young woman, and an assumption of some responsibility to his name and station.

Ian laughed as he read the letter, infuriating his brother. Well, the two of them, his father and brother, would say that he had his just deserts. Forced into an unwanted marriage by the very sins of which they accused him. How hateful to be coerced into the situation his father insisted. But at least he need not, could not, wed the insipid Maria Atherton.

"How convenient that this ultimatum should arrive at such a moment. I am indeed going to be married, but not to Maria Atherton. I am on my way now to offer my hand and heart to a lady of unimpeachable virtue, whom you will both find more than acceptable," he sneered, raising his eyebrows at Arnold, who stood stolidly by, awaiting his opportunity to protest. Well, at least he had startled Arnold out of that odious complacency which he enjoyed.

"And may I ask the name of this fortunate lady?" Arnold replied, his lips thinning at the thought of some undesirable parti. He could not acquit his brother of foisting some demirep upon the family, knowing his predilection for such women.

"Her name is Ariel Frazier. She is the orphaned daughter of one of Wellington's officers, and the cousin of Sir Robert Mackenzie, seconded to Castlereagh from the Foreign Office. No doubt you are acquainted with the estimable Sir Robert," Ian returned coldly.

"Yes, I know Sir Robert. I cannot believe that he will give his approval to the match. Your reputation has preceded you, even to Vienna, I vow." Arnold was unwilling to admit that his brother could contemplate matrimony with any respectable female.

"Well, we will see. I am about to call on the gentleman, who expects me to offer for his cousin." Ian eyed his brother with barely concealed dislike. What a pompous pettifogging creature Arnold was. So sure of his own position and so critical of any other.

"Do not let me keep you. I can only conclude that you are entering the wedded state reluctantly, probably because you have compromised the girl. And I suppose you think a decent marriage will ensure you the position on Wellington's staff that you covet," Arnold concluded, now heartily disgusted that he had wasted his time and energies on this journey.

Cocking his shako at a rakish angle and smiling cheerfully at his brother, Ian left his rooms, eager to put distance between him and Arnold, realizing that his arrival had only compounded his troubles. Now he had no choice but to offer for the chit. Until this unexpected complication, he had hoped that he might brush through the coming interview without committing himself to marriage. God knows he had taken every care in the

39

past to avoid just such a mess, ignoring the debutantes and virtuous girls dangled before him and confining his attentions to ladies who understood what he wanted. Well, no doubt Miss Frazier was no more eager for the match than he was, and might extricate them both from this contretemps.

Ian frowned as he strode through Dom Grasse, and across the square before the great medieval church of St. Stephen's, down the Kärntner Grasse, and to the left toward the Mackenzies' temporary mansion home. The walk in the brisk early November morning did little to clear his head, which still pounded unmercifully from last evening's excesses and the meeting with his brother, but little of his discomfort showed in his tanned, cleanly shaven face. He paid little attention to the beauty of the palaces and government buildings which lined his path, but his soldier's eye noticed, not for the first time, the crumbling fortifications which had failed to keep Napoleon from entering the city some years back. Inadequate and in poor repair, the redoubts were typical of this charming, irresponsible, and fascinating city, whose king could barely afford the lavish entertainments which he hosted nightly in the regal Schönnbrunn Palace beyond the inner city's environs. The Austrians were a plaguey lot, trimming their sails to the prevailing political winds, little assistance as allies, and a dashed nuisance. While he enjoyed the dissipations Vienna offered, Ian Montague scorned the feckless society which preferred to dance rather than negotiate.

He paused for a moment before the impressive palace which housed the Mackenzies, feeling his stomach lurch sickeningly at the thought of the coming interview. How could he have let his warm flirtation with Lady Fiona bring him to such a pass? Well, there was no evading the consequences. Straightening his shoulders beneath the heavily braided green uniform, he marched up the steps as if going into battle. And indeed the emotions were similar.

None of the young officer's trepidation showed on his face when he entered the library where Sir Robert and Ariel awaited him. He greeted his host with his usual insouciant air, and bowed briefly over Ariel's hand, his eyes raking her with an intimate, almost insulting stare.

"There is little need to waste words, Captain," Sir Robert opened the interview with a repressive frown, seated behind the large desk which gave him a commanding position. "I believe you have come to offer for Ariel's hand, and she has no recourse but to accept."

"Well, I would not force the lady into an untenable stand. Last night, I fear, I was somewhat carried away both by her charms and an inordinate amount of brandy. Normally I would not think of such outrageous behavior." Ian smiled at the pair, hoping to lighten the grave atmosphere.

Ariel, watching him from beneath her eyelids, could scarcely believe his attitude. Was he so accustomed to seducing women that he considered it a matter of little importance? What a

41

scoundrel he was, his much-vaunted charm now exercised in extricating himself from his own imprudent actions. Did Robert really believe he had intended to seduce her, when it was quite obvious that for the past few weeks he had been pursuing Fiona with every sinew? She had suffered through a rather nasty interview with Fiona before the equally distasteful encounter with Robert this morning, and she heartily wished the three of them to Jericho. She had no intention of wedding such a rake under duress. Rather take up a post as a scullery maid before entering into such an alliance.

"I am prepared to accept Captain Montague's apology for his disgusting attentions last night, and prefer to forget the whole business," she said with some hauteur. He needn't think she was grateful for his casual dismissal of last evening's events. Before she could rush into speech, Sir Robert interceded.

"I think you must listen to the captain's offer, Ariel. If any word of his behavior, and yours, became common gossip, your reputation would not be worth a farthing. Vienna society may be dissolute but there are some things which will not be countenanced. I had no idea you had been conducting a liaison with this scapegrace. I am ashamed that you could conduct yourself so."

Before Ariel could protest, Ian sent her a speculative glance, noticing her flushed cheeks. Would she reveal all and push Sir Robert into challenging him? No coward, he had little fear of facing the wronged husband across a dueling ground but the scandal would ruin his career. Damn, but the girl was quite attractive under that demure air. This might not be such a distasteful task after all, bringing that prim statue to life. Before she could make any explanation, he hastened to put his offer.

"I regret exceedingly that I have compromised you, Miss Frazier, and I am eager to offer you my hand and heart." He tendered the proposal with a mocking air, waiting then for her eager assent. Surely the girl would not be such a pea goose as to refuse him. No such luck. She was probably hanging out for a husband, obviously living on the charity of her cousin. She could not have expected to net such a catch.

"No doubt you think I should be grateful for your condescension, Captain, but I have no intention of wedding you. Robert, this scandalous situation was not of my making. I have as little interest in becoming Captain Montague's wife as he has of wedding me. This only reinforces my intention to return to England and find some respectable employment, which should not be too difficult if we ignore this whole affair, and you give me a testimonial," she insisted, her temper rising at the way these two men hoped to settle her future without any consideration of her own wishes.

"I don't believe you will be able to keep this . . . this escapade a secret, Ariel. Servants talk, you know. But I can see there is no use in my arguing with you now. Perhaps Captain Montague can persuade you of the necessity of this

43

marriage. I cannot in good conscience allow you to go off to some position in England where you will be forced into some impecunious employment or worse, no matter how much you deserve it," Sir Robert argued. "But now I must leave you as I am overdue at the Hofburg for a conference."

Ariel, watching him gather some papers into a bundle, conceded bitterly that naturally her future, her reputation, her welfare mattered far less to him than the affairs of state which he considered his chief responsibility. He left hurriedly after giving the couple a scornful stare.

"Sir Robert is quite correct, you know," Ian argued. "However disagreeable the thought of matrimony with me is to you, I don't believe you have a great deal of choice. Somehow I can't see you as a meek companion to some doddering dowager, or teaching some country squire's brats." He gave her a wicked grin, lounging against the mantel, obviously amused by her childish objections.

"I think you refine too much on the effect of gossip. And you cannot want this marriage any more than I do, Captain Montague," Ariel replied, determined not to let him see how his arrogance and careless indifference angered her. This ruthless devil was too accustomed to getting his own way, and she was no grateful supplicant for his favors.

"Unfortunately I have a great deal more experience than you in the ton's ways, and I, too, have a reputation to consider. Although I am sure you are convinced that I take the seduction of virgins in my stride, I assure you I feel some compunction about the difficult position in which I have placed you. I owe you some gratitude for not revealing to Sir Robert the real object of my visit last evening."

"You did not seduce me. I doubt very much if you have ever given me a second glance, and if Fiona had not chosen this despicable way of extricating herself from difficulty, you would not now be offering me a marriage neither of us wants," Ariel snapped.

"Oh, I don't know. You are far from unattractive, my dear. You would certainly pay for dressing, and you are an uncommon type with hidden depths, I'll warrant," he countered outrageously, not one whit upset by her disdain.

"Let us have no more of this fruitless conversation, Captain Montague. I refuse to discuss it further. I will not marry you. You have done the proper, but you cannot force me to the altar," Ariel responded, not assuaged by his mocking appraisal of her charms, and conscious that she was looking far from her best in an old blue morning gown.

"I can see there is no moving you, but I think before many days have passed you will regret your refusal. I will bid you good morning as I see my presence is only annoying you." He bowed curtly and left abruptly.

Ariel gasped back a protest at his sudden departure. She had expected he would argue more vehemently, but no doubt he was only too eager to leave before she changed her mind. Very lowering to her self-esteem, she thought a bit grimly as she contemplated what lay ahead. This humiliating position was none of her making, but she would be the one to suffer. Fiona had escaped any retribution and now the perpetrator of her trouble was allowed to continue his womanizing without any discomfort. Her only revenge would be to confess all to Robert, but pride, and gratitude toward her cousin, prevented her from doing that. Well, she would just have to suffer stoically whatever was in store. She could not believe that the story of what Robert referred to as "the escapade" would soon be the on dit of every fashionable gathering. Surely what had happened could be kept between these walls. She could rely on Captain Montague to keep silent about this infamous conduct and certainly Fiona would not want the matter broadcast. Whatever Robert's suspicions, he would gloss over the implication if he wanted to keep his marriage intact. What hypocrites they all were, and she could not be absolved from guilt. Oh, why had she ever come to Vienna? She should have refused Robert's invitation, knowing she was unsuited to this shallow tawdry social life. Sighing, Ariel left the library for an interview with Fiona. She had promised to let her know how Sir Robert had handled the situation. It would give her great satisfaction to see that lady suffer, and the disreputable Captain Montague, too, but she doubted she would enjoy that revenge.

Chapter Four

Ariel's faint hope that Ian Montague's invasion of her bedroom, and the construction put upon that shocking incident, would pass unnoticed by Vienna society was soon dispelled. Emerging from St. Stephen's Church one afternoon two days after the event, she was cut dead by one of the doyennes of the Congress, the Princess Esterhazy, wife of the Austrian ambassador to England, whose social prestige was unrivaled. That afternoon Fiona had suggested Ariel absent herself from Lady Mackenzie's "at home" as her presence would titillate the gossips, and she would feel a veritable pariah. Ariel, furious that Fiona could be so irresponsible, and ignore her own guilt in the affair, had no recourse but to agree, although she would dearly have liked to embarrass her cousin's wife and all of Vienna by brazenly parading about as if there was no foundation for their suspicions. Fiona's haughty reminders that Ariel owed them some gratitude for rescuing her from poverty or worse did little to soothe Ariel's anger at her invidious position. With little to do but gossip and speculate, the avid rumor mongers were having a field day. As usual, it was the woman in such affairs who suffered. The only satisfaction Ariel gained was the knowledge that Fiona's affair with the libertine captain had come to an end, an outcome Fiona found frustrating in the extreme. At least Sir Robert was now convinced his wife had not betrayed him. In this conclusion Ariel felt some relief from the general sending to Coventry which was now her lot. Although Robert continued to treat her with the grave courtesy which had been his wont, she was only too aware of his displeasure and disgust at what he thought were her abandoned ways. Of Captain Montague she saw nothing, a cause for some satisfaction, she decided, unaware she was deceiving herself.

Her daily life, which before had offered little happiness, was now almost insupportable, but before she could put her plans of escape into action, she received a visitor who completely overset her firmest decision. Four days after the episode with Captain Montague, as she was counting linen for the household, the butler announced that Lord Castlereagh had called and requested her presence in the drawing room. Even Franz was impressed by the august Foreign Secretary, and Ariel found his manner amusing even as she speculated about the unprecedented attention of England's chief delegate to the Congress. Surely he had matters of graver moment than an interview with Sir Robert's lowly cousin.

She entered the drawing room, allowing none of her surprise at this unexpected caller to show on her well-schooled features.

"Good morning, Lord Castlereagh. I fear I must have misunderstood the butler. He insisted you had asked especially to see me," she greeted the Foreign Secretary in puzzlement.

Lord Castlereagh's well-bred features showed no disgust or scorn as he returned her salutation with equanimity.

"Your servant, Miss Frazier. I remember your father well. I was with Wellington during the last campaigns and was much impressed with Major Frazier's bravery and dedication to duty. You must mourn him, but have pride in his exploits, I know." Lord Castlereagh smiled at her with the charm he could exercise on occasion.

"How kind of you, Lord Castlereagh. Of course, I do miss Father dreadfully. And I miss following the drum with him. Life was much simpler then. I know what a relief it is to have finally settled Napoleon but I wish my father could have been spared to me." Ariel responded to any appreciation of her father, for in her new life there was no one to confide and comfort her as he had.

"I know your present situation is an unhappy one, compounded by the spiteful gossip which can only cause you great pain," he offered, his manner all sympathy.

Her pale complexion reddening at the reference to the recent episode, Ariel tried to think of something to say, to explain her innocence, but she was tongue-tied. How dreadful that this distinguished cabinet officer knew of her shame.

"It is because of your father, and because of the gossip, that I have come to request your help. I believe I have found a way of extricating you from what is now unendurable, and at the same time relieve me of a burden," Castlereagh explained gravely, careful to ask for no explanation and casting no judgment.

"I do not understand, Lord Castlereagh, what you want of me," Ariel replied, puzzled by his diffident approach.

"I know, as a soldier's daughter, you would want to cause confusion to our late enemies. Unfortunately, even with Napoleon on Elba, his supporters have not ceased in their conspiracies and attempts to bring to naught all our efforts to settle the peace of Europe. I have every reason to believe that at this moment a plot is being hatched in London to rescue that madman and even to assassinate Wellington. Already the Duke has narrowly escaped death at the hands of a disgruntled enemy, and we cannot expect the conspirators to abandon their plans after one failure," he explained, a troubled frown settling over his distinguished features.

Ariel said nothing, waiting for whatever Lord Castlereagh wanted of her, although she was puzzled that the Foreign Secretary would take such pains to discuss his responsibilities with her.

Studying her with a thoughtful air, Castlereagh seemed reluctant to continue, almost embarrassed at what he was about to request. Then he continued.

"Vienna is a hotbed of gossip, which can come as no surprise to you, and Captain Montague's imprudent behavior the other evening has now become the current on dit, on the tongues of every silly woman in the city. I know nothing of the real events, and you owe me no explanations, but I have talked to the captain, who assures me he has done the honorable thing and offered you marriage to save your reputation, and you have unaccountably refused." Castlereagh put the matter baldly, finding the whole subject disagreeable. But he was not here to make moral judgments but to acquire Ariel's acquiescence to his plans. He rather admired her stoical silence, her unwillingness to make excuses or explanations.

"I cannot believe your Excellency has any interest in the tittle-tattle of Vienna gossips," Ariel said finally, aware to her dismay that a slow flush was reddening her cheeks.

"Normally, no. But what I am asking you to do, Ariel, concerns this scandal. I want you to marry Montague and accompany him to London next week. I understand you have some connection with the Comte and Comtesse de Villefranche, through your mother, I believe, and we have some reason to think that plots dangerous to the security of the country are emanating from their London home. As a new bride, you would be expected to call on your relations, to introduce your new husband, and be accepted into their

51

circle. You will then be in a position to learn if the suspicions of the War Office and Foreign Office are correct." He hesitated a moment and then went on, a warmer note creeping into his voice. "I cannot think your present position is a comfortable one, and although this marriage of convenience may be distasteful, it would surely be better than what you are enduring now."

"Yes, I feel like a social leper. But that is of no importance. Since my father's death, I have found that the role of an indigent relative has exposed me to insult and humiliation. This is just one more cross to bear," Ariel agreed, then shaking off her embarrassment, she found herself seeking assurance from this grave and kindly statesman. "I take it you have discussed this with Captain Montague."

"Of course. His own usefulness here is finished, and as he wants a position on Wellington's staff, he must do all he can to cooperate, otherwise his career is blighted. His family, too, finds his recent behavior unacceptable. He wants this marriage, even if possibly for the wrong reasons." Castlereagh made no attempt to gloss over the indignity of the situation of Ariel forced to accept an unwelcome husband through misleading circumstances. "Selfish though it appears, I must grasp this opportunity to place a spy in the Villefranche menage, in order to ferret out a conspiracy against His Majesty's government, and I may say, one which could affect the peace of Europe, which your father fought so bravely to secure." He added the last argument as the ultimate persuasion.

Here was no giddy young girl eager to secure a place for herself in the ton, but a soldier's daughter who understood what was at stake. He paid her the compliment of confiding his doubts, fears, and anxieties, which he normally kept hidden. She was not proof against his appeal.

"You must know, my dear, that most marriages in society are made for reasons not so noble as this one, for place, for land, for fortune, for heirs. This at least has the merit of being for your country."

"I had planned no such marriage, my lord, but hoped to secure a relatively quiet situation in the country, where I would no longer be the cynosure of gossips and conjecture," Ariel confided, relieved to be able to explain her unhappiness.

"Captain Montague may be a devilish fellow, but he comes of good family, and has proved a gallant soldier. He is not unattractive to women, I gather. Surely it is not so terrible a fate," Castlereagh joked gently, impressed by the pride of this reserved young woman who was attempting so valiantly to gain some ease and security for herself. He had done all he could. He could not force her against her inclinations. He could only appeal to her patriotism. "I am not denying there is some danger in what I am asking. These conspirators are a ruthless company. But Captain Montague will do his utmost to protect you. Will you do as I ask?" He was becoming impatient and somewhat ashamed at coercing such an innocent, but the opportunity to introduce her into the Villefranche household was too fortuitous to miss. He wondered briefly what her relationship with the bold captain had really been, but that did not concern him.

"If you appeal to my love for my country, I cannot deny you, my lord. I will marry Captain Montague and do my best to discover what you want to know," Ariel said firmly, relieved in a way to have her unhappy situation solved in a manner which would do justice to her pride.

"Thank you, my dear. I believe you will not regret it and I suspect you will learn that these tumultuous emotions will prove less important as time passes. It has been so long since I experienced the passions of youth, I forget how overriding they can seem. A happy marriage is based on so many other factors." He sighed, remembering his own felicitous union.

"Let us hope that Captain Montague shares your views, Lord Castlereagh," Ariel replied somewhat tartly, recognizing that however sympathetic the Foreign Secretary appeared, his demands upon her were made for political reasons, not from any real feeling for her dilemma. He was a man obviously accustomed to being obeyed, she decided cynically, and not above using whatever means came to hand to secure cooperation for his plans.

"Thank you, Miss Frazier. I will explain matters to the captain, and hope that the ceremony can take place without delay, at the embassy, I think. For it is vital you travel to London as soon as possible. I want this conspiracy thwarted before the Duke of Wellington replaces me in Vienna. He should be here soon after

Christmas, and I must return myself for the new session of Parliament. I assume your cousin will stand up with you. I will leave the arrangements to him, and to Captain Montague." Castlereagh was all business now that he had persuaded her.

He took his leave shortly afterward, leaving behind a girl relieved but troubled. She did not fear the danger he had warned about so much as the new relationship which could prove far more threatening than any attempt to foil a French plot. She had never met her Villefranche relations and she wondered how they would receive her. Much better to think of that confrontation than the loveless marriage which loomed before her. A shiver of repulsion she could not subdue shook her when she thought of what she had agreed to do. How had events come to such a pass, and would Ian Montague honor the arrangement imposed by his ambition and his careless actions? Could she withstand him if he decided to make the marriage a reality? Banishing all thoughts of what might be implied by that decision, she turned her thoughts to how she would explain her change of mind to Fiona and Robert.

by his sincerity, but then she remembered Elaine

Chapter Five

"Well, you have managed to catch yourself a very acceptable husband, Ariel," Fiona accused her cousin, behaving as if the whole business had little to do with her.

"I might remind you, Fiona, that this distressing state of affairs, which can cause me nothing but a great deal of grief and unhappiness, was brought about by your own imprudent behavior," Ariel replied, eyeing her cousin's wife with dislike. How dare Fiona imply that she had maneuvered to bring about this unpalatable arrangement? Fiona seemed determined to ignore the real cause of Ariel's submission to events of which she was the innocent victim.

"You cannot deny that Ian is a charming and exceptional lover, far more exciting than any parti you might have attracted without my intervention," Fiona said complacently, patting her hair. But beneath her scorn and displeasure Ariel sensed real pique at the outcome of her

57

endeavors to save herself. Seldom had Fiona been the one abandoned in a love affair and the situation was not acceptable. She disliked exceedingly having her enjoyable affair with Ian Montague terminated by this marriage of convenience to a girl she considered beneath her notice. She had never wanted to admit Ariel into her household, and had done her best to see that the girl's position was as humiliating as possible. But she had not been above using her when her own safety was threatened.

"I could, of course, try to explain matters to Robert, throw myself on his mercy, and tell him what really happened that evening," Ariel suggested smoothly, knowing how unlikely such a resolution of her problem would appeal to Fiona. Lady Mackenzie enjoyed her lovers but she would be terrified at having her indiscretions revealed, being forced to surrender her wealth and standing, to be judged as an erring wife. Ariel doubted that Fiona cared a fig for Sir Robert but she reveled in the assets he commanded. She would not willingly sacrifice her current role for that of an abandoned woman, treated with contempt by the very society in which she had queened over her rivals. Oh, no, Ariel knew Fiona would never allow that to happen, no matter who suffered. But it might serve her well to think she had not emerged safely from this mishap. A few sleepless nights, on the other hand, would be little enough revenge—that and the realization that she had lost Ian Montague were far less than she deserved.

"Robert would never believe you. He loves and

trusts me and he would only despise you if you attempted to extricate yourself from this scandal by such a paltry story," Fiona returned smugly.

Reluctantly Ariel conceded that Fiona was probably right, but the knowledge did nothing to calm her. Why should this tawdry woman get off without any payment for her sins?

"The only bonus to this whole unfortunate predicament is that I will no longer have to suffer your condescension and demands, Fiona. I have not enjoyed being a member of your household any more than you have enjoyed having me here. I will bid you farewell with the greatest of pleasure." Ariel knew she was being as spiteful and petty as her tormentor but she could not allow Fiona to treat her in this careless fashion.

"You are an ungrateful chit. Didn't we rescue you from destitution? You would have probably ended up on the streets where you belong, if Robert had not intervened," Fiona replied viciously, now thoroughly aroused, her normally languid manner rapidly disappearing under Ariel's goad, hard ugly lines drawing her face into a parody of her usual beauty.

"Somehow I feel that would be preferable to living under the domination of a foolish harpy such as you, Fiona. If your various admirers could probe beneath that charming facade you turn to the world, they would be vastly surprised. But what's the use? There is no way you will be brought to account for your iniquitous ways. My sympathies are all with Robert. I only pray this has been a warning to you and from now on you

59

will treat him with the respect and affection he deserves." Ariel sighed, knowing this to be a doubtful prospect. Why brangle with this odious woman? No good would come of their exchanging insults, although she had a certain satisfaction in bringing their relationship into the open. It hardly mattered now, and she had more important concerns to attend to. She left Fiona to her brooding without more ado. She would keep her distance from that shrew for the few days she had to remain beneath her roof.

Fiona would have liked to indulge in a temper tantrum, but remembering that such displays of passion were ruination to the complexion, she restrained herself from hurling a Meissen figurine at the departing figure of her cousin by marriage. After all, there were other delightful men thronging around her here in Vienna, more than ready to flirt and dally. She regretted the loss of Ian, but felt she had brushed through the calamity of Robert's suspicions very well. Instead of railing at her, Ariel should have shown a proper gratitude that her own clever plan had resulted in such a fortunate conclusion. Certainly the dowdy chit would never have attracted such a husband without Fiona's intrigues. Actually she should be thanking her. And Robert had been most assiduous lately, rewarding her with a new string of pearls as a sop for his suspicions. All in all, events had turned to her advantage, she concluded, and she could ignore Ariel's contempt for she would soon be gone, probably the most felicitous result of all. Now she must visit her modiste—that last ivory ball gown did not hang properly and the seamstress must be made to alter it immediately. Consoling herself with the ephemeral delights which were her wont, Fiona dismissed from her mind the recent confrontation with her annoying cousin.

Ariel, too, decided to waste no more energy on the shallow Fiona. Her fangs were leashed, and no matter how spitefully she wished to behave, to thwart this marriage, she had no recourse but to accept it. Much as Ariel herself was forced to. She had determined on her attitude to the coming marriage and she would not be persuaded from it. She must concentrate on the mission which Castlereagh had asked of her, and look upon the wedding as just an interlude of little import, for she had decided she would adopt a cool, reserved attitude toward her bridegroom. Not for one moment would she allow him to entertain the notion that her feelings were at risk in this venture.

Determining to send his cousin off in fine fashion, no matter the reason for this marriage of necessity, Sir Robert insisted that Ariel buy herself a suitable wardrobe. The modistes of Vienna enjoyed the patronage of Europe's most stylish women, and the Kärntner Strasse was thronged with shops devoted to milady's toilette. The Congress was providing a bonanza for the dressmakers, and Ariel decided she would, for once, abandon her prim styles and dress according to her taste, with no expense spared. She did not favor the sprigged muslins and proper white

61

silks so popular with unmarried women, but chose a deep nile green silk, opened to show a figured cream levantine underdress. Her pelisse had to be warm enough for travel, and the matching green wool cloak lined with sable was frogged much like an officer's uniform. With it went a matching military-styled bonnet, set off by a dashing plume of ostrich feathers, and a huge sable muff. Not perhaps in a bridal mode, but then she felt so little like a bride. The outfit showed her tall, slim figure to advantage and the plainness of the style accented her carriage, her hazely green eyes, and her creamy white skin. She would not go to the ceremony looking like a dowd, and her choice pleased her. For the first time since leaving France, she felt able to hold her own in the modish set the Mackenzies frequented. How her bridegroom would view her new apparel caused her little interest.

The interview with Ian Montague which took place the day after her meeting with Castlereagh passed off more smoothly than she had anticipated. Whether he was disappointed at her decision to take him as a husband, she could not discern. She received him in the morning room, and was rather amused at his firm dismissal of Fiona, who obviously wanted to question him and attach his interest once more.

He bowed low over the hands of both ladies and complimented them on their good looks. Then he turned to Fiona, who could barely conceal her avid concern.

"My dear Lady Mackenzie. How kind of you to

receive me. I am sure it is through your good offices that Miss Frazier has been persuaded to change her mind about accepting me," he said suavely, well aware of Fiona's frustration at matters, and deriving an unholy enjoyment of her dilemma.

"I see no reason to wrap this mess up in clean linen. You were forced to offer for Ariel because of what passed between us the other evening. I never thought that my suggestion you take refuge in her bedroom would result in this fiasco," Fiona replied, her resentment obvious as she plucked at the bodice of her elaborate aqua silk morning dress.

"Just what did you expect, milady? That I would risk discovery by Sir Robert? Your charms are many, but not enough to cause me to lose my head, and perhaps my life, in defending your honor. What recourse would we have had if I had faced Sir Robert! I doubt very much if you would abandon all for love, my dear," he countered brutally, his eyes staring her down boldly. "I enjoyed our amorous encounters as you did, but not enough to sacrifice myself on the altar of your conceit."

"You are a cad, sir, to lure me into a liaison and then desert me," Fiona argued, unwilling to take any responsibility for the situation.

"As I recall, Lady Mackenzie, you did most of the running, ungentlemanly as it is for me to admit. But I see no reason for all these soul-searchings. We must pay the piper. You have come out of all this just as you planned, with your reputation unimpaired, which is more than you deserve. It is your cousin, and myself, who must shoulder the burden of your impetuosity," he explained coolly, not one whit disturbed by her fulminations. "I deplore this raking over the past. And it cannot be comfortable for Miss Frazier." Turning to Ariel, who had watched Fiona's set-down with pleasure, he said, "I must really endeavor to call you Ariel—such a delightful name."

"You will regret this cavalier attitude, Ian," Fiona riposted angrily, her face marred with displeasure. Ariel doubted that the captain had seen his late love in such a mood before and could only enjoy the scene. But how smoothly he handled the difficult confrontation with no recourse to protestations of thwarted love. It was as she had suspected—the affair between the two had been purely a sensual gratification. Their emotions were not involved, although Fiona perhaps felt more than he did.

"Now, perhaps, you will leave us, Lady Mackenzie, to get on with our plans. Ariel and I have much to discuss which could only bore you, and I am sure the amenities will be preserved. I will accept your good wishes, although they have not been offered, and bid you adieu. No doubt we will meet in London," he concluded, leaving Fiona no recourse but to do as he had bid, since he held open the door for her, waiting for her to obey his orders.

Eyeing him warily once they were alone, Ariel made no push to engage in conversation. Let him make the first move, she decided. He seemed more than adept at handling matters to his own satisfaction, either brutally or with a certain rakish charm.

"Not an auspicious beginning to wedded bliss, I am afraid," Ian suggested, propping himself against the mantel and eyeing Ariel quizzically.

"I am not expecting wedded bliss, nor are you, I am sure, Captain Montague. We have been forced into this marriage of convenience by events, and by Lord Castlereagh's request for help, as you very well know. I understand that unless you comply, your military career is in jeopardy, and that your family are insisting that you mend your libertine ways," Ariel reproved, eager to set matters on a proper footing.

"Oh, I don't know, Ariel. I think this union might offer an unexpected bonus. And my name is Ian. It is quite quelling to be addressed in such repressive tones by one's fiancée," he teased, pleased at getting a rise from the reserved Miss Frazier.

Ariel subdued a shiver, unwilling to let him see that her composure was threatened by his innuendo. "Let us not play games, Captain Montague. We are entering into this charade at Lord Castlereagh's demand and because of rash and imprudent behavior on your part. I have no wish for a husband who is constantly chasing after some other woman, nor do I find you in the least attractive." As she set out the terms of the marriage, Ariel wondered if he would accept the limitation she was insisting upon.

"Ah, but with such an exceptional wife, I will

have no need to pursue other women, my dear. Surely it is your duty to do your utmost to keep me faithful as we cooperate on this spy caper," Ian argued, enjoying her discomfort.

Thoroughly angry now by his mocking efforts to turn aside the serious nature of their situation, Ariel rushed into heedless speech. "I do not understand to what you are referring, Captain, but I must make it clear this marriage is strictly a necessity, imposed by Lord Castlereagh, and in no way engages our feelings." She felt like a prim schoolmistress reproving a wayward charge, but she could not allow him to think she found him in any way alluring.

"Oh, dear. You have taken me in dislike. I will have to exert myself to change your mind. I don't want a wife glaring at me from the nuptial altar. You really must try and make it look as if this marriage has your approval. It would never do for your Villefranche relatives to think it was all a hum, and suspect our real motive."

"Yes, well, I will endeavor to play my part convincingly, just as long as you understand that it is a charade. I doubt you can act a loving bridegroom in any case, and you, too, must try to leash your normal appetites in order to make our masquerade seem a reality," Ariel answered, repressing an urge to slap his insolent face.

He crossed the room to her, where she was standing and holding tightly to the back of a chair in an effort to retain her composure. Before she could gasp a protest, he had taken her in his arms and kissed her lingeringly, ignoring her struggles to free herself. His lips were warm and ardent, but ruthless in their demand for her response, which despite herself, she felt rising beneath his practiced caresses.

"Just a little dress rehearsal for our play, my dear. I will see you at the embassy two days hence. In the meantime, do not let the vindictive Fiona overset you. She is of no importance. It will all work out, you will see. And I am not such a bad fellow," he said audaciously, kissing her in a friendly fashion on her forehead and removing himself from the room before she could offer any more argument.

Chapter Six

Settling herself with a sigh of relief against the velvet squabs of the traveling coach, Ariel wondered, not for the first time, at the startling change in her life. As the coach rattled over the cobblestones on the boulevard taking them from Vienna, she studied her new bridegroom, who was sprawled opposite her. He did not seem to share her nameless fears about what lay ahead.

"Plaguey things, weddings. Too much champagne and too many gratuitous words of advice. But I must say, Ariel, you do me proud. I always knew you were hiding your good looks under those prim collars and dowdy dresses. You look very handsome, my dear," he complimented her casually.

Flushing under his appraising stare, but not believing one word of his praise, Ariel refused to be beguiled. "How long will it take us to reach Calais, do you think?" she asked, hoping to distract him from any more insincere words. She did not think he cared what she looked like for one moment. Unlike herself, he had endured the brief wedding ceremony under the eyes of the small company with a careless gaiety which was such a contrast to her own grave demeanor. She had never expected to be repeating the marriage vows with a man who had been forced into taking them. Despite her practical no-nonsence appearance, she had hoped someday to wed a man who would love her as her father had loved her mother. Thinking of her beloved parent brought tears to her eyes, but she resolutely banished them. She must think of this marriage as an expediency, a way to expose the enemies of her country. That was what Castlereagh had asked of her, and what had precipitated this state of affairs. To dream of any other outcome was foolish in the extreme, even if Ian Montague was the type of man to encourage such romantic fantasies.

"A week, at least. And damn confining, pent up in this wretched coach. Still, since we are forced into each other's company, we will perforce have to make conversation. A priceless opportunity to get to know one another. You are somewhat of an enigma, Ariel," he mused, looking at her with the same appraising stare she found a bit unnerving.

"No more so than you, Captain. Until recently my life was bound up with the fortunes of the army. My father took me from a Devon convent when I was twelve, and ever since, until his death last year, I followed the drum with him. I found it an exciting time, full of the tragedies of war, but having a reality I never found in Vienna," she

70

explained, for some reason eager to explain the fortunes which had formed her character.

"Yes, war is not all posturing and gallantry, but a miserable bloody business. Such an experience makes you see the tawdriness of the social round we have both found so exasperating lately. My father would have preferred I go into the Foreign Office or at least found some sinecure in the War Office as Arnold has done, but I could never endure all that diplomatic clap-trap. I enjoy the army and intend to make it my life," he revealed, for once all traces of frippery gone from his manner.

"I cannot see you as a diplomat," Ariel observed, thinking he must have made a rash and courageous officer, daring death and emerging triumphant.

"Yes, I don't envy Charles Stewart. He's Castlereagh's half-brother, you know. Perhaps that is why he left the army for this post as ambassador, but he must miss the action. Wellington never thought much of him, but he appears to have made his mark here."

"He was very kind to lend us this coach, and he behaved very prettily today at the ceremony. I had not met him before," Ariel chatted on, amazed at how easily they were conversing. She could abandon the reserved manner she had adopted for many weeks past to protect herself from Fiona's condescension and scorn. At least she and the captain shared the memory of bivouacs and battles, which was some bond as they entered this new war. Surprisingly he

71

seemed prepared to treat her in a friendly manner, and that rather frightening gallantry which he had assumed before the marriage was absent. She had decided to treat him in the frank comradely way which she had used toward her father's fellow officers and hoped it would serve to get them through any awkwardness imposed by their new relationship.

"Do you share Castlereagh's opinion that the traitors who are planning to rescue Napoleon and plotting Wellington's death are headquartered in the Villefranche household?" she asked, reminding him of their reason for this journey.

"I can only respect the Foreign Secretary's source of information. And I sincerely hope we can confront the devils. Without Wellington we are in real trouble, but I do not envy him what he faces in Vienna. Peace still seems as elusive as ever. But I would prefer to challenge the French across a redan rather than ferreting around some London drawing room, trying to discover their secrets. I am not much of a conspirator," he confided, his face drawn into a scowl. "But we must do our best with our assignment."

"I doubt that either of us is devious enough to make a good conspirator," Ariel admitted. Then deciding that since Ian seemed to be in a receptive mood, it might be wise to put to him some of the questions which had been dogging her.

"Your brother Arnold did not appear to take our marriage in good part. I don't think he believes I am a proper wife for you."

"Arnold's general character is gloomy, and he

72

rarely approves of my exploits," Ian explained indifferently. "But do not be cast down by his manner. It is of little moment."

"I always wanted a brother or sister. It is sad that you cannot be friends." Ariel plucked at her reticule nervously. She was a bit intimidated by Ian's scowl. Obviously the subject of his brother was one he did not welcome. But she wanted to know about this family which she had so summarily joined.

"Be grateful for your lack of family ties," he replied bitterly. "They can be very constraining. I get along no better with my father. Like you, both Arnold and the governor think I am a lost cause."

"Perhaps marriage will be a sobering influence," Ariel offered, realizing that she was entering deep waters. She wanted to make it plain to Ian that this marriage, not of her seeking, must remain one of convenience, but she hesitated to put her fears into words. She hoped they could be friends if nothing else, but she would not be used by her new husband just because events had forced them into this strange alliance.

"If you believe that, my dear, you will be shortly disabused. I doubt I have the qualities which make a good husband, although who knows? You might be able to tame the beast. Does the prospect appeal?" he asked mockingly, noticing her blush at his hints.

Ariel was conscious that she was reddening under his provocative stare, and furious that he could send her up in the boughs so easily, she tightened her mouth and answered repressively,

"I am not up to your touch, Captain Montague, and it would be well if you remembered that we married on Lord Castlereagh's request in order to unmask these traitors for him. That is our only concern." She faced him down although she felt her heart beat erratically. If he forced his attentions upon her, she had little recourse but to resort to scorn and ridicule. Obviously, he was unaccustomed to women rebuffing his advances, but she would not become one of his legion of amours just because circumstances had placed her in his path.

"Oh dear, back to the schoolmarmish chill, I see. You really must try to call me Ian. If we are to play our parts convincingly, you will have to show a little more warmth, Ariel. And be careful of throwing out challenges. I always take up a dare."

"Hypocrisy is not my forte," Ariel snapped back, vexed that he could tease her thus. She would not allow him to get beneath her guard, for she feared that he could easily override her principles. She would not be bedded as a convenience, and if that made her a silly romantic, so be it.

"A little hypocrisy is necessary in this game we are venturing upon, I suggest. But enough of that, I am cruel to mock you. I suspect you rue the day I embroiled you in this deception. But we must just make the best of it," he relented, realizing that the past few days had been a trial to her. She was trying to hide behind her natural dignity, but that aloof air she wore so habitually was a challenge to him. He did not enjoy her condemnation of his life-style no matter that it was deserved. They might both come to regret this marriage but for the moment they must try to achieve some truce.

He set about trying to win her to a more relaxed and acceptable state of mind, and as the miles lengthened from the Austrian capital, he believed he was succeeding. His first reaction to the reserved Miss Frazier had not been favorable, but he was fast revising his opinion. In her fashionable wedding clothes she seemed a far different girl than the repressed dowd he had met in Lady Mackenzie's drawing room. Actually she was a damned attractive piece and he wondered about the real woman beneath the serene facade she turned to the world, which had treated her so unkindly.

Looking at the cool schooled expression on her face, he glimpsed not for the first time the passionate nature she kept so well concealed. Here was no flighty miss, intent on casual flirtations, fashions, and fribbles, but a woman of stern principles, much like his Scottish forebears. What lay underneath might prove exciting. For the first time since he had reluctantly spoken the vows that tied him to her, he believed this marriage might have a chance of success, a felicity he had never contemplated, but he would have to go carefully. Her initial dislike of him was strongly entrenched, and would not yield easily to the ploys of a practiced seducer. Well, it did not pay to worry about the future. Unlike Ariel, Ian took life and its pleasures pretty much as he found them, without too much examining of morals or motives. Experience suggested that few women could resist him if he set out to conquer them. Why should she prove an exception? It did not occur to the arrogant officer that he might be defeated, but sufficient unto the day. They would be thrown together in a situation of intimacy, and he had no doubt he would prevail if that was what he desired. And studying her calm, withdrawn demeanor, he decided that he desired it very much.

They stopped for the night at a small town, just over the border of Austria on the edge of the Bavarian forest. Ariel, happy to leave the confines of the coach and stretch her legs, could see little of the surrounding countryside as the late autumn sunlight had faded into a murky twilight. But she was relieved to escape for a while from the dangerous privacy of the carriage. Rooms and a private parlor were engaged for the couple, and she hurried to her chamber to repair the ravages of the journey, feeling more than a little apprehensive of what lay ahead on this, her wedding night. She did not trust the captain to abide by the terms of their marriage of convenience, and the hours loomed ahead of her, making it impossible to relax.

However, when she met him in the private parlor for dinner, it appeared he would make no inordinate demands. He set himself out to be pleasant, talking of inconsequent matters, their journey, the weather, the sights of Vienna. She noticed that he drank heavily from the wine the innkeeper served, and he pressed wine upon her, but she was determined to keep a clear head. Finally the meal came to an end, and they were left alone at the table with only the sputtering candles to light the dark room. Ariel decided she might retire to her chamber and rose to take her leave.

"I am feeling quite tired, and I assume we will make an early start in the morning with so many miles to cover, so I will say good night," she said brightly, but she could not resist curling her fists in tense expectation of his reply.

"Yes, we have hours in that damnable coach again. Good night, my dear." He rose gallantly and escorted her to the door, eyeing her with a wickedly amused expression. He had little doubt but that she feared his advances, and he enjoyed her confusion.

Muttering her good-nights, she fled from the parlor to her own chamber, chiding herself for her embarrassment and fear. Obviously he was not going to take advantage of her. After all, they barely knew each other and he did not find her attractive. Why that devoutly wished happenstance should cause her such annoyance she did not know. After all, if he had found Fiona alluring, he would hardly be prepared to accept her dowdy companion as a substitute. She must always remember the reason for this marriage and the task that lay ahead. She had nothing to fear from the arrogant womanizing officer, and she had made her own opinions on the matter quite clear.

Donning her white flannel nightgown, a necessity against the winter chill, she brushed her hair and thought determinedly of her Villefranche relatives. She knew little of them, only that her mother had not been eager to pursue the ties of kinship, which made her wonder if the Villefranches were unreceptive. That might pose a problem. She was no actress, and would find it difficult to force herself upon them if they did not welcome her.

Finally abandoning all conjecture, she got into bed, relieved to discover the sheets had been warmed. She read for a while by the light of the candle, hearing muted movements from the adjoining chamber, which she believed signified Ian had retired also. She was more than surprised when the door dividing their rooms opened and he appeared in the entrance clothed in a handsome red silk dressing gown.

"What are you doing here?" she gasped, angry that she sounded shocked and amazed but unable to mask her fear.

"Well, where else would a bridegroom be on his wedding night but in his wife's chamber?" he answered in that devilish tone which irritated her.

She was not about to be the object of his amusement. She watched him warily as he crossed to the side of the bed, where she sat bolt upright, ready to flee if he attempted any liberties.

"I do not want you here. Please leave immediately," she protested, pulling the sheets up around her neck.

"Oh, come now, Ariel, surely you realize we cannot pose as devoted newlyweds if you flinch whenever I come near you. I understand you are nervous of the delights of the connubial bed, but let me assure you you will enjoy them once you become accustomed to them," he persuaded her smoothly, taking her in his arms, and ignoring her stiff outraged stance.

Furious at his casual attitude, his intention of bedding her without any avowals of affection, but just because she was available, Ariel's pride rose to the fore. "I will not become your wife in reality. This is a marriage of convenience."

"Ah, but it is convenient to me to make the marriage a reality. We are truly shackled and must make the best of it. I anticipate enjoying it, once you abandon your virginal shrinkings." He released her, frowning at her rebuff.

He made no move to touch her again although his glance was disturbingly intimate. She could not know he was moved by the sight of her vulnerability, her black hair streaming over her shoulders, her tense closed face, the enveloping nightgown buttoned closely to her creamy throat. He had little experience in persuading reluctant virgins into bed, and his first reaction was one of anger and a strange disappointment.

"I am not a monk, my dear. If you deny me your bed, I will have to take my pleasure elsewhere, and that could be humiliating for you," he argued softly.

Ariel felt her throat close tightly. She did not know what to say. Finally she stammered, "I understand what you mean but I cannot go to bed with a stranger, even if he is, by the force of circumstances, my husband. Perhaps, when we get to know one another better...." Her voice trailed off uncertainly.

"By all means, let us come to know each other, but do not rely on my patience, Ariel. It is an uncomfortable emotion, frustration. I will bid you good night." He leaned over and gave her a quick hard kiss on her trembling mouth and strolled from the room.

Ariel, unaware that she had been holding her breath, let out a sigh of relief and then took refuge in anger. What an arrogant conceited rake he was. And he needn't think he could try his wiles on her. But how she could prevent him from exerting his rights she could not imagine. Blowing out her candle, she snuggled down into the bed, aware that she had handled the interview badly, like a silly shrinking miss. And along with relief that she had postponed the promised consummation of the marriage came a niggling feeling of dissatisfaction and anticlimax. Her principles suddenly appeared cold comfort as she drifted off into lonely slumber.

Chapter Seven

Ariel had been away from England for seven years, and she had to become reacquainted with the cool green and quiet of the countryside as their carriage rumbled through the low rolling hills of Hampshire and Surrey en route to London from Southampton. She had plenty of time to remember and brood as the miles lengthened from the port, for Ian, evidently weary of her company, had abandoned the coach to ride a horse he had procured the moment they landed after a turbulent Channel crossing from Calais. Since the confrontation on their wedding night, he had retreated behind a polite mask, treating her with all consideration but rebuffing her efforts to learn more about the man beneath that sardonic facade. So much for her attempts to learn about the real man, to grow closer to this reluctant husband. Hurt by his reserved demeanor, she did not offer further overtures and, in her own turn, retreated to the cool prim manner which had served her in Vienna.

When the coach entered London, she threw off her melancholy, entranced by the city's air of bustling excitement, hearing the hawkers' cries, watching the crowds in the streets, trying to ignore the dirt and disorder but appalled by the obvious poverty of the people living cheek by jowl with the splendor and rich variety of the aristocrats' mansions and state palaces. They were bound for Stephen's Hotel in Bond Street, a haunt much favored by the military, as the Montague House in Grosvenor Street was closed. She felt it would not have done to impose on her Villefranche relatives without warning, and until Arnold returned from Vienna, Ian's family house would not be available. His wife, Harriet, preferred to spend her time in the country, on the Strathcairn estate in Northumberland on the Scots border. The Montagues did not appear to be very uxorious. From the little Ian had revealed, the marriage seemed to have been an arranged one, rather like her own, she conceded bitterly. And there were no children of the union, one of the reasons Ian's father, the Earl of Strathcairn, had been so eager to see his younger son shackled to the amenable Maria Atherton, no doubt. Well, he would be disappointed in this marriage, for no heirs would result from their sterile pact. Ariel threw off her despondency, determined to make the best of matters, as they drew up in the crowded courtyard of the Stephen's Hotel. Dozens of equipages jostled on the cobblestones, and the hostlers and page boys rushed to and fro, aiding the travelers who were too intent on their own business to notice the arrival of yet another couple of guests.

Ian bustled her into the hotel, an imposing building whose reception hall was thronged with officers. Several of the men nodded to Ian, and raked her with those appraising arrogant glances she found so disturbing. But within moments the obsequious host had ushered them into the suite Ian had reserved and she realized how relieved she was to have at last reached the quiet sanctuary of their rooms.

"We will have to find you a maid, and see to a new wardrobe for you," Ian suggested as he looked about the comfortable appointments with approval. "We will not want to stay here for long. Perhaps your Villefranche relatives will offer us hospitality once you have made yourself known to them."

She looked at him as he stretched out in an armchair before the fire, seemingly at ease in this intimate setting and not one bit discomposed by their situation. If only she could behave with such assurance.

"Do you think that would be wise?" she asked, removing her bonnet and passing a distracted hand through her hair.

"Perhaps not wise but intriguing. We would have a much better chance of discovering their intentions if we are right on the scene, I suspect. I suppose the thought of living in such intimacy among your relatives poses some problems, but you will just have to learn to dissemble, my dear, hide your distaste of me," he answered with an outrageous grin.

"I do not find you distasteful, just arrogant and unfeeling," Ariel hastened to reply, somewhat unwisely as it gave him just the opening he was seeking to embarrass her.

"Hardly unfeeling, my dear, as I think I tried to show you on our strange wedding night. As I recall, you were the one who had such doubts about displaying any unmaidenly emotion," he reproved, looking at her suggestively and seeming to enjoy the blush she could not restrain, to her annoyance.

"Ian, if we are to deal together satisfactorily in this unusual alliance, you must restrain your more ... more obvious appetites. You may be able to find some relief in bedding any woman who comes your way, but it is not quite that easy for me," Ariel explained breathlessly, looking at his boots stretched out toward the fire, unwilling to face him with her fears. He need not think she was ready to fall into his arms like a ripe plum. No doubt he expected to take full advantage of their forced union and could not understand her reluctance to be bedded in such a cavalier fashion. Well, she was not one of his doxies, to be coaxed into the nuptial bed just to satisfy his lust.

Ian raised a skeptical brow at her demurs. He found her virginal shrinkings quite amusing, but was prepared to indulge her for the moment.

"If we are to persuade your Villefranche relatives that we are indeed what we seem, a newlywed couple madly in love, you will have to prove a better actress than I have so far glimpsed, Mrs. Montague," he said, his devil roused by her austere manner. Clearly the chit did not find him attractive, which was salutory to his conceit, probably, but damned insulting.

"The French take a very practical view about marriage. They would not be surprised to find us on formal terms. And I understand, too, it's considered bad form to be living in one another's pockets when you are wed. We would not want to display bad manners," she argued, facing him now and determined not to let his teasing, provocative airs affect her.

"I can see I am batting on a losing wicket with you, but I don't despair. Still, I am cruel to tease you now, when you are fatigued from the journey, but we must come to some resolution before we face these Villefranches. Decide on how we are going to proceed." Ian's brow furrowed as he thought about what lay ahead. The whole masquerade suddenly seemed ridiculous, and his forced marriage with this iceberg a grievous mistake. He rose impatiently to his feet. "While you repair the damages of travel and unpack, I will toddle around to the War Office. There are a few chaps there I must consult. I will see you at dinner, my dear, when we can continue this fascinating debate," he promised, and bowed to her before quitting the room in some irritation.

Left to her own devices, Ariel faced her unpalatable situation, determined to come to some sort of accommodation with her disturbing husband. She might hold him responsible for the events which had forced their marriage, but it was now an accomplished fact, and no good could come of their constantly sniping at each other. Then, too, there was the Villefranche confrontation which she must meet with some composure. Resolutely turning her mind to how she could approach these unknown relations who might not welcome her enthusiastically, she decided her best plan would be to write requesting an interview, apprising them of her arrival with her husband in London, and await their convenience. Perhaps she should confer with Ian before penning the missive, but surely the sooner she put matters in hand, the better. She could not hide in her hotel room hoping to postpone the task which Castlereagh had requested of them. The thought of spying on her unknown relatives caused her some disquiet, but if the Foreign Secretary was correct, they deserved little consideration, acting treacherously toward the country which had offered them refuge. Perhaps she might prove his suspicions wrong, and that would be a great relief, but somehow she had an uneasy feeling that Castlereagh's suspicions had some basis in fact.

Resolutely she wrote a short, polite note requesting an interview with the Villefranches, addressed to the comtesse, giving her address and stressing its temporary nature. Perhaps this might provoke an offer of hospitality. Ariel gave a small moue of disgust at this ploy, unwilling to force herself upon reluctant relatives, but realizing she must sink her scruples if she were to comply with Castlereagh's request. Sending off the letter with a footman, she paced the private parlor with impatience. When would Ian return? Would he be annoyed that she had taken matters into her own hands and contacted the Ville-franches? Well, he would just have to accept it. He might be her husband but that did not prevent her from some independence of action. The sooner they settled this conspiracy, the better. She would have liked to take a leisurely walk about London, reacquainting herself with the town, but she realized she could not go unescorted and quelled her impatience by unpacking their effects—beginning her marital duties, she conceded somewhat ironically—and then tried to curb her resentment by ordering a bath and dressing for the evening ahead.

She was stitching angrily at a piece of embroidery, normally a soothing occupation, when Ian returned as the evening was drawing in. His earlier mood of irritation had changed to one of jaunty aplomb as he hailed her.

"Ah, my somber bride, looking lovely and unapproachable as usual, I see," he greeted her, entering the room and crossing to the fire, where he put one booted foot on the fender and raised a sardonic eyebrow at the picture she made sitting sedately in a slipper chair.

Ariel decided not to antagonize him, suspecting that he had been celebrating his return rather heavily. She looked at him calmly.

"I have sent a note to the Villefranches, letting them know of our arrival and requesting a meeting at their convenience. I hope that meets with your approval?"

"Quite right, my dear. As usual you have done the proper. We must lose no time in investigating these suspected traitors. I have had a very interesting afternoon with some old comrades at the War Office. They had a great deal to tell me about the machinations of the émigrés here in London, and your Villefranche relatives were mentioned," he said, abandoning his provocative tone.

"Then Lord Castlereagh has a definite basis for his suspicions." She frowned, not liking what she was hearing.

"He usually does. Did you believe he was solely motivated by an avuncular interest in your reputation, determined to put you right before the world? A real innocent, aren't you? No, my dear. The noble Foreign Secretary is a hard-headed realist, I'm afraid, more than willing to barter your virtue for information," Ian explained cynically, watching her reception of his news lazily.

Ariel was aghast at his implications. "I think it is hateful, if true. After all, England offered them sanctuary, has received them kindly. How could they be so ungrateful, so wicked?"

"They have lost their estates, their position, a great deal of their wealth, with the prospect of losing even more, their sugar plantations in the West Indies," he explained patiently. "They will brook at nothing to regain them."

"I can't imagine an Englishman behaving so," Ariel argued, shocked at his easy acceptance of such chicanery.

"Oh, I can. I would not sit tamely by if some upstart tried to wrest the Strathcairn acres from my family," he said, smiling grimly at the prospect. Ariel could well believe he would make a formidable foe if thus challenged, rather a surprise, as she had believed he cared little for his family, roistering his way through life, living for the moment, with little care for the responsibilities entailed by his birth and ancestry.

Rising to his feet, Ian looked down at her quizzically.

"Since you seem to have difficulty in believing me, I have called on some reinforcements. Castlereagh has enlisted the services of an old comrade of mine, Alistair Glendenning, who has some experience in these affairs. Formerly an officer in the King's Dragoon Guards, he has been detached for intelligence work, and is now serving as a liaison between the Foreign Office and the War Office. Alistair is a rogue, but a courageous officer. We have been in some tight places together. With women he is not to be trusted, but in battle he is a tiger, and a reliable ally in this different kind of fight. I have asked him to join us at dinner, and we can have a council of war." Ian waited for her reaction, and when none was forthcoming, he sighed and continued, "On the Villefranche matter he is to be completely trusted, but don't take his flirting seriously. He's a devil with women."

Abandoning her embroidery, Ariel rose, smoothed down her skirt, and studied her husband with a jaundiced eye. "Just like you, Ian. It takes a rogue to recognize one, no doubt."

"You malign me, my pet. I am now a sober, respectable husband." He laughed, seeing her skeptical expression. "But come let us repair to supper, call a truce for the nonce, and see what Alistair suggests."

Chapter Eight

Alistair Glendenning was all that Ian had promised, a tall chestnut-haired Celt with deep blue eyes, which widened with appreciation at the sight of Ariel. She had dressed carefully for this meeting in a magenta silk gown, cut low to show off her creamy white shoulders, and flattering to her midnight dark hair. She disdained the pastel muslins so favored by the demure misses of the day, realizing that those insipid colors did little to enhance her regal appearance. Ian did not compliment her on her gown, but his eyes narrowed as he noticed the admiring glance his fellow officer raked over his wife.

"My dear, this graceless mountebank is Captain Alistair Glendenning, who I hope will prove a helpful ally in this mission we are undertaking. A paltry fellow, but of some use to us, perhaps." Ian made the introduction wryly, not unmindful of his friend's unmistakable attraction to women.

"I am delighted to meet you, Captain Glendenning," Ariel acknowledged, feeling a bit like a delicious bone between two quarreling dogs. What a pair these two were, not a farthing between them when it came to outrageous behavior, she suspected.

Alistair Glendenning bowed low over her hand with practiced address, his gaze hotly appraising. "Charmed, madam. How unfortunate that this mean dog should have seen you first. I am sure he does not realize what a jewel he has captured," he said audaciously. Then turning to Ian, he remarked, "I never thought to see you leg-shackled, my friend, but upon meeting your bride, I am not surprised. You are to be congratulated."

"Thank you, Alistair. I am not sure Ariel completely agrees, but I warn you, I am a jealous husband. No poaching. I remember your penchant for married women." Ian spoke lightly but with an undertone of possessive menace which quite shocked Ariel. Did he think she was ripe for dalliance with his friend? How typical. He did not really care for her himself, but would never allow another to gain what she denied him.

"A challenge, Ian. You know I cannot resist that," Glendenning teased, still eyeing Ariel with that speculative air, wondering just how far he could go.

"You are quite outrageous, Captain Glendenning. But I am not some gullible miss to be taken in by your flattery. Come let us have dinner and discuss the matter which engages us all," Ariel said severely, determined to put the situation on a dignified footing.

"Ah, a set-down. How disappointing. But it is early days yet. I am sure we will become fast friends, my dear Mrs. Montague," the captain countered, not one whit dismayed by her disapproval.

Despite herself, Ariel smiled, earning a stern look from her husband, but who could resist this engaging scamp? She could well believe he had caused havoc among the credulous females exposed to his winning ways. Well, she was well armored against such practiced seducers. Wasn't Ian just such another?

Ian had engaged supper in their parlor, believing they needed the privacy to discuss events. But for the first part of the meal, an elaborate fare with several removes, the talk was light and whimsical. Not until the waiter had cleared the dishes and set out a bottle of port did the conversation turn to the French conspiracy.

"Well, Alistair, enough of this London gossip. To our task. What have you heard at the War Office about all this French conniving?" Ian spoke casually, toying with his wineglass, but frowning as if the whole affair was distasteful to him.

Glendenning spoke angrily. "Well, there is little doubt that the clever devil, Fouché, has his minions everywhere. He may have appeared to accept the changed regime, but there is every reason to believe he is in contact with Napoleon. And as he is his master's former chief of police, you may be sure his network of spies is still reporting our every move to him. Nasty character, that one. His methods defy description. Give me an out-and-out enemy every time. This slipping in and out of boudoirs garnering tidbits disgusts me."

Ariel had heard a great deal about the notorious Comte Joseph Fouché, sometime Duke of Otranto, who had served his former master, Napoleon, well. A cruel, ambitious man, whose lascivious appetites were well documented. Napoleon trusted him and relied on his loyalty. He was an adversary to be respected and feared as much today as when he had commanded Napoleon's secret police.

"Come now, Alistair. You are quite adept at ducking in and out of bedrooms yourself. Don't fault the man for that activity," Ian quipped, ignoring Ariel's movement of distaste.

"I have not yet been forced to Fouché's methods of seduction, my friend," Alistair responded in some heat. "He promised his victims clemency if they warmed his bed, and then after the seduction, callously turned them over to Madame Guillotine or the Bastille."

"We are shocking my bride," Ian reproved, noting Ariel's disgust. "What I want to know is if his spies are still reporting to him, and if you think he is the ringleader of this plan to rescue Napoleon from Elba," Ian pressed his friend.

"Little doubt of it. Not only planning the escape but also involved in this effort to assassinate the Iron Duke," Alistair said. "Valentine—you know him, I think—has just gotten his step up to general and he is convinced of it. And he has a deal of experience in chasing French spies."

"Yes, well, what about Ariel's Villefranche relatives? How do they come into it? And what evidence do you have that they are the headquarters of the spy ring?" Ian was deadly serious now, intent on wresting from Alistair hard information. Gone was the careless, philandering beau of the ballroom; Ariel believed she was seeing the dedicated officer, readying himself for a battle as fierce as any he had fought on the Peninsula.

"No hard evidence. That is where you and your wife will prove so valuable. You will get it for us. Every émigré in London gathers at the comtesse's salon, and much of society besides. It's not just the Frenchies themselves we are concerned with, you know. They have connections in the War Office, the Foreign Office, the highest seats of the government itself, Valentine believes, and so do I. This is not just a band of disgruntled exiles, biting the hand that feeds them, but English traitors, damn them, plotting against His Majesty's government," Alistair explained angrily, his blood as hot as his fellow Scot's about this native treachery.

"I understand from Castlereagh that the villains have already tried to kill Wellington, and they will try again. Without him we would be in a sorry case," Ian mused. Like all serving officers, he was a great admirer of the Duke.

"That is why we must move quickly to apprehend them. And your contribution is vital. How will you infiltrate the Villefranche household?" Alistair asked.

"Ariel has already taken the first steps in that

95

direction," Ian replied. "We are hoping they will extend their hospitality to their newly discovered relation and her husband. Once in the house, we should be able to ferret out their intentions, if indeed they are involved. Nasty job, spying on one's hosts, but justified, I think." Ian rose to his feet in some impatience, the idea of the subterfuge obviously causing him disquiet.

"Well, you must just put aside any gentlemanly instincts and get on with the job. As you know, I have been delegated to assist on this affair, and will offer you all the help I can. . . . Now, tell me about Vienna." Alistair turned the conversation, somewhat to Ariel's dismay. She did not want Alistair to learn about the scandal which had brought about their marriage, pride preventing her from exposing the truth to this old friend of Ian's. Just such a one as her husband, she thought. He would probably find the whole story vastly amusing, and she would become an object of pity. The tale would not reflect well on Ian either. But he evidently shared her view, for his tales of Vienna, ribald and shocking, did not include any mention of the luscious Lady Mackenzie.

Finally the evening ended, to Ariel's relief, for fatigue was overcoming her. Alistair Glendenning left, professing himself her devoted slave, and raking her with one of those audacious glances which wreaked such havoc in the more susceptible hearts of London's beau monde. They were a pair, Ian and Alistair, and she needed all her determination to guard her from Ian's assault without succumbing to the flirtatious advances of

Captain Glendenning, irresistible as he felt he must be. Obviously Ian, too, was aware of the danger. Bidding his comrade a hearty farewell, he returned to his stance before the fire, and looked consideringly at Ariel.

"I hope your tender feelings are not affected by that graceless scamp. Alistair is not to be taken seriously by any woman. He is quite adept at luring whomever he fancies into a liaison and then becoming bored with the whole affair, impervious to heartrending avowals of undying love. I believe that currently he is pursuing the young second wife of the Marquis of Bletchford, but that does not prevent him from casting his net into other waters. He finds his current assignment rather frustrating, would far rather be shooting some Frenchmen, so he alleviates his boredom in the boudoir." Ian eyed her carefully. So difficult to tell what Ariel was really thinking with her aloof touch-me-not air—maddening, too. He would like to tear aside that prim facade she donned as a protection and find the woman beneath. But she had not yet learned to trust him, which roused his basest instincts. If he had his way, he would carry her off to bed, rip aside that cool dispassionate manner, and discover what was in her heart. But Ian was a skilled campaigner, in matters of love as well as war, and he realized tonight was not the evening to satisfy his desires. But how long could he resist, especially in the intimate situation in which they found themselves? Patience was the answer, but damn it, he was not a patient man. While he was biding his time, he did not want Alistair luring her into an affair. And good friends though they were, he did not trust that scoundrel when it came to women.

Ariel had a good notion of what was passing through her husband's mind, and an equal scorn of what he was planning. She would not be taken to bed just to soothe his conceit or to give him a fleeting pleasure. But she, too, wondered how long he would be content with their sterile marriage, and how she could prevent him from asserting his rights to her person.

"You are rather harsh in your assessment of Captain Glendenning's character, Ian, for a man who has rarely denied his own appetites. I found him charming, but I am not such a fool as to become embroiled with another rake. I know how to protect myself." Ariel eyed him severely, quite pleased that he should consider Alistair a threat, while at the same time annoyed that his possessiveness should give her such satisfaction. What did she care how he felt? Really, she was behaving like a vaporish female, prone to idiotish fancies. Where were all her good resolutions about treating Ian in an aloof, no-nonsense manner?

"I am fast renouncing my rakish ways, didn't you know? Marriage has made me a veritable pattern card of respectability, but alas, I seem to find you hard to convince," he teased, but the smoldering eyes had softened and he watched her expectantly.

Under that warm gaze, Ariel felt her resolution to treat her husband circumspectly weakening. Oh, he was clever. Since his friend had found her attractive, he had decided to reassess his own actions. Perhaps she was worth his practiced addresses. Ariel could not believe he acted from sincerity, an effort to translate this strange union into a marriage based on friendship, a community of interests, as well as passion and a common goal. She doubted Ian was capable of love—his past told so strongly against him. Suddenly she felt tired to death of all the badinage, the repartee which hid their real thoughts.

"I am extremely tired, Ian, and if you have nothing of consequence to discuss, I believe I will retire," she said, covering a simulated yawn.

"Take refuge if you must in your chaste couch, my dear Ariel. Tonight is obviously not the hour to woo you with soft words and protestations of passion, but you are putting up a magnificent fight against the inevitable. I commend you, but warn you, too, it is but a rearguard action. I intend to win," he promised, in all earnestness now.

Ariel would not give an inch. "I am not a redoubt or a hill to be taken, Ian. You might override my scruples by sheer strength, but I hardly think rape is your style." She faced him courageously although her palms felt wet and she barely repressed a shudder.

"It would not be rape, my dear. Give me a little more credit than that. But come, I am a devil to tease you so. Off to bed, and tomorrow all will seem brighter," he said gently, and surprised her by crossing the room and giving her a swift kiss on her forehead, a brotherly salute totally at odds with the hot glow of his dark eyes. Then he walked casually to the door of her bedroom, opened it, after taking the key from the lock, and held it out to her.

"See, a proof of my good intentions. You may barricade yourself in." He grimaced at her look of relief. Taking the key from his hand, she sailed through the door and closed it behind her. Then he heard the key turn in the lock.

Damn the woman. Had she no feelings? A well of frustration rose in him. He was unaccustomed to denying his appetites, and he did not intend to. If she refused him her bed, others would not be so unwelcome. Tugging at his cravat with one hand, he picked up the decanter of port with another and entered his own chamber, slamming the door with irritable force.

Ariel slept surprisingly well, considering the events of the previous day and the challenge which lay ahead. She had thought she might lie awake worrying over the future, both of her marriage and the coming meeting with the Villefranches. But as soon as her head touched the pillow, she was off into slumber. Looking at her husband the next morning over the breakfast table, it was obvious he had not shared her untroubled night. He returned her cheerful greeting with a mutter, a black scowl signifying he wanted no casual conversation. Ariel shrugged her shoulders and began her meal with a hearty appetite, surrendering to his wish for silence.

At last he finished eating and, pushing aside his

dish with a grimace, finally broke the silence. "Thank God you are not one of those women who chatter in the morning. I cannot abide aimless drivel over a meal this early. I am surprised you did not prefer to breakfast in bed," he growled, ready to argue at the slightest provocation.

"Oh, that is a sluttish habit I have no use for. I always rise for breakfast. I am sorry you do not approve," she answered brightly. "Of course, gentlemen rarely feel well the morning after a night's dissipation. My father was just the same. I became used to it and acted accordingly."

"Perfect in this as in all things, or almost all things," Ian said sarcastically. Then, somewhat regretting his bearish manner, although he held her responsible for his miserable head, he continued in a calmer tone. "I suppose we can make no move until we hear what your Villefranche relatives have to say in response to your note. No doubt, we can expect some reply this morning."

"I would think so. Perhaps, you might ring for the waiter to remove these dishes, and inquire as to any messages," Ariel suggested in a practical manner. She wondered just how much assistance Ian would be in insinuating himself into her relations' good graces if he continued in this sarcastic mood. He did nothing to allay her apprehensions over the coming meeting.

The waiter did appear with the expected note at last. Ariel was beginning to despair of spending the whole day sequestered in these rooms, with nothing to do but brood, and trying to keep from arguing with Ian. The Comtesse Francoise de Villefranche's response was couched in formal terms, but at least, she showed no reluctance to meet with this unknown relation.

"Ma Chère Madame," the missive opened, written in very correct French. Ariel translated as she read the letter to Ian, who scowled and paced the room, listening to the invitation to take tea that afternoon.

"Not exactly enthusiastic," he muttered when she had finished, tugging at his cravat as though it choked him.

"What did you expect? She knows nothing about us. She could not be expected to extend a glowing welcome to unknown relatives turning up out of the blue. She might think we will ask her for money, or some other outrageous request," Ariel reproved sharply. Really, he was proving very uncooperative. If he was going to sulk and protest, they would have a thin time of it.

"This is not going to be as simple as Castlereagh made it out to be, insinuating ourselves into the Villefranche household," Ian complained. "I hate all this conniving."

"Yes, well, we will just have to remember what our purpose is, to discover if the Villefranches are running a spy ring from their South Audley Street house. We will not be going there to enjoy ourselves, you know."

He rubbed his forehead. "Yes, you're right, as usual, a most irritating trait, my dear. Well, I am not going to sit about here waiting for the appointment. I must get some air, and rid myself of this damnable head."

"Ian, I should like to get out myself, renew my acquaintance with London, and obviously it is not the thing for me to stroll about unescorted. I will have to get a maid, I suppose. But do you think . . ." Ariel's voice trailed off, uncertain how he would receive her request.

"I will not trail around to the shops, if that is what you have in mind, but I am not averse to showing my wife the sights of the town. Might put us both in a better mood. Come get your bonnet and we will be off." He smiled, his dark mood banished as if by magic. Ariel, happy to see his lighter spirits, hurried to comply. At least they could postpone arguing and speculating for a few hours, and perhaps deepen their companionship. She did not know why she viewed this prospect with such delight, but prepared to join him with a determination not to cast a blight on his sudden change of mood.

Chapter Nine

The Villefranche house in South Audley Street near Grosvenor Square surprised Ariel with its opulence. A typical James Wyatt house with flat Doric columns against the mellow red brick and a projecting balcony overlooking the street, it had a classical elegance which spoke of wealth. Ariel wondered how an émigré family could afford such a fashionable London address. But her musings were cut short as the massive mahogany door was opened by a very proper butler, who took their names with impassive gravity and informed them that Madame, the Comtesse, was expecting them. He ushered them into a salon on the right of the spacious black-and-white-tiled entrance hall, threw open the double doors, and announced them in a voice of solemn gravity.

Rising to meet them from a chair before the fireplace was a woman of indeterminate years, stylishly gowned in aqua silk with the new double flounces at the hem. Her hair, arranged in the à la

Grecque mode, was a striking titian and she was covered in diamonds. Her impeccable appearance rather startled Ariel, who had not been expecting such a cold beauty, but the comtesse, eyeing Ian approvingly, was all graciousness.

"*Bonjour, mes amies*. How delightful to meet unknown relations. I welcome you to London. Now come sit down and tell me all about Vienna, a charming city which I once knew well." Francoise de Villefranche's warm welcome was somewhat belied by the assessing look in her rather small blue eyes, which she used to maximum effect.

Ariel, uncertain of how to proceed in the face of this fulsome greeting, took her cue from Ian, who upon meeting such an accredited beauty, displayed his most charming manner.

"Delighted, madam, to meet you. I cannot understand why Ariel did not mention such a fascinating connection before this. If I had known about you before, we would have made even greater haste to London to meet you. But, of course, we have been much occupied with defeating Napoleon." He bowed low over the comtesse's hand, raking her with that practiced seducer's eye, much to Ariel's irritation. Really, he could not resist flirting with any attractive woman. And certainly the comtesse was stunning, if a trifle mature, Ariel concluded spitefully. She had an air about her that reminded Ariel of Fiona Mackenzie, which did not endear the comtesse to her newfound cousin.

"*Mais oui*, it is indeed strange we have not met before. Of course, events on the continent precluded such a reunion. But now all is settled, peace at hand. Did you see much of my cousin, Prince Talleyrand, in Vienna?" she asked, settling down gracefully into her chair again, and signifying that they, too, should be seated.

"The ubiquitous prince was everywhere," Ian replied smoothly, crossing one booted foot over the other, and continuing to eye the Frenchwoman with admiration.

Ariel, piqued at being ignored, rushed into the conversation.

"Have you been in London long, madam?" she asked in her usual forthright manner. If allowed, these two would be conducting a flirtation right under her nose, and she would not have that.

"Alas, we fled from France during the worst days of the Terror. We have been here quite a dozen years. But we long to return to Paris, and perhaps, this will now be possible. Not that the English have not been all that was welcoming, but I find them a trifle cold to *les étrangers*," she said smoothly.

"I quite understand, madam, being a Scot myself," Ian agreed, playing her game. "A devilish arrogant lot, these English."

How outrageous of him, Ariel thought, falling in with the comtesse's criticisms, when he was far more English than Scots. How devious he was, willing to ignore his ancestry in hopes of flattering his hostess.

Before Ariel could protest, the door opened and the butler entered with a massive tea tray, which he deposited on a Pembroke table by the comtesse's side. Much time was then spent in pouring out the tea, requesting their pleasure, and pressing upon them a vast array of delicacies.

"I find myself quite enamored of this English fashion, and *le thé* has become my daily habit," the comtesse explained, sipping daintily.

"Quite right, to adapt to the customs of the country," Ian said in that pervasive manner Ariel found so annoying.

"Now, I must hear all about the wedding. I take it you have not been married long," the comtesse asked, gazing in approval and some surprise at Ian, as if in wonderment that such a dashing officer should have made a mesalliance.

"Yes. We were wed but a bare fortnight ago, at the embassy in Vienna," Ariel interceded, tired of being ignored.

"And now you have come to London. Do your duties bring you here, Monsieur Montague?" the comtesse asked, still directing her attention to Ian.

"I have received a London posting, which causes some problems as my family house is shuttered, my father, the Earl of Strathcairn preferring to live on his estates, and my brother, Viscount Montague, still in Vienna on Foreign Office business," Ian explained, hinting delicately at the reason for this visit. "We are staying at Stephen's Hotel."

The comtesse hesitated a moment, then obliged with the invitation they had hoped for. "Of course, you must come here. I would be charmed to entertain such attractive relatives, and I know

mon mari, Philippe, will be equally insistent."
She smiled fulsomely, but the cold eyes did not
warm.

"We would be delighted, would we not, my
dear," Ian accepted quickly, turning to Ariel with
a specious smile. "The hotel is not a proper milieu
for my wife, too crowded with rough military
types."

Ariel, who had spent most of her adult life with
military types, and found them most congenial,
agreed sweetly, hiding her anger at Ian's picture
of her as a timid little mouse. But then, if she had
her way, they would never become the guests of
the Villefranches, subjecting themselves to this
condescension. Just as well to remind herself of
the reason for their eager acceptance of the
comtesse's offer of hospitality. She suspected the
worldly comtesse had her own reasons for extending it. She did not appreciate the provocative
manner in which the Frenchwoman eyed Ian.
Obviously she believed Ariel no threat to what she
had in mind for that gentleman. And Ian was
doing little to discourage her intentions.

They chatted casually for a few more moments,
about Vienna, and life in London, saying little of
moment. But now that the coveted invitation had
been extended, there remained little to discuss
except the projected move. Ian, thanking the
comtesse, promised they would remove themselves from the hotel the following day and would
be with their hosts for dinner. He had completely
won over the comtesse, but Ariel found herself
prey to all sorts of confusing emotions, an un-

warranted jealousy chief among them. Asserting herself for the first time, she suggested that perhaps the comte might find their presence an intrusion.

"*Au contraire, ma chère*, he will be thrilled. We have adapted quite nicely to London life, but it will be so agreeable to have close relations to entertain. I must give a reception to introduce you," the comtesse demurred.

"Too kind of you," Ariel answered amiably, playing her role of the accommodating wife. Beneath her surface politeness, she was figuratively gritting her teeth. Was she expected to welcome this experienced matron's attempts to lure Ian into a flirtation? She wondered anew about the comte. Was he as sophisticated as his wife, willing to turn a blind eye to her *affaires de coeur* while pursuing his own desires? And as for Ian, she had a few things to say to that womanizer. Playacting strained her patience and she wondered how she would go on once they were established in the *maison* Villefranche.

With assurances of gratitude and promises to meet on the following day, the Montagues took their leave of the comtesse, Ariel barely restraining her irritation as Ian bowed suggestively over the Frenchwoman's hand, and received her expressions of delight. Obviously, she was of little account to these two, both experienced at playing the game of dalliance.

Once outside the South Audley Street house, Ariel's tenuous grasp on her temper relaxed. In the hackney going back to the hotel, she taxed Ian with his attitude.

"Really, Ian, need you have been so excessive in your compliments? Hardly the attitude of a new bridegroom," she reproved, casting all discretion to the wind.

"Well, my dear, you were little help. If it had been left to you, we never would have received an invitation, our sole purpose in coming to London, if you remember," he replied silkily, removing his tall beaver hat and running his hands distractedly through his hair. "The comtesse is a clever woman, obviously to be watched. She would never have been taken in by your prim manner and it is no good going into the sullens just because I charmed her. One would think you jealous of the lady's charms, if I did not know such a paltry emotion is beyond you," he sniped. "You must learn to dissemble a bit. It would never do for our hostess to think you have taken her in dislike."

Ariel's lips tightened. How typical of him, to blame her for an attitude she had little choice but to adopt with the two of them simpering over one another and virtually ignoring her. He would soon discover she was not the acquiescent little wife, content to follow in her husband's train.

"I am not going to stand by tamely while you carry on one of your flirtations with our hostess," she objected, sounding just like the shrew he accused her of being.

"There is a remedy for that," Ian countered smoothly, eyeing her with that devilish glint in his eye which promised an outrageous revenge for her complaints.

"And just what would that be?" she asked, realizing as the words were out of her mouth just what she was inviting.

"If you are prepared to be a complaisant wife to me, I should have no need to seek satisfaction in other women's beds," he replied, enjoying her loss of composure at his suggestion.

"For how long, I wonder. I am not about to be used to gratify your desire, sir, and then be abandoned when you become bored," Ariel replied tartly, knowing she had been lured into a trap. But he needn't think she would agree to his sexual blackmail. Somehow the thought of allowing him to make love to her in the coldhearted, passionless way he suggested, although it should have repelled her, brought a blush to her cheek as she imagined what such an encounter might entail.

"Just as you wish, my dear, but don't complain about my attitude toward more accommodating partners," he answered in a bored tone, dismissing her objections and staring out the window of the hackney as if the whole subject had become tedious.

Ariel repressed her angry reply. What was the use of brangling with him? He always emerged the victor, leaving her with the frustrating feeling that she counted for little except as a necessary facade in this dangerous game on which they had embarked. They had married not through choice but through expediency, and she should be relieved that he had accepted her terms for the marriage, instead of accusing him of all

112

sorts of perfidy. She sighed wistfully, remembering her dreams of a loving companion, a solace for the loss of her father, a bulwark against life's hazards. Confusion and regret warred with her normal caution and cynicism. Had she learned nothing during these last turbulent months? Retreating behind the armor she had donned to protect her from hurt, she said no more and, in her own turn, stared out the window, refusing to admit her disappointment.

On arrival back at the hotel, Ian escorted her to their rooms and then left her, saying he had business to conduct and suggesting she make ready for their departure the next day. He would probably not join her for dinner, as he had promised some fellow officers his company. Nodding brusquely, and implying she was happy to be rid of him, he departed, leaving her prey to some disturbing thoughts.

As he strode down St. James Street later en route to Brooks, he cursed to himself. Why could he not accept this marriage for what it was, a convenient vehicle to unmask Castlereagh's traitors, a sop to his father's demands? And need he behave in such a paltry manner toward Ariel? It could be no more pleasing to her, having to accept a bridegroom who behaved so, when she must have dreamed of a far different union. But she got his back up with her touch-me-not airs, and her obvious disdain of him. Why had she taken him in such dislike? Other women seemed eager to welcome his advances. How long could he desist from making her his wife in reality? God knows,

113

he was not a monk, and he found her reluctance frustrating and insulting. She attracted him. There was no denying that, though what an idealistic ninny she was, expecting some great romantic passion instead of settling for what they could have, a satisfying physical relationship. Well, he would abide by her rules for the moment, but the new Mrs. Montague would soon see he was no tame puppy, happy to accept the sterile companionship she had imposed. He was no brute, but damn it, the chit would drive him to rape if she continued to fend him off. Never had a woman proved so difficult, and he would wash his hands of her if they had not agreed to this masquerade. He suspected that the comtesse might prove another problem, too. She had a come-hither eye. And that would only complicate matters. He smiled grimly as he entered the club. Well, it was his own fault for dallying with that stupid Fiona. He would just have to pay the piper. And Ariel, although an innocent victim, might just have to pay too.

His humor was not lightened by meeting Alistair as soon as he entered Brooks. Why he should find his former comrade so irritating he could not fathom, and he resolutely banished his suspicions about that maddening officer as they settled down to broach a bottle of Madeira together and discuss the latest political maneuverings.

The Montagues' reception at the Villefranche

house the next day was flattering in the extreme. The comtesse herself was on hand to welcome them and escort them to their rooms. She had ordered adjoining bedrooms, laughing gaily at the arrangements.

"I assume you would not wish to share accommodations, *mes amies.* Modern marriages being what they are. So tiresome to always be under one another's feet. I cherish my privacy, and suspect you do too. Philippe is such a bad sleeper, his tossing and turning disturbs me. Often the case, *n'est-ce pas?* But I hope you will forgive my frankness. I forget you are such a new bride, *chère* Ariel." She spoke disarmingly, but with a glitter of curiosity in her blue eyes, as she glanced at the pair appraisingly.

"Quite right, madam. We will be most comfortable, I am sure," Ariel replied, trying to ignore her cousin's speculative tone. Rushing into speech to hide her confusion, she asked, "And are we to meet the comte this evening?"

"Yes, of course. I insisted he be home to greet you. He spends a great deal of time at the War Office, you know, helping our hosts to decipher the news from France. Of course, we all breathe easier knowing that devil Napoleon is incarcerated on Elba. What a monster the man is. But now happily removed from danger," the comtesse said with every impression of sincerity, crossing to the long windows and twitching the draperies, as if dissatisfied with the crimson velvet hangings. The room was decorated in the most luxurious fashion, with the latest Sheraton mahogany fittings, several bouquets of spring flowers, and a brilliant-colored Aubusson rug. Ariel wondered not for the first time where the money had come from for all this opulence. Had the Villefranches managed to spirit their money from France when they fled years ago, or did the source of their income have a more sinister background?

Ian raised a warning eye at Ariel. Then he put the question Ariel was eager to ask. "How fortunate you were, Comtesse, to be able to bring your assets from France when you fled. So many of your compatriots left with barely the clothes on their backs." He looked at his hostess innocently, but there was a nuance to his tone Ariel felt her cousin must find puzzling.

"Yes, we rely for much of our comfort on the proceeds from our West Indies estates. But the sugar plantations could be forfeit now. It is a great worry," she confided, then as if regretting admitting so much, she added, "But so depressing all this talk of money and politics. I try not to think of the disagreeable events in my homeland, and be grateful to your countrymen for providing such a delightful haven." She faced them boldly. Her apparent artless manner was no clue to the reality of the situation. She appeared to accept Ian's rather probing question at face value, but then she was a sophisticated and experienced woman, not apt to make careless disclosures.

"Well, I will leave you to settle in. My maid will be up soon to unpack for you, *chère* Ariel. I must call you that now, for Madame Montague sounds so formal, and you, too, Captain Montague, I hope

116

I can call you Ian?" She turned away from Ariel and looked winningly at Ian, much to Ariel's annoyance.

"Thank you, dear comtesse, and may we return the compliment and call you Francoise, since we are practically family? I understand you and Ariel are related through Prince Talleyrand, a most astute champion of France, as we learned in Vienna," Ian replied to Ariel's dismay. Really he was not at all subtle. If he was not careful, he would ruin their whole pretense.

"Alas, too true, a misalliance on our ancestor's part, I fear, for the man is a veritable mountebank. Not to be trusted," the comtesse responded, evidently not at all overset by Ian's knowledge.

Still smiling, she bid them *bonjour* and departed. Ariel waited a moment to be sure she would not hear, and then turned angrily to her husband, who was lounging against the mantel.

"You will give the game away if you ask the comtesse such probing questions. She is not a fool, you know."

"No, but she is a vain and ambitious woman. I am convinced that Castlereagh is correct. There is more here than the usual émigré story. I do not believe her dislike of Napoleon or Talleyrand is so deeply rooted. A clever, devious woman, the lovely Francoise," he suggested, amused at Ariel's railing. She was such an innocent herself she would find it hard to accept pretense in another, but he had learned to his cost how disingenuous women such as the lovely comtesse could be.

Ariel, for once in agreement with her provoking

117

husband and heartened by his assessment of the comtesse, which matched her own, smiled at him, causing that gentleman to narrow his eyes. How lovely she looked when she was not scolding him, quite an enticing picture in her warm green merino walking dress. With the light from the dying sun glinting on her heavy black hair, she had a strange appeal—not an obvious one, but compelling for all that. He felt drawn to her in a way that for the first time was not physical but combined a yearning to protect and cherish. This peculiar partnership on which they had embarked could prove to be exciting in more ways than he had expected.

"I wonder what the comte is like. As sophisticated and worldly as his wife, I suppose," Ariel, unaware of Ian's speculation, wondered, settling on the sofa and smoothing her skirt abstractedly.

Shaking off his thoughts, Ian shrugged. "Well, we will discover soon, no doubt. We must change for dinner." For some reason he wanted to prolong the moment in this dim room, lit only by the fire blazing in the grate.

"Yes, of course," Ariel answered, rising to pull the bell for the maid. "I must see about securing an abigail, an unnecessary expense but expected, I vow."

"I think my pockets can run to that and a new wardrobe for you. You must do me proud," Ian urged, surprising Ariel somewhat.

"Well, I bought some clothes in Vienna, but I have never had a very extensive wardrobe. That will be pleasant, although I doubt if I can

118

challenge the comtesse. She certainly seems to have the funds to indulge her every whim. I wonder if, indeed, the Villefranche wealth does come from the sugar plantations, or from some other less respectable source."

"That is one of the things we must discover," Ian said, and abruptly left the room, wary of extending the intimacy of this twilight scene which was provoking such odd fancies in his normally uncomplicated mind.

Alone, Ariel brooded over the coming meeting, her musings finally interrupted by the entrance of the maid, an austere Frenchwoman, who responded coldly to Ariel's overtures. She quickly unpacked Ariel's possessions, not at all impressed, and asked her if she could assist her in dressing. Ariel, preferring to be left to her own devices, finally dismissed her. Yes, she would have to hire her own abigail. This frosty Frenchwoman would not suit, and she probably was in her mistress's confidence, not a situation Ariel found comfortable. But then there was little in her current circumstances that offered comfort.

Chapter Ten

Comte Philippe de Villefranche was not quite what the Montagues had expected. At least twenty years older than his stunning wife, he was a man whose experiences and dissipations had etched deep furrows on his pale face. Of middle height, he had sparse white hair covering a thin-boned aristocratic head, cold gray eyes, and a formal, correct manner. His dress was foppish, with high shirt points hiding a wrinkled neck, and a waistcoat which defied description so heavily embroidered was the canary silk. However, Ariel could not fault his welcome. He bowed low over her hand and eyed her appreciatively from under his heavy lids, his thin lips breaking into a fulsome smile.

"My dear madam, what a pleasant surprise. When Francoise told me of finding a long-lost relative I had no idea she would prove to be such a charming addition to our household. How fortunate that you decided to make yourself known to us, and how pleased we are to welcome you, and your so gallant husband."

Not quite knowing how to accept this unctuous speech, Ariel smiled shyly and turned to Ian, as if seeking his support.

"It is too kind of you to have us, Comte," she replied. "Aside from my husband I have little family, so it is a great pleasure to meet my long-lost cousins." She looked beseechingly at Ian, hoping he would add his own gratitude to hers.

He did not fail her. Dressed in severe black evening clothes, he could not have provided a more stunning contrast to the dandified comte. And he was more than equal to the occasion.

"I do hope this is not too much of an imposition, Comte," he said suavely, shaking the Frenchman's hand heartily. "We are really at *point non plus*, with my family's house under the dust sheets. But we will not burden you with our presence too long. My brother, Arnold, will be arriving from Vienna shortly, and we will be able to join him and my sister-in-law at Grosvenor Square. Unfortunately my father, the Earl of Strathcairn, does not like London and prefers to remain on our estates in Northumberland." Smoothly, Ian had let the Villefranches know that he was no parvenu, but a member of England's most distinguished aristocracy, a point well taken by their hosts, Ariel was certain.

Exchanging news about common friends in Vienna, the quartet moved on into the dining room, where the comtesse apologized for the intimate dinner, reminding them that she hoped to provide more exciting entertainment for her guests before too long. Ian played up to his hostess, flattering her in the manner Ariel found so detestable, but she had to agree that Francoise seemed to accept his compliments in good part, thawing under his smooth gallantry. He was a master at these specious exchanges, and no doubt it was necessary to win her confidence, but Ariel did not like his practiced flirtations.

The evening went off well, although Ariel believed that the comte was not as receptive to Ian's courtesy as was his wife. On the other hand, Ariel did not appreciate the comte's efforts to touch her, his manner quite effusive. A lecherous old roué, she decided, and she must watch her step with him, playing the naive wife, while her husband pursued the comtesse.

Later in Ariel's bedroom they compared impressions. Ian seemed much more inclined to suspect the comte of double-dealing than his wife, but Ariel felt of the two, the comtesse was the more capable of conspiracy.

"You do not want to suspect Francoise, because you find her attractive," she complained, despising herself for sounding like a jealous shrew.

"Not at all. But remember that our host is the one with access to the War Office, in the confidence of a score of generals and policymakers. Alistair has had his eye on the comte for some time, and I must take his judgment seriously," Ian reproved, a twinkle in his eye. If Ariel was jealous of the comtesse, all to the good, as long as it did not impede their investigations.

"I thought you viewed Alistair with a jaundiced eye, believing him too involved with womanizing to be a serious ally," Ariel riposted, annoyed that Ian should defend the comtesse, although she realized she was being petty and spiteful.

"Whatever Alistair's proclivities in that line they do not prevent him from being an astute observer and courageous officer. I would trust him with my life, if not my wife," Ian explained in some amusement.

"Really, Ian, you are quite insulting. Do not excuse your own libertine ways by trying to foist a flirtation upon me. Besides, I do not think Alistair would try his ploys on me. You are old comrades, are you not?" Ariel spoke crossly, annoyed that he should turn the conversation in such a way.

"Old comrades, true, but old rivals when it comes to women, my dear. But come, I am a monster to tease you. You are tired, and worried about this masquerade upon which we have embarked. I am making no judgments yet. Both the comte and his charming wife bear watching, and that is what we are here to do, remember." He turned toward the adjoining door to his own room, wrenching at his cravat. "I will bid you goodnight, unless there is anything more you have to say, a request for me to stay, perhaps?" he offered whimsically.

"Good night, Ian," Ariel said almost absent-mindedly, her attention concentrated on her assessment of the Villefranches.

"Alas, refused again. You make it devilishly difficult for a man, my dear," Ian answered, hesitating at the door and smiling at her in a beguiling fashion.

"Don't be ridiculous, Ian. You like to provoke me, but we must take this situation seriously. Within weeks Castlereagh will be in London and we must have discovered if his fears are justified," she reproved.

"Quite right. But you cannot fault me for trying to come to a better understanding with you. And remember, Ariel, if you are reluctant to assume your marital duties, I might be forced to look elsewhere for my pleasure," he said mockingly, and was through the door into his own room before she could reply in the scathing manner his remark deserved.

But later, tossing restlessly in the big bed, she had to concede that he had some justification for his warning. A husband denied his rights, and such a one as Ian, would not long suffer rebuffs. But could she give herself to him in a soulless coupling just because he had legal rights over her body? He could cajole and flatter, but his attentions meant little but sop to his consequence. He did not entertain the idea of being denied by the one woman he had reason to think owed him compliance. To Ian she would just be one more woman to be bedded, available and convenient. She could not surrender to casual lovemaking, when it meant little more than an easing of his physical aches. Once he had made her his, she might find the association so binding, might even fall in love with him, and in that way lay heartbreak. No, she must continue to refuse him,

125

for this marriage had been entered into for all the wrong reasons, and she would not be used thus. Her decision, though, was fraught with perils.

How would she feel when he began to pursue some other woman? Her pride would suffer and perhaps more than her pride. She must remember the reason for this strange marriage, and take each day as it came. To hope for other than friendship from this alliance would be foolish. She reminded herself, not for the first time, that she had always considered herself a sensible person, who accepted that life would not be a romantic dream. Romance would not be found with the enigmatic Ian Montague.

With a determined effort she wrested her thoughts from her husband to the Villefranches. She had not made any judgments about that pair as yet. They might be what they seemed—well-to-do émigrés, interested in London's social round, content to forget their previous life in France, grateful for the sanctuary they had found in England. But there was a quality of opportunism in the couple which disturbed her. Perhaps on closer acquaintanceship she might be able to solve the questions which now had no answers. Resolutely she banished the welter of problems which threatened her tranquillity and finally fell asleep.

The next morning brought calmer counsels to Ariel, and she greeted Ian with composure and decision when he entered her bedroom. She was enjoying her breakfast looking young and vulnerable with her midnight black hair tumbling over her shoulders, faint shadows under her emerald green eyes, a bit embarrassed that Ian should see her in her dishabille.

"Good morning, my dear. I trust you had a comfortable night," he said, eyeing her mockingly, as if he knew how troubled her slumbers had been. He looked his usual arrogant self, dressed for riding in cream britches and hessians with a claret-colored riding coat.

"Good morning, Ian. I am being shockingly lazy. Usually I do not indulge myself with breakfast in bed, but the comtesse seemed to expect it. Have you need of me today?" she asked, toying with her chocolate cup. His raking stare made her aware of the intimacy of the scene.

"I am sure you are normally a veritable paragon of industry, so it will not hurt for you to have a relaxing morning. However, I thought we might make a plan for our investigations. The sooner we begin our enquiries, the better. I have a notion that events are closing in on us. My sources at the War Office appear nervous. After my ride I intend to go around there and try to set in train some deeper searches into just what our host's responsibilities vis-à-vis the government are. He seems to be privy to a lot of information, and I wonder if that is wise." Ian, having abandoned his teasing pose, was all seriousness, obviously not too disturbed by the provocative picture his wife made.

"Yes, well, I must employ a maid. Perhaps your batman might know of a suitable person. I do not

127

want to trust the comtesse to suggest an abigail. My maid must owe her loyalty to me, or we would encounter trouble. And I suppose I must try to get Francoise to confide more deeply in me, although just how I am to do that I am not sure." She sighed thinking of all the problems which lay ahead.

"I am sure you will contrive, although deception is not in your nature, I am afraid," he warned, sitting down on the edge of the bed. Ariel had all she could do not to shrink back from his disturbing closeness. "You might visit the modistes together. Fashions are a common bond between females, I have discovered. But be careful. I do not think the lovely Francoise is one for girlish confidences."

"No," she agreed sharply, "men are more her targets. But I will do my best."

"Puss, puss. You are too hard on the charming lady. I must try to find out about those West Indies plantations where their wealth is founded. It's deuced puzzling. They certainly live well, much better than most émigrés. And Villefranche seems up to snuff on all the army activity. Sometimes I wonder about the boffins at the War Office. Security is very lax." Ian, in common with most serving soldiers, had little but contempt for the armchair generals who decided the fate of the men in the field.

Shaking off his unease, he leaned over, imprisoning her with his arms. "I will bid you good day, and be about my business." He gave her a gentle kiss, raising a wry eyebrow at her flush. "Privileges of a husband, my dear, although not quite

128

the ones I hope to enjoy before too long." And before she could retort, he had strolled casually from the room.

Ariel, her appetite gone, and in some confusion, rose to make her toilette, prey to a welter of emotions, the strongest being annoyance that Ian could move her to such a tempest.

Later that morning she approached Francoise with a plea for some assistance with her shopping, and the two made the round of Bond Street and the Pantheon Bazaar, where Ariel bought carefully, wondering if Ian had the resources to pay for her new wardrobe. She knew he had debts, gambling ones no doubt, and she must talk to him about their finances, but on this gray January day, her first duty was to win the comtesse's confidence by seeking her advice and playing the ingenuous relative.

Her artless questions about the Villefranches' past were parried deftly. She discovered that her hostess appeared to take Napoleon's defeat as a blessing, castigating the emperor as a monster and sighing with relief that France had shaken off such an ogre.

"But do you think he is really safely incarcerated in Elba?" Ariel asked as the two rode down Piccadilly after their tiring morning of shopping.

"I certainly hope so. But one never knows with that wily upstart. Still, it is of little matter to us. We intend to remain in England. There is little left for us in our poor tortured homeland, even with a Bourbon once more on the throne," Francoise answered, seemingly sincere in her detestation of the man who had destroyed her country and much of Europe.

"Is there any possibility of your regaining your estates, in Normandy, I believe you said?" Ariel queried. "It seems strange I know so little of my mother's people." She hoped that excuse would serve for her curiosity.

"Well, a great deal will depend on my cousin, Prince Talleyrand, a clever man, as I am sure you will agree," Francoise replied, apparently accepting Ariel's interest. "You saw him at Vienna. Did he seem to be making much progress in winning concessions from the victors?"

Ariel, beginning to feel that she was the one under the inquisition, murmured something innocuous, relieved to see they had arrived at the South Audley house. Really, she was not an efficient conspirator, and felt a bit ashamed at quizzing her hostess, who had offered such generous hospitality. If only she could be certain that Francoise was just what she seemed, an innocent victim of France's turmoil, and not an intriguer. As the women descended the carriage, they met Alistair Glendenning walking down the steps. He raised his hat and smiled charmingly at them both.

"Ah, Ariel, well met. I just called on the hopes of finding you at home. And the charming comtesse, of course." He eyed them both with that rakish smile which made him such a threat to women.

"Captain Glendenning, is it not?" Francoise sparkled, pleased to be the cynosure of the officer's admiring stare. "How charming to see you again. Will you not come in, and perhaps join us for luncheon?"

"Alas, duty calls, but I had hoped Ariel might honor me with a tool around the Park later this afternoon, and you, too, if you would be so kind, Comtesse," he invited smoothly.

"Unfortunately I am promised to Lady Sefton this afternoon, but I am sure Ariel will find the escort of such a dashing gentleman acceptable. Will you not, Ariel," she said in a rather patronizing manner which set her cousin's teeth on edge. "Naughty of you though, Captain, to send out lures to a new bride," the comtesse teased, impelling Ariel with an unaccountable desire to smack her.

"I would be delighted, Captain Glendenning. At what time?" Ariel said.

"Oh, four o'clock, I think, if that is convenient." He bowed and left the ladies, springing into his phaeton and driving off with a flourish.

"An attractive man, the captain," Francoise said to Ariel as they proceeded into the house.

"An old comrade of my husband's," Ariel explained, irked that she felt the need of an explanation.

Over luncheon the comtesse continued to quiz Ariel about the dashing Captain Glendenning, much to her displeasure.

"Really, Francoise," she said as she peeled a peach. "The captain is only paying a courtesy to his old friend's wife. I understand he and my husband share memories of childhood days as well as a regimental association. They go back a long way together, and I assume Captain Glendenning is just doing the proper."

"But do take care, my dear," Francoise persisted, eyeing her cousin reflectively. "The captain has a fearsome reputation with women, has fought several duels, challenged by irate husbands, and is about to find himself in like case again over his liaison with Lady Bletchford. Of course, he is quite irresistible." Francoise had come to her own conclusions about the Montague marriage, and believed neither of the pair was greatly enamored of the other. If that was the case, it might prove vastly amusing to send out lures to Ian herself. He was quite wasted on this prim maiden.

"Not to a new bride, Francoise. And I do not think Ian would be very pleased to hear such hints." Ariel answered, a flush rising to her cheek as she tried to restrain her temper.

"Ah, but your husband himself is quite a rake. I understand they make the most possessive of husbands. But come, I am unkind to tease you, but I felt a word of warning as your cousin, and a woman who has seen a good deal more of London life than you, might not come amiss." Francoise was amused that Ariel's defenses could be so easily breached. Could she really care for Ian under all that reserved English gentility? Francoise tended to judge most women by her own appetites, which were avaricious and did not include compassion or kindness. She did not really like her own sex, much preferring the company of sophisticated men who shared her tastes for flirtation. Normally she would never have welcomed the Montagues as houseguests, but her reasons for extending the invitation were complicated, compounded by her own attraction to Ian, and political incentives which the comte also endorsed. She was a shrewd woman with a fancy for intrigue as well as a desire for money, with little interest in anything beyond the satisfaction of her own needs. She was perfectly willing to endure Ariel's presence in her household but she would entertain no competition from such a dull and prim matron.

Ariel, who was finding it difficult to restrain her anger at the comtesse's patronizing and sophisticated jibes, bit back a hot retort. She was not here to indulge her own fancies, and it was her duty to behave with circumspection, to show gratitude for the comte and comtesse's hospitality. If she found her new relatives uncongenial, she must mask her feelings for the purpose which had brought her to this sterile house. Her own inclination, to flee from all this conspiracy and conniving, must be set aside. Since the night Ian had burst into her bedroom, her life had become a welter of confusion and out of her direction. She could only pray that events would come to a climax before she lost her control and told all the protagonists in this affaire exactly what she thought.

Summoning up an agreeable air, which was quite an effort, she turned the conversation to the morning's shopping, aware that Francoise suspected that she was disturbed. Well, she must just struggle on, hoping that her meek manner would deceive not only the comtesse but all the characters she must face in this new life on which she had embarked so reluctantly.

Chapter Eleven

While Ariel was attempting to soothe her hostess and disguise her own unease, Ian had reported to the War Office for a conference which emphasized the seriousness of the quest to which they had committed themselves. He learned from General Lucien Valentine, now head of the Army Intelligence Service, that Wellington had narrowly escaped death on his departure from Paris.

Valentine, a handsome man in his mid-forties and a veteran of countless European campaigns, had vast experience in chasing spies, and some notable successes in catching them. Ian had met him but once before, during the Peninsular Campaign, and found him most impressive. They were joined in their interview by Alistair, who seemed privy to all the ploys Valentine had introduced to get to the bottom of the current conspiracies.

"It is vital that few know of what we have learned," Valentine said to the two young officers.

"Castlereagh is quite right to suspect a dangerous leakage of information, but whether the culprits are in his department or ours is the problem. No matter how successful our efforts in unmasking these networks, another springs up almost as soon as we capture one group. Fouché had spies everywhere in London during the late war, and we have reason to believe he has not abated his intrigues now that we are at peace. We have been too generous in welcoming these émigrés into our midst. Some of them no doubt are sincere in their hatred of Napoleon, but many of them will commit any folly to ensure their estates are returned to them."

"And you believe, sir, that the Villefranches are among these traitors," Ian said.

"Castlereagh believes so, and I cannot fault his intelligence. The Villefranches, unlike many of their countrymen, seem to have emerged from the revolution with their wealth intact—very suspicious. Most of the funds come from the plantations in the West Indies, and now the Allies wish to wrest those islands from French domination. That is reason enough for the Villefranches to conspire with Napoleon's minions. And do not forget Talleyrand, to whom the comtesse has family ties. He is capable of the most sophisticated of intrigues in aid of his own ambition. They are very likely agents." Valentine eyed the two officers wearily. He envied them their uncomplicated soldier's view, for he would have much preferred to fight the French or any of his country's enemies on the battlefield than busy

136

himself with these complicated ruses in London's drawing rooms.

"What news do you have of the Duke's danger, sir?" Ian asked, well aware, as were all three of them, how injurious to their cause the loss of Wellington would be.

"Four assassins were arrested outside Paris, before they could attack the Duke's coach en route to Vienna," Valentine replied. "It is the second attempt, and there well might be more. It seems our late enemies much prefer Napoleon to a Bourbon. They have not welcomed the monarchy with much enthusiasm. I was against imprisoning Napoleon on Elba, much too near the mainland, and others share my view, but it is too late to worry about that now. But you may be certain that Napoleon is in touch with all that goes on in Paris and Vienna. He is not accepting his exile calmly, and continues to plot for his return. The death of the Duke would ensure that any opposing armies would have a much harder time defeating him again. We cannot allow Wellington to be immobilized."

A frown darkened Alistair's usually insouciant countenance. "And you believe that the plots to assassinate the Duke, to free Napoleon from Elba, originate in the Villefranche household?"

Valentine deliberated for a moment, as if wondering whether he could completely confide in the younger officers. "Evidence suggests there is some reason to suspect them. Every émigré of any note has entree into the Villefranche establishment, and the comte is on intimate terms with

137

a number of high-placed sources in the War Office and the Foreign Office as well as the Horse Guards. I am reluctant to accuse the man without incontrovertible evidence, and it is just that information we hope you can secure for us, Captain Montague. We must move carefully, for the comte has the ear of the Prince Regent, and accusation of his treachery must be backed up with hard facts, not easy to obtain, I warrant." A man who normally had no difficulty making decisions, Valentine seemed this time almost tentative, colored by doubts and the pressures from unseen but powerful forces. He stabbed crossly with his pen at a paper on his desk. He did not like trusting these junior officers to do the job he would have preferred to undertake himself.

"Have you any ideas as to how we will secure these hard facts?" Ian asked, barely restraining his impatience with all this cloudy supposition.

Valentine hesitated. "I believe we must offer him some vital papers, perhaps depositions of troops in case of another uprising in France. Then it will be your job to see what he does with them. Have you the chance to take a look at his correspondence, do you think?" He stared at Ian straightly, aware that the officer would loathe such an assignment. Spying was a dirty business, but necessary.

"I could make the opportunity, General," Ian said, frowning.

"You understand that if you are caught, accused by the comte of a grievous abuse of his hospitality, we can do nothing to protect you?"

Valentine insisted, uneasy at asking such a favor. Captain Montague was a brave serving officer, unaccustomed to the nasty complications of spying. Did he have the talent for deception? Valentine wavered, not liking to offer his next suggestion. "I understand Lord Castlereagh has explained the situation to your wife. Perhaps it would be more expedient for her to do the investigating. Women often are more adept at this type of thing."

"I would prefer Ariel not become involved, although I am sure she is eager to aid us in every way. It's not a job for a woman," Ian argued, suddenly angry at the thought of what she might have to face. Again those unexpected feelings of protection rose to haunt him. He wanted to keep her out of it.

"The Montagues are newly married, General. Naturally Ian wants to protect his wife," Alistair intervened, eyeing his friend with tolerance.

"I am afraid we cannot afford the normal niceties in these circumstances, gentlemen. But for the moment, we will hold a watching brief. If you discover anything suspicious in the comte's household, we can then proceed to put a plan in motion. And notify me immediately if you do find anything which denotes unusual communication with the French. Glendenning will assist you in any way. Unfortunately too many people are already privy to our plans. Our chief purpose now is to keep our plans secret until we can pounce on the traitors. If it were only the Villefranches and their émigré friends we suspected, I would be more sanguine, but I greatly fear the leakage of information begins with one of our own, a home-grown traitor. In my experience, bribery casts a long shadow. Even Englishmen will do a great deal for money," Valentine said in some heat. He had vast experience in the avarice of his country-men, who placed greed above patriotism.

"I will do my best, sir. I admire the Duke and loathe Napoleon. Like you, I fear we have not heard the last of him, and events in Vienna right now seem to be going the Frenchies' way, chivied along by that mountebank, Talleyrand," Ian answered, remembering the maneuvering he had seen in Vienna.

"Castlereagh arrives within the week. I would like some concrete news for him by then." Valentine finished the conference, standing to bid good-bye to his aides. It had been an unpleasant interview, but then uncovering spies was an unsavory business always. "Good luck and thank you, Montague." He smiled winningly, trying to lighten the atmosphere.

"Yes, sir, and good-bye for the moment." Ian resumed his usual adroit manner, unwilling to let the general know how worried he was by the interview. The two officers left Valentine's office, each with his own budget of anxiety.

"Well, Alistair," Ian said as they left the War Office, "we are now engaged in a vastly different kind of war than we have fought in the past, and one which promises trouble."

"Yes, and spying on one's host is a dastardly game. I feel for you. I know little of the

Villefranches, although I see the luscious comtesse everywhere. Her husband is an unknown quantity. However, I hope to correct that situation. I have every excuse, since they accept that you are an old comrade in arms and will expect me to be a frequent caller while you are in residence. As a matter of fact, I have set events in train by inviting your wife for a tool around the Park this afternoon, and perhaps she will allow me closer acquaintanceship." Alistair was well aware that Ian would not like his encroaching behavior, but he could not resist goading his old friend.

Ian's eyes blazed. "Stay away from Ariel, Alistair. She is not fair game for you, and I understood you were heavily occupied elsewhere." Damn the fellow, could he not keep his hands off any available female?

"Can it be that the prim and proper Mrs. Montague has pierced your defenses, my dear chap? I never thought I would see the day when you would be caught in any woman's toils, even a wife's."

"A wife is a bit different than a light-o'-love, Alistair. We Montagues know how to protect our own. I am warning you, do not send out lures to Ariel." Ian knew he was reacting badly, rising to Alistair's jibes, but could not seem to stop himself.

"The role of benedict does not suit you, Ian. Oh well, I suppose it comes to us all, but I have so far steered clear of that trap. Not to worry, my dear man, I am only doing the proper and escorting your wife on an innocuous ride. No need to call me out." Alistair laughed, amused at Ian's fierce reaction to his teasing. But he was a bit surprised. He had assumed the marriage was one of convenience, for he had heard gossip about the contretemps in Vienna and Ian's previous pursuit of the incomparable Fiona Mackenzie.

"Oh, have it your way, Alistair. But take care. I might just respond by trying to cut you out with the lovely Lady Bletchford. You are delving in dangerous waters there, my fellow," Ian riposted as the two walked down Whitehall.

"Not your style, Ian, the lovely Olivia," Alistair answered carelessly, hiding his irritation at his friend's implied criticism. "I am a man of many talents, and cannot confine my attentions to one lovely. There are too many ladies out there awaiting consolation. And I am only too willing to oblige. La Bletchford is just one of many. You must not believe every on dit, you know."

"Let's cry pax, Alistair. We must just agree to differ about your many amours. Have a delightful ride with my wife. I will hear all about it, no doubt." Doffing his hat to Alistair, Ian strode off down the street, ignoring his friend's laugh. He had not found Alistair's quips enjoyable. Whatever their necessary cooperation over this spy business, he did not want Glendenning exercising his famous charm on Ariel. But how was he to prevent it?

Ariel, not quite so naive as her husband believed, had a notion that Captain Glendenning had invited her on this afternoon's ride as much to annoy her husband as from any desire for her company, but she intended to enjoy herself all the same. It would do Ian no harm to understand that other gentlemen found her company attractive, although why she should care what her husband thought was puzzling. She had not realized that his indifference piqued her so much, but Alistair Glendenning's obvious interest in her was flattering. Of course, he was a shocking flirt, but on the whole it was pleasant to be the object of his practiced addresses.

She had dressed carefully for the outing, in a bottle green wool gown under her sable-lined pelisse with a fetching plumed bonnet. It added to her consequence to play the fashionable matron after years of looking a dowd. Ariel had little conceit, not realizing that her serene appearance represented a challenge to a man such as Alistair, who wondered about the passions hidden by her proper facade. Her looks were uncommon, far from the vacuous blond and blue-eyed beauties who were currently the rage. Ariel neither simpered nor flirted, but her cool brunette elegance promised a passion Alistair was too experienced not to find challenging. He was too clever to pay her obvious compliments, but his eyes were admiring and his conversation just rakish enough to keep her entertained and relaxed.

As they drove through Hyde Park behind his team of dashing chestnuts, he kept up a running commentary on the fashionable throng who congregated at this popular hour.

"See, Ariel, there is Harriette Wilson, the most infamous of all the demimondaines, some say the *chère amie* of the Iron Duke himself. Of course, the gossips insist she toys with men's affections but her heart was given long ago to Lord Ponsonby, who abandoned her. So she now takes her revenge on all us luckless souls who yearn for her *beaux yeux*," he claimed outrageously.

"Should I be shocked, Captain Glendenning? Alas, I am well aware of the fickleness of men's affections, and that marriage does not mean fidelity," Ariel responded, eyeing him severely.

"So lovely and so cynical. How have you come by such bitter reasonings? I am sure you have never suffered a rebuff from your cavaliers," Alistair countered, deftly turning his horses down a shaded path.

"I am not some school miss on the catch for a husband," Ariel said airily, "nor a society matron up to all the rigs and starts of the ton, but years following the drum have inured me to the false promises and seductive offerings of you so-called officers and gentlemen."

"You are a most uncommon type, my dear, and I am quite jealous of that dog, Ian, for scooping you up before the rest of us could have ar. inning." Alistair, not one whit abashed by her set-down, raked her with a hot stare.

"Save your ploys for more credulous women, Captain Glendenning, and tell me something of your army career," she said, hoping that she would learn a bit more of Ian and his exploits, "for

144

I am a veteran campaigner and like nothing more than to recall those years following my father in the Iron Duke's train."

"Ah, what a stubborn woman you are, impervious to all my charms, I see. Well, courtesy demands that I answer your request," Alistair acceded, and proceeded to give her an amusing if not entirely accurate account of his army years in the Peninsula. Ariel realized she was hearing a lighthearted and embellished tale but was astute enough to recognize that beneath his careless jesting lay a dedicated soldier, who had endured the hardships, danger, and weariness of campaigning, much like her father, and her heart warmed to him. There was much to admire in the insouciant Alistair, no matter how he tried to disguise his devotion to duty beneath that cloak of womanizing and rakehell indifference to society's dictates. Somehow she felt she could trust him, that she had made a friend.

Interrupting one of his scurrilous tales of regimental thievery in Portugal, she said seriously, "Captain Glendenning, I know you are privy to what Ian and I hope to attempt for Lord Castlereagh. What is your impression of our hosts, the Villefranches? I know it is reprehensible of me to discuss them when they have offered us such generous hospitality, but our mission is so important." She turned to him, her emerald green eyes lustrous with sincerity.

"Ariel—I may call you that, I trust?—and do call me Alistair—Captain Glendenning is so quelling—how can I answer you? I do not know the Villefranches, having met them only casually at the various functions one attends. I naturally tend to suspect most émigrés. Very few of them would not sacrifice their principles to regain their estates, and although many of them deserve their fate, having treated the peasantry so ruthlessly, I think they have paid dearly for their selfishness. Some of them, of course, are innocent victims, but in any revolution, even the innocent suffer. But somehow I doubt if the Villefranches can be numbered among the innocent. Not much help to you, but they are my views, paltry as they may be," Alistair finished soberly, for once his light-hearted manner in abeyance.

Impressed by his sincerity, Ariel felt that her revised opinion of this casual rake was confirmed. There had been nothing of the indifferent society dandy in his analysis.

"Thank you, Alistair. I echo your sentiments. I must simply restrain my natural instincts and get on with this investigation, I suppose. Perhaps I can free my cousins from suspicion. But if they are guilty, I want them to be punished. I saw enough of the havoc that ogre Napoleon imposed on his own people, as well as the Portuguese and Spanish. Too many good men died to bring him to justice." She stared directly into Alistair's cobalt blue eyes, impressing him with her honesty.

For his part, Alistair realized for the first time that here was no simple innocent but a woman of compassion and warmth, who cared about larger concerns than furbelows and ton gossip. A woman of strong convictions and an old-fashioned morality, whom his friend, Ian, could neither cow nor charm. Their union promised fireworks, and he for one thought they both had some lessons to learn if they were to settle into marital accord. His friendship for Ian did not prevent him from exercising his mischievous streak. He would quite enjoy employing his meddlesome talents in their affairs. Ian should not have matters all his own way.

Handing Ariel down from his phaeton before the South Audley house, he pressed her hand suggestively and promised another meeting soon. "It would never do to let Ian have a clear field with you. 'Tis doubtful if he appreciates you as he should. But we are destined to become warm friends, I know, and when I have proved myself to you, perhaps you will honor me with your confidence. Until then, *au revoir*, my dear lady." Leaping up into his phaeton, he gave her a quizzical smile and was off, steering his horses skillfully down the street toward Piccadilly.

Ariel chuckled, then sobered as she was admitted to the house. Taking off her bonnet and handing her cloak to the butler, she wondered just what Alistair had intended to convey by his parting remarks. Had Ian told him the circumstances of their marriage? Or had he guessed some of their difficulties? He had too much knowledge of women and too much experience not to realize that theirs was hardly a love match. Could he be trusted? She badly needed a friend, but was Alistair a wise choice, or just such another as her libertine husband, unable to refrain from bringing any female he met under his spell? Obviously her new life in London society held other perils than acting a role before her Villefranche cousins and delving into their secrets. How she yearned to return to the uncomplicated life of the campaign, where at least one had no difficulty in recognizing the enemy.

Chapter Twelve

Ian found no opportunity to search Philippe de Villefranche's study in the next few days. He wondered if the wily Frenchman suspected his interest in his host's concerns. And he had an equal lack of success in establishing a closer relationship with Ariel. He could not break through that aura of reserve and suspicion which she donned to prevent him from any deeper intimacy.

He had quite determined now that he wanted to make her his wife in reality, but he did not want to force her. Cynical and wayward, Ian did not admit that what he felt toward Ariel was anything like that inconceivable emotion, love. Ian doubted if he was capable of that romantic feeling the poets raved about in their sonnets. Passion, desire, physical gratification, he had experienced them all at one time in his pursuit of the gentler sex, but a love which inspired an unselfish desire for the loved one's happiness before his own, a strong enduring affection, a basis for a lifetime companionship was a notion he had never entertained. He doubted he entertained it now, but it was devilishly hard to live in such close proximity to an attractive woman, moreover his own wife, and not try to tempt her into bed. Frustration was making him irritable, and the lack of progress in his effort to discover just what the Villefranches were plotting did little to ease his discomfort.

And then there was Alistair, hanging about flattering Ariel, suspicious of the marriage, and hoping to take advantage of the couple's estrangement. Damn him. Ian had seen his old comrade in hot pursuit before, and rarely had any of his quarries refused him in the end. Did Ariel find the captain appealing? Hard to tell. She enjoyed his company, but gave little away. Maybe he should try Alistair's tactics, try wooing his wife as he had Fiona and a long list of lovelies before her. Why was Ariel so stubbornly refusing to consummate their marriage? Did she find him so repulsive?

Confused and tormented by his own feelings and his inability to discover hers, he became increasingly discontented and irritable. With the knowledge that both Castlereagh and his brother Arnold would soon be arriving on the scene, he decided he must solve at least one of his problems before many more hours had passed. They had been in England a week now, with little to show for it. Not given to indecision, always preferring action, Ian decided on this bright winter morning to tackle the least challenging of his two problems, and sought out his wife in their rooms.

Although Ariel appeared to be her usual composed self—dressed in an elegant morning gown of cerise merino, which was suited for the inclement weather—she was coping with her own problems, chief among them being her attitude toward her provoking husband. She greeted him coolly, wondering what he had in mind. For once his mocking, indifferent air seemed in abeyance.

"Ariel," he said, taking up his usual stance before the fireplace, "I have been giving a great deal of thought to how we might proceed to find the evidence which Castlereagh seeks. Time is passing and we are no closer to unmasking the Villefranches, if they are indeed the traitors we seek."

A frown darkened her creamy complexion as she toyed nervously with the embroidery she was holding. "Yes, I know, and I cannot conceive of a plan to expose them. Do you have any suggestions?" she asked.

"I have been conferring with General Valentine, who is in charge of intelligence at the War Office, and an experienced spy chaser. He thinks we must at least make a stab at examining the comte's correspondence. A nasty chore, I agree, but we cannot expect to fulfill our responsibility and still observe the niceties of polite behavior."

He waited for some demur from her but, receiving none, continued, "If I am caught in his library, it might prove more awkward than if you were the culprit. The comte obviously fancies you, finds you pleasing, not to be wondered at, but still we must use the opportunity to hand. Can you possibly see your way to doing this disagreeable task?"

"Why not? That is what we are here for, after all. But I doubt if he would be so foolish as to leave incriminating documents lying around for our discovery. Still, I agree we must make some push to find out if he is truly our culprit. I am more inclined to believe that Francoise is our traitor. Of the two, she seems more suited to intrigue," Ariel mused.

"Females, all of you are devious. Is it that you think Francoise is a rival in any way, my dear? Let me assure you she is not," Ian replied, returning to that cynical mocking manner she found so provoking.

"Don't be ridiculous, Ian," Ariel said sharply. "I do not share your constant preoccupation with dalliance and flirtation. If you intend to practice your wiles upon Francoise, it is no concern of mine, although I might remind you that the last time you indulged in such romantic pursuits, you paid a heavy price."

"Ah, but it should be your concern. And let me remind you that if I had a loving wife, I would have no need to chase after more complaisant females," Ian jeered, enjoying as always the telltale blush that rose in her cheeks.

"I doubt if I threw myself into your arms and confessed an undying passion you would be pleased. What irritates you is that I do not find you irresistible. And little wonder. Have you given me any reason to think you would make a faithful husband?" Ariel was annoyed that she would rise to his baiting but was unable to restrain the sharp retort.

Ian sighed, abandoning his provocative manner. "Quite right, as usual, my dear. I see I must use different tactics to prove my devotion, but are we not straying from the matter in hand?"

"Yes, but you delight in provoking me. I will undertake to examine the comte's correspondence, but you must see to it that Francoise does not interrupt me. Could you not invite her for a drive or some other ruse?" Ariel responded firmly, determined not to surrender to his challenge.

Suddenly tiring of trying to win from her any response, Ian turned away, annoyed at her constant rebuffs. Was the woman made of iron? Did she have no softer feelings? Despite himself, he admired her stubbornness, her unwillingness to be bedded as a convenience, but the more he saw of her, the more intrigued he became with her intransigence. Not for a moment did Ian wonder why it had become so important to him to win his wife's affection. In the beginning he had entertained no such notions of behavior. But he found her obdurate resistance to his attempts to consummate their marriage maddeningly frustrating. Surely she was not so naive as to expect him to declare his undying love, play the romantic besotted suitor. She must realize that most ton unions were based on far more practical reasons, and that love was a game for fools.

153

"Well, Ian, I think we must not delay," Ariel remarked, wondering what ideas her husband was harboring behind that cool mask he donned. "If you remove Francoise on some errand, I will try to make the effort today. Nothing will be gained by postponing the disagreeable chore."

"Quite right. I will approach Francoise immediately, and let you know the plan," he answered, trying to restrain his dislike of what he had asked of her. These protective scruples would avail him nothing. She was quite capable of handling the situation, and he was stupid to allow his distaste of involving her in such a dangerous task cloud the issue. Bidding her a curt good-bye, he left her bedroom, afraid of remaining longer and letting her see how the necessity for this action bothered him.

Ariel crossed the hall toward the library, keeping a wary eye out for any observers. Ian and Francoise had left for their ride in Hyde Park a quarter of an hour ago, and she could not postpone her intention any longer. Francoise had accepted Ian's invitation for the late afternoon, wishing to parade her attractive cavalier at the fashionable hour when all of London's beau monde would be taking the air. Ariel could only hope that the comte would not return early from his War Office duties, but that seemed unlikely. He put in long hours at his desk there, although just what occupied him to such an engrossing extent remained a mystery.

Darting into the library, she gave a heavy sigh. No use in taking a disgust of her actions. She must remember the greater good at stake. If indeed the comte was involved in treachery, the sooner he was apprehended, the better. If through her tardiness in bringing him to book any danger befell the Duke, she would never forgive herself.

She took a quick look around the vast room, lined with impressive volumes behind their glass doors. Perhaps she had best choose a book, just in case she was surprised by some intruder. Giving a comprehensive glance over the array of leather-bound books, she took out a novel from the Sir Walter Scott set and laid it on the desk. There were no papers in sight. Possibly the comte locked away any incriminating correspondence, and if that were the case, just what she could discover was problematical. But the drawers were unlocked. She opened each quickly, finding in one receipted bills, and more that were unpaid, several with demanding notes attached. The comte owed a great many tradesmen, but that need not prove he was beneath the hatches. Most of the nobility delayed payment of such debts for months, believing that tradesmen should curb their demands while more honorable debts were paid. Still the Villefranches did not appear to be in too deep. Where did they get the funds to provide this luxurious life-style?

Finally in a bottom drawer she saw a bundle of letters from the West Indies. Gingerly untying the correspondence, she saw to her surprise that the island factor was reporting on distressing conditions at the island plantation. Crops had failed, workers were lazy, sugar prices had fallen. All in all the plantation did not appear to be showing a good profit, and the factor demanded an infusion of money to set it on its feet. That did not jibe with Francoise's description of their island estates.

Ariel frowned as she retied the bundle. If the sugar plantation did not supply the funds, they must be coming from somewhere else. Could this be the evidence she needed to prove the Villefranches were in the pay of Napoleon's minions? The other drawers had little of interest, filled with writing paper, pens, and stamps. The final drawer in the center of the desk was locked. Whatever secrets the comte possessed must lie there, and how could she gain access to them? Did he carry the key with him? Probably. Which meant that either she or Ian must somehow secure it. She stood irresolutely before the desk, planning her next move, when suddenly the door opened, and the comte entered the room.

Seeing the intruder, his eyebrows rose, then lowered, but Ariel had glimpsed the ugly expression in them which he quickly masked.

"Ah, my dear Mrs. Montague. Can I be of some assistance?" he asked suavely.

"Oh, do forgive me, Comte, for the intrusion. I was looking for a book, and have found one, this copy of Sir Walter Scott's *Waverley*. I am a passionate admirer of his and eager to read this latest effort. Do excuse me for being so bold." Ariel lifted the book as if to show him her interest,

156

all the while sounding to her own ears like some simpering fool.

"Of course, my dear Ariel. I am delighted to share Sir Walter Scott with you. But don't you find him a bit farouche, so violent and impetuous the Scots, I think," he countered with a wealth of meaning beneath his smooth tones.

"Not at all. You forget that my husband is a Scot. Very exciting creatures in my experience," she prattled on, wondering if he would ask what she was doing standing by his desk when the bookshelves were across the room. She sought frantically for an excuse, but was unwilling to venture an explanation if he did not require one.

His face told her nothing, for his expression was bland and polite. But she had had that one glimpse of ferocious anger when he had first entered the room. She doubted she would come out of this encounter easily. She watched him warily as he crossed the room to her side, not liking to provoke him but wondering how soon she could escape.

"I am happy to see that you regard my home as yours, *chère* Ariel. You are an intriguing lady, with many unsuspected talents. I wonder if your gallant husband appreciates you. I find soldiers on the whole so concerned with their martial exploits, the camaraderie of like-minded men, that they have little time to spare for the gentler sex. It takes a Frenchman to understand a woman. The English are so hearty, so devoted to their sport and their clubs. And then you are half-French yourself, are you not?" His hand came out to caress her cheek. Ariel repressed a shudder at the touch of this aging roué. Did he really believe she would accept his disgusting advances?

"Frenchmen are indeed romantic, but for husbands, I believe the more practical British have advantages. And Scots, of course, have Celtic blood, which is vastly seductive. Ian is a very paragon of husbands," Ariel declared, crossing her fingers behind her back.

"Ah, I forget, you are still such a new bride. I hope disillusion will not overcome you too soon. But I am always available to advise you on the pitfalls of marriage. Consoling pretty matrons is one of my talents." He eyed her with that lascivious glance. Then suddenly, as if tiring of this game, his tone altered, his glance became colder. "Just remember, *chère madame*, that there is danger in identifying too closely with your husband's interests." The comte's words held a threat of which Ariel was not unmindful. Just how much did he suspect and did he have a great deal to hide?

"I cannot believe that a wife should not be supportive, Comte. I must identify with my husband in all things," she countered, aware that she was perhaps showing her hand, but she would not allow him to intimidate her. Now more than ever she suspected the Villefranches were not what they seemed. Lord Castlereagh's suspicions were well founded and she would prove them correct. Whatever cousinly gratitude she owed this pair did not extend to forgiving treachery against her country.

"Now I must retire to my bedroom. I understand we are having guests to dinner tonight, and I must dress." She turned away, eager to leave the comte's presence.

His hand shot out to restrain her, capturing her wrist. "Just remember, *ma chère*, that your beauty will not protect you if you find yourself in troubled waters trying to aid your so gallant husband. *Au contraire*, I doubt if he will be able to offer the protection you need. You would be well to confine yourself to the usual pursuits of embroidery and novel reading." His tone was steely and his grasp on her wrist tightened cruelly, as if to promise retribution should she attempt any further investigation of his affaires. "I make a bad enemy, Ariel, but a most doting . . . ah, shall I say, friend."

"And I hope I can rely on that friendship, Comte. Now you must excuse me." Ariel smiled, as if not understanding his double entendre. Holding her breath, she made her way slowly to the door, her back rigid. Once she was in the hallway she sighed in relief. She believed she had brushed through that contretemps well, but she realized now that Philippe de Villefranche was not the foppish lecher she had thought, but a dangerous man, and she would be wise to tread warily in any attempt to discover his secrets, and that in itself was intriguing. She walked slowly to her room, in a deep study of what the interview had revealed.

Ian, coming in from his rather tedious ride with Francoise, found Ariel brooding before the fire in

159

her bedroom. Halfway to being dressed for dinner, she made an enticing picture, her long straight ebony hair hanging down her back and her figure confined in an emerald velvet dressing gown. Watching her unobserved from the doorway which connected their rooms, he wondered not for the first time at his patience in not making her his. Every day she became more alluring to him, compounded by the long abstinence his marriage had imposed upon him. That was all it was. She was attractive, and it had been weeks since he had bedded any woman. He did not consider why this one particular woman had suddenly made any other seem undesirable. That was a path down which he refused to stray.

"Well, Ariel, what have you to report?" he asked brusquely, coming to stand before her, a bit disturbed by her stillness. She looked up as if interrupted in a loathsome reverie.

"How was your ride, Ian? Were you able to wrest any significant information from Francoise?" She eyed him curiously, not replying to his question, more in the nature of a severe nanny, he thought, than a loving wife. But then Ariel was hardly that, and little prospect of her becoming one, he decided gloomily.

"A great deal of intemperate gossip about the ton, some amusing on dits, and a long tirade against her modiste. Not very revealing," he concluded with a lugubrious sigh.

"You must be losing your touch. I thought you would have masses of incriminating detail from her," she quipped, and then chided herself for

160

sounding like a jealous harpy.

Ian refused to rise to her baiting. He seemed content just to loom there in the flickering firelight and look at her in that disturbing way. She should have dressed, not allow him to see her in her dressing gown. The intimacy of their situation might lead him to expect favors she had no intention of granting.

"What is bothering you, Ariel? Has something untoward happened?" he asked, ignoring her allusion to his attempts at a flirtation with their hostess. He would not give her the satisfaction of hearing that he found the comtesse's mature charms not at all delectable.

"What has happened is that the comte surprised me in the library," she said sharply, nervous under Ian's admiring stare, conscious of her own vulnerability.

"In the act of rifling his desk?" Ian said in some dismay.

"No, fortunately I had completed that, or as much as was possible without a key to a locked drawer. And what I found was proof of a sort. The Villefranche fortunes are not founded on their sugar plantations," she reported, and then went on to describe the contents of the correspondence she had read.

"Well, that is significant, and an indication that their funds must come from some other, no doubt less honorable, source. If the comte did not catch you in the act of rummaging through his papers, what is the trouble?" he continued, puzzled by her distraught air.

Ariel hesitated. If she told Ian that their host had made advances to her, what would be his reaction? Not that he would be jealous, but hotheaded he certainly could be, impetuous and apt to precipitate a situation she did not want.

"Well, I may be reading more into the conversation than it warrants, but it seemed to me he suspects you of taking an inordinate interest in his affairs, and he warned me not to join you in such undertakings. He offered to comfort me if you strayed with more accommodating females, too." She laughed, tossing off the last remark lightly.

"Old lecher," Ian growled, then looked at her almost inimically. "Did you imply that I am an indifferent husband, Ariel, and that you would be happier in his senile embraces?"

"Of course not, Ian. I suppose it is just his manner, to flirt with any available female, but I found his attentions quite repulsive. And I am afraid I have made him angry with my obvious repulsion," she explained meekly, looking at him nervously from under her eyelids.

"Well, we must just prove him mistaken, show him that you are deeply captivated by your adoring husband. And I think a little practice might not come amiss," Ian replied, his hands grasping her shoulders and pulling her up from her chair into his arms.

Before she could resist, her mouth was crushed beneath his passionate kiss, then his lips roamed down to the deep cleft revealed by the gaping dressing gown. Ariel's blood rose under his warm caresses, and for the first time she made no effort

162

to struggle, a feeling of lassitude overtaking her, her hands instinctively going around his neck and clasping him with as much ardor as he was exercising. She felt her control slipping as his kisses became more demanding, his hands more insistent.

At that moment, her abigail walked into the room. Shocked to see the intimate embrace, she gasped out her apologies.

Ian, releasing Ariel, looked rueful and more than overset, a hot light in his eyes as they roamed over her flushed cheeks and swollen mouth, an unholy satisfaction in his countenance causing her to turn away in humiliation. How could she have been so brazen, encouraging his lustful possession?

"A beginning. We must continue your tutelage later this evening, madam," he mocked. He pressed a hard kiss on her palm and strolled nonchalantly to the door leading to his own chamber.

Chapter Thirteen

Surprisingly, in view of Francoise's advice about Alistair Glendenning, he was among the guests invited to that evening's dinner party. Hanging on his arm when he entered the drawing room was a young beauty with limpid blue eyes, blond ringlets, and a lovely figure, fetchingly arrayed in a sky blue silk gown edged with seed pearls. She was introduced as Olivia Bletchford, and her husband had not accompanied her. She must be the latest of Alistair's flirts, Ariel thought, and could not wonder at his attraction. She discovered that Lady Bletchford had little conversation and spent most of the evening gazing intensely into Alistair's eyes, despite the fact that he did not return her soulful looks.

Ariel much preferred General Valentine, whom she knew to be in Ian's confidence, his superior in the War Office and a soldier of proven courage and distinction. His ebullient wife, some ten years younger—and an American, she was quick to point out—charmed Ariel from their introduction, discussing her travels, her two children, and the joys of country living. Since General Valentine and Alistair were both involved in their attempts to unmask the French spy ring, Ariel wondered at their presence. Had Francoise invited them in all innocence, knowing that they were friends of her houseguests, or because she suspected their interest and hoped to learn a bit about their inquiries? If so, she gave no signs of it, chatting easily of mundane topics.

The other two couples which made up the dozen were obviously colleagues of the comte, one an émigré pair who had escaped the Terror and were vehement on their disparagement of Napoleon, the other typical innocuous London society folk, the gentleman having some connection with the Foreign Office. A strange assortment, Ariel thought, and wondered anew at Francoise's boldness in inviting the enemy, if that was what she considered them, into her home.

Whatever the loyalties of the guests, no politics were discussed at the lavish meal which followed. Ian, sitting next to Lady Bletchford, lost no time in exerting his charm on that receptive young woman. Lady Bletchford had explained that her husband rarely came to London, preferring to remain on their Wiltshire estates, but, he must be a complaisant husband indeed to allow such an incomparable loose among the bucks and rakes of the ton. Alistair seemed to take Ian's flirtation with his light-o'-love, if that was what she was, in good part, paying little attention to Ian's pursuit

166

of the lady. Ariel did not find it so easy to ignore her husband's efforts to captivate Lady Bletchford. She found her appetite for the turbot, pigeons, and petit pois which followed quite meager. He was paying her back for her rejection of him, she was convinced. And remembering their tempestuous embrace before dinner, she tried to consider him with contempt, a practiced womanizer who cared little about the object of his attentions as long as they soothed his consequence. In this assessment she made a mistake. Ian, never able to ignore an attractive woman, and especially one who had ensnared Alistair, considered La Bletchford fair game but he had no serious intentions other than to make Ariel jealous. Alistair, on her left, took equal advantage of the situation.

"Ah, Ariel, what *bonne chance* to find you as my dinner partner. Since Ian is so well occupied, I can feel free to charm you. You are looking particularly lovely this evening," he said, eyeing her audaciously.

"Thank you, Alistair, but I look upon your compliments with some cynicism. Like my husband, you are an experienced philanderer, and not to be taken too seriously. Do you never tire of this shallow pursuit of women?" she reproved him with a smile, sipping carefully at the champagne that accompanied the sweet confection signaling the end of the meal. She had been very sparing in her indulgence, finding the wines served throughout the meal a little heady, and unaccustomed to spirits in such abandon, she felt her head beginning to ache.

"You pain me, Ariel. Here I am endeavoring to fix your attention on my humble person and you spurn me. Rarely have I met such a cruel, if beautiful, lady," he answered, his eyes dancing, not one whit abashed by her put-down.

"You would be better served concentrating on your duties than in this ceaseless round of pleasure," she said, trying to be severe. It was difficult to be harsh with Alistair—he was such an engaging rogue—but no doubt perfectly willing to break some poor girl's heart and then go merrily on his way. She could not deny his charm, but she was not going to encourage him no matter how Ian tempted her to retaliate in view of his own casual flirtation.

"Too true, dear lady, but when duty is combined with pleasure, I take the utmost advantage. Now tell me, how are you and Ian enjoying your visit with your cousins? Myself, I find the formidable Francoise quite intimidating, although I admit she does have a certain mature attraction," he mocked, but beneath his light tone she sensed some other emotion.

"The Villefranches have been most gracious. But I fear we will outstay our welcome. Soon, I understand, we will remove to the Montague townhouse. I am most anxious to meet my new relations. Having had no one but my father, it is heartwarming to know I am now a member of a larger family." She spoke hesitantly. She wanted to know more about Ian's family but for some reason was reluctant to question her husband. She suspected he would not entertain her questions benevolently.

"Oh, Arnold, his brother, is a dull dog, forever prosing on about Ian's duties to his family. Not that Ian has ever paid much heed, I warrant. And Lady Montague is not much better, a veritable dowd, and would not say boo to a goose. The earl, of course, is a far different case, an old dragon. He will be pleased with you, I know, because he has wanted Ian to marry a respectable girl for ages." Alistair eyed her mischievously, to see how she responded to the quelling description of propriety.

"I doubt that he will think my respectability makes up for the lack of other assets. I have no fortune, and although my background is respectable enough, it is hardly top of the tree." She sighed, realizing that the doughty Earl of Strathcairn must have hoped for a far different match.

"You will bring him around in a trice. I have no fear of that. Ian is a fortunate fellow. I wish I had seen you first. I knew I should have requested a Vienna posting," Alistair complained, making her smile at his cajolery, spurious but soothing all the same.

Before she could give the him answer he deserved, Francoise indicated it was time for the ladies to retire, leaving the gentlemen to their port. Ariel felt only relief—jesting with Alistair could become tiring, and the fact that he was paying her such marked attention was embarrassing while both Ian and Olivia Bletchford looked on.

In the drawing room, Ariel sought out Sarah

169

Valentine, who looked a comfortable and easy woman, which indeed she was. Passionately devoted to her general, she appeared well content with her married state, although Ariel suspected she would kick at any attempts at undue domination. Her conversation was not confined to domestic affairs. She talked soberly about the conflict between America and her adopted country, impressing Ariel with her grasp of the issues at stake in the late war, criticizing both sides for their stupidity.

Their fascinating discussion was interrupted by their hostess, who claimed their attention with an innocuous question about a new dressmaker, and then turned the conversation adroitly to General Valentine's duties at the War Office. But Sarah was too clever to give away any secrets, if that was what the comtesse intended.

"The general is such a distinguished man, so well regarded, and responsible for Intelligence, Philippe tells me. How worrying for you, dear Lady Valentine," Francoise cooed, looking innocent.

"Not at all. I have every confidence that he can keep his own counsel, confound our enemies, and emerge victorious, much like the Iron Duke. Now there is an admirable man," Sarah countered, turning her glowing topaz eyes on her interlocutor.

Ariel smiled, watching the two women sparring. She admired Sarah's ability to counter Francoise's leading questions, and her adroit introduction of Wellington, the hero of all London.

"Ah, yes, the great Duke, the conqueror of Napoleon. How much we owe him. But he is so vulnerable. I understand that there have been several attempts on his life by my disgruntled, ungrateful countrymen," Francoise probed, looking guileless.

"Much exaggerated, Comtesse. I do not know how these rumors begin, but we must not pay them much heed," Sarah answered, completely at ease.

Ariel noticed that Francoise looked a bit annoyed but only briefly, and then her expression returned to her usual one of social blandness. She could not resist trying one more ploy. "Ah, Lady Valentine, how clever you are not to interest yourself in these taxing political matters. Much too complicated and tedious for our poor female brains, I fear."

If Sarah Valentine was irritated at the accusation leveled, that of behaving like a shallow uncaring ninny, she did not show it. Ariel, whose own temper was rising, admired her poise. But before Sarah could answer, the gentlemen entered the room, and Alistair crossed to her side.

"Have you missed me, dear lady, or have you and your companions spent the time raking over our misdeeds?" he asked her, hoping for some reaction.

"Your brief absence scarcely allowed us time, Alistair. I am certain your sins and transgressions would need hours rather than these few moments," Ariel responded, noticing that Sarah Valentine smiled at the young soldier, who bowed

171

in acknowledgment of Ariel's hit.

"Quite right, Ariel. But I would be charmed to allow you all the time you need. But perhaps Lady Valentine will put in a few kind words for me, show you that I am not the fribbly fellow you suspect," he answered, his blue eyes challenging both ladies.

"My husband tells me you are a brave soldier, Captain Glendenning, if not to be trusted in the drawing room, or among gullible girls," Sarah joked, well accustomed to dealing with officers and their gallantries.

"Lady Valentine is a very paragon of a wife, following dutifully in her general's footsteps," Francoise interrupted, her tone a bit acid, and then excusing herself, she crossed the room to talk to her countryman, the distinguished émigré, who looked rather uncomfortable at finding himself in such alien company.

"Our hostess seems a bit piqued. Have you been twisting her tail?" Alistair asked outrageously.

"Not at all, Captain Glendenning," Sarah assured him, her poise undisturbed by his banter. "We were just assuring the comtesse that she can sleep safely in her bed, unmolested by Napoleon's minions."

Olivia Bletchford honored the company with a few selections on the pianoforte, insisting that Alistair turn the pages of her music, which that young man did with élan, ignoring her meaningful glances. Ariel, who neither played nor sang herself, and was ill suited to judge the performance, could not help but think Lady Bletchford's

172

only charm was her beauty, for she had little conversation and her musical talent was minimal, but then she chided herself for her spiteful opinion. But she was rather disappointed in Alistair. She would have thought he would pursue a far more dashing type.

The evening ended soon after Olivia's performance, much to Ariel's relief, for she found her headache increasing. But she was pleased that Sarah Valentine took a moment to urge a further meeting, inviting her to a tea a few days hence. Ariel's first impression of the Valentines was all that was favorable, for she thought the general and his American wife both intelligent and warmhearted, with a sincerity not often found among London's society personages.

Allowing her abigail to relieve her of her gown, Ariel dismissed the girl to her bed. She thought it an iniquitous habit, expecting servants to wait up to all hours when they had to rise so early. She had easily won the devotion of the fresh-faced country girl that Ian's batman had secured for her, by her unusual consideration, and normally she enjoyed chatting with Nancy about her country background. But tonight she was not only tired but apprehensive about Francoise's peculiar attitude, and she half expected Ian to resume the conversation which had ended so unsatisfactorily before dinner.

She gazed pensively in her mirror, idly brushing her long black hair and brooding about their dilemma. It was only by concentrating on the mission which had brought her to this uncomfort-

173

able pass that she could banish more disturbing thoughts about her husband. She considered what she had learned in the Villefranches' library today, trying to bring some order to the news of the financial problems of their West Indies estates. Obviously they were not receiving funds from the sugar plantations. Then where did the money come from, to support this extravagant life? Could they have managed to bring out jewels or gold, enough to pay for all this, or were they indeed in the pay of Fouché or Napoleon? Perhaps Talleyrand had helped them, but that wily statesman was not known for his philanthropy. He did not pay out valuable coin without expecting some return. And why had her hosts invited such a strange melange of guests to this dinner tonight? Ariel would like to believe they were inspired by kindness, ensuring that the Montagues would find the company to their taste, but Ariel doubted that was the reason. How nasty and suspicious she was becoming.

Before she could continue her ruminations, the connecting door to Ian's bedroom opened and he entered unceremoniously.

Crossing to stand behind her, his eyes met hers in the mirror, and he took the heavy brush from her hands and slowly stroked down the heavy tresses.

"What lovely hair you have, Ariel." His voice held a gentleness she had rarely heard from him before. Was he trying to woo her with tenderness, to which she was vulnerable, having had little of it in her life since the death of her father?

Trying to gauge his mood was difficult, and she was suddenly afraid of misinterpreting this change from the mocking cynical stance more habitual to their encounters.

Putting down her hairbrush, he drew her up slowly into his arms, looking at her with those unfathomable dark eyes which hid his feelings. She felt her heart pounding rapidly; surely Ian, too, was aware of that tale-tell signal of her agitation.

"I hope this docility means you are coming around to viewing me as less of an ogre, Ariel. Surely we can do better than we have in these past days. I want our marriage to be more than just a partnership through which we discover these pesky traitors. Can you not endure the thought of becoming my wife in reality? For we cannot go on this way, you know that." He spoke quietly, all the while holding her gently, his hand moving over her hair, soothing her into acquiescence.

"You think I am behaving in a silly, missish fashion, don't you, Ian?" She raised her head from his shoulder, her clear emerald eyes revealing her anxiety and a plea for understanding.

"No, I respect your reluctance to trust your life to a graceless rogue such as I have proved to be. I cannot erase my past, and we got off to a poor start, but I want to change all that." His sincerity touched Ariel, his admission that their union had begun under the worst possible circumstances. But he did not mention love. And she craved some assurance that what he felt was more than physical passion. Every instinct led her toward

175

surrender, but still she hesitated.

"If only . . ." she began, but he put a finger on her lips and then kissed her tenderly, with none of the hot passion which had marked his previous efforts to seduce her. Here in the quiet intimacy of this darkened room, lulled by the warmth of the soothing firelight, Ariel felt her defenses weakening, the blood coursing through her veins under the impetus of his skilled lovemaking. His hands roamed seductively down her back, bringing her close to his aroused body, and his mouth wandered down the white column of her throat. She was fast losing control, but before she could answer his unspoken question, a knock came at the door.

"Ariel, *chérie*, are you asleep?" Francoise's voice interrupted them and then she appeared, scarcely giving them time to separate.

Taking in the scene, the comtesse had the grace to apologize although she should not have been surprised. "Oh, forgive me, I thought . . ." Her voice wandered off in some confusion. Ariel would have been amused by her cousin's embarrassment in other circumstances but she was too overset by the recent storm of emotion to protest. Looking at Ian's rigid face, she saw his barely concealed anger at the untimely intrusion. However, politeness forbade her from showing her own turmoil.

"Not at all, Francoise. Is there something I can do for you?" Ariel asked a trifle sharply. She suspected her cousin had some ulterior motive for this late-night visit. Did she hope to discover the real truth of their marriage? If so, her suspicions

176

had not received confirmation.

"I just wanted to discuss the evening. Nothing that can't wait until morning. Forgive me." Francoise backed hurriedly out the door, her normal sophistication destroyed by the obvious construction she put upon the tableau which had greeted her. She shut the door sharply, as if in pique, which Ariel found surprising. What had her cousin expected?

"Damned interfering jade. I know what she was after, trying to see if our marriage was all that it should be. Well, I hope she was convinced. Too clever for her own good," Ian growled, furious that his campaign, which had appeared within an ace of succeeding, had been thwarted.

Valiantly subduing her still aroused senses, Ariel answered frostily, believing he had intended to lure her into his bed from the basest of motives. "Just as well, perhaps. We have now lulled her suspicions, if indeed she had any." She turned away, ignoring his hand outstretched as if in supplication. She may have temporarily lost her inhibitions, but she had herself well under control now and would not allow him to resume his seduction. She doubted that his intentions had been inspired by any real affection, just the determination not to be rebuffed, and a certain inability to accept failure, which disgusted her. And she had almost surrendered.

Ian swore under his breath. "The sooner we leave this cursed house, the better. I do not think we will discover any more telling evidence against your cousins, and right now I don't care

177

one way or the other. This whole idea was ridiculous, and I want to be rid of the business."

"I am fatigued, Ian, and want to retire. Perhaps we can continue any discussion of our future plans at a more opportune time." Ariel walked across the room and opened the door connecting their rooms, hoping he would take his dismissal without any argument. The headache which had dogged her all evening had returned with a blinding force. He seemed to accept that the climate for further approaches was not favorable, and giving her a curt nod, walked through into his own bedroom, giving her nothing more than a disgusted glance.

Ariel sighed with relief. Really, it had been a most exhausting evening, what with all the undercurrents at the dining table. Francoise's probing questions to Sarah Valentine, and the knowledge she had ferreted out some of Philippe de Villefranche's secrets. She did not need her husband's attempts to seduce her.

Doffing her dressing gown and climbing into bed, she wondered if sleep would prove illusive, what with all the apprehensions her current position imposed. Beneath her relief that she had brushed through the last encounter without too much damage was disappointment. Really, she was becoming a veritable wanton, eager to succumb to Ian's skillful lovemaking.

Expecting to suffer through another disturbed sleepless night, she dropped off almost immediately, worn out by the events of the long day and

178

with no resolution to her various problems.

Arriving for breakfast the next morning, her armor well in place, Ariel hoped the ravages to her emotions had been skillfully hidden by her peaceful night. She was a bit overset to see Ian before her, eating a hearty meal of grilled kidneys. Taking a less filling plate herself, she sat down, wary of his mood. But he seemed amazingly cheerful.

"Good morning, Ariel. You are looking most fetching this morning, legacy of an untroubled night, I suppose," he greeted her in his usual mocking manner.

"Yes, I slept quite well," she returned imperturbably. She would not allow him to get beneath her guard. And she did look most appealing in a warm cashmere gown of teal blue, its rather severe lines accenting her fine figure and giving her an air of confidence.

"When you are finished, perhaps we can have a sensible chat about our next move. I have received a letter I wish to discuss with you," he said smoothly, noting her closed-up expression and determining to ignore it. He indicated an open missive by his plate.

Ariel felt her appetite dissolving. Now what had the clever devil decided? Obviously he had come to some decision, and she doubted if she would approve of it. Restraining her impatience, she forced herself to finish her frugal meal and drink her chocolate with a composure she was far from feeling.

"After you, my dear," he indicated, rising with some impatience as she sipped the last draught. She had no recourse but to accompany him from the room, and toward the stairway.

"I believe we will find a modicum of privacy in your boudoir, although after last evening's strange visit from our hostess, even that is arguable," he said sardonically as they mounted the stairs and walked along the hallway.

Once in her room, which had been tidied by the chambermaid, Ariel sat down, her spine not touching the chair back, girding herself as if against attack.

"Don't look so apprehensive, Ariel. I have come to a decision about our future plan of action. And I intended to put it before Valentine this morning. You have done your part nobly, but I feel that the comte probably suspects your visit to his library was not just to find a novel. We cannot take the chance of his surprising you there again. I believe we must try another method, and I want to put it in train this morning. But you need not be bothered with that. I received a letter from my father today, and he and Harriet, my sister-in-law, are en route to London. He wants to meet you, and of course, will open the Grosvenor Street house for his London stay. He expects us to join him there, and frankly, I want it, too. I think we have outlived the Villefranches' hospitality." Ian paced up and down as if impatient with events he could not control. Ariel suspected he did not view the coming meeting with his father with equanimity. Neither did she.

He continued, still pacing up and down. "And Arnold is on his way back from Vienna. A reunion with my family is in the cards." He frowned ferociously. "It only needs that to complicate matters. How I wish I were back with the regiment. All this intrigue is not to my taste, and I am damn bad at it."

"Oh, I don't know, Ian, you seem to be handling affairs well. I must say I look forward to meeting your father and sister-in-law and renewing my brief acquaintance with your brother," Ariel said soothingly. She suspected that the coming meeting disturbed Ian more than he was willing to admit. Whatever their differences, there must be some affection between Ian and the formidable Earl of Strathcairn. What she feared was the latter's reaction to her, since Ian had failed to marry the girl the earl had chosen for his younger son.

"I commend your optimism, my dear, even if I cannot share it," Ian said, coming to a stop by her side and looking at her searchingly, his expression unfathomable. "You amaze me, Ariel, with your deceptive serene air, your ability to control any untoward emotion. But I fancy it is all a mask, and that underneath that prim manner you are a woman of raging passion." He smiled then, changing his somber expression and making Ariel catch her breath with shock. Had she revealed too much to him last night?

"What do you want me to tell Francoise, Ian?"

she asked, determined not to let him under her guard. She would not be caught again by his undeniable charm, used whenever he found it expedient.

"I believe you must give her our grateful appreciation for her hospitality and tell her we will be leaving within the week. Has she said anything more about this reception she intends to give? I wonder whether she has had second thoughts. It might prove vastly expensive if they are under the hatches," he murmured, though his thoughts were on this enigmatic wife of his. Ariel was getting to him, insidiously working on his desire and his determination to wrest from her some reaction to his attentions. By God, she was alluring, not in the usual mode perhaps but appealing for her very difference, that cautious, guarded facade which hid her real temperament. Last night he had almost breached her defenses but now they were well in place again. He would prefer not to force her, but he wondered how long he could restrain himself. He wanted to make love to her, although he would not admit to himself, and certainly not to her, that any deeper feeling impelled him. No woman would trap him into such an admission, but her vulnerability tempted him. Was he such a cad that he would take her if she resisted? He was disgusted with himself, but there it was. He had always gotten what he wanted, particularly when it concerned women.

"No," Ariel replied, mercifully unaware of his thoughts, "and I hope she has abandoned the idea. I would not want to be that beholden to her. It is bad enough we have entered her house under false pretenses, and spied upon her." Ariel frowned, disgusted at the role she had been playing.

"Such ideas of polite behavior must be abandoned when we deal with traitors," Ian insisted.

"But we are not sure that they are traitors, only that there is something suspicious about the source of their income," Ariel protested, reluctant to make accusations founded on so little evidence.

"There is something havey-cavey about them, and we will find out. They are a devious pair, not at all what they pretend to be, I warrant. But enough of that. I will know one way or the other before the week is out. Just take care not to arouse their suspicions while we remain under their roof. I am off to see Valentine and lay my plan before him." He bent over and gave her a brief hard kiss on her mouth before she could demur and left the room in his usual brisk way.

Deciding to face Francoise without any delay, Ariel relegated Ian to the back of her mind with some difficulty and sought out her cousin. Ascertaining that Francoise was still in her bedroom, Ariel sent a maid to see if her cousin would receive her. On obtaining the necessary permission, she entered the bedroom to be greeted by Francoise, who was still abed, sipping chocolate and reading her post. Without her makeup, she looked every one of her thirty-odd years. She was frowning over a letter, which she put aside and looked at Ariel without much enthusiasm. She did not like being seen before she had donned her social face and dress, but she masked her displeasure and

183

greeted her cousin cordially.

"Good morning, Ariel. As you see, I am having a lazy morning. You reproach me with your dewy cheeks and bright eyes." She looked somewhat distracted. "I assume you had a blameless night." The innuendo in her tone embarrassed Ariel. Did her cousin think she would give her an account of the scene she had interrupted the previous evening? In her reticence Ariel was more English than French and she felt a blush redden her cheeks, but she was not going to divulge any of her secrets for her cousin's delectation.

"Yes, indeed. I am sorry to disturb you, Francoise, but I thought I should give you our news immediately," Ariel said, feeling awkward as she stood just inside the door, taking in her cousin's casual dishabille.

Pushing her letter to one side, Francoise patted the bed. "Come sit down and tell me, Ariel." She placed her hand over the letter, concealing it from her cousin. Ariel wondered if she thought her low enough to try to read her correspondence. She sat gingerly on the side of the great bed, disarranging the satin comforter.

"Ian has received a letter from his father announcing his arrival in London before the week's end. He insists we join him at the Strathcairn house in Grosvenor Square . . ." She spoke abruptly, a little nervous although she did not quite know why. Surely there was nothing exceptional in the earl's requesting their presence at the ancestral home.

"*Hélas*, you must take your *congé*. We will miss

you. Come let me arise and dress and then we will discuss your plans." Francoise rose, sweeping her letters into one hand. In her sheer batiste nightgown she showed no embarrassment, but Ariel was relieved when she donned her peignoir. The informality of the scene reminded her of an intimacy she found disturbing, although she did not know why. Francoise crossed to the bell and rang for her maid. The woman must have been right outside the door, for she quickly appeared and swept her mistress into the dressing room, leaving Ariel alone, sitting on the bed. It was then she noticed that Francoise had dropped one of her letters. She picked it up, intending to return it to her, but found herself looking inadvertently at the signature, a bold black scrawl. Talleyrand. Why was the prince writing Francoise, when the Villefranches pretended to despise Napoleon's lackey?

The letter, curt and demanding, requested that Francoise improve on her latest budget of information or her allowance would be curtailed. Obviously, the prince was not satisfied with whatever mission he had asked her to accomplish, but what was even more frightening to Ariel, he warned her cousin about Ian, suspecting his presence in her home. Hearing some movement from the dressing room, Ariel quickly concealed the damaging letter beneath the bed linen and tried to compose her face. Her heart was pounding with both excitement and anger. This was the proof Ian needed. How fortunate they had made plans to leave. Ian's life could be in danger, hostage to this wily politician who demanded action in return for his generosity, and that action could mean harm to her husband. She gave not a thought to her own predicament. Somehow she must disarm Francoise, and hurry to give Ian the damaging news.

"Now, *chérie*, I am at your service." Francoise entered the room, giving a sharp look at her cousin, who had walked to the window and was looking out onto the street, trying to bring some order to her frantic senses. Finally, Ariel turned, fearing her cousin could read her dismay in her face, but she must have been a better actress than she had thought for Francoise seemed to notice nothing as she sat at her dressing table and rummaged through her jewelry case, searching for the fruits of her treachery, Ariel thought bitterly.

"You have been most kind to entertain us, Francoise, and both Ian and I are most grateful, but we will be leaving soon, and you will be relieved to have your house to yourself." Ariel said stiffly, her eyes averted. She was no great hand at deception and she feared her cousin would discover her secret.

"I quite understand, Ariel. Naturally the earl will want to meet his son's new bride, but just because you are transferring to his house does not mean we must lose you entirely. We will meet often, *n'est-ce pas?*" Francoise queried, wondering why her cousin always behaved in such a restrained fashion. Really, she was a thorny one, so hesitant and proper, and a veritable clam about her personal affairs. Francoise was quite relieved at her news, although she wondered how this removal would affect her own plans.

"Yes, of course, Francoise. We are bound to see a great deal of you, and we will want to return your hospitality. But I must be on my way. There is much to do," Ariel answered, anxious to get away from her cousin's questions.

"I hope we will have many more pleasant evenings like last night. I am sure you have found a friend in Lady Valentine. Quite an engaging lady, although her devotion to her husband is a bit cloying, and not at all the thing. How boring to live in one another's pockets like that. And I wonder if he does not find it a bit of a problem, having a colonial wife, what with the recent war with America straining her loyalties," Francoise said spitefully.

"I think they understand one another well, and I am old-fashioned enough to think such devotion between partners rather refreshing," Ariel answered tartly. She respected the Valentines and did not like discussing them in such a fashion.

"Really, *chérie*, you sound so straitlaced, one would never know you had French blood," Francoise remarked, annoyed that her cousin turned aside her attempts to gossip. But she was not deterred. If Ariel would not talk about the Valentines, there remained the scapegrace Alistair.

"And how did you find La Bletchford? Rather a disappointment and I hope Captain Glendenning takes care. She appears most clinging," Francoise said, determined to cast her barbs.

But Ariel would not be drawn in, although she was inclined to agree with Francoise's assessment of Alistair's *chère amie.* "I am sure Alistair is wide awake on all suits and knows exactly what he is doing. Lady Bletchford is most attractive, and a bit lonely, I suspect, with her husband in the country." Whatever her cousin's reasons for attacking the Valentines and Alistair, she would not join her in disparaging them. Now that she had proof of the Villefranches' duplicity, all Ariel wanted to do was put as much distance as possible between them and herself and Ian. Despite Francoise's efforts at friendship, Ariel now knew the reason for her spurious kindnesses. She was in the pay of that master of deception, Talleyrand, whose only concern was for his own advancement, uncaring of what or whom he used to satisfy his own ambitions. He was not to be trusted for a moment, and neither were her cousins. She felt despoiled by their relationship, and worried as to what their various conspiracies meant for the future of England and all Europe. However, she must dissemble until she could put this house and its masters behind her.

Bidding Francoise a restrained farewell, Ariel left the bedroom, eager to contact Ian. He would know how to deal with this latest revelation. On her departure, Francoise cursed softly. Ariel's rebuff of her gossip had annoyed her, but thank heaven she had not seen the letter. Francoise rummaged through the bed linen and retrieved the damaging missive, reading it again with anger. If they lost Talleyrand's support, their creditors would make life a misery. She cared little for politics, and not a whit for Napoleon, but she had become accustomed to luxurious living, and she would not happily abandon her comforts for any foolish ethical imperatives. Greed had forced her into complying with Talleyrand's demands and she could not contemplate surrendering the tidy allowance he paid them for information about their English hosts. And if Napoleon should escape from Elba and regain control of France, she and Philippe had every chance of winning back their estates, then she could leave this cursed country and return to her rightful place. Despite the Valentines and the Montagues, she would win through and Philippe, silly fool that he was, could not persuade her to abandon their schemes. She was a match for them all. He would see and so would that wily fox, Talleyrand. Having settled matters to her satisfaction, shrugging off the slight unease her cousin's appearance had instilled, she settled at her escritoire to answer Talleyrand's letter.

Chapter Fourteen

The remaining few days of their stay with the Villefranches seemed interminable to Ariel. Ian had received her news about Francoise's provocative correspondence with Talleyrand quite coolly, much to her chagrin, for she felt she had discovered an important clue to the identity of the conspirators. However, his own ploy to catch Philippe in the act of spying had proved disappointing. He was now inclined to dismiss the Villefranches as their targets. He explained to Ariel that with General Valentine's cooperation, he had drawn up a document outlining possible troop movements and strategies in the case of a spontaneous uprising which would bring Napoleon again into the field. Of course, the document was false, but to any conspirator it should be so tempting he would be inclined to spirit it away for his master. The list was quite complicated. It would be fruitless to try to memorize it. An interested party would have to copy it, but although the damning paper had lain on Valentine's desk for two days in full sight of Philippe, who was often in the general's office, he did not disturb it. Since he had failed to fall into the trap so cunningly laid, both Ian and the general were inclined to believe in his innocence.

Ian had duly reported Ariel's discovery of the Talleyrand letter to headquarters, where it was received dubiously. It was known that Francoise and the prince were related. Perhaps Ariel had misunderstood and the letter was innocuous, for despite Francoise's publicized dislike of the wily Frenchman, their secret exchanges could be of no import to the larger issue. Ariel was not convinced but had to admit she knew far less of the matter than such experienced spy chasers as Valentine and Alistair. She tried to put the whole puzzling affair from her mind, but she was far from convinced of the Villefranches' innocence.

Both Alistair and Ian were distracted by increasingly disturbing news of activity at Elba. Ian had a theory about Napoleon's incarceration on that very accessible island. He believed that certain members of the delegations at the Congress of Vienna wanted Napoleon to escape so that he could be assassinated or recaptured and then exiled to St. Helena, a much safer refuge. Wellington had arrived safely in the Austrian capital, but his appearance had not brought the disputing parties any closer to agreement. The Tsar was preoccupied with his Holy Alliance, which the British felt was impractical and visionary although they conceded it could do little real harm. Castlereagh and Wellington were both determined on wresting from the Congress delegates some assurances for the future neutrality of Belgium, which the French wanted returned to their control, and the Tsar had aspirations toward annexing Poland. All in all, little of any real worth was being accomplished while the French continued with their intrigues and plots. Castlereagh had returned to London and was busily occupied with helping Liverpool stave off the attempts of the Whigs to regain political power. With him had come Arnold Montague, and Ian and Ariel prepared to join his family in the Grosvenor Street house.

While Ian was encountering so many frustrations at the War Office, he was finding little surcease in his strained relationship with Ariel. Neither of them was prepared to compromise. Ian saw no reason for Ariel's refusal to consummate their marriage and she, for her part, believing his efforts were motivated more by satisfaction of his physical desire than any real affection, continued to rebuff him, retreating into the cool reserved facade which had protected her in the past. She was apprehensive, too, about the coming meeting with the earl and Arnold and his wife. How would they manage under one roof? If the earl suspected the real state of their marriage, he would probably press for an annulment since she could hardly be the match he had hoped for for his younger son. By the time they had packed their effects and removed to Grosvenor Street, she was in a rare state of nerves, not responding to any overtures Ian made, and hurt by her attitude, he, too, retreated into the impassive sardonic mood which had initially repelled her. His reception of her news about Francoise had further alienated Ariel, and all in all she was tempted to abandon this sterile marriage and flee to her old governess's cottage in the country. Only her promise to Castlereagh, her deep sense of patriotism, and her knowledge that her father would have expected her to do her duty as a good soldier's daughter prevented her from escaping her intolerable situation.

Finally, the morning came when the Montagues could bid good-bye to their hosts. Francoise behaved with that easily assumed charm which she could don when the occasion demanded it, promising frequent meetings and assurances that they must not forget the ties of kinship. In the landeau that was transporting them away from Audley Street, Ariel sighed with relief at putting the whole episode behind her, and relaxed the guard she had put upon herself.

"Thank goodness we are away from that house. If the Villefranches are the only relatives I can claim, I would be better without any," she told Ian as they turned down Grosvenor Square.

"Be thankful you do not have a clutch of relatives. Frankly, I am more than happy that you are an orphan. Family can be the devil," Ian growled, then thinking better of it, realizing that Ariel had no one to depend on but himself, and a distasteful husband he had proved to be, he took her hand and tried to comfort her. "It will not be so bad, this meeting with the governor. He can be a stiff old party, but I am sure you can get around him. I hope you will be happier in the future, Ariel. You have had a pretty thin time of it lately," he said kindly.

She blinked back the sudden tears that rose to her eyes. Ian, in this gentle mood, disarmed her. She felt so vulnerable, ashamed that she could not be stalwart. After all, her lines were not laid in such a bad road. She might have been cast adrift with no protector at all, and Ian's own position was not an enviable one. Despising self-pity, Ariel rallied her emotions and accepted the olive branch he was offering her.

"I am a silly goose to be so overset. It is not entirely your fault that we are in this scrape, and I am sure we will come about. I should not be so concerned with my personal situation when grave matters that threaten the nation are worrying us all," she said resolutely, half expecting some ironic rejoinder from her husband.

"You are a brave girl, Ariel. I am not unmindful that most of the responsibility for our present unhappy situation lies at my door. I regret that you have been dragged into all this just because I was fool enough to respond to Fiona's ploys," he answered her with a warm sincerity, far removed from his usual mocking air. He waited for a moment, hoping for some response from her, but she remained silent. "Shall we have a truce, and try to cooperate on our common mission? I will do all I can to shield you from Father's wrath, although I believe that once he comes to know you, he will realize what a treasure he has gained as a daughter-in-law. He might have had to welcome a far more disappointing bride. I am not known for my good taste in women," he concluded ruefully, remembering some of his past adventures.

Unaccountably cheered by this far from passionate endorsement, Ariel threw off her malaise with a determined effort. "Friends, Ian? That is a strange relationship for you with a woman, I warrant," she teased.

"It will do to go on with, my girl. But I am still determined that this marriage will prove successful. It does my consequence no good to be disliked by my wife, you know," he answered, relieved that she had abandoned that disapproving manner which had prevented him from breaching her defenses.

She smiled at him, grateful for his understanding, but before she could say more, the carriage stopped at the Strathcairn townhouse, a regal residence well suited to its neighbors with its pedimented front and broad smooth stuccoed facade.

"Very impressive, your home," she decided, giving it an apprehensive glance.

"Not so much of a home, and it will all be Arnold's before too long. My father appears to be in ruddy health, but he suffers from the gout and the increasing onset of age's ills, which contribute to his testy manner. But I will protect you, never fear," he promised, disarming her with his continued friendliness.

"Good morning, Lufton," Ian greeted the portly

butler who welcomed them as they entered the house. "This is my wife, and this, my dear, is Lufton, who has shielded me from justified punishment more often than I care to recall."

Lufton smiled, his jowls wobbling with delight. "How pleased we are to welcome your wife, and you, too, Master Ian, after all those battles. I often feared you would not come through, but I should have known that you would triumph, and now you are home safely and with a new bride, too. Delighted to meet you, madam." He smiled at Ariel, easing much of her discomfort with his warm welcome.

"The earl is awaiting you in the library, Master Ian. Will you go right in, or would Mrs. Montague want to repair to your rooms to freshen up first?" Lufton asked, taking Ariel's cloak and Ian's greatcape and hat.

"Might as well beard the lion in his den and get it over with, eh, Ariel?" Ian suggested, taking her arm and shepherding her toward his father's sanctum.

The huge high-ceilinged room, lined with glass-fronted bookcases and filled with massive furniture, would have dwarfed a lesser man. But the Earl of Strathcairn would stand out impressively in a palace. Taller than his son by several inches, ramrod straight, with a shock of white hair and beetling brows overhanging dark piercing eyes, he was indeed an intimidating figure. He stood at their entrance and raked Ariel with a keen glance as Ian introduced her.

"Well, madam, I must congratulate you. You

have accomplished what no other female has been able to do, lured this graceless son of mine into the parson's trap," he growled, taking her outstretched hand and subjecting her to a fierce stare.

Ariel, determined not to be cowed, answered sharply, "It was not all my doing, my lord. Circumstances forced our hand." She bit back a gasp, looking at Ian's amused face. The words did not convey her meaning, and she could only hope that the earl did not take them the wrong way.

"Does that mean that you are *enceinte?* And Ian was caught by the oldest ruse in the world?" He chuckled as if the thought of his son being trapped in such a fashion was an occasion for delight.

"Not at all, sir," Ian said sardonically, obviously enjoying both Ariel's embarrassment and his father's indignation. "You will have to wait for your grandchild, for our marriage was not a matter of my paying the piper for unbridled lust."

Ariel, by now in a rage at both of them, turned a haughty stare at her two adversaries. She knew she must make her position plain from the start. Otherwise she would soon be playing the role of cat's paw between these two dominant men, neither one willing to give an inch.

"I resent your implications, my lord. If I am not the bride you would have chosen for your son, that is unfortunate, but I do not intend to apologize for my existence nor to endure any insults," she said stiffly, clasping her shaking hands behind her back.

"Not a meek little wife. Good, I hate these milk and water misses. It seems you will have a turbulent union, which I will enjoy watching. Well, Ian, there is no denying that I wanted you to be wed, although I had chosen another match for you. Stubborn fool that you are, I suppose that alone would have forced you into your present pass. You look a sensible girl, madam, a soldier's daughter, I understand, and I only hope you understand where your duty lies. That dowd Arnold has been riveted to these past four years is a barren chit. I want a grandchild." He scowled at them both. "There have been Strathcairns at Northdale Hall for three centuries, and I want the line to continue."

"I am not a brood mare, sir. I would like children, but I will not be chivied into it to serve your dynastic ambitions," she retorted.

"Well, Ian, judging by your past performances, I should think you could accomplish the deed." The earl chortled rather crudely, bringing a flash of temper to his son, who until now had watched the duel between his wife and his father with some amusement.

"As far as I know, I have no bastards littering the countryside, sir, but I thank you for your faith in my abilities," he answered in that outrageously provocative manner which he knew would irritate his father beyond bearing. God knows, he would not be forced into bed with the girl just to breed an heir, although he might thoroughly enjoy the coupling. Ian smiled at the thought of Ariel meekly allowing herself to be used in such a fashion. He wanted badly to possess her but not on the orders of his irascible father.

"That will do, Ian. Not fit language for a lady," the earl protested, aware that the interview was not going his way.

"I have heard worse on the campaign trail, my lord. And Ian does not always choose his words with the strictures of polite society in mind. No doubt he comes by his frankness and his obstinacy naturally," Ariel insisted, smiling at the two of them as if they were mischievous schoolboys. Now that she had the earl's mettle, she thought they might deal very well together.

"Um. I can see you are not easily intimidated, my girl. Well, enough of this. Let us sit down and I will hear what you have been up to in Vienna and how this amazing marriage came about." The earl indicated chairs before a warming fire. Ian raised his eyebrows questioningly at Ariel but did as he was bid, sitting beside her on a deep leather sofa. He then launched into an expurgated version of their meeting and subsequent marriage, but said nothing about Castlereagh and the business which had brought them together. Gratefully, Ariel understood he intended to shield her from his father's wrath and make it as easy as possible for her.

The earl's reaction to the tale was not what she had expected. He laughed, a deep, enjoyable chuckle, as he heard of the hurried ceremony. He was not yet convinced that his scamp of a son had not been forced to the altar, but had decided not to pursue his suspicions. At the conclusion of the sketchy tale, he nodded, prepared to accept the fait accompli. Turning to Ariel, he grinned, satisfied that for once his son had behaved in an acceptable fashion.

"Well, we will have to see the new Mrs. Montague launched appropriately into society. Since I have been forced to come to this accursed London, I might as well try to enjoy myself. We will give a ball to introduce you, my dear, but I fear you will have to supervise most of the doings. That Harriet, she's hopeless, such a little mouse, scared of her own shadow."

Ariel realized that like most bullies, he only respected adversaries who could give as well as they got, and she had every intention of standing up to this determined curmudgeon. They would probably deal very well together, if Ian did nothing to provoke his father.

"My cousins mentioned some such idea, sir, but I believe it might prove more acceptable if you acted as host. Then the ton would see that I am a proper daughter-in-law, which would assure my position," she said calmly, expecting the outburst she knew her words would inspire.

"Of course, you are a proper daughter-in-law," he sputtered. "Nothing wrong with your background—the daughter of a brave officer of our King. Pay no attention to any slights from these popinjays. Parvenues most of them, grasping for a place in society. I still have some influence, and I intend to use it. No need for involving foreigners in our affairs. Sorry, my dear, but French relatives are not an asset."

"Thank you, sir. I am happy to have allayed your suspicions." Ariel smiled at the old man, ignoring Ian's growl of disgust. Somehow she would reconcile these two, victims of their own

201

stubborn unwillingness to be coerced. Really, they were so much alike, and Ariel, looking at the earl, realized she was seeing Ian as he would be in thirty years. If she was around to observe, she conceded bitterly. The earl might have accepted her, grudgingly or not, but his son was still an unknown quantity. Ian's mercurial temperament, so like his father's, was not to be relied upon in any circumstances. Who knew what he was thinking, as he sulked by her side?

Suddenly weary of all these deceptions, Ariel stood up and indicated she would like to see their rooms. Thanking the earl prettily for his reception, she reached up and kissed him saucily on the cheek.

Escorting her from the room, Ian looked at his serene bride with some respect. She had tamed the old devil in an amazing fashion. Quite a woman, his wife, but she would not bring her husband so easily under her thumb. He was no doddering old fool to be couzened by an attractive wench into trailing at her skirts. But he was not displeased. Whatever his differences with his father, he had not enjoyed being at daggers drawn with the old man. And he wondered how Arnold would accept this change in the family fortune. An unholy smile lit his face, causing Ariel to wonder what her husband was hatching in that devious mind of his. Well, he might be in for a few surprises himself. For the moment, at least, they were in unusual charity with one another.

Chapter Fifteen

Harriet, Viscountess Montague, proved to be as meek and dowdy as the earl and Ian had promised. Ariel suspected that she had come from as intimidating a household as that to which marriage to the heir of Strathcairn had brought her. She wore her mouse brown hair in the plainest of styles, and her round, stocky figure was garbed in a succession of dun-colored gowns which did nothing to improve her plainness. Her best feature was her doelike deep brown eyes, which gazed fearfully at life, as if expecting the rebuffs she constantly encountered. Of sallow complexion and meek demeanor, she had little to recommend her, but Ariel tried to make friends with her sister-in-law, who seemed surprised by her attempts.

Obviously the match was an arranged one, and Ariel learned later that Harriet's family lands marched with the earl's, so that the marriage had cemented that crusty gentleman's holdings, a matter of paramount concern to him. He cared little whether the couple's feelings were involved. Harriet said little about her husband, who treated her in a casually indifferent manner but with polite circumspection. Ariel's easily aroused sympathies went out to the poor lady, and she did her best to try to become her confidante, but with minimal success.

Arnold was an even thornier proposition—aloof, disapproving, and determined to extend his resentment toward Ian to include his wife. Ariel, an only child who had always yearned for the intimacy of a family relationship, wondered how such an estrangement between the brothers had happened. Granted their temperaments were violently opposed, but surely they must have felt some bonds of kinship. She did her best to soften the troubling animosity between them, but found her task formidable. While the earl obviously preferred Arnold, she felt he had a sneaking respect for Ian's independence and swashbuckling manner. For the moment, an uneasy truce existed at the house on Grosvenor Street, but Ariel doubted such careful observance of the amenities would last.

The earl ordered his daughters-in-law to get on with preparations for the ball which would introduce Ariel to society, and the arrangements took up most of her time, as Harriet seemed either unwilling or unable to cope with the invitations, caterers, florists, musicians, and other merchants whose services would ensure a triumphant debut for the newest Strathcairn.

Ian, uncomfortable under his father's roof, spent a great deal of time at his club or the War Office, renewing old acquaintances and, Ariel suspected, roistering with his fellow officers. Left to her own devices, she saw a great deal of Alistair, who appeared to have plenty of leisure to squire her about to various entertainments and to satisfy her desire for sightseeing. Ian made no demur, but the tentative rapport between them did not progress to the warmer relationship Ariel coveted. Her pride to the fore, she made little attempt to alter their sterile pact, and since they had separate, although adjoining, bedrooms, she saw even less of her husband than she had when they were living under the Villefranche roof. That this situation could continue much longer she doubted, but did not know how to change matters.

When she did meet her husband, they talked mostly of their spy investigation. Ian was disgusted at the lack of progress, and conceded that he and his superiors might have been too quick to discount the evidence of the Talleyrand letter to Francoise. He suggested that she seek out her cousin and try to discover more from that enigmatic lady about the affair. Ariel, reluctant to trade upon her relationship with the Ville-franches, nevertheless made an effort to comply with his demands. But Francoise proved strangely elusive. Ariel wondered if she suspected Ariel's motives. She did not trust her cousin and was convinced Francoise felt the same toward her.

Only with Sarah Valentine could Ariel really

relax. In that warm and affectionate household, she found some surcease from the problems which troubled her, although she could not bring herself to confide in her new acquaintance. Sarah, an astute observer, was concerned about her friend's marriage, but did not quite know how to broach the subject. One afternoon as they were gossiping idly over the teacups, she steeled herself to mention her disquiet.

"I notice, Ariel, that you are seeing a great deal of Alistair Glendenning. I know he is an old friend of your husband's and I am sure behaves with proper respect toward you, but London is such a hotbed of rumor. People adore to speculate and cast judgment. I am loath to interfere, but do you think it wise to see so much of him?" Sarah asked gently.

"Alistair has proved a good friend," Ariel answered a bit bitterly. She found the rules of London society false and hypocritical. "His flirtatious ways are mostly a facade, I think. I doubt if he has a heart to be touched. Certainly he feels nothing but the most lukewarm of emotions toward me. He just cannot help sending out lures to any woman in his neighborhood. I believe he is really deeply involved with Olivia Bletchford. She is the one you should warn."

"Oh, I know it is considered unfashionable to show any affection toward one's husband. But you and Ian can hardly be accused of living in one another's pockets. I do not wish to pry or censure you, dear Ariel, but I know how easily circumstances can lead to misunderstandings when a little plain speaking would clear up matters. Pride can be such an obstacle. I suffer from an inordinate amount of it myself, and once it almost led me into deep waters," Sarah confided, hoping to lure Ariel into revealing the trouble which obviously beset her.

Ariel met her friend's warm gaze ruefully. "I have never told you the reason for our marriage. It is a tawdry tale, and reflects badly upon us both. But I need advice and support urgently." She hesitated a moment, twisting her hands together nervously, while Sarah waited calmly. Then taking a deep breath, Ariel related the circumstances of the hurried Vienna wedding, the reason for it, and Castlereagh's request.

"Yes, I see. That explains a great deal. But I do believe you are for Ian, and he for you. He needs the steadying affection of a loving wife," Sarah offered, wondering if she had gone too far. "I almost lost Lucien through an excess of pride, and I would not want you to suffer a similar fate."

Ariel looked at her friend in some astonishment. Nothing could testify to domestic tranquillity more than the relationship of the Valentines. "I cannot believe you and Lucien ever were at odds with one another. You seem so devoted."

"Yes, now our problems are all behind us. But believe me, we had our share, especially the difference in our loyalties. The war between our countries tested our love but we have had fifteen years of felicity and our beloved children who brought us through to calm waters. I may seem the most contented of matrons but I can be aroused to a fury over injustice and criticism toward my native land. I am sure Lucien despairs of me sometimes." Sarah laughed, secure in the knowledge of her husband's devotion.

"Well, I must simply hope for a happy outcome to my difficulties, but now they seem almost overwhelming, even though I am far from faint-hearted," Ariel said. She wanted to be comforted by Sarah's assurances but she saw darker days ahead.

Sarah, realizing that she had done all she could to alleviate her friend's distress, talked of less turbulent matters, but hoped she had given Ariel some ease of mind. She admired Ariel's independence of spirit, having a great deal of that commodity herself, and wished she could do more to bring about a happy ending to Ariel's tempestuous marriage.

Much warmed by Sarah's concern, Ariel returned to Grosvenor Street determined to try again with Ian. Somehow they must resolve the distance between them even if she had to lower her pride and confess her confused feelings toward him. But she shuddered at the thought of tendering her feelings and suffering a rebuff. Her emotions had undergone many ups and downs since she and Ian had first met in Vienna, but now she had to admit that she wanted more than their present state of affairs. Somehow she must signify to him she would not be loath to consummate their union as he demanded. But lately she wondered if his desire for her had lessened. Perhaps he no longer wanted her. And even if this were not true, was it possible for Ian to forsake his libertine ways and become a faithful husband? Somehow she doubted it, and doubted even more her own attractions. He had so many temptations, and she felt his current boredom and restlessness at their present life must drive him even more distant from her.

Arriving at the Strathcairn house, she resolutely decided to put her decision to force matters to the test. But upon her entrance all thoughts of her marriage left her when Lufton handed her a message from her cousin. Francoise was demanding to see her on a matter of some urgency. Ariel responded that she would attend her cousin the following morning, barely restraining her impatience to know if Francoise's summons had any bearing on the investigation which had reached a stalemate.

That evening Ian, for once at home for dinner, noticed his wife's distrait air. He had not been unaware of her growing intimacy with Alistair and wondered if she was falling in love with that scapegrace officer. Damn it, he would not stand for her refusing him and taking up with Alistair.

The earl, whose gout was causing him pain, exacerbated the strained relations within his family by deliberately goading the brothers.

"Well, Ian, we are honored by your presence this evening. Perhaps your wife does not find your activities unsettling, but I confess for a new bridegroom you are very cavalier in your treatment of her. It's all of a week since you have dined at home." He glowered at his son, who remained impassive under his father's sarcasm.

"My wife seems well able to endure my absence, and I cannot feel that you and Arnold require my attendance," he replied, his eyes on Ariel, who found herself shifting uncomfortably under his enigmatic gaze.

"This modern indifference to proprieties disgusts me. It would serve you right if she ran off with that graceless Glendenning who seems to be always underfoot," the earl growled.

Ian frowned, his father's words only reinforcing his own suspicions, but he would not give his father the satisfaction of knowing he had scored. "I am sure Ariel is mindful of her position, and behaves most circumspectly. Isn't that so, my dear?"

Not willing to tangle with Ian beneath the eyes of his disapproving family, Ariel refused to dignify his remarks with any soothing nostrum, but to her surprise, Harriet leaped to her defense.

"Naturally Ariel needs an escort, Ian, and if you are not available, she must rely on your friend," Harriet said firmly. Both Arnold and Ian looked at her with some amazement. For Harriet to take issue with anyone was a shock, and to defend her sister-in-law so vehemently even more astonishing.

"I stand reproved, dear Harriet. I must mend my ways and be more attentive, I see," Ian replied wryly.

Arnold frowned at his wife, his thin lips tightening in distaste. "I am sure Ian has many demands on his time. He does not need your

210

advice on how to conduct his marriage, Harriet."

"On the contrary," Ian replied. "I am delighted my family is so concerned with my behavior, critical though my dear sister-in-law may be. But I have yet to hear that my wife finds my company as desirable as that of Alistair's."

"Harriet is only voicing what we all wonder, Ian," the earl said, obviously eager to stir the waters. "Since we are about to launch your wife upon the ton just a sennight since, the least you could do is show a little interest."

"Well, Ariel, what do you say to all this concern about my lack of attention?" Ian asked with a dangerous smile. "Do you wish more of my company, my dear? I rather gathered you were happy with your current cavalier."

"You will do as you see fit, Ian, and I doubt if my wishes will influence you," she answered repressively, furious at them all.

"On the contrary. But perhaps we can discuss our wishes in private. I do not enjoy our affairs brought out for Arnold's delectation." Ian rose as he spoke, then he crossed around the table to grip Ariel's hand and force her to stand up. "You will excuse us, I am sure," he finished with a haughty stare at his family and, without more ado, dragged Ariel with him to the door. Arnold and Harriet said nothing, but Ariel thought she heard the earl chuckle as her husband escorted her so summarily from the dining room.

Marching her upstairs to her bedroom, Ian appeared to be in a fine rage, and Ariel hesitated to challenge him, although she could not but wonder why he was so angry. Could he be jealous of Alistair's attentions to her? Once inside the privacy of her chamber, Ariel waited for her husband's outburst, becoming more and more enraged herself.

"Well, madam, I hope you are satisfied. You have made me look a fool before my family. I certainly did not enjoy that little exchange at dinner, although my father and Arnold both seemed to find it amusing," he growled, staring at her with hot ruthless eyes.

"Really, Ian, you are creating a scene over nothing. I am not inclined to defend myself when I have done nothing to incur such criticism. If I chose to dally with some man, I would certainly not take up with Alistair, who is just as much a rake as you are, and more than occupied in other directions. He has been a good friend to me, escorting me when you seem heavily committed to your own amusements." How dare he criticize her behavior when his own was far from creditable? She faced him fearlessly, her green eyes flashing.

"Yes, well, that's all very well, but you are damned attractive, and Alistair is no saint. Perhaps I reacted too easily. If so, I apologize. You would try any man's patience with that prim air of yours, although I must admit when your temper is roused, you show signs of some human passion," he quipped, suddenly changing his attitude to one of cynical amusement, much to Ariel's confusion. "All right, I will beg your pardon most humbly, if my suspicions were unfounded," he concluded, a lingering doubt still

212

apparent as he regarded her quizzically, hoping for some more satisfactory rejoinder.

Taking up a lounging stance before the fireplace, he watched her as she struggled to bring her emotions under control. "You know, Ariel, we would not brangle so if we were not both suffering from frustration, brought about by your determination not to become a real wife to me," he said quietly, watching her closely.

"We have had this discussion before, Ian, and I think you know my feelings on that subject. I am not some doxy to be bedded to soothe your ego or satisfy your physical needs. I find your attempts to consummate our marriage rather disgusting when your affections are not engaged," she responded, knowing she sounded like the frigid spinster he accused her of being, but she could not forget Fiona or his reluctance to spend any time with her in preference to his roistering ways.

"I have never said my affections are not engaged, but if you are waiting for some impassioned declaration of love, you will be disappointed my dear. No woman will get me into her toils to become her lap dog," he countered.

"Well, we seem to have reached a stalemate then," Ariel said crisply, unwilling to admit to the disappointment she felt at his callous manner. He would not change and she would not surrender. She looked at him steadily, hoping he would not guess at the welter of emotion he evoked in her. "I realize that this situation is difficult for us both, but I cannot accede to what you ask. I am sorry if I have caused you embarrassment before your

213

family, but I think you must bear equal responsibility for that," Ariel said, hoping to conciliate him. "This marriage has been a trial to us both and I can see no way of solving our dilemma, but let us not make matters worse by arguing. At least we can be friends," she pleaded.

"There is no such thing as friendship between men and women. Do not be so naive, my dear. And remember I will not be a complaisant husband, willing to deny myself what you might offer others. But enough of this. We are both on edge because of this nasty situation with the spy ring. We make no progress, and that is an added frustration," he conceded.

"Yes, well, perhaps the situation will change shortly. I have received a peremptory note from Francoise requesting an interview. She seemed quite overset. I cannot imagine what she wants but I am seeing her tomorrow morning," Ariel explained, eager to discuss a less provocative subject.

Ian frowned as if wishing to pursue the matter which exercised him. How lovely she looked, standing there defiantly, almost daring him to take her. If only they could put all this business behind them and sort out their problems, preferably in bed. But he could not force her. She deserved better from him.

"Be careful, Ariel. She is a dangerous woman. She may not be the ringleader of our spies but she is up to some havey-cavey work, I'll warrant," he insisted, worried now at the danger Ariel might be facing.

"I thought you believed, as does General Valentine, that the letter I discovered meant little, that she was not conspiring with Talleyrand."

"I don't know, but I suspect she is delving into matters which would bear investigation. Her husband might be unaware of what she is doing, for he appears to be innocent of any treachery. So far they have avoided any traps set for them, but that does not mean they are cleared of suspicion. Someone is sending privileged information to our enemies. And we will expose the varlets yet." He crossed the room to her and, putting his hands on her shoulders, looked searchingly into her eyes. "You are ill fitted for all this deception, Ariel, and I regret exceedingly embroiling you in this masquerade. But I have hopes we will come about before too long. I suppose we would do well to postpone our own personal problems until we have solved the country's greater need. And I promise to be more of a husband. Tomorrow I will escort you to whatever entertainment you see fit after your interview with Francoise. You see, I have surrendered entirely," he teased, his eyes warm and understanding.

Disturbed by his nearness and the sudden alteration in his manner, Ariel felt her defenses weakening. If only he were always so gentle, he could completely disarm her. But she must not forget that his desire was not based on any lasting emotion. He did not love her and she would not submit as long as he remained obdurate against loving her. But she would not reject this latest overture.

"Thank you, Ian. I would like that. And I will need your support and advice after I hear what Francoise wants of me. I have a feeling that the interview might be unpleasant." She smiled at him gratefully.

"You disarm me, Ariel, with your gentleness. But I see I must resist persuading you for now. It's damn difficult," he added wryly. He raised her hand to his lips, kissing it tenderly. "Good night, my dear. I hope you sleep well. I know I shall not. Until tomorrow." And he was gone, leaving her to mull over their conversation and finding little in it to assuage her doubts.

Chapter Sixteen

Ariel faced the day ahead with trepidation.
Somehow she felt that Francoise's demand—it
could hardly be called a request—could bring
nothing but more problems, and she was bedeviled
enough without her cousin's intrigues. And beneath her worry about the Villefranches was the
constant ache of her unresolved situation with
Ian. At least she did not have to face him this
morning. He had ridden out early. For this she
felt some relief as she dressed for her meeting.
Beyond her window, the gray late January day
offered little surcease from her dark mood, but
she resolutely banished her disquiet and donned
her bonnet and cloak, anxious to be away. As she
left her bedroom and passed down the hall, she
heard sounds of distress from a chamber some
doors away from her own. Surely that was
Harriet sobbing. Ariel hesitated, then knocked
gently. Receiving no answer, she opened the door
to see her sister-in-law sprawled across her bed

crying her eyes out. Ariel crossed to the bed and laid a hand on Harriet's heaving shoulders. Whatever was the matter? The afflicted woman stifled a last desperate cry and turned to face Ariel.

"Oh, Ariel, I did not hear you." She tried pathetically to staunch her tears, but her poor face was swollen and streaked with misery.

"Whatever is wrong, Harriet? Can I help in some way? Are you in pain? Should I call a physician?" Ariel asked, distressed by the agony she saw in Harriet's face.

"No, no physician can help me. Thank you for your concern, but no one can ease me. I am such a failure. You would not understand, Ariel. You are so strong, so able to cope with your problems, while I am a fainthearted ninny, prey to all kinds of fears," Harriet gulped.

Ariel sat down on the edge of the bed. Obviously, she could not abandon her sister-in-law to whatever tragedy had beset her. Francoise would just have to wait. This trouble of Harriet's, whatever it was, must be alleviated. Ariel, accustomed to thinking of her sister-in-law as a meek, long-suffering wife prey to the domination of her austere husband and crusty father-in-law, realized that a crisis had occurred and had to be dealt with before all else. She could not abandon the wretched woman to her pain.

Harriet swallowed and tried to wipe her tears away ineffectually with one shaking hand. "Thank you, Ariel, but there is naught you can do. It is Arnold," she confessed, her words tumbling out in

218

despair. "I know I should not complain about my husband. I should be loyal, but I am beside myself. Perhaps I am not the wife he wants. I know he cares little for me, and is disgusted that I am unable to breed. He wants an heir. He is jealous of Ian, you know, and fears if I do not produce a son, the title will go to his brother, and he could not abide that."

Her normally taciturn sister-in-law, burdened by her worry, was indeed suffering. "But Harriet, it is not your fault," Ariel said with some embarrassment. "I am sure you want a child, but we must accept what life brings us, I am afraid. Surely Arnold understands. You must both just be patient."

Now that the floodgates had opened, Harriet was eager to unburden herself. "Arnold hates me, thinks I am a poor milksop of a woman. He has found someone who responds to him, gives him all that I cannot. He has taunted me with my inadequacy. I have tried, Ariel, but I know when he takes me to bed he is only doing a duty. He is so cold, so cruel, so uncaring."

Ariel hesitated. She knew so little of the marriage bed, of physical relationships between man and woman—how could she advise her sister-in-law? Surely the fastidious and proper Arnold did not share the womanizing proclivities of his brother. He showed no signs of being a libertine, indeed, appeared to find Ian's adventures disgusting and unpalatable. Harriet must be mistaken.

"I am sure you misunderstood, Harriet. Arnold would never take a mistress. He disapproves of all licentiousness." Ariel could see that her sister-in-law was still convinced of her husband's perfidy. What a coil.

"He told me. He has someone, whom he says is warm and loving, so different from me. He laughed at my efforts to be a good wife, says I am cold and frigid, do not know how to please a man. He is right. But how can I learn to satisfy him? He rejects any attempts I make to mend matters between us. Oh, what will happen to me? He will cast me off, send me back to my parents. I could not face the disgrace," Harriet wailed, a fresh burst of tears overcoming her.

"Nonsense, Harriet. The earl would never allow that. I know that wives sometimes have to endure their husband's infidelities, but you must take heart. The wife, in these cases, has the advantage. Arnold would never abandon you," Ariel soothed and reassured, but her astonishment at this turn of events made her less than convincing. Harriet had little to attract a man, and now she seemed sunk in such unhappiness she would never rouse herself to fight for her husband. Still, Ariel tried to hearten her sister-in-law, made her lie quietly with a cloth soaked in eau de cologne on her head, covered her with a light blanket, and urged her to sleep.

"I have an urgent appointment, but I will return and we can talk further. You must try to rest now. I am sure all will seem brighter in a short while. No doubt Arnold regrets causing you distress. You will come about. Please try to compose yourself, dear Harriet." Ariel bustled about settling Harriet into some comfort, but was appalled by the revelations she had heard.

"Thank you, Ariel, you are so kind. I know you think I am fainthearted, but then you would never succumb to such misery. You are too strong, too resolute. Oh, if only I could be like you," Harriet said pathetically, about to burst down again.

"Nonsense, Harriet. I am not impervious to sorrow or trouble. But we must face up to it, not allow our men to cast us into the boughs. They must respect us, listen to us, support us. You will learn to cope with this difficulty, I am sure. I will help you all I can. But I must be off now. Try to rest." Ariel leaned over the woman stretched out on the bed and gave her a gentle kiss on the cheek. Poor girl. How could she help her? All her life Harriet had bowed to others, subjugated her own will to that of her parents and husband. She was totally incapable of standing up to Arnold. Ariel wondered if there was any truth to her accusations that Arnold had become embroiled with another woman. It seemed so out of character. Well, she would have to postpone this latest budget of bad news until she had met Francoise.

Ariel went on her way, leaving behind the painful problem that Harriet had offered, confused as to what she could do to assist her sister-in-law. Not for the first time Ariel felt her anger rise as she realized how vulnerable women were to the men who controlled their lives. Only a deep abiding love made such relationships possible, but the sterile marriage, made for fortune and prestige, seemed the normal condition in London society. Harriet was just such a victim, and if she did not take precautions, she herself would be in a like case. As Ariel stepped into the carriage which would carry her to the Villefranche residence, she felt more determined than ever to thwart Ian's loveless possession of her.

Her cousin, dressed as usual in the latest stare, in a gown of deep crimson silk, greeted her formally when she entered the drawing room. Ariel refused to allow herself to feel intimidated but Francoise's expression boded ill for a comfortable cose. Obviously she had serious matters on her mind.

"Ah, good morning, Ariel. I see you understand the importance of our meeting, although you are a bit tardy in arriving," Francoise complained waspishly. None of her fabled address was exerted for this interview. She must feel she was dealing from strength.

"I was delayed by a domestic crisis. What can you want of me, Francoise, which is so important?" Ariel responded calmly, determined not to be put on the defensive.

"I have been aware for some time that your efforts to trade on our relationship had deeper motives. You accepted our hospitality and intended to spy on us, a most ungrateful and despicable return for all we did for you. But now I have learned the real reason for your strange marriage, and I intend to have my revenge." Francoise spat her words from a face suddenly marred by vindictiveness.

Ariel, astonished by her cousin's attack, did not

know how to respond. What could Francoise mean? And how should she respond to her accusations?

Rallying, Ariel drew herself up and faced her adversary coldly. "I have no idea as to what you refer, Francoise, but I dislike your tone. I do not deserve such censure."

"Can you deny that you entered this house with the intention of proving Philippe and I were members of some conspiracy?" Francoise said shrilly.

Determined not to be cowed, Ariel decided that the moment had come for plain speaking. "I admit that you and Philippe are objects of some suspicion from the government. You live well on funds that appear mysterious. You lied to me about your relationship with Prince Talleyrand. I feel there is every reason to doubt your gratitude and loyalty to the country which offered you a safe refuge from France's Terror. If I am wrong in these suspicions, you must excuse me, but there is much in your life that causes disquiet." Ariel looked her cousin squarely in the face, noticing that her eyes dropped before Ariel's assault. So there was reason for her doubts. Francoise might pretend to take offense at Ariel's explanations but she did not evidence the horror and surprise that an innocent would have shown.

"You are the spy, not me. But I have the means to put a stop to all that. If you do not cease this investigation into our affairs, deny to your superiors the doubts of our loyalty, I will ruin you. I know you were forced to marry Captain Montague because of imprudent behavior and I am not loath to let London society hear the real story. You will be a laughing stock, and your august father-in-law will not find that to his taste," she sneered.

"You refine too much on scurrilous gossip. Do not threaten me, Francoise," Ariel said with more firmness than she felt. Here was a nasty situation. How could she thwart her cousin's intentions?

Suddenly Francoise's manner changed, and she became softly cajoling. "There is no reason for us to be at odds with one another. I am willing to keep silent if you will cooperate with me. Philippe and I must regain our lands, and only Prince Talleyrand can aid us. I am not asking you to betray your country, only to give me some information on some of the government's leaders. He pays well for gossip and tales about such men and we need the money, now that our sugar plantations are in such sad straits. You are in a position to get me that information with your close ties to the Valentines, and you are privy to all sorts of talk at the War Office. I need to know these things. Surely it is in both our interests to cooperate," Francoise pleaded, now beguiling and tempting in her efforts to win her case.

Furious at her cousin's attempts to bribe her, Ariel answered with scorn. "I will never do what you ask, Francoise, and I abhor your conniving and ingratitude. I am sorry for your plight, but I owe you little. From the beginning you had your own motives for welcoming us, and whatever I did to discover your machinations I feel no regret. Do your worst. Shout the circumstances of our marriage to the housetops if you wish. But I warn you, these ploys of yours will rebound on your head. You do not frighten me and I feel nothing but disgust at your attempts to blackmail me. I am sure that the War Office will find them equally despicable." Ariel, who had not sat down during this tempestuous interview, straightened her bonnet and prepared to depart, unwilling to stay one moment more in the presence of this hateful enemy.

"Oh, you may talk bravely, but I am sure on second thought you will accede to my requests. I will give you some time to change your mind, but not too long. Your father-in-law is giving a ball to introduce you to society and that would be a perfect occasion to expose your scandal to the world. I promise you I will do it," Francoise snarled, irate that her threats had not brought Ariel to her knees.

"Good-bye, Francoise. I do not envy you when Ian and General Valentine hear about your infamy." Ariel whirled and left the room without more ado.

No matter how stalwartly she had confronted her cousin, she felt distinct unease. This new complication could only endanger Ian's plans. And he would blame her, she knew, for not handling her cousin with more address. She must find him immediately and confess the results of this uncomfortable meeting. Perhaps she should have pretended to acquiesce, to draw Francoise into further indiscretions, but somehow she could not summon the resolution to act so deceptively.

She wondered where Francoise had heard the story of her marriage. No one but Fiona Mackenzie knew the real facts. Could she be the culprit?

Ariel sighed. Really, her once calm, even dull, life had altered beyond all expectations. Why had she yearned for excitement, for an alteration of the commonplace, if humiliating, routine which had been her wont when under the Mackenzies' protection? Here she was embroiled in a spy conspiracy with its attendant dangers and mysteries, a marriage which seemed headed for disaster, a relationship with the troubled Harriet for whom she felt pity, and increasing suspicion of everyone whom she met. Even Alistair posed a problem. She did not think his flirtation serious. He could not resist trying his wiles on any attractive woman, especially a married one, with whom he could not be called to account. And was there more to that young man than the rollicking, insouciant manner which he turned to the world? Was he really as feckless and irresponsible as he appeared or was that just a convenient role which masked more devious intentions? Would General Valentine trust him, allow him access to so much privileged information if he was nothing but a meretricious womanizer? But certainly he was in a position to betray government secrets. Could he be the culprit, the unknown agent in the War Office who was using a position of trust to betray his country? Ariel tried to subdue her doubts. She would as soon suspect Ian as Alistair but she felt surrounded by intrigue and hypocrisy. Well, she would have to just struggle on and do her best in the confusing maze in which she found herself. But her first duty was to confide this latest problem to Ian and try to learn how this might affect their investigation.

On returning to the Strathcairn house, she was relieved to learn that Harriet had left on a shopping expedition. At least that domestic crisis could be postponed. Also, Ian had returned, for which she was grateful. His absences were becoming more prolonged, perhaps because he wished to avoid her. Well, he would have to smother his distaste for her company and listen to what she had learned from Francoise. On entering the morning room, she found him bent over some papers, but he stood with alacrity to welcome her.

"There you are, Ariel. I have been waiting for you to hear the outcome of your interview with your cousin," he greeted her cheerfully, taking her cold hands in his and rubbing them briskly. "You are chilled to the bone. Come near the fire and tell me all," he commanded, drawing her to the sofa near the hearth, which blazed with a cheerful fire.

"Yes, well, it was not completely unexpected. She tried to bribe me to secure information about certain government officials, and threatened to noise the real story of our marriage about the ton if I refused," Ariel blurted out, anxious to unload the sordid tale onto his broad shoulders. For once his ruthless, domineering ways seemed to offer protection, not annoyance. She was unaccustomed to sharing her burdens, and the knowledge that she had a supporter gave her unexpected relief. But she could not get into the habit of relying on Ian. She had stood alone since her father's death and their current relationship was too fragile for her to open her heart. Staring at him in some confusion, she chided herself for accepting the comfort and assurance he offered. But she found she trusted him despite all evidence to the contrary. She looked at him expectantly.

"Well, Ariel, it seems you were right to suspect Francoise, a clever conniver, that one. Perhaps her husband is innocent but she has at last come out into the open. I suppose she learned of the true circumstances of our marriage from Fiona, the only possible source. The Mackenzies have returned to London and Fiona lost no time in taking her revenge, I see."

"What will we do? Naturally, I treated her suggestion with scorn and refused to do what she wanted, but how can we prove she is dealing with Talleyrand? If only I had taken that letter," Ariel moaned, remembering the revelations in that document.

"We must simply try to bring her perfidy to the attention of the authorities. Even without proof she could be persuaded to leave the country, I think. And just because Talleyrand has bullied her into collecting gossip does not mean that she is our culprit. I doubt if she has the brains to run an intricate spy ring, and we are now convinced the perpetrator is nearer home, in the War Office or Foreign Office itself. I wonder if we have made a mistake about Philippe. He might have been clever enough to realize the trap we set and ignore it," Ian theorized, running through the various possibilities.

"But what about her threats? Your father will be furious if I embroil the family in a scandal," Ariel insisted, unreasonably piqued that Ian should be more concerned with the larger issue than their personal affairs.

"Our family is no stranger to scandal," he replied brusquely. "And it would be no more than a brief tempest, fuel for the gossip mongers but of no real import. We might have to endure a few raised eyebrows, some social stigma, but since you dislike society and find most of these ton leaders of no account, I cannot see that it would matter."

"Yes, all very well for you. But I remember that in Vienna, I was the target of the rumors. It was my reputation which suffered. You did not incur any censure," Ariel replied bitterly.

"It is the woman who pays, as you know only too well, Ariel. You are no doubt right, but we can scotch these rumors, Francoise's nasty tongue, even Fiona's spite, by acting the devoted lovers. A role I quite fancy," he teased, but underneath his joking tone she sensed a certain determination.

"Francoise promises to tell her tale at the ball if I do not come up with the information she needs," Ariel reminded him, ignoring his reference to their relationship.

"Let her do her worst. But somehow I do not think she will endanger her own position. Astute people might question her motives, and she does not want to put herself in jeopardy. Forget her threats. I will tell Valentine of her approach to you. He is our best protection. And I don't think Fiona will cause trouble. Robert would be disgusted and she depends on his good opinion. No, I think Françoise was just trying to see what you might reveal about our mission, hoping to learn something to her advantage but not willing to risk her own safety in the attempt." Ian soothed her, aware that her precarious life in the Mackenzie household had left her insecure and unwilling to trust anyone to protect her. He yearned to reassure her, to comfort her, and to gain her confidence. Life had taught her to rely on no one but herself. He would have to alter her perception of him as a fribbly, reckless fellow with no finer sensibilities, content only to gratify his own wishes. Only then would she be willing to surrender her future and her person to him. Ariel would never love a libertine and mountebank, only a man upon whose devotion and fidelity she could rely. Somehow he had to persuade her he was that man, for this marriage had come to mean more to him than he could ever have dreamed. They would win through, he was determined. He looked at her down-bent head, wondering what was going through her mind. He was more than startled by her next question.

"Ian, are you sure of Alistair's loyalty? I know it is shocking, but I have come to suspect everyone, and he is in a position to give much dangerous information to our enemies," Ariel offered tentatively, almost ashamed to voice her doubts of Ian's friend and longtime comrade.

"I am as certain of Alistair as I am of myself. Do not bother your head about him. He may be a rake and a philanderer but he is not a traitor," Ian answered, surprised that she could challenge his fellow officer.

"I am foolish, suspecting everyone, but we seem surrounded by treachery. No one is what they seem." She sighed, remembering Harriet and her revelations about Arnold, but she did not feel she could confide her sister-in-law's trouble to Ian. There was too much bad feeling between the brothers, and this latest problem would only make matters worse.

"Come, Ariel, luncheon is about to be served. Try to put Francoise out of your mind. It is all a tempest in a teapot. You will see. Concentrate on the ball. I hope you have bought a ravishing gown, and we will confound all our detractors on the night," Ian quipped, eager to restore her to her usual poise and serenity.

She smiled wistfully but nodded agreement, taking his comforting arm as he escorted her from the room. If only she had his ability to live in the present and not brood about tomorrow with its hidden traps and unfaithful friends.

Chapter Seventeen

Ariel looked at herself critically in the cheval mirror as her maid put the finishing touches on her hair, which was braided high on her head into a thick cornet. The wickedly expensive gown appeared to pay for the cost, in her favorite green, a watered silk more the shimmering color of the sea, falling in severe folds from beneath the high waistline, the bodice shockingly low but showing off her creamy shoulders to advantage. The only decorative accent was a row of intricate ruched ribbon trimming the neckline. She wore no jewelry but some pearl earrings which had belonged to her mother, the plainness of her attire depending for its effect on the clever cut. Madame Claude had been quite right, assessing her client's elegant figure and insisting that she would be wise to ignore the frills and furbelows so beloved by her less-favored customers. Ariel dismissed her maid with thanks and wondered if she should seek Ian's approval before descending into the hall to await their guests.

Instead she made a visit to Harriet's room, hoping that her sister-in-law had taken her advice and decided on the azure blue silk and lace Ariel had selected. For once she was determined her sister-in-law would look her best, on this night of the ball the earl had insisted upon giving for his new relation, when they would be the cynosure of all eyes. On entering Harriet's room, Ariel was relieved to see that she had indeed chosen the blue silk, and for once her maid had outdone herself, dressing her mistress to best advantage. Flushed with excitement, her sallow complexion flattered by the color, Harriet looked her very best. Although she would never be a beauty, she at least looked like a proper viscountess instead of a dowd.

"Harriet, you look lovely. I was sure that gown would do the trick," Ariel reassured the girl, who stood hesitating in the center of the room. She was holding a lovely circlet of sapphires in her hand, unsure as to this addition to her costume.

"Thank you, Ariel. I am so grateful for your suggestions, for taking me to Madame Claude. I have never had such a lovely gown. Do you think this necklace will do?" she asked, her brow furrowing as she looked at herself in the glass.

"Just the perfect touch. Arnold will be proud of you," Ariel agreed. She hoped to give Harriet some needed confidence before she faced her critical and cold husband. Little had been said between them about Harriet's tearful disclosures some days past, but Ariel was determined to instill some confidence in the insecure girl. She

234

certainly had made the most of her assets, and now she must be persuaded to act accordingly.

"I don't suppose he will even notice. And next to you, I am quite cast in the shade. You look so elegant and poised. How I envy you," Harriet mourned, looking at their two images reflected in the mirror.

"Nonsense. We set each other off. You will have a triumph. Just hold your head high and face the world with assurance. I am sure you will surprise everyone," Ariel encouraged. "Now let us go down."

They left the room together, and Ariel let Harriet precede her down the wide staircase to where their menfolk awaited them. The earl and his two sons stood in the hall, watching as they descended. In his formal dress the earl looked every inch the aristocrat, his snow white hair and proud stance indicating his rank, his proud hawklike face a testament to his lineage. Arnold, his black evening coat and white knee britches set off by a blue waistcoat, looked more impressive than usual, and his eyes widened with surprise at his first glimpse of his wife. Ariel hoped he would reassure Harriet, and for once he behaved with some gallantry, bowing over her hand and telling her that he admired her gown, receiving a look of shy gratitude in return. However, all thoughts of Arnold and his wife faded as Ariel faced her husband, whose hot dark eyes glowed with desire as he raked his wife with a stare which brought an unwelcome blush to her cheek. Then his lids dropped over that gaze and she thought she might have been mistaken at the sensual stare he had given her. Dressed in his formal uniform of the King's Dragoon Guards, he made a dashing figure, quite casting his companions into the shade. She remembered with a pang that other ball in Vienna when he had so mockingly requested a dance. There was nothing mocking in his smile now as he looked at her with that appraising stare which promised so much. Before he could make any comment, the earl leaned over and kissed her on the cheek.

"You look beautiful, my dear. You will have all the young bucks in a twitter. I knew I could rely on your taste. You will honor an old codger with a dance, I hope." He smiled, lightening his usual severe expression with the admiration which she inspired. "You had best keep a close watch on your wife, Ian. She will break hearts this evening."

Ian scowled. He did not need his father's words to realize what a beauty he had taken to wife. What a far cry from the humble companion he had met in Fiona's drawing room. This vision was a woman he barely recognized. But before he could add his compliments to his father's, the earl intervened.

"But that gown demands some impressive jewelry. Come into the library before our dinner guests arrive. I have just the thing." The earl took her arm and escorted her across the hall.

Ariel, bemused by Ian's sudden anger, followed in his wake. Once inside the room, the earl went to his desk and took up a velvet case lying there, opening it to show her a glittering parure of

236

emeralds and diamonds with matching earrings.

"The Strathcairn emeralds are famous, Ariel. And you are just the one to set them off. I will be pleased if you will accept these as a token of my esteem," the earl said gruffly.

Ariel, overcome with emotion, felt the tears rise to her eyes. This was the old man's effort to signify his approval of the marriage and his acceptance of her. Turning to him she took the necklace from his outstretched hand and found herself too touched to speak.

"Let me put this on for you, Ariel. The governor is quite right. You will add luster to them," Ian said gallantly, fastening the jewels around her neck, his finger on her skin causing her an electric tingle. "And the earrings." He handed her the matching gems and watched her beneath lidded eyes as she removed her pearl drops and substituted the emeralds. "Yes, now you look even more beautiful, if possible," he concluded with satisfaction.

"Thank you so much. I will take the utmost care of them. I never expected such an honor." She smiled at the father and son, basking in the warm regard she saw in both pairs of dark eyes.

"Shall we go? I believe our dinner guests are arriving," the earl said, breaking into the tender moment. Ariel took Ian's arm and they left the room together. His warm glance raised her hopes. For once he was not wearing his enigmatic smile; his glance had seared her with its promise of passion. Could he be at last seeing her as she wished him to? Well, she conceded wryly, underneath all these fine feathers, she was still the soldier's daughter, the prim girl who had rebuffed his lechery, his intention to lure her into his bed. But a faint anticipation stirred within her. Perhaps he was looking at her in a new light, with affection more than friendliness, with appreciation and even a deeper emotion. How she wished that this evening could culminate in their true marriage.

As they welcomed the two dozen guests who had been invited to dine before the ball, it was all Ariel could do to retain some composure, to behave as if this evening were naught but an unexceptional entertainment, but her excitement was not easily restrained. Even the arrival of Fiona and Sir Robert could not dampen her spirits. The earl had insisted on their inclusion in the exclusive dinner party because they were Ariel's closest relations. She found herself amused at Fiona's unbelieving stare as she faced her former victim. The haughty beauty for once looked overset, aware of a rival to her own cool blond looks. Sir Robert, of course, was all affection and delight at their reunion.

"Well, Ariel, I am so pleased to see you looking so handsome. Marriage certainly agrees with you. I am delighted your lines have fallen on such pleasant places," he said as he kissed her on the cheek.

"Thank you, Robert. I feel an imposter in all this finery, but I must say I enjoy it," Ariel returned his greeting, touched by his reception.

"Yes, Ariel you have done well for yourself. Those emeralds are magnificent. I would never have believed a mere soldier's daughter would appear to such advantage," Fiona commented snidely.

Ian's eyes narrowed. "I for one am not surprised, Fiona. I suspected all along that Ariel had hidden depths. Unlike so many of the ton's incomparables. She has a rare quality of sincerity so lacking in the usual women one meets on the social round."

"You should know, Ian, with all your experience," Fiona replied, irritated to be criticized by one whom she had once believed to be at her feet. Sir Robert, fearing an outbreak of his wife's temper, whisked her away before any more damage could be done, not liking the unholy delight at her jealousy he saw in Ian's eyes.

Ariel welcomed the Villefranches with some temerity, wondering if Francoise would make a double-edged remark, but that lady was all graciousness, thanking the earl for including them in the dinner party and smiling seductively at Ian. Her husband took advantage of the situation to leer at Ariel suggestively, recalling their interview in his library. She was relieved when they were succeeded by the Valentines, whose appreciation she recognized as sincere. Alistair, too, was all flattery and she smiled easily at him, her doubts about his loyalty for the moment in abeyance.

Ceding to Harriet the role of hostess, which, for once, she accepted with calm, if shy, assurance, Ariel settled to the table with the rest of the guests, finding herself with Lucien Valentine on one side and an old friend of the earl's, Lord

Inchcomb, a distinguished portly gentleman, on the other. To her relief the dinner proceeded with no mishaps, the conversation concerned mainly with politics, and the satisfaction over the recent peace engaging all the guests. It was General Valentine who cast doubts on the solidity of the recent decisions of the Congress of Vienna. But even his suggestions as to the frailty of the current balance of power in Europe did not unduly disturb the tenor of the conversation. Ariel found herself responding to the sophisticated conversation easily, even taking part in it, and watching Ian, down the table looking at her with approval and admiration, she felt an unaccustomed glow of happiness. If only Francoise would not realize her threat, this evening could indeed become a triumph. And it seemed her cousin was content to play the part of a grateful guest, acting with all circumspection.

The glow of the dinner party remained with Ariel as the ball opened, the Grosvenor Street house burgeoning with the influx of guests who had been bidden to welcome this newest addition to the Strathcairn family. Whatever the rumors about her background and this surprising marriage, society was only too eager to accept the august earl's new daughter-in-law when it was obvious he approved of the match. After a few hours in the receiving line, she began the dancing with the earl and then was claimed by her husband for a waltz. As his arm tightened about her waist and they swung into the throng of dancers, Ariel believed her fears for the evening had vanished and she thrilled to the intimacy of his ardent glance.

"You are a raging success, my dear, as I knew you would be. All of London has come out to do you honor. I am more than proud of my beautiful wife," he murmured as they danced in perfect harmony.

"Not quite all, Ian. I fear Fiona is quite put out by my respectability. And there is Francoise. She might still be planning to create a scandal," Ariel warned, reluctant to believe all would continue in such an idyllic fashion.

"Fainthearted, Ariel?" he queried, looking at her mockingly. "Not like your usual indomitable attitude. I would back you against Francoise and a dozen like her," Ian said as he reversed her smoothly through the dancers.

"I am grateful for your confidence in me, Ian. But I am prey to some overwhelming doubts. No one is who they seem. There are Francoise, Fiona, Alistair, poor Harriet, and even you, sir," she tried to answer lightly, but suddenly the morass of intrigue in which they moved seemed almost insurmountable.

"Society is intrigue, rumor, gossip, the lifeblood of this community. Not like the army, although even there place-seeking abounds. I fear your innocence and honesty will lure you into deep waters, my dear. You must learn to take people as you find them, and not expect too much," he warned.

"Yes, I must not prose on about morality or I will be quite out of fashion," she replied in some

241

chagrin, seeing in his words disapproval of her attitudes.

"But come, this is not an evening for such grim thoughts. Sufficient until the day our efforts to resolve our problems. What do you think of the reigning queen of this fashionable world, Lady Jersey? I see she is in fine form tonight, chattering away, destroying reputations and thoroughly enjoying herself," he mocked, indicating the ebullient lady, who had been dubbed "Silence" just because she talked incessantly, questioning her victims, purveying and initiating gossip, and jealous of her rule, allowing no other dowager to rival her firm grasp of the social code. Ariel looked at the lady in question, who was dancing with a grim Arnold, and laughed. She would have her work cut out to pry any secrets from her austere brother-in-law.

Abandoning herself to the pleasures of the evening, to the thrilling feel of Ian's arms holding her closely, Ariel pushed all thoughts of their various dilemmas from her mind. Tonight she felt carefree and amazingly happy; even Fiona's thin-lipped disapproval did not disturb her joyous mood. And later it was a merry group that settled down to the lavish supper of lobster patties, cold meats, and jellies that was provided. Alistair, in particular, appeared to be in a rollicking humor, for once not burdened with the cloying Olivia Bletchford and instead squiring a young debutante, of impeccable family and pert blond good looks. Even Harriet and Arnold, who joined their party, appeared to be enjoying themselves in a sober way, Harriet flushed with excitement and more forthcoming than usual. All in all the evening proved to be most successful and Ariel thanked her father-in-law as they left the supper room for providing such a stunning debut to her social introduction. The earl seemed gratified, then removed himself to the card room, where he was more content in the company of a few cronies.

Toward the end of the evening, Alistair claimed his dance with Ariel, who would not confess to disappointment that Ian had not favored her with another waltz. But he seemed engrossed with a stunning brunette, who flirted shockingly with him as they twirled through the steps of a country dance. Pleading exhaustion, Ariel suggested they sit out the next number, and Alistair offered to escort her to the conservatory, where they might find some privacy. Laughing at one of his sallies, she agreed, not noticing Ian's frown as he watched them leave the dance floor.

"A triumphant evening for you, Ariel. I see even the mighty Lord Castlereagh honored you with a request for a dance," Alistair said as they settled comfortably on a settee beneath a shielding palm tree. Fanning herself, for the tropical heat of the conservatory was oppressive, Ariel smiled at her companion.

"Yes, all has gone amazingly well. I did not think I could be seduced by such frivolity but I must have a giddier nature than I realized. I have quite enjoyed all this attention," Ariel agreed somewhat ruefully.

"You deserve some gaiety, Ariel. Your life until

243

now has not been exactly filled with light-minded pleasures," Alistair answered kindly, watching his companion with affection. She did indeed seem to glow with an inner excitement this evening, her usual reserve conspicuous by its absence. What a lovely lady she was, admittedly of an uncommon type but all the more enticing because of that. Ian had made a fortunate choice, if only he appreciated his luck. Alistair sighed, thinking of his own misfortunes in love.

"What is wrong, Alistair? You seem strangely distraught, quite unlike yourself. Affairs of the heart or of state bothering you?" Ariel asked idly, wiggling her tired feet in their slender satin slippers.

"Both, I believe. But it is Olivia Bletchford who is causing me heart searchings," he admitted, for once serious. "She is becoming quite demanding. I am fond of her, and sympathize with her situation, but I am not willing to be caught in her toils. I began the affaire not suspecting it would prove to be so troubling."

"She is a lovely woman, but married, Alistair, and not willing, I think, to give up her respectable position, even for you. You would be well advised to end your relationship before it endangers your career," Ariel replied, wondering not for the first time if Alistair had a heart to be won.

"Ah, yes, the lovely Olivia is a temptation, but I am not one for throwing my cap over the windmill. Now if it were you, Ariel, I might have a change of heart," he teased, unwilling to let the discussion continue in deeper waters.

"You are quite safe from my lures, Alistair, as well you know. But I do wish you would find a suitable girl, one you could love and would follow the drum with enthusiasm. Army life has many advantages, but it does not appeal to some women. I found it quite adventurous, and far removed from all the hypocrisy and intrigue of what is accepted in polite society," Ariel confided, watching her companion closely, her mood suddenly altered. She knew so little of the real Alistair, under the flippant face he turned to the world. There had to be more to him than his handsome face and whimsical manner. Otherwise he would not have gained Lucien Valentine's confidence. Perhaps it was just with women that he showed his capricious side, unable or unwilling to expose his deeper feelings, fearing that he might be hurt. She knew little of his family, but Ian had hinted that, like his own situation, Alistair and his relations did not get on well.

"Ah, Ariel, you are such a comfort. All is black and white to you. You would never be tempted to behave in a shoddy fashion or compromise your principles. Alas, we are all not so stalwart," Alistair said wistfully.

"Well, I hope I let my conscience guide me to behave as my father taught me. He was such a fine man, and I miss him, although I never forget his teachings," Ariel agreed, sobered by the reminder of the parent she had loved so deeply.

"You are fortunate in your memories. Mine are not so happy. Well, as usual, you have cheered my megrims. Your standards are high ones, but admirable. I doubt I can find a female to rival you," he said, gazing at her with unaffected friendship, for once not playing the part which hid his real character from the world.

Ariel smiled at his kind words, for she did not think herself exceptional. But this talk had lightened her suspicions of Alistair. She hoped that now indeed they could be real friends, not just partners in a silly flirtation. She rose, indicating that they must return to the ballroom, and Alistair, retrieving her fan, looked at her in admiration.

"Thank you, Ariel. I feel we have established a real bond. Greatly to be prized in this nasty welter of plots and social game playing," he said sincerely, and bending over, drew her into his arms, kissing her lightly in gratitude. Surprised by his warmhearted sincerity, Ariel did not struggle.

Unfortunately their position appeared quite compromising to Ian, who interrupted the tender embrace.

"Is this how you repay my friendship, Alistair, by trying to seduce my wife?" Ian said silkily, his face flushed with anger and his hands tightening into fists.

"Don't be an ass, Ian," Alistair said, surprised and unwittingly displaying some guilt as he faced his friend. "You misunderstand."

But Ian was not to be cajoled into a calmer frame of mind. "If it would not cause the most almighty scandal, Alistair, I would call you out. I know you think any female is fair game for your lechery, but my wife is not one of that number. I have warned you before and I am within an ace of teaching you a lesson." Ian, misinterpreting the shock he saw on their faces, his mercurial temper fueled by what he read in Ariel's stunned silence, turned to his wife. "And you, madam, I have had enough of your excuses and your rebuffs. Come, before some eager gossip monger discovers us, I will escort you back to the ballroom. Our guests are leaving and we must do the proper. But you have not heard the last of this, either of you."

Alistair hesitated, unwilling to part from his friend in such circumstances, and even more reluctant to surrender Ariel to his wrath, but she shook her head at him. They could not brangle here where any casual guest might discover them and judge the facts to their detriment. Viewing her husband's scowling face and realizing his tight-lipped control was in danger of breaking through the proprieties, she bit back her own retort and accepted Ian's arm. Beneath his uniform sleeve she could feel the muscles bunching, as if he might even now give in to the overmastering rage at what he thought he had surprised, his best friend and his wife in a liaison. That dangerous Scots temper was barely leashed, and unless she soothed his suspicions, they could all be embroiled in a horrible mess.

"Really, Ian, you are acting in a ridiculous fashion. Alistair meant nothing but friendship in that embrace. You mistook appearances," she said under her breath as they approached the hall, where some of the guests were bidding farewell to the earl.

"Do not lie to me, madam, I know what I saw, and I will not stand for you cuckolding me with that damned fellow. We have not finished with this, you and I," he raged. Composing his features quickly, he accepted the thanks of Lord and Lady Castlereagh, who were waiting for their carriage.

Ariel, seeing that this was not the time for further remonstrances, joined in bidding farewell to their departing guests, marveling at the facade Ian could don so quickly. Oh, he was a master deceiver, and how dare he threaten her and accuse her of dallying with Alistair. Ariel, usually slow to anger, felt a welter of rage rise in her breast to equal that of her husband's. She would not be treated thus, and if he continued to doubt would pay for his transgressions, she vowed, feeling beneath her anger a growing disappointment at yet another breach between them. Would they never be reconciled and deal with each other honestly? At the first opportunity she made her good-nights and fled to the sanctuary of her bedroom, too tired and unhappy to contemplate dealing with this latest misunderstanding.

Chapter Eighteen

Ariel dismissed her maid after the woman had unhooked her dress and wrapped her into her dressing gown. Then, she unclasped the emeralds and laid them carefully on her table, intent on returning them to the earl on the morrow. She could not keep them. She did not feel entitled to them. As she thought back over the evening and its disastrous ending, she wondered what she could do to reassure Ian of the innocence of the scene he had interrupted. His anger seemed all out of proportion. Perhaps when he had slept on the matter, he would see how insulting and unbelievable his reaction had been to both Alistair and herself. But she could not think how to deal with his unjustified wrath now. Her head ached and her whole body throbbed with weariness.

She donned her nightgown and went to the chair before the smoldering fire. She doubted that she could sleep with such a burden upon her. In the morning all might appear less ruinous, but now she could not cope with what Ian had implied. His Celtic temper was driving him, and as long as he allowed his anger full rein, she might be wise to avoid him. And her own anger threatened to overmaster her. How typical that he should be moved to such violence. He indulged his own desires, went his own way, and then when he suspected that she might be acting in some indiscreet fashion, was quick to criticize and blame. She must not come between Alistair and Ian, whose friendship meant more to both of them than either man's feelings for her—of that she was convinced. And her own reaction? She had believed she loved Ian, or was coming to feel that overwhelming need of him—of his support, his tenderness, his approval—but now it had all vanished in a stupid muddle of misunderstanding. How could she retrieve the situation? She sighed, her burden almost more than she could bear. She rose and climbed into bed. She doubted that sleep could be wooed but no good could come of brooding in the dark. She needed to rest and face tomorrow with resolution, if she could.

As she was restlessly trying to settle, the door to the adjoining room crashed open and Ian stood on the threshold. She bit back a startled gasp. She would not show her fear, but as he crossed to her bedside, she realized that he had been at the brandy bottle.

"What do you want, Ian? It is very late, and I am not in the mood for your recriminations." Ariel sat up in bed, clutching the bed linens around her.

She did not like the menacing look in his hot eyes, or the flush of rage on his face. There was nothing of the gentle supportive friend in his stance. He looked as if murder were his intention.

"I have respected your virtuous rebuffs long enough madam," he sneered, his voice harsh and cruel as he raked her with a sensual stare.

She hesitated, not knowing how to conciliate him. He was in the grip of a terrifying anger fueled by the brandy he had been drinking and would not be easily turned from his purpose.

"You wanted a marriage of convenience. Well, it is convenient for me to make it a reality. I have waited far too long, respecting your prudish objections. I will not stand by while you give to another what is mine by right," he said, throwing off his shirt and grasping her by the shoulders.

She gasped and averted her eyes. She had never seen a man unclothed before, and his obvious maleness, his broad chest covered with black curling hairs tapering down to narrow hips, shocked her. But he would have none of her shrinking. With a hard hand he turned her face toward him and kissed her brutally, his hand roaming down the neck of her nightgown to fondle the curves of white flesh beneath its folds. She struggled desperately beneath him. He effortlessly tore her nightgown open, leaving her breasts exposed to his bold stare.

Trying to elude his roving hands and seeking mouth, Ariel fought ineffectually against him as he forced her back upon the pillows.

251

"Don't do this, Ian. It will be rape," she pleaded, frightened by the determined lust she saw in his face.

"I doubt it, my dear. You are far from the innocent I believed you to be. Much as I hate taking Alistair's leavings, I will not be put off any longer," he murmured, his lips fastening on hers again with a hot drugging kiss. He pulled her beneath him, his kisses deepening, his body subduing her struggles. Despite herself, and heedless of the violence of his caresses, she felt herself responding to the urgency of his desire, her limbs leaden and her flailing arms stilled under his expert handling. She knew she should repell him but a strange lassitude filled her, and she despised herself for responding to his hands and mouth. He chuckled bitterly as he sensed her arousal.

"What a little wanton you are, Ariel, under all that starched facade. Well, I intend to enjoy the fruits of your initiation into the delights of the connubial bed." His knee forced her thighs apart and his hands moved down her body with insulting familiarity.

As he moved her more completely beneath him, she felt his surging manhood pressed against her. She gasped in surprise and shock. Then he was within her, his penetration causing her to cry out in pain at the unaccustomed invasion. He hesitated for a moment, as if in wonder, and then he could no longer control the frenzy of his passion, his grip tightening and his movements inducing a throbbing pressure within her. His breathing

252

quickened and she knew by his hunger-ridden face that he had lost all restraint, taking his pleasure from her in one overmastering gust of passion.

He collapsed upon her in a sigh of gratification seemingly unaware of the tears which coursed down her cheeks. For a moment he remained immobile, then he raised himself to look at her searchingly.

"I am sorry, Ariel. I did not mean it to be this way. I did not believe you were a virgin," he said in gentle remorse.

"You did not care. You were only intent on punishing me, and you have done that," she sobbed, turning her head away from his probing eyes.

"I was angry. I am a devil when aroused, and you suffered for it." He rolled off the bed and donned his dressing gown. "But it had to happen sometime, Ariel. I only regret that I took you in such a rage. It will be better next time, I promise."

"There won't be a next time. I hate you. At least leave me alone now," she cried, overwhelmed by humiliation and pain.

"Forgive me, Ariel. My damned temper rode me, but I can see you wish me to hell. Perhaps that is where I will end," he conceded, looking at her streaked face, ashen and agonized. He wanted to take her in his arms and console her, give her the tender reassurances she was entitled to, but he knew she would not respond to him now. The damage was done. He bent over her, ignoring her shrinking, and kissed her gently. "Try to sleep. It will all seem less horrible in the morning," he murmured, but she made no sign that she had heard him, and he turned away, realizing she was in no condition to listen to him. He crossed the room and shut the adjoining door softly behind him, leaving the unhappy girl alone to face what had happened to her.

Ariel awoke from her drugging sleep at the sound of her maid pulling aside the draperies on the gray February morning. She stretched languidly, and then remembering the events of the previous evening, groaned, a deep blush flooding through her. Sleep had restored her bruised body but returning consciousness erased the healing qualities of sleep.

"What time is it, Nancy?" she asked, determined to put a calm face upon matters, but wondering if her maid noticed her unease.

"Almost noon, madam, but Captain Montague insisted you be allowed to have your sleep since you retired so late," the girl answered, bustling about the room putting it to rights. Spying her torn nightgown by the side of the bed, Ariel wondered what her maid would think. She shuddered at the memory of what had happened in those final hours before dawn. Pulling the bed linen around her naked form, she hoped the girl would notice nothing amiss, but doubted that her dishevelment and confusion would escape the maid's sharp eyes. She could only pray that Nancy was not one to gossip in the servant's hall. Eager to avoid any semblance of the unusual, she sent the girl for her breakfast and bath and then rose gingerly from her bed, hastily wrapping her dressing gown around her. She must try to act with some degree of normalcy. Regrets and recriminations could come later. Ariel had always faced up to what life had dealt her with courage, and in this, one of the most traumatic experiences she had ever endured, she was determined to do no less.

Later, looking at her shadowed eyes and pale face in her mirror as she finished her toilette, she wondered how she could ever face Ian again. Her body ached from his brutal possession. He had exercised none of his fabled skill as a lover last evening. No doubt he was unaccustomed to bedding virgins, she conceded cynically. Her struggles had been unavailing and had made the ultimate violation more painful, but she would never forgive him. She had wanted to become a real wife to him, but not in such a fashion, to be used as the vehicle of his anger and lust. But sulking in her bedroom would avail her little. She must behave with some composure, try to dismiss the anger and hurt of the experience, but she would not forget, and she would not be used in such a fashion again.

Deciding that what she needed was some brisk exercise to dispel her unhappiness, she donned her riding clothes and descended into the hall, intent on leaving the stifling atmosphere of the house. She hoped she would have an interval of peace to restore her equilibrium before she met her husband, and in that she was fortunate. She met no one as she waited for her horse to be brought around, and she mounted the spirited mare quickly, eager to ease her disquiet in hard exercise. She wished she could dismiss the groom who must accompany her, but realized that riding alone would not be tolerated. Once in the Park, almost empty at this time of day, she let out her horse, welcoming the brisk breeze which brought color to her pale cheeks and some surcease to her troubled thoughts. Leaving her groom to follow as best he could, she put the mare to a hard canter along the bridle paths. The early gloom of the morning had lifted and a watery sun peeked through the scudding clouds, raising her spirits somewhat. After a half hour's brisk exercise, she reluctantly turned her horse homeward.

To her dismay, as she trotted the mare gracefully up to the entrance of the Strathcairn mansion, she saw Ian pull his phaeton to a stop before the house. He jumped down and tossed the reins to his tiger before striding to her side and lifting her down from the horse.

"If I had known you intended riding, I would have accompanied you, my dear," he said wryly, looking at her aloof face beneath the olive green Hussar-style hat she wore.

To her dismay, Ariel felt her face flooding with color, and she could not meet his eyes, his hands on her waist recalling his far less gentle touch of the night before. But she could say nothing before the servants and they walked silently into the house together.

"We must talk, Ariel," Ian murmured.

"If you insist, Ian," she responded repressively, handing her hat, gloves, and whip to the waiting Lufton, and making her way toward the morning room.

"Luncheon has been served, madam. But if you would like some refreshment, I can bring something to you," Lufton offered.

"Nothing, thank you, Lufton. I had a very late breakfast. Perhaps some chocolate," Ariel said, clasping her shaking hands behind her back.

"And bring me some Madeira, Lufton," Ian ordered, watching his wife's straight back as she marched across the hall. He smiled grimly to himself. This would not be easy. Her defenses were up, and after all, how could he excuse his actions?

"Well, Ian." She turned and faced him once they were alone behind the closed doors of the morning room.

He looked at her closed expression. She would grant no quarter—that was evident.

"I apologize for my brutal possession of you last evening. But damn it, Ariel, why were you dallying with Alistair, allowing him to fondle you in such a manner?" Ian demanded.

"Appearances are not always what they seem, as you should know. I seem to remember that your abrupt entrance into my bedroom in Vienna was capable of several interpretations," Ariel answered with some asperity.

Ian, restraining a hot reply, crossed to her and took her in his arms, raising her downbent head

257

with a gentle hand. "Your initiation into wifehood could have been much easier, and I regret forcing myself upon you, but you know, Ariel, my possession of you was inevitable. I just regret it was so violent." His voice was tender as he watched her struggle with her embarrassment and anger.

"It was nothing more than rape," she answered, still in the grip of powerful emotion.

"I did not mean it to be rape. I care for you, Ariel, and would wish our relationship to be otherwise, but frustration and jealousy, no matter how displayed, are poor companions. I behaved abominably, and can only plead for your forgiveness, and promise that next time it will be different," he soothed her, seeing little in her expression that offered forgiveness.

Before she could answer, Lufton entered with a tray of refreshment and perforce their conversation could not continue while he was in the room. Ariel, brooding, decided she must somehow accept Ian's overtures. They could not deal with each other as enemies. What had happened was past, recriminations would not change it, and they must struggle onto some acceptable footing.

"I see no need to continue hashing over what transpired Ian," she said after Lufton had left the room. "But I insist that you leave me alone in the future. I would not entertain a repeat of your shocking behavior." She thought she sounded like a repressed spinster chastising a wayward charge but what could she say? She wanted to forget their violent union, relegate it to the farthest reaches of her mind, although she doubted she would be successful in banishing it entirely. How differently she had once thought they would consummate their marriage. But it was not to be. Ian might feel regret and a certain humiliation at his outrageous actions but that in no way altered his feeling for her. He was incapable of the real affection she wanted and his desire merely a satisfaction of his senses. It would do no good to reprove him for that.

For a moment it seemed that Ian would protest, but realizing that further explanations could only harden her rejection of him, he appeared to accept her decision, and hurried into a less personal discussion.

"I talked to Valentine this morning about the Villefranches. He has decided they must be banished before they cause further trouble. Either back to France or to the West Indies, but they cannot remain here to continue their dealings with Talleyrand," he said, changing the subject in hopes that Ariel could be brought around to discussing their alliance against the traitors with some equanimity, the only bond between them now, he conceded unhappily. Although he regretted exceedingly what his temper had impelled, his invasion of her virginity, he was not willing to admit that his regret implied any deeper feeling. He felt some unnamed emotion for his wife, but he could not bring himself to expose his doubts and unhappiness at their strained relationship further. She would not listen now, at any rate, and he must deal as best he could with her justified intractability. More angry and disappointed with himself than with Ariel, he retreated behind the armor of engimatic indifference which was his usual style, not realizing that she took his attitude for one of unconcern for her own troubled feelings.

"Another, rather grave indication of treachery has surfaced to cause us disquiet," he continued. "A messenger, probably one of Napoleon's vast number of agents, has been discovered drowned off the Sussex coast with a sodden document in his possession. It is, as we expected, an outline of arrangements for Napoleon's escape and landing in Italy, ships, military dispositions, France's reaction to the Bourbon king, all the most telling evidence that plans are well advanced for the escape with the connivance of traitors here, in France, and in Vienna. Valentine has sent Alistair to Sussex to try to discover more, but he is certain that the documents originated in the Foreign Office. We know that agents of both Napoleon and our own have been visiting Elba for the past weeks, despite what we do to prevent them. Even fishing vessels have been prohibited from landing on the island, but I fear our methods are not stringent enough to prevent the man from effecting his escape. He promised to return, you know, carrying violets ... the mountebank," Ian growled, indignant at how events were conspiring to overturn the fragile peace of Europe.

"But surely the French will not rise to his standard. And what Englishman would cooperate to loose that terror again?" Ariel exclaimed, distracted from her own worries over this greater threat.

"Money is a great assuager of conscience, my dear. And whatever the Villefranches' loyalties, they must not be allowed to continue their intrigues. I am delivering Valentine's ultimatum to them this afternoon. Once their fangs have been leashed, we can concentrate on the homegrown villains, damn their eyes. If you are worried about Francoise's threats to reveal the story of our marriage, I think you can discount them. She will have no time to spread her poison. She will have to look to her own safety and future, and so I will tell her."

"Well, that's a relief, but I suppose it is paltry of me to be so concerned about our personal affairs when the country is teetering on the edge of another debacle. If Napoleon does escape, it will mean war again, many innocent lives lost, and a general tragedy for all our countries," Ariel mourned, remembering her father and all the brave men who had died to prevent this very occurrence.

"Yes. Wellington will have to take the field, and I pray I will be with him. That might relieve you of your most pressing problem, Ariel," he mocked.

"Don't be nonsensical, Ian. I do not want you dead on some battlefield. That is no answer. But I suppose the chance of winning glory in some engagement has its attraction. You men are all the same, bloodthirsty wretches, always hoping to test your courage in some vainglorious engagement. I have no patience with it," she answered, now thoroughly aroused.

Amused at her castigation of men's folly, he nodded agreeably. "Quite right, Ariel, we are a pesky crew. You ladies cannot live with us, or without us, I vow. But come, let us part on a happier note. I must be off to tangle with your cousin. I anticipate it will be a stormy interview. But I am happy to see you have mollified your anger against me somewhat," he said, a question in his tone.

"I am not so selfish, or so heedless, to be completely engrossed in my own problems when more grave matters are afoot. Good luck with Francoise, Ian. I will await your report with some eagerness," she said, ignoring his implication of peace between them, but wearily conceding that again he had disarmed her. What a clever rogue he was, so convinced that his fabled address would always win the day. Well, she was not defeated yet. There were other battles to be fought than the impeding contest with Napoleon. She would not let Ian dominate her so that she became a mindless object of his loveless possession. Somehow she would win through to happiness, with his cooperation or without it.

Chapter Nineteen

Despite her determination to face the myriad problems which life had dealt her in such succession the past few days, Ariel, in truth, found it difficult to concentrate on her next move. For the moment she must await events, a spectator rather than an executor in the drama, a role she did not find to her taste. She felt she had lost control of her life, surrendered it with her virginity to the ruthless Celt who held her in sensual bondage. Disgusted with women who used the excuse of overpowering passion to explain their disregard of convention and honor, now she was in danger of submitting to the very thralldom she had always despised. Well, she would not, could not allow Ian to dominate her in his careless fashion. Any regret he evidenced for their painful union seemed rooted in his lack of expertise, rather than in the soullessness of the act. No doubt his possession of her had somewhat soothed his self-esteem and his physical needs, but for her it had been far different. She refused to remember her involuntary response to him—that was just the result of a temporary loss of control, induced by fatigue and probably too much champagne. After all, she had normal appetites, even if she did not want to satisfy them without love and tenderness. Well, she could not remain here, cloistered in her bedroom, reliving those tempestuous moments in the very bed whose smooth counterpane showed no evidence of the traumatic experience which had left her defenseless and disappointed. She must find some activity to take her mind from it all. As if in answer to her plea, a knock came at the chamber door and Nancy, her maid, entered.

"Madam, Lady Montague requests your presence in the drawing room. Several guests from last night's ball have arrived to tender their thanks and she wants your support to receive them. Will you change your gown now?" Nancy asked timidly, looking askance at Ariel's riding costume and her rumpled hair.

"Yes, of course, Nancy. I will have the lavender sarsenet. Let us hurry. I would not want to keep Lady Montague waiting," Ariel said, knowing how unsure and inadequate her sister-in-law felt in the face of fashionable company.

Some twenty minutes later she joined Harriet in the vast drawing room, even its imposing magnificence now dwarfed by a throng of the ton's most august personages. Harriet, looking a bit harassed at handling this influx, was ensconced behind the tea table, trying to pour numerous cups while answering the questions of Lady Jersey, who stood by her side.

"Good afternoon, Harriet. Forgive my tardiness, but I went for a ride to blow some of the cobwebs from my head after last evening's dissipation." Ariel greeted her sister-in-law and gave a more formal acknowledgment of Sally Jersey, who gave her a searching look, her eyes bright with curiosity and a bit of malice. That doyenne of society was enjoying her usual sport, prying into other people's business, hoping to find some nugget of scandal. Poor Harriet was no match for her.

"Let me relieve you of your duties here, and you can circulate among our guests," Ariel suggested calmly. Harriet rose, barely concealing her relief, and crossed the room to talk with a rather dowdy dowager whom Ariel could not remember.

"Dear Harriet, so shy and modest. I know she must rely heavily on you to assist her with her hostess duties," Lady Jersey purred.

Ariel, feeling no need to disagree, smiled abstractly, and busied herself with the teacups.

"Last evening was such a triumph for you, dear Mrs. Montague. And you looked so well. I must ask you for your modiste, that gown was so unusual," Lady Jersey chirruped on, her eyes darting to and fro, afraid she might miss some tidbit being discussed among the various groups of guests but unwilling to lose this opportunity of quizzing Ariel, an unknown quantity to her.

"I believe everyone enjoyed themselves. It was kind of the earl to give me such an overwhelming introduction," Ariel replied, wondering what Lady Jersey hoped to glean from her, but well able to parry her inquisitiveness. "Can I refill your cup, and perhaps offer some of these sandwiches?"

"No, thank you, my dear. I must watch my figure. So many festivities are ruinous to me, I fear," Lady Jersey answered, and in truth, she was putting on weight, giving her the appearance of a bustling pouter pigeon. "I see Lady Mackenzie has her usual train of admirers doting on her every word," she commented spitefully, drawing Ariel's attention to Fiona, looking as elegant as usual, and flirting with a trio of young officers by the window.

"Lady Mackenzie is a very paragon of beauty who puts us all to shame," Ariel agreed, hoping Lady Jersey would not pursue the subject, but a warning bell rang in her mind. Now why should Lady Jersey introduce the topic of Fiona?

"Of course, she is a relation of yours, by marriage I believe, so you know her well. Did you not live with her in Vienna?" Lady Jersey asked avidly, leaning toward Ariel in hopes of hearing some damaging admission.

"Sir Robert is my cousin, and they were both very kind to me after my father's untimely death," Ariel replied curtly, refusing to be drawn.

"Yes, I had heard you followed the drum, all through the Peninsular campaigns, so adventurous, but just a bit sordid for a gently bred girl, I suspect," Lady Jersey probed.

Now how am I supposed to answer that, Ariel

wondered. Either I must confess I found it stimulating, which gives a lie to any pretension of gentle breeding, or confess that I found army life disgusting, which makes me appear an unfortunate, pewling, poor thing, buffeted by the misfortunes over which I had no control. Since neither admission would be true, Ariel said nothing. She preferred to keep her own counsel rather than confide in this gossip seeker.

While she parried Lady Jersey's questions, several guests came up to the tea table to proffer their thanks for the entertainment, and Ariel did her best to receive their gratitude with composure. How superficial London society was, ever intent on their dress and manner, few exhibiting any emotion but the most blasé ennui, constantly on the watch for some titillating item which would relieve their boredom. Only with two fellow officers of Ian's did she feel at ease, for they asked her about some of her Peninsular experiences and she enjoyed sharing memories of those days with men who had participated in them. Busy with her hostess duties, she did not notice the entrance of Francoise de Villefranche, who joined Fiona and her train at the farther end of the room. But in the midst of one of the officer's rather racy tale of a bivouac in Spain, Ariel was suddenly conscious that Fiona had joined the group about the tea table, accompanied by Francoise.

"Dear Lady Mackenzie has just been telling me about her recent sojourn in Vienna, Ariel. So interesting, being included in all the exciting events of the Congress. And Vienna, so cosmopolitan, so dashing. I am afraid London must appear a provincial backwater to you," Francoise interjected smoothly, her tone hinting at some secret.

Ariel startled and looked up in surprise at the two women, both of whom were looking at her with venom. Remembering Francoise's threats, Ariel braced herself for what was coming, and she was not disappointed.

"You really took advantage of your opportunities, Ariel, didn't you, while you were sheltering under the Mackenzies' roof?" Francoise insinuated.

Since Ariel refused to answer, Fiona turned to Lady Jersey and let loose her bombshell.

"Did you know, Sally, that Ariel lured Ian into her boudoir with the tawdriest of excuses and then arranged that Robert would catch them there? Why else would dear Ian have married her? We all know how dexterously he avoided becoming leg-shackled before this, when so many eligible girls laid traps for him in vain. Clever Ariel, using our patronage for such a ploy!" Fiona's voice had risen during this malevolent exposition, so that it fell throughout the suddenly quiet room with a stunning impact.

Lady Jersey, thoroughly enjoying the revelations, was temporarily silenced, as was Ariel. But Francoise eagerly added her comments to reinforce the story. "Yes, Ariel is an ungrateful chit, only too willing to take advantage of her relatives' patronage, as I found to my sorrow."

Her face flushing with anger, Ariel refused to

bow down before her inquisitor's malice. "It seems I have little be to grateful for in my relatives, a tawdry lot who punish a defenseless orphan, an easy target," Ariel replied to her tormentors, but knowing that the harm was done. Taking a deep breath, she was about to continue when her husband's suave tones interrupted.

"How surprising to see you here, Francoise. I understood you would be busy packing." He stared at his former hostess, raising a mocking eyebrow, and then turned to Lady Jersey, who was almost beside herself with excitement at this budget of scandal. "The Villefranches have been invited to leave the country, Lady Jersey. They have not proved to be loyal and grateful guests of His Majesty's government. We should soon see the backs of them or they will be accepting less salubrious accommodations in Newgate Prison, or perhaps even the Tower." He smiled silkily at the assembly, dumbstruck by such delectable news.

"As for you, Fiona, what shocking bad ton to speak so disparagingly about one who is entitled to your charity. I don't think Robert would approve. But then he would not condone the real story of your intrigues, would he? Shall we just agree to deny Francoise's nasty insinuations, made mostly from chagrin that we have found her out? And can it be that your own remarks come from a fear that your cousin by marriage rivals you in attraction?" Ian tossed the words out with a certain insouciance, implying that both Fiona's and Francoise's behavior was rooted in jealousy,

269

not truth. He looked at Fiona challengingly, as if daring her to refute his explanation, but that lady was speechless—whether from rage or embarrassment, who could say. She tossed her head, but looked away from his insultingly measuring stare. Seeing that he would get no argument from his thoroughly routed victims, he smiled sardonically and offered his arm to Ariel.

"Come, my dear. You have devoted enough time to your tea table chores. Let us go talk to Lady Castlereagh, who wishes to bestow her thanks for last evening."

Ariel, only too happy to escape Lady Jersey's sharp eyes, and the animosity of her two protagonists, accompanised him to where Lady Castlereagh was standing, ignoring the buzz of comment in their wake.

"Is Sally stirring up trouble again?" that matron asked as they reached her.

"No more than usual, and to give her justice, she had some cooperation," Ian growled, his irritation surfacing now that he had routed Ariel's foes. "But then what drawing room in London is without its tittle-tattle? By God, I would like to get some of these popinjays in the field."

"Ah, Ian, my boy, so impetuous. You would never make a diplomat. But let us just hope you will not be drawn back to your blood-ridden battlefields. Affairs look grave indeed," said the warmhearted matron. Not unaware that Ian had just rescued Ariel from some embarrassing encounter with two of the ton's most haughty beauties, she wanted to soothe his lacerated spirits.

Distracted by her reference, Ian followed her lead gratefully and they discussed the current status of Napoleon's exile. Ariel stood by silently, still covered with mortification at the recent exposé of her private affairs. Pleased as she was that Ian had extricated her from what could have been the most humiliating and disturbing situation, she disliked sheltering under his protection. A welter of emotion was bubbling in her breast but she played her part prettily, acting the perfect wife, she conceded cynically. Instead of welcoming Ian's championship, she felt smirched and ill at ease. She must not grow accustomed to his protection, for who knew when it would be withdrawn? She should have stood up to Fiona herself, but consoled herself that she would not have abashed that spiteful woman nearly so effectively. Oh, what a tangle that episode in Vienna had caused, and was there to be no end to it?

Ariel could only feel relief when Ian told her that evening that he would be leaving in the morning to join Alistair in Sussex. He approached her as she was preparing to retire for the evening, and she wondered if he intended to reaffirm his possession of her that night. But sexual indulgence appeared to be the last thing on his mind.

"Well, my dear, you will be relieved of my

presence for the next few days. Valentine thinks I should help Alistair with the problems in Sussex. That agent with the incriminating papers is just one among many, we fear," he said somewhat abstractedly, staring into the fire.

"Was he murdered, do you think?" Ariel asked, distracted by his introduction of this new problem, and wondering what he had in mind.

"No, I don't believe so," Ian answered, his brow furrowed. "He drowned while trying to reach a fishing boat which was to take him off to France, but the boat, and its occupants, may be lingering in the vicinity, and perhaps another agent may be dispatched with more information. If so, we want to be on hand to apprehend him."

"Will there be danger?" Ariel asked, suddenly thinking of what Ian might be facing.

"Very little, I suspect. Are you hoping some one of our enemies will dispatch me to free you of my attentions?" he asked acerbically.

"That was not what I meant. Much as I hope you will discover what plots are afoot, I would not want you to be wounded or killed in pursuit of your duty," Ariel replied astringently, a bit surprised by his bitterness.

"Generous of you, my dear, when I fear I have made myself quite obnoxious to you." Ian searched her face as if trying to pierce the careful facade she had erected.

Ariel sighed and, taking her courage in her hands, faced him with resolution. "I feel I am as much at fault as you, Ian, for what happened last night. I know we cannot go on as we have been, always at odds with each other, and I regret that our marriage has come to such a pass."

"And now how do we retrieve matters? Are you suggesting a separation? An annulment is out of the question. You might be carrying my child," he suggested, watching her expectantly.

"I doubt it. And I do not think we can resolve our difficulties tonight. We must postpone our personal problems until you have returned. We will both benefit from a respite, I think," she proposed, meeting his glance bravely, although she felt the blood rushing to her face.

"I had no thought of ravishing you this evening, my dear," Ian said in that sardonic tone which always raised her hackles. She did not reply, but turned away from him, unwilling to show her confusion and embarrassment at this reminder of their previous encounter, which he could treat so casually.

"I will be leaving at dawn tomorrow, so will say *au revoir* now. Take care, Ariel, and do not worry about Francoise. Her fangs have been drawn, and she and Philippe will be leaving London soon. He had quite a difficult interview with Valentine, and even if he was innocent of intrigue, the poor fellow is now paying the price for his wife's conspiring with Talleyrand. I wonder just how much damage she really did. You can console yourself with the thought that at least we flushed them from their lair."

"I did not thank you, Ian, for coming to my rescue this afternoon and routing Fiona and Francoise so effectively. I can only hope their

273

tongues will be stilled now, and I cannot cause you and your family any further embarrassment," Ariel apologized, feeling that somehow her own timidity and fear of a scene had allowed her opponents to challenge her in such a disastrous fashion.

"You were not at fault. If blame must be assigned, I imagine I should bear most of it. I rue the day I ever saw Fiona, the designing harpy, but I fear we have not experienced the last of her spiteful tongue. Try to stay out of her way, a difficult task since you are related and, I suppose, feel some fondness for Robert. She entertains the most revengeful feelings toward you, I fear, due to my reckless behavior, no doubt." He shrugged, as if acknowledging that his past transgressions should be lightly dismissed, and Ariel was roused to argument but she bit her tongue. No good could come of reviving that Viennese adventure now.

"Good night, Ariel, and good-bye for the nonce. I should return before the week's end, if all marches well in Sussex. That should give you time to consider your position, and when I return, we must put our affairs on a more comfortable footing." Ian bowed and left the room by the connecting door.

Ariel had tensed at his words. What did he mean by that last remark, uttered in the cool casual tone which signified he had become bored with the discussion. She did not know what she had expected, but she had hoped for a more affectionate leavetaking, and she was far from understanding her husband's motives, or even her own for that matter. Certainly they must resolve their relationship, and for Ian, obviously love would not be the foundation of any life they eventually led together. Could she endure that? She could so easily love him and suffer agonies in a marriage which was based on nothing more than expediency and passion. Somehow she must find a basis to deal with this tumult of feeling he aroused and not let him swamp her emotions with the magnetism he exerted when his own emotions were not at risk. Feeling used and discarded, Ariel prepared for bed, damning all men and her own foolish hopes.

Chapter Twenty

Ariel stepped briskly out of Bread Street, her maid, Nancy, trailing in her wake. She had been to visit one of her father's veterans and dismissed the carriage, hoping the exercise would relieve her mind of the burdens which were dogging it. To her right, the Thames moved sluggishly toward the sea, its murky waters clogged with ships of all sorts, and to her left, the majestic dome of St. Paul's rose temptingly. She considered stopping for a glimpse inside the church before continuing on to Grosvenor Street. The solemnity and peace of the church would soothe her mood on this gray February afternoon.

Her interview with Sergeant Perkins had cheered her enormously—listening to that doughty soldier's praise of her father, and enjoying his cheerful wife's prattle about long-ago days in the Peninsula, had been just the tonic she needed. Sergeant Perkins had been wounded at Vitoria, and although not fit for active service, accepted his fate with admirable stoicism. Ariel wanted to put him in the way of some profitable employment and promised to give the brave pair some aid, although they were reluctant to accept charity. A tough, dedicated professional, he worried primarily that he would not be able to fight again, but withal his spirits were high. Ariel was pleased she had made the effort to contact the pair, whose acceptance of their lot contrasted so strongly with the frivolous types she had met since entering London's social round.

As she turned toward St. Paul's, she noticed a couple just ahead of her on the corner by a flower seller's stall. Surely that was not Arnold? But she could not mistake him. And clinging to his arm was a flashily dressed woman Ariel did not recognize. She stopped, momentarily confused, but unwilling to let the couple see her. Just why she was reluctant to make her presence known to Arnold she could not say, but she sensed he would find a meeting now uncomfortable. This had to be the woman Harriet had alluded to in her distraught confession, Arnold's mistress. How surprising. Ariel had not thought for one moment that Harriet's suspicions were based on fact. Who would have thought that the proper viscount, so critical of his brother's womanizing, could have been attracted to such an obvious bit of muslin? Her lush figure was wrapped in a startling crimson velvet pelisse trimmed lavishly with ermine, and her rouged cheeks and brassy blond hair bespoke her calling. Did Arnold find such a bold piece to his taste?

Ariel hesitated. Should she approach her brother-in-law? She thought not, for he would find her knowledge of his intimacy with such a woman distressing, and the encounter could only embarrass them both. There was no doubt that the pair were on very intimate terms, for as Ariel watched, astounded, the woman bussed Arnold heartily as he pinned violets on her shoulder, their color clashing hideously with her costume but obviously giving her pleasure. She laughed a hearty chuckle, and they turned away to hail a passing hackney. So involved with each other were the two that Ariel need not have feared discovery, but she was astounded at the warm and suggestive look Arnold bestowed on his companion before they were whirled away. Suddenly all thoughts of seeking the shelter of St. Paul's disappeared, and frowning at the meaning of the unexpected encounter, Ariel decided to return to Grosvenor Street. She must think about what this latest turn of events implied. Arnold had cleverly duped them all with his cloak of propriety. Poor Harriet!

While Ariel was brooding over Arnold's deception, Ian was fully occupied with the business which had brought him to Sussex. He met Alistair at the coaching inn in Newhaven, determined to ignore their personal problems and concentrate on the matter at hand. For the first time there was a distance between the two old friends, which each hesitated to breach. Ian believed he had jumped to false conclusions about Ariel's relationship with Alistair, but he could not

279

bring himself to question his old comrade further. Was he deluding himself that Ariel felt nothing for Alistair but friendship? His own past came back to haunt him, for his experience had not inspired any trust in women. He had found them only too willing to succumb to the seductive offers of any attractive man who pursued them. He had thought Ariel was of a different stamp, had believed in her integrity, and the shock of discovering her in Alistair's arms had aroused a scorching jealousy in his heart which had led him to take her in such a brutal fashion. But she had been a virgin and his ruthless possession of her had scarred both of them. She would never accept now that he entertained softer feelings for her, would never believe he sincerely loved her. And Ian was too proud to offer love and be rejected. What a coil! But he would not let her go. Somehow he would make her return his love. If she could not, then tragedy lay ahead. For the first time his checkered past seemed disgusting to him. Why should she give her heart to such a faithless libertine, and why should she believe he had been transformed by his feeling for her? But she would be no better off with Alistair.

Hiding his doubts and frustrations behind a businesslike manner, he brushed aside Alistair's hesitating attempts to return to their old footing.

"Well, Alistair, have you made any progress in tracing the villains who tried to take that agent to France?" he asked as the two shared a bottle in the inn's parlor.

"The citizenry about here are very close-mouthed. They care little for our efforts to thwart the spy ring. I suspect most of them have close ties with the Continent, for they are smugglers, you know," Alistair confided a bit bitterly. He had been in Sussex for three days and met with little success in his attempts to secure information.

"Just what have you discovered?" Ian asked, depressed at the thought of yet another fruitless mission.

"Only that the papers found on the agent, one Henri Solignac, came from the Foreign Office, which does narrow our investigation somewhat. I have them here, relatively undamaged and readable. There is little doubt that Talleyrand is behind most of the conniving to get Napoleon off Elba. But the discouraging aspect is we have no real proof of his involvement, clever devil that he is. Talleyrand is more than adept at dealing with both sides while protecting his own skin," Alistair concluded, twirling the stem of his glass in irritation before taking a deep draught.

"And we have no idea how much damage Francoise de Villefranche has done," Ian said. "She adroitly parried our questions, while admitting that she had corresponded with her cousin on purely family matters. I wish Ariel had stolen that damning letter. Then we would know where we stood. The haughty Francoise insisted that we were maligning her, persecuting a poor beleaguered exile. Our only recourse was to order her from the country, but although that may stop her intriguing, it does not lead us to the real culprit, who Valentine now insists is a high-placed Englishman, and from your evidence, probably in the Foreign Office."

Alistair, conscious of the restraint in their relationship, did not want to bring up their last meeting, but felt somehow they must reach an understanding and try to get back to their old comradeship. Giving Ian the papers, he stood up impatiently and walked to the window, his back to Ian in tense expectation as the latter studied the documents. Ian read them carefully, having little difficulty in deciphering them for they had been wrapped in an oil skin pouch which had kept the water from damaging them. They were a detailed exposition of what had transpired at a recent Foreign Office meeting, with Castlereagh's suggestions as to what could be done to thwart Napoleon's supporters from rescuing him, as well as instructions to Wellington in case the escape was attempted. Obviously they were copies of the minutes of a high-level meeting, and Ian found the writing vaguely familiar. He had read that hand before, although he could not put a name to the perpetrator. Finally, he looked up, his eyes going to Alistair's still figure before the window. The rigid set of his friend's back told him that Alistair still had something on his mind, and Ian did not believe it had to do with the papers. He sighed. They must talk it out, no matter how painful the revelations were to him.

"Alistair, these documents prove that whoever is betraying the country is well versed in Foreign Office affairs, privy to the most secret negotiations of Castlereagh and the arrangements with the Duke. It is very worrying," he said, although not just the treachery toward the government was causing him concern. Treachery of another sort was paramount in his mind.

Alistair turned, and for the first time, met Ian's gaze frankly. "To hell with the French. I cannot allow this estrangement between us to continue, Ian. You must believe I had no ignoble intentions toward Ariel. I had been telling her my troubles the other evening and she was just trying to comfort me. You have a very loyal wife, and I have been guilty of a little light flirtation, as is my wont, but I certainly received no cooperation from Ariel," he said, sincerity in every lineament.

"You looked more than friendly when I interrupted that scene," Ian protested, but he was aware that his jealousy had provoked him. If Alistair really cared for Ariel, how could he stand in their way?

"Believe, me, Ian, even if I wanted to begin a liaison with Ariel, she would have none of it. Surely you know your wife is not of that legion of light-minded women, whose only recreation is attracting some man," Alistair responded in surprise. "You have a jewel of a wife, and should appreciate her." He was treading carefully, unwilling to risk a further quarrel although he wanted some assurance that Ian had not punished Ariel for what had been a momentary lapse in her usual cheerful comradely attitude toward him.

"Do you love my wife, Alistair?" Ian finally asked, the words forced out of him. He braced himself for the answer, realizing how important it was to him. If Alistair said he did, how could Ian reprove him? He had carelessly tossed aside her overtures toward him, and ruined any hope he had of winning her love and fidelity. He knew now that he wanted to not only possess her but win her heart. At last he faced up to what she had come to mean to him. If only he were not too late.

"I am very fond of Ariel, but I do not love her in that way, please believe me, Ian. My stupid philandering in the past does not speak well for me, but in this I am sincere. I would never want to be the cause of misunderstanding between you. Come, old friend, in this you must trust me, although I grant I have given you every reason to doubt me." Alistair had abandoned his insouciant air, his usual careless cynical manner toward affairs of the heart, in his desire to persuade Ian that his fears were groundless.

Ian gave Alistair a straight look. He wanted to believe him. Their long friendship was at risk, but Ian knew that he must handle this crisis with sense or all would be lost. He must trust Alistair and accept his explanation. And somehow he knew that his friend had been honest with him.

"I seem to have behaved like a credulous jealous fool, Alistair. Forgive me. Friends still?" Ian held out his hand, smiling with that charm he could exert when he chose.

Alistair, relieved that they had solved their difficulties, shook the hand extended heartily. "Thank you, Ian. I knew I could count on your good sense in the long run." He hesitated. He wanted to ask if Ian had been as charitable and understanding toward his wife but did not dare.

"Let us now return to the matter in hand. Between us surely we can apprehend these varlets," Ian said, eager to put his personal affairs behind him. "Did you bring with you that platoon Valentine promised? We must be prepared if another agent attempts to deliver these documents."

Alistair, no less eager to dismiss their quarrel, hurried into an explanation of the preparations he had made for just such an eventuality.

"It looks as though we will be here for a time yet, and I wanted to return to London before too long. It has been more than a week since the discovery of the body. Do you think the man's masters have heard of his death yet and made other plans?" Ian asked, aware that beyond the task at hand was a barely restrained impatience to return to Ariel and beg her forgiveness and put the question which was consuming him. With difficulty, he turned his attention to Alistair's arrangements in the event the fishing trawler returned to pick up another agent.

Ariel would have been much eased in her mind if she could have known that Ian and Alistair had settled their differences, but for the moment she had relegated to the background her fears for a future with her mercurial husband. The encounter with Arnold was nagging at her mind, but she could not bring herself to tell Harriet about that unexpected meeting. Since the ball, her sister-in-law had seemed more cheerful, less shy and retiring. To tell her that Arnold had indeed betrayed her, had been entrapped by a light-skirt would reverse all the progress she had made toward coming to terms with her marriage. Arnold had told his wife that he had another woman, but Ariel had tried to calm Harriet's fear of abandonment. Could she now tell her sister-in-law what she had seen?

How the sober and circumspect Arnold could have become embroiled with such a creature Ariel could not understand. And surely even if he was not keeping his liaison from his wife, he would not want his father to be privy to it. The earl's precarious disposition would become completely out of hand if he learned what his elder son had done. Then another aspect of the situation occurred to Ariel. She knew that Arnold, like Ian, received an allowance from his father. Was it enough to support another establishment, and a, no doubt, greedy mistress? Even if the woman was not inordinate in her demands, she still had to cost Arnold a tidy sum. Where was he finding the money? And was it any of her business? Should she face Arnold with her discovery? Somehow that idea did not seem very attractive to Ariel. Should she tell Ian? Would he think the matter serious enough to confront his brother, an interview which could only widen the breach between them, if not put them completely at odds with one another? Ariel paced up and down in her room, prey to all sorts of misgivings. It was with some relief that she welcomed Nancy's interruption.

"You have some callers, ma'am. Sir Robert and Lady Mackenzie are in the drawing room,"

Nancy announced.

"Thank you, Nancy. I will be down directly," Ariel said, waving her maid away. It only needed this to add to her budget of problems. What could the Mackenzies want? How dare Fiona face her after her performance in the drawing room two days previously? And Robert, too. Had he discovered the real truth of what had happened in Vienna? Bracing herself for the uncomfortable encounter, Ariel smoothed her hair, looking critically at herself in the mirror. Upon meeting Fiona she must look her best, for she needed all the armor she possessed to face that spiteful lady. Ariel had little reason to suspect that Fiona had come on an errand of friendship, but she did not show her distaste and apprehension when she greeted her cousins a few moments later.

Fiona was dressed, as usual, in the height of elegance, her dove-covered velvet gown edged with chinchilla, accented by a matching bonnet faced with fur, but her expression lacked its usual haughty disdain. She appeared apprehensive and subdued. Robert, on the other hand, appeared unusually severe, although he greeted Ariel with a cousinly kiss.

"You might be surprised at this call, Ariel, in view of Fiona's regrettable lapse of decorum a few days ago in this very drawing room," Robert began, obviously ill at ease but determined to waste no time in apprising her of the reason for their visit.

"It is always pleasing to see you, Robert, and we have not been honored with much of your attention since your return from Vienna," Ariel replied, ignoring Fiona. She could not pretend to social niceties in that despicable woman's presence even to soothe Sir Robert.

"Yes, I have been quite remiss in that direction, and in several others it seems," he said. If Ariel had not known Robert so well, she would have believed this interview was making him unduly nervous, even embarrassed.

Remembering her duties as a hostess, she indicated they should sit down and so conduct their talk with some semblance of propriety.

Robert, however, disdained her invitation, and paced back and forth in some anxiety, eyeing her closely. Fiona settled herself on the settee, tossing her head as if to repudiate any further interest in the conversation. Then thinking better of it, she said bitterly. "No doubt you do not care to receive us, Ariel, but Robert was most insistent."

The look Robert cast to his wife surprised Ariel with its evidence of disgust, so at odds with his normally affectionate and gentle manner toward her.

"Fiona's shocking behavior the other afternoon demands she make some apology to you for placing you in that invidious position," Robert ground out, as if the whole affair caused him the gravest unrest.

"I am sure Fiona regrets her imprudent words, and perhaps it would be best if we forgot the matter. It does not reflect well on any of us," Ariel responded, her honest searching gaze on her cousin, wishing she could spare him any further disquiet. Robert was as much a victim as she was in this cruel dilemma.

"I fear that none of us will escape being the target of scandal mongers so easily. Sally Jersey has bruited the business all over London. In view of Fiona's vicious calumny, reparation must be made," Robert insisted, unwilling to let the matter alone. His innate sense of fairness, his Scots integrity, would not allow his wife to escape so easily the results of her folly. He looked at Ariel with affectionate kindness, reluctant to proceed but steeling himself to the effort.

"Since hearing what happened at the tea table, I have taxed Fiona on her role and forced her to admit the truth of what happened that night in Vienna. I can only tender my sincerest apologies that you should have suffered such indignity under my roof. I should have known you were the innocent party in that wicked deception," Robert said painfully.

"Oh, we all know that Ariel would never be tempted to behave in anything but the most respectable fashion," Fiona interjected spitefully.

Robert gave her a quelling glance which caused her to flush. "It does not behoove you to criticize Ariel, Fiona, and I am waiting for your apology to her for all the humiliation to which you have subjected her," Robert said sternly to his wife.

"Really, Robert, you are making a fuss about a mere bagatelle, and after all, it won Ariel an eligible husband, whom I doubt she could have entrapped otherwise," Fiona objected, loath to admit any wrongdoing.

"I don't consider the assassination of Ariel's reputation to protect yours a mere bagatelle, and the subsequent result of your shocking deception could not have brought her any ease of mind," Robert reproved. Too reticent to ask Ariel about the state of her marriage, he was obviously disturbed at the thought that Fiona's actions might have added to his cousin's burdens, but he wondered if this imprudent marriage had caused her deep unhappiness. Shaking off his doubts, he turned to his wife and looked at her in dislike. "I am waiting for your apology to Ariel, not that words will erase what you did," he said repressively.

Fiona tossed her head, furious that her husband was forcing her to humble herself to her odious cousin by marriage. But Robert would not be denied, and Fiona realized for the first time that her cajolery and winning ways would have no effect on her obdurate husband. She had supposed when he had pried the real story from her that she could talk him around, minimize her role in the proceedings, but for once Robert was not won over by her tricks. Eyeing her composed enemy with venom, Fiona muttered, "I am sorry, Ariel, that you had to shoulder the burden of my duplicity. Please accept my regrets." She rushed the words out, obviously not feeling any real remorse.

Although Ariel knew she should feel some satisfaction that at last Fiona was paying for her transgression, all she wanted was to see the last of this devious, selfish harpy, and only her deep gratitude and affection for Sir Robert prevented her from rounding on his wife with bitter words of accusation.

"I think it best we no longer discuss this. I owe you too much, Robert, to place you in an invidious situation and I deeply regret that you should have suffered from the revelation of all this. I wanted to spare you," she said to the man who had rescued her from poverty and despair.

"You are more than kind, Ariel. But you will have no further trouble from Fiona. I am escorting her to the country, where she will remain for the rest of this year," he promised.

Knowing that exile from London's glittering social round was the worst punishment he could inflict on his wife, Ariel felt a certain satisfaction that her erstwhile tormentor should suffer such a retribution.

"It was more than kind of you, Robert, to ease my mind with this confession. I am only sorry that you should suffer, too, but let us try to relegate it all to the past now. London will soon have some other juicy rumor to chew upon, I'll warrant." Ariel rose, signifying the difficult conversation was at an end. She could not bear to watch poor Robert's humiliation. He would protect his wife as well as he might, but perhaps Fiona had learned a lesson and would deal more honestly with her devoted husband from now on. The role of a rejected wife was one she would not play with any dignity and that was her real punishment, for Sally Jersey and her coterie would gain vast enjoyment from Fiona's banishment.

"Thank you, Ariel, generous as always," Robert

said. "I wish you every happiness, you know. You are certainly deserving of it, and I only hope you will find it with your husband, no matter the damaging events which caused your wedding him." Robert's tone expressed both a doubt and a question, but Ariel would not satisfy either. Kissing him on the cheek, she thanked him again and gave a heartfelt relief as she saw him escort his erring wife from her sight. Fiona's absence from London could only offer her limited surcease from her troubles. It would not solve them.

Chapter Twenty-one

Roaming restlessly around the drawing room following dinner two days after Ian's departure, Ariel could not settle to her embroidery. Both Arnold and the earl had been in their most taciturn mood at dinner, and Harriet was her usual subdued self. Watching her sister-in-law over the coffee cups later, Ariel decided that she had recovered amazingly from her unhappiness over Arnold's defection. When the earl and Arnold left to discuss some business in the library, Ariel decided to quiz her sister-in-law, about her tranquil state, so removed from the hysteria and tears before the ball.

"You seem in good heart, Harriet. Have you come to terms with Arnold?" Ariel asked, settling by Harriet on the settee when the men had left the room.

"Not really. We have not discussed it again. But oh, Ariel, I had the most exciting talk with Hannah More recently. And since then I have attended some of her readings. She is doing such wonderful work, and her book, *Christian Morals*, is so uplifting." Harriet positively glowed with fervor of her new faith, her sallow cheeks flushed and the light of the evangelist in her eyes.

Ariel wondered where Harriet could have met the famed religious reformer whose tracts had become best-sellers, rivaling Byron's poems in popularity although their message was a paean against wordliness. Ariel had read her book and commended her sensibility and good taste, and her charity in founding a school in Somerset. But she was more than surprised that Harriet found Miss More's tracts and conversation inspirational.

"Where did you meet Miss More, Harriet?" Ariel asked, curious to know how the sheltered and shy Harriet had made the acquaintance of such a controversial woman.

"In Hookam's Library. She dropped her glove and I retrieved it and then we began to talk. She invited me to her rooms—she is staying with Mrs. Garrick, the great actor's widow, while in London. And there I met such a fascinating group of people. All dedicated to furthering the new morality," Harriet bubbled on, the words tumbling helter-skelter from her as she explained.

"I am happy that you have found such a congenial interest, Harriet. I, too, admire Miss More, and her work. And she and her friends can only ease your troubles," Ariel answered gently, hesitant to remind Harriet of her unhappy marriage.

"She says women must raise the level of

morality, persuade men into a more religious frame of mind. She believes not one member of Parliament has any real faith."

"I am sure she is right, but alas, we have a big task ahead of us if that is the case. Society seems much more interested in vice than virtue, I fear." Ariel did not want to depress her sister-in-law's enthusiasm but was not convinced that her reforming zeal would have much affect.

"Miss More offers me much comfort, Ariel. Pray do not discourage me," Harriet said firmly. "I find I can contemplate Arnold's horrid manner toward me with much more equanimity now." Harriet looked defensively at her sister-in-law.

"Then I bless Miss More," Ariel responded cheerfully, but wondering how long this new ardency would last.

Harriet prosed on, full of her enthusiasm, and Ariel listened kindly, letting her sister-in-law air her views, while her mind followed its own path. Obviously this would not be the moment to tell Harriet about Arnold's light-o'-love, if that was what she was. Finally, the two women parted for the evening, since it seemed obvious that neither Arnold nor the earl would be joining them.

Ariel, in her room, dismissed her maid. She was not ready to retire yet. She could settle to nothing, although she should have written some letters. Perhaps a novel would distract her, and surely the men had finished their discussion in the library. She would not want to interrupt them. Deciding to venture downstairs again, Ariel left her room and descended the stairs, pausing outside the library. The door was slightly ajar and she heard angry voices emanating from the room. Arnold was arguing with his father. Ariel hesitated. She did not want to eavesdrop but then she heard a mention of Ian's name.

"I suppose you have increased Ian's allowance since his marriage. You seem ready to excuse all his excesses now that he has taken that soldier's brat to bed," he remonstrated.

"That is no way to speak of Ariel, a thoroughly respectable and lovely girl, and she will be the making of Ian. Since they have been wed, he has moderated his behavior a great deal. And perhaps soon they will provide me with a grandchild, a notion you appear to scorn," the earl replied, thoroughly aroused.

"How can I get a child from that milksop you persuaded me to marry? The fool is barren," Arnold answered coarsely. "Are you saying that only if Harriet becomes pregnant will you increase the funds you allow me?"

"I see no reason to throw my blunt around carelessly, and I do not like your tone, Arnold. You will have no more money from me and that's the end of it. Now leave me. You have caused my gout to flare up again. No respect for your father's ills," the earl complained.

Ariel, realizing that both men would be furious if they caught her spying upon them, whisked into the drawing room, peeking from the door in time to see Arnold storm from the library and call for Lufton. Obviously he was going out at this late hour, to seek solace from his lady friend, no doubt.

This was her opportunity to find out more about that relationship.

Arnold took his coat and hat from Lufton, ordered his phaeton, and left almost at once. Knowing that he would have to wait for the horses to be put to, Ariel rushed to her bedroom and donned a dark serviceable cloak, hiding her face in the hood, and slipped downstairs again. Somehow she felt compelled to follow Arnold and see where he was going. In her determination to discover the identity of his woman, she did not heed the recklessness of going out at this time of night. Both Ian and the earl had warned her about being abroad without protection since the streets were filled with rabble protesting the Corn Law and agitating for reforms. But ignoring the danger, she waited impatiently behind the drawing room door until Arnold had leaped into his carriage and ridden away. Looking wildly up the street, she noticed a hackney discharging a passenger some houses farther down, and hailed it frantically.

"Follow that carriage," she ordered as she almost fell into the seat and gripped her hands tightly as the coachman careened after Arnold. They rode in this tempestuous fashion for some time through the deserted streets until at last the hackney drew to a halt. Peering out, Ariel did not recognize the neighborhood, but saw Arnold tether his horses to a hitching post and rush up the steps of a modest dwelling, whose door opened to his key.

"Please wait," Ariel ordered the coachman, who

grumbled a bit but cheered when she offered him a guinea. "You shouldn't be out alone at this time of night, ma'am," he murmured, but promised to wait on her assurance that he would not be the loser for it.

Ariel approached the door of the strange house carefully, wondering if she would be able to gain entrance. In the rush of events she had not paused to consider the precariousness of her position. Trying the door, which was locked, she was about to hammer on the portal but then she hesitated, prudence overcoming her first inclination. If she met an enraged Arnold, who knew what he might do? No, she would do better to take note of the address and return in the morning. Retracing her steps, she came up to the coachman.

"What is this street? Where are we?" she asked the man, waiting patiently on his perch.

"St. John's Wood, ma'am. I did not take note of the street in my haste," he answered, curious as to her actions. Here was a coil. Perhaps a betrayed wife seeking vengeance, although she seemed a cool customer.

"Yes, well, let us ascertain the street and number of this house. I will not disturb the occupants tonight," Ariel decided. "You may take me back to Grosvenor Street."

All the way back to the Strathcairn house with the address committed to memory, Ariel pondered her next move. The shrouded darkness seemed more menacing now, and as they turned into Piccadilly, she saw from the window a rough crowd running pell-mell down the avenue, bound on some mischief. Thank goodness she had not tarried. How would she explain being out at this hour if some mischance fell upon her? No, she had used caution. Arnold's affairs could wait until the morrow. And she needed time to decide how she would approach the woman, if that was indeed whom he had hurried to meet. After all, this was none of her business, but she felt certain that Arnold's atypical behavior would answer some important questions, and she would have a very disturbing budget of news for Ian. But she could not accuse his brother of deception until she had proof. This evening's strange occurrences had cast another light entirely on that pattern card of propriety. He could no longer attack Ian and remain unscathed himself. She had made her mind up to that, and perhaps now the earl would look more kindly on his younger son, if he understood that Arnold was not what he had always supposed him to be.

Arnold had to be under the hatches if he had pressed his father for money, and he must have gone in debt to finance his liaison with the woman. If he was paying the rent on her house, supporting her, then indeed he needed every penny he could wrest from the earl. But Arnold had always appeared so circumspect, living in a sober fashion. How had this deviation from his normal mode occurred? Ariel frowned in deep perplexity. If Arnold could suddenly alter his accustomed habits to take a mistress, did this mean he was deceiving them all in other matters as well? Certainly the Viscount Montague was not at all what he seemed. The face he turned to the world was not his real character. Well, tomorrow she would have more clues to his conduct.

Ariel had some difficulty in evading Harriet the next morning. Since her sister-in-law had confided in her about her friendship with Hannah More, Harriet wanted to introduce Ariel to this absorbing new interest. Miss More's stay in London was limited and Harriet insisted that Ariel must meet the impressive lady and listen to her plans for reform. Pleading a prior engagement with her modiste, Ariel was able to escape to carry out her own plans.

She dressed in her most impressive green merino morning gown, with the accompanying sable pelisse and muff. She must awe Arnold's mistress with her consequence, overwhelm her with her position. Ariel suspected that the woman, from what she had seen, had a certain rough style which would not bow easily to intimidation. She directed the Strathcairn carriage to drive her to Madame Claude's emporium on Bond Street and then dismissed the coachman. Hiring a hackney she made all speed to St. John's Wood, hoping to surprise the woman before she had put on her defenses for the day. She did not think the woman was an early riser.

In this she was quite correct. A rather slatternly maid admitted her to the house, the plain neat dwelling's outer facade not in tune with the rather tasteless overdone interior. She gave her name,

Mrs. Montague, to the maid, who did not completely grasp it, and seated herself firmly in the parlor, which was decorated in a tawdry imitation of the Egyptian decor considered the latest crack, a medley of imitation sphinxes and water lilies scattered about the room. All matters pertaining to the culture of the Nile had come into style with Nelson's victory and obviously attracted Arnold's mistress. After a short wait, in which Ariel tried to formulate some plan of attack, she was greeted by the brassy-faced woman she had seen at the flower stall.

"How d'ye do, Mrs. Montague. I am Flossie Baines. I understand you have some business with me," were the woman's first words. She was still in her dressing gown, a magenta silk trimmed with rather dirty marabou, but her round face and small blue eyes glowed with good nature. Overly plump, she showed a good deal of flesh and was obviously wearing little beneath the gown.

Ariel returned Flossie's smile with one of her own. She did not intend to antagonize Flossie, who appeared a friendly woman with the easy manners of her class. Despite her distaste at her errand, Ariel could not help warming to the woman.

"How kind of you to receive me, Miss Baines. Or is it Mrs.?" Ariel asked, extending her hand, which was shaken heartily.

"Well, I use Mrs. But it is really a courtesy title. In my business it is the usual thing," Flossie confided artlessly, looking over her distinguished visitor but not at all cowed by this very proper member of the ton. She must have realized that

301

Ariel had some connection with her protector but cannily waited for her visitor to make the first move.

Ariel did not betray any discomfort at her position, but launched immediately into the reason for her call. "You must excuse the informality of this intrusion. But I felt I must meet you. I am Viscount Montague's sister-in-law, and quite by chance saw you with him a few days ago, near St. Paul's." She paused for a moment, hoping Flossie would make some explanation.

"So you know about me and Arnie, and I suppose have blown the gaff to his toffee-nosed wife," Flossie said with undiminished good humor, crossing her legs and showing off her white calves to some effect.

"I have not mentioned this call or your whereabouts to Lady Montague, but I fear Arnold has not been so close-mouthed," Ariel said.

"He's a downy one, is my Arnie, but he didn't ought to have done that. I mean the poor lady no harm, but every cove needs a bit of comfort and cuddling, and she's no doubt too starchy to give him what he needs." Flossie nodded her head as if her suspicions were confirmed.

Ariel restrained her amusement at Flossie's picture of Harriet as an imposing dowager of demanding manners. "I am certain of that, Mrs. Baines. But Arnold cannot really afford another establishment, you know."

"Well, he comes up with the blunt easily enough. He seems to have plenty for a flutter at the tables, too. He's very warm in the pocket. Not that I am always gouging him for presents and such. But he's very accommodating." Flossie tossed her head, causing her somewhat disheveled brassy blond curls to tumble into even further disarray. Despite her rather overblown charms, there was a certain earthy attraction to Flossie which Ariel could not deny. She could see what Arnold found so engaging, for Ariel had none of the scorn of the lower orders so typical of the London society matron, and Flossie's honest explanation of her profession did not shock her. The camp followers in Wellington's Peninsular Army had possessed just the same crude honesty and goodwill which Flossie evidenced. She did not exactly know how to proceed, for she was not in a position, nor did she desire, to threaten the woman.

"I wish you no bad fortune, Mrs. Baines. And I would not venture to insist that you break off the relationship, but I had to assure myself of Arnold's interest." Ariel hesitated, wondering what Flossie's reaction would be if she had threatened her with exposure.

"Well, it's no great thing. Most men have a little piece tucked away somewhere, but I suppose his high-toned family might object," Flossie conceded, realizing that Ariel could disrupt her comfortable life.

"Yes, I am sure they would if I should reveal your situation, but I am not convinced that would be in all our interests," Ariel answered gently. Really, Arnold did not deserve such an obliging mistress. She had feared she might meet a

303

demanding harpy who was bleeding him for money but Flossie was far from that, just a comfortable not very ambitious woman who took life as she found it.

"Well, what do we do now?" Flossie asked in some perplexity, beginning to wonder what this unusual lady wanted of her.

Ariel sighed. She did not feel she could ask Flossie to break off with Arnold. It was not her business. And Harriet had come to terms with the situation. Really this interview had solved nothing. "I suggest you do not mention my call to Lord Montague. I suppose you must just continue as you are, although you must realize that your relationship with him cannot go on indefinitely. Arnold cannot afford you, you understand."

"If you say so, ma'am. But I don't think he would be pleased that you have meddled in his affairs." Flossie, knowing now that Ariel did not represent any danger to her comfortable situation, was taking the initiative, and Ariel could only concede she was dealing from strength.

"You must look out for yourself," Ariel said. "Perhaps it would be wisest if you did not mention my call to him. I can see no good would come of it, just cause unhappiness and turmoil to us all. And I will undertake to keep the matter secret, if I can. I shall not promise not to confide in my own husband. But Arnold and Ian are not on intimate terms. Naturally, I will say nothing to Harriet until I have decided what is best."

"His sister-in-law, are you? I wondered. Well, I know there is no love lost between him and his

304

scapegrace brother, but that's your business. I will certainly say nothing to Arnold. It would not be in my interest, and a girl has to look out for herself, you understand." Flossie stood up, obviously eager to see the back of her visitor. She had made no attempt to plead with Ariel, or to blackmail her with exposure of Arnold's deception, although she must have known she could further her own ends in some way.

Ariel, realizing that there was little more to be said, and aware that the advantage had passed to Flossie, prepared to make her farewells. She had found Flossie practical and ungrasping, with a down-to-earth philosophy, a cheerful acceptance of a morality that Ariel should have found repugnant, but did not. This blowsy coarse woman was too good for Arnold with his pettifogging suspicious attitude, and Ariel found herself hoping that the amiable Flossie would not suffer when her protector finally severed their connection. Ariel had little doubt that Arnold would not pursue the relationship, no matter how comfortable he found it, if his father should discover it and threaten to cut off support. Certainly if the earl knew about Flossie, he would soon put a stop to the affair. For Arnold, Ariel had little sympathy. Of the two, Ariel much preferred Flossie.

"Thank you for being so patient with me, Flossie, if I may call you that. I doubt we will meet again, but if you should find yourself in evil straits, do apply to me," Ariel said sincerely, drawing on her gloves and preparing to leave.

"That's good of you, ma'am. I thought you might

305

interfere, being shocked by me and all, but I can see you are a fine charitable lady. Don't you worry, we will come about," Flossie answered cheerfully, now that she was assured Ariel meant her no harm. They parted on the best of terms, but Ariel had a sneaking feeling that Flossie had emerged the victor in this inconclusive interview.

Chapter Twenty-two

Ian's continuous absence left Ariel plenty of time to worry about him, their relationship, and the problem of Arnold. She needed Ian's support and advice, for this was a matter she could not solve on her own. And she wondered about Arnold's deception in other matters. If he had managed to hide his relationship with Flossie so skillfully, and for such a long time, what else could he be concealing? It was obvious that Flossie's menage was one of long-standing, which meant that Arnold needed money to keep that establishment going. He was undoubtedly finding himself quite purse-pinched; otherwise he would not have dared to approach his father. Arnold had always castigated Ian for his expensive tastes, his excesses of riotous living, and all the time he had had this secret himself. How typical of Arnold, and how hypocritical, but he would do anything to keep his father from learning of his true nature. At least Ian had never tried to cloak his behavior in a sanctimonious facade of morality. If the earl learned of Flossie, Ariel had no doubt that Arnold would be banished to the ancestral acres with Harriet and the unhappy couple would never resolve their differences.

And Harriet. She had managed to find some peace in her new interests, which would be denied to her in Northumberland. How could Ariel hurt her? Until Ian returned, she would have to keep what she had learned to herself, but she had every intention of learning more about Arnold. There was Flossie's allusion to his gambling. At the time, Ariel had paid little heed, but now the woman's words came back to cause her disquiet. A mistress and a penchant for gambling. There was much to Arnold that bore investigating.

But for the moment, Ariel bided her time, impatient with events which puzzled and distressed her. She had almost decided that she should confide in Sarah Valentine, who could keep her own counsel, when all her notions were overset by Arnold. The day after her interview with Flossie, while Ariel was still debating her course of action, he approached her after breakfast. Harriet usually took that meal in her room, and the earl, succumbing to the pain of his gout, had grumblingly taken to his bed with his leg elevated, disturbing the whole household with his complaining.

"I would like a word with you, Ariel," Arnold requested in his most formal manner as she sipped her chocolate.

She raised guileless eyes to his. "Yes, Arnold?

What can I do for you?" she asked, not liking the look in his eyes.

"Let us go to the library. I don't want any witnesses to this conversation," he answered sternly, rising and indicating that she should precede him from the room.

Ariel, refusing to be cowed by his manner, could only concede that he had learned of her visit to Flossie. She did not believe that Flossie had told him of the visit, but suspected he had learned it from other sources.

There was nothing of the polished London gentleman in Arnold's stance as he ushered her into the library, first taking a narrow look about the hall to ensure there would be no observers to the scene which he intended to take place. Once inside the room, he made no concessions to polite manners, taking up his stance behind his father's desk, his hands clasped behind his back. Ariel realized he was in a towering rage, barely controlled.

"How dare you spy upon me, poking your nose into affairs which are no concern of yours!" Arnold accused her, his tone menacing even if his voice remained soft.

Ariel, ignoring his breach of politeness, settled herself calmly in a leather chair facing the desk and folded her hands in her lap, taking her time to answer his charge. Arnold was in no position to ring a peal over her.

"I made it my concern when I discovered Harriet in a taking over your cruel treatment of her. She deserves better of you, Arnold," she said firmly.

"Interfering between husband and wife, not a very attractive stance for someone who claims to be so prudent and well behaved," Arnold sneered, but unable to completely conceal his astonishment that she should receive his rebuke so calmly.

"I have never claimed to be either prudent or well behaved, and I discovered your liaison quite by accident. I saw you and Mrs. Baines near St. Paul's the other day and in view of Harriet's tearful confidences I thought I should try to find out if there was any truth to her outpourings," Ariel explained, not one whit disturbed by Arnold's blustering. She was dealing from a position of strength and she knew it. "I am rather surprised that Mrs. Baines apprised you of my visit."

"Oh, Flossie has too much sense for that. I heard of the mysterious Mrs. Montague from that tweeny who serves her. She was only too eager to display her knowledge," Arnold confirmed, but then realizing that he was being forced on the defensive, continued. "How I discovered your conniving is not the point. You take a great deal upon yourself, madam, for a come-by-chance soldier's brat. You cozened my brother into the parson's trap with your taking ways, but you will get no change from me."

"Attacking my parentage will avail you little, Arnold, and in no way alters the fact that you have been deceiving Harriet, which I suppose can be expected in this worldly society you frequent," Ariel said, despising his hypocrisy. He had, it was true, been guilty of no more than many other men in his position, but his cloak of propriety, his criticism of his brother, roused her wrath. Ian, at least, had not had a wife when he had embarked on his scapegrace ways. However, what Ariel really found so shocking was Arnold's attempts to widen the breach between Ian and the earl by exposing every youthful peccadillo of that young man's while playing the role of a respectable, righteous pillar of society himself. Such duplicity disgusted Ariel although she did not see how her assessment of Arnold reflected on her changed opinion of her husband. Arnold had taken him to task for the very conduct which she herself found so abhorrent, but at least Ian had never pretended to be what he was not. Ariel had vastly altered her view of Ian since her first experience of him in Fiona's Viennese drawing room, a reversal she was not quite sure she understood.

"And what is your price for keeping this knowledge you gained by trickery to yourself, may I ask?" Arnold persisted, eyeing her with disfavor.

"Do not judge everyone by your own standards, Arnold. I will not blackmail you, but I believe, in consideration of your circumstances, you could deal with Harriet with a little more charity," Ariel responded.

"Are you suggesting that if I play the devoted courtier to my dowd of a wife, you will not reveal Flossie's whereabouts to my father?" Arnold asked, prepared to make concessions although he hated being placed in this humiliating position, and by his brother's wife.

Ariel, well aware that Arnold was more intent on protecting his secret than in justifying his conduct, was not yet ready to allow him to escape from his dilemma.

"Perhaps. And, of course, you must stop trying to worsen conditions between Ian and his father. You are hardly in good straits to continue that maneuver, are you?" she said boldly, wondering just how far she could go with Arnold. However, now that she had him at her mercy, she could almost feel some compassion for the wretched man. All his life he had probably felt inferior to his dashing brother, and his jealousy and ill-will had forced him to protect his own interests by denigrating Ian. It had brought him little satisfaction although he had acquiesced in every demand of the earl's in order to ensure his position as the favored son, even to marrying a woman he disliked. Both Harriet and Arnold were victims of the earl's domineering ways, and she pitied them.

"Do you mean that you will not expose me to the earl?" Arnold pressed, not understanding her hesitation to take advantage of the knowledge she had gained. He would never have been so foolish.

"I will make no promises, Arnold. But I suggest you soften your attitude to both Ian and Harriet," she advised sternly, and then made the mistake, in her triumph, she would deeply repent. "Who knows what other chicanery you have been up to? If you could hide Flossie's existence so successfully, rail at poor Harriet for her inadequacies as a wife, what other secrets are you hiding?"

she mused.

For a moment real evil shone from Arnold's opaque eyes, but he quickly masked his start of surprise and anger. "I assure you, Ariel, Flossie is my only sin, and not such a deep one after all," he said smoothly. "You must realize that marriage does not automatically ensure lifetime felicity. I suspect Harriet and I can jog along without too much trouble if we are left to our own devices."

"As I said, Arnold, I cannot commit myself to a course of action. Much depends on events, but you would be wise to take my advice and cease your criticism and carping of those who deserve better of you." Ariel, now weary of this, wanted only to be quit of the devious Arnold. She did not like playing the righteous accuser, but Arnold's pose of propriety while he behaved little better than most libertines had roused her indignation, and then there was poor Harriet to consider.

"We will just have to see who emerges the victor in our little duel, Ariel," Arnold said. "You may feel you have the upper hand now, but the situation could alter. I warn you to take care." Arnold refused to play the humble supplicant to this woman even if she did hold the advantage for now.

"We are not at war, Arnold. I dislike being out of charity with you, but now that we understand one another better, I think we can come to some accommodation. Now you must excuse me. I have an errand to perform." Ariel rose at those words, determined to put this uncomfortable interview to an end. She had hoped it would not come to a

313

confrontation with Arnold, and she was not certain she had handled matters with skill, but for better or worse, she had made her position plain and had not committed herself to any course of action. It would be best to leave Arnold wondering, off balance, but she realized she had made an enemy, and one who would not accept defeat tamely. In that he was much like his brother. She left the room disturbed by the encounter, and feeling that little had been resolved between them. Arnold remained an enigma, and one she should have been warned not to solve.

Ian had been gone five days when March finally made its appearance on a gust of bitter rain and chilling wind. Ariel had kept to the house, the inclement weather an excuse for her lassitude. She felt suspended between two worlds, unable to settle to any sensible occupation. Since her confrontation with Arnold, he had modulated his manner somewhat, treating Harriet more kindly and avoiding any of those barbed remarks about Ian which had been his wont. But Ariel suspected he was biding his time, waiting for her to make some untoward move. She had no intention of using her knowledge of Flossie to cause further trouble, but he could not be certain of that. The atmosphere in the Grosvenor Street house reflected the capricious mood of the weather, and finally Ariel decided she must rouse herself to some constructive work. She remembered she had promised to renew her contact with Sergeant

Perkins and his wife. Involving herself with others who were far less fortunate and yet so cheerful in their adversity would remind her that her own life did not lie in such miserable ways. It could only serve to help her put her problems in perspective. That evening at dinner she told the family about Sergeant Perkins, and mentioned that she would be calling upon the veteran the next day.

The earl commended her for her thoughtfulness. "Good of you, my dear, to take such an interest," he said gruffly. "I fear the soldiers of our grand campaign against Napoleon have a dim future before them. The government insists it cannot afford to pay the subsidy they deserve. Private charity is their only hope."

"Yes, well, Sergeant Perkins would not accept charity," Ariel replied. "I only hope his wife is not so proud. They are in dire circumstances I think. At any rate, I will do what I can."

The next afternoon, after receiving a note from Ian saying he would be arriving within the day, she tempered her impatience by gathering a basket of necessities and proceeding on her mission. Ian's note had been brief, informing her that he and Alistair had made little progress in Sussex but that he was more concerned with his personal problems, which they would discuss, speculative words that caused Ariel some apprehension. But she could do nothing about their relationship until Ian returned. She could only hope there was some basis for a resolution which would bring them both comfort and relief.

315

She invited Harriet to accompany her to the Perkinses' rooms, needing the distraction of even that lady's docile presence, but Harriet had business of her own, and in the end Ariel was forced back on the company of Nancy, who was more than reluctant to face the nasty weather even on a mission of mercy. Nancy had caught a cold, and her sniffling and red nose proved she should not brave the elements. Ariel excused her maid from accompanying her, insisted she take to her bed until she felt more the thing. For once, ignoring the proprieties, Ariel set forth alone. Surely the escort of the coachman and footman would be protection enough, not that she needed such a safeguard.

The Perkinses greeted her effusively, although they were embarrassed by the gift of provisions. Mrs. Perkins insisted on providing a cup of tea from their slender resources and Ariel could not be so churlish as to refuse. How bracing was the attitude of this brave pair, who had sacrificed their futures for an ungrateful country. She would prevail upon Ian or even General Valentine to come to their rescue, she decided. And she reminisced happily with the pair, comforted by their sound good sense and calm acceptance of their lot. An hour or so passed in their company while Ariel listened to tales of past campaigns in which she had been an observer, but Sergeant Perkins a participant. He was a typical man of his trade, red-faced, burly, although a bit less hearty since his wound. He brushed aside her inquiries about his health, assuring her that his shoulder had all but recovered, and he hoped to pass his medical, which would return him to duty.

"I don't like this idling about, Miss Ariel, and I need my pay. But I see the doctors next week, and I am sure they will pronounce me fit for duty, a good thing, too, as I don't doubt that pesky Napoleon will be up to his old tricks before long," Sergeant Perkins said eagerly. Obviously he yearned to return to the fighting, where problems disappeared in the heat of the battle. His simple philosophy was one which Ariel sometimes echoed, but she feared for the carnage which would result if his prognostications came true.

"Let us hope that peace has settled on Europe. The people have suffered enough," Ariel said sadly, remembering all the tragedy she had seen.

"Quite right, ma'am," the usually cheerful Mrs. Perkins endorsed soberly, nodding her head in agreement. "Alf here just thinks of all the fun and games he gets up to. Doesn't see the horrors, babies and mothers starving and that. It's a crying shame, that it is."

"Well, I dare say it will all work out, but I must take my leave now. I will try to return next week, to see how you are getting on." Ariel made her farewells, reluctant to leave this uncomplicated couple who accepted their lot with such bracing faith in the future.

She went off to seek her carriage and the return to Grosvenor Street feeling much improved by her visit, insisting that Alf not accompany her down the shabby stairs. No sooner had she left than Mrs. Perkins noticed Ariel had left her gloves on a nearby table.

"Here, Alf. You catch up with Miss Ariel. There are her gloves, mighty fine ones, too. She would not want to lose them, even if she probably has a dozen or more pairs." Mrs. Perkins thrust the gloves into her husband's hands and sent him after Ariel.

Ariel, descending from the depths of the dark house into the street, equally forbidding, did not see the Montague carriage. She had told the driver to return for her in an hour and she had overstayed her time but surely the carriage must be nearby somewhere. She looked up the street but could see nothing but a shabby hackney. As she walked toward it, two rough men loomed up out of the shadows and accosted her, one of them pinning her arms behind her. The other, standing in front of her, his face covered by a grimy scarf so she could not see his features, placed a dirty hand over her mouth as she attempted to scream. Neither of the men said a word, but their heavy breathing and determined stance were more frightening than any words. She struggled vainly to evade their grasp, realizing that she was being abducted.

Suddenly from the house she had just left, Sergeant Perkins hurtled to her rescue, laying about the two men with a will. A seasoned fighter who took the men off guard, he felled one of the villains with a mighty blow, but was having a more difficult time with the other. Ariel hit the man with her reticule, a hard blow to the face, scarring his mouth. Swearing, the man backed off, just as his companion struggled to his feet. Deciding that flight was more in their interests than continuing the fight, they ran off toward the hackney, boarded it, and clattered into the fog.

Sergeant Perkins, breathing heavily, his hands still clenched, hastened to Ariel's aid.

"Did those varmints hurt you, Miss Ariel?" he asked anxiously as Ariel tried to put herself to rights.

"You arrived most opportunely, Sergeant Perkins. No, I am fine. What about yourself?" she asked, remembering his wounds.

"Ho! Those two mangy curs could not deck me. Quite enjoyed the little tussle. Not much bottom to those two. I've always thought this a most respectable neighborhood. And what happened to your carriage?" Alf Perkins asked, rubbing a small bruise on his cheekbone while he peered up the street.

"I have no idea. I told the coachman to wait here for me. He must have misunderstood my directions." Ariel frowned, trying to recall what she had told the man.

"Well, ma'am, I am going to escort you to St. Paul's and find you some safe conveyance, not that I think those cowards will return. Now who could want to harm you so, Miss Ariel? I can't think they were just an idle pair of thugs, hoping to rob you," Sergeant Perkins considered shrewdly.

"Thank you, Sergeant Perkins. I am sure they will not return, and I cannot think what they had in mind. But I am grateful for your intervention. How did you come to follow me?" Ariel asked as they walked toward the church. She was more than relieved to have the sheltering bulk of the sergeant by her side, for the encounter had upset her more than she was willing to admit to him.

"You forgot your gloves, ma'am, and Molly sent me after you with them. Here they are, a bit worse for wear, I fear," he explained, tendering the crumpled kid gloves.

"It's of no matter. I almost lost something far more valuable." Ariel shuddered, reaction setting in. Who could have planned such an attack? She also doubted that the two ruffians were idle layabouts, seeing a well-dressed victim who might possess some valuables. They had intended to drag her into that hackney and spirit her away to a fate she did not want to think about now. And where was her carriage?

Refusing Sergeant Perkins's offer to escort her back to Grosvenor Street, she summoned her courage and bade him an affectionate farewell, after he had assured himself that the carriage he hailed from the church courtyard was a safe vehicle.

Shakily she tried to gather her senses together and puzzle out what had occurred. There seemed no rhyme or reason to the attack, but she wondered if somehow a member of the French spy ring could have threatened her. Or perhaps Francoise was taking her revenge for the Ville-franches' exposure and exile. Upon reaching the sanctuary of Grosvenor Street, she asked Lufton to inquire about the coachman. When he appeared, she questioned him closely. He insisted that he had had a message from a small boy who had told him to return to the stables as his mistress would be some time yet, and with a care for his horses stamping impatiently in the cold damp air, he had acquiesced. He was most upset to learn of her plight and blamed himself for not being more wary.

"No harm done, John, thanks to Sergeant Perkins, but in the future perhaps you had better be more suspicious," Ariel said. "There are so many ruffians hanging about, it's best to be prudent." No good would come of prosing on about the mishap. She had been warned and would now be on her guard. She feared she would be unable to discover the perpetrator of the incident. Obviously some unknown enemy had hired the two men to abduct her. However, she knew now that she was in some danger and would take precautions.

Chapter Twenty-three

In Sussex, Ian and Alistair had met with no success in capturing the fishing boat crew who had attempted to take off the French agent, and Ian chafed with impatience to return to London. Deciding to leave the investigation in the capable hands of Alistair, he hoped to pursue a thin lead the papers had offered by rooting about in the Foreign Office, where the two were convinced the culprit lay. But before Ian and Alistair could put a new plan in train, events six hundred miles distant came to a climax which would alter all their strategies.

On February 28, 1815, supported by twelve hundred soldiers aboard seven small ships, Napoleon eluded his captors and sailed from the quay at Elba, cheered by his loyal adherents. Successfully avoiding the British Navy, which was looking out for him, he made straight for Provence. News of his escape did not reach Vienna until March 7. Wellington was the first to hear of the disaster from a naval commander, Sir Neil Campbell, who had arrived at Elba to check on the fretful Corsican. Wellington immediately contacted Talleyrand, who heard of the escape while he was making his toilette and listening to his niece's plans for a play rehearsal at the Metternich Palace. Talleyrand and the Iron Duke met to discuss the problem. Both agreed that Napoleon was probably making for Italy as he would not dare to land in France, where the Bourbon's soldiers would recapture him. They expected he would seek aid from his brother-in-law, Joachim Murat, King of Naples, the rash and courageous cavalry leader of his many successes. Murat was at odds with Talleyrand and the Congress over the question of Austrian claims to his land and in any event was not to be trusted.

The shock of Napoleon's escape drew the Allies together. Even the Tsar of all the Russias realized the importance of the news. Hearing of Napoleon's flight, Tsar Alexander laid his hand on Wellington's shoulder and intoned solemnly, "It is for you to save the world again." The Duke agreed he had no choice. The partying and bickering in Vienna were over. He prepared to leave for Brussels for the Allies expected that Napoleon would make his first priority to reclaim Belgium for France. The beleaguered country was the linchpin of Castlereagh's attempts to secure the peace of Europe.

Napoleon, eluding the British ships more by luck then clever ruse, sailed safely into the Gulfe de Juan and raised his standard near Antibes. Marshal Ney, sent to apprehend him, promised that he would capture the former emperor and put him in a cage. Would France rise to support Napoleon? Castlereagh believed so, and sent word to Wellington that he must leave Vienna post haste for Brussels with as many troops as he could muster. As Napoleon rallied his countrymen with stirring words about past glory—"the eagle and the tricolor shall fly from steeple to steeple to the towers of the Notre Dame"—the Congress proclaimed the upstart Corsican an outlaw. The Allies—Russia, Prussia, and England—rushed to gather their armies, but Wellington could only rely on thirty thousand British veterans, "an infamous army, very weak and ill-equipped," he wrote.

In England, which had been peace-mad since the year before, only the Guards were prepared for immediate embarkation. Wellington would have to depend in large part on the crude, hard-drinking Marshall Gebhard Lebrecht von Blucher and his Prussian troops. The Prince Regent, in Brighton, deluding himself with martial dreams, donned his own field marshal's uniform and anticipated taking command of an army himself. The common folk of London, appalled at the specter of Napoleon loose again, gathered in Leicester Square to see a model of the cage in which Ney promised to incarcerate Napoleon, while at Westminster Parliament hurried to vote a twelve-million-pound subsidy for the campaign. In Paris, where the weather refused to cooperate, English visitors scurried pell-mell into flight and the Bourbon King, Louis XVIII, shivered in fear.

The Hundred Days had begun.

Both Ian and Alistair, recalled to London, felt a certain relief that they could abandon the thankless task set them and contemplate returning to the field. All private problems were abandoned for the emergency. Even the apprehension of the spy in their midst now seemed of minimal importance.

After a brief stop at the War Office, and a consultation with Valentine, Ian made for Grosvenor Street. He arrived as the family was sitting down to dinner. They greeted him with a host of questions about Napoleon's escape and the possibility of another battle.

"I know little more than you do, except that Ney has been sent to capture him in Grenoble," Ian informed them gravely as they tried to eat, their appetites impaired by his news. "But it is touchy. Napoleon still commands the loyalty of many Frenchmen. We should have sent him to St. Helena or the Azores. Indeed, plans were afoot to do just that, but he learned of them, which spurred him to leave Elba. That and the stupidity of not paying him the yearly indemnity promised by the treaty sealed our fate. So Valentine tells me."

He watched Ariel with a strange expression. She could not fathom his mood, although she realized she should not be trying to gauge his attitude toward her when more serious matters were afoot.

"Will Wellington take the field?" Arnold asked his brother, his expression concerned.

"Of course, and I intend to be wtih him," Ian replied firmly, averting his eyes from Ariel. She shuddered, remembering past engagements and her father's death. Repressing her instinct to plead with him not to go, she asked quietly, "Will you be leaving soon?"

"I am awaiting orders," Ian told her, wondering if she feared for his safety. "The Guards have left for the embarkation point, but I must have Valentine's permission to rejoin the Dragoons. Perhaps the Bourbon can stop him, but I doubt it."

The earl, suddenly aware of his years and the peril to his youngest son, frowned. "Damn it. Why should you have to take the field again?"

"Because someone has to do it, and it's my job," Ian said, sensing his father's concern and strangely touched by it.

Later in the drawing room, they discussed the disturbing turn of affairs exhaustively, without reaching any conclusions. Ariel sensed that Ian was impatient with all the talk and strained for action. She could not blame him, but she said little, leaving the earl and Arnold to do most of the talking. Just before retiring, the earl gruffly requested that Ian join him for a private interview in the library.

Ian crossed the room to where Ariel was chatting desultorily with Harriet and said to her quietly, "I don't suppose the governor will keep me long. Wait up for me."

Ariel made no demur, but nodded her acquiescence. Some quarter of an hour after the two men left, she bid good night to Harriet and also Arnold, who indicated that he thought he would go around to the Foreign Office to learn further developments, since officials there would be working well into the dawn. Ariel gave a passing thought to Arnold's remarks, wondering if, in truth, that was where he was bound. With all the excitement about Napoleon's escape, she had temporarily forgotten her discovery of Arnold's liaison. Now she remembered she had not decided whether to tell Ian or not. Surely he should not be bothered with an affair of such small consequence when the shadow of war threatened them all. Arnold's liaison with Flossie, his treatment of Harriet, even her own encounter with those two ruffians who had tried to abduct her, seemed irrelevant in the face of this common danger. Ariel was much more concerned about Ian and what he meant to say to her after this absence. She had been able to tell little about his mood when he had greeted her with the rest of the family. And he did appear distracted and apprehensive about the inevitable battle. She did not believe he worried about his personal danger but some problem was bothering him, and she felt it concerned her. Was he going to tell her that he thought they should separate? Could she bear that?

Nancy, sniffling as she helped her mistress disrobe, brought Ariel's mind back to the task in hand. She insisted her maid return to her bed, and kindly hoped her cold would improve. Ariel treated servants with great consideration, having a sympathetic understanding of their position. As a result, she received generous service in return and in the servants' hall the verdict on Master Ian's wife was one of enthusiastic approval.

Seated by the fire, she mused ruefully that she spent a great deal of time waiting upon some significant conversation with Ian, but rarely did these anticipated discussions resolve their personal dilemma. Why could she just not accept the arid terms of this marriage, and not expect a true meeting of minds and hearts? But that was abhorrent to her. She could not live out her life in the sterile way so many of London's couples managed. She wanted more than that, and if she could not have it, must plan a far different future for herself, one that would offer peace of mind if not happiness.

As the minutes passed slowly, she could not settle to anything. Her current novel had little appeal in light of the momentous events happening on the larger world stage. She picked up her embroidery, usually a soothing task, but soon threw that down in disgust and took to pacing about the room. What was the matter with her? She must get herself in hand. Finally when she was on the verge of screaming with impatience, Ian came, having paused to change into his dressing gown. He looked tired and drawn, gravely serious, too.

"I am sorry to have been so long, Ariel, but the governor had a great deal on his mind. After all these years and all the campaigns I have endured, he suddenly appears to care that the next battle might be my last." He hesitated, crossing over to the fire and staring down into it unhappily. "I suspect he is mostly concerned about the succession, rather than my safety," he concluded bitterly. "Not that I am unaware that this time I might be leaving a hostage to the future. If you should be pregnant and the child is a son, there is every possibility he might be the next earl."

Ariel did not know what to answer to this cynical assessment. She disliked being considered a brood mare, fit only for producing children, but she hesitated to begin a quarrel with Ian. "Do not concern yourself with your father's desire for an heir, Ian. You have other, more important worries." She twisted her hands together in some agitation, wondering how to proceed. The knowledge that Ian was about to embark on a dangerous course tempered her attitude. How could she refuse him, no matter what his motives, on the eve of a battle? She yearned to tell him of her love and her fears for him, but believed he might reject her confidences. Could she risk a jeering refusal of her feelings while granting physical possession of her body? Why was her pride such an obstacle?

"Listen to me, Ariel. We have not dealt honestly with each other in the past. My jealousy and anger are poor excuses, but I must tell you I know now that you and Alistair were not deceiving me. I am a fool, I suppose, but it has not been my habit to trust a woman. For that I beg your forgiveness." The words were wrenched out of him with obvious difficulty. His Celtic stubbornness rebelled at admitting a fault, and Ariel dropped her eyes before he could glimpse the tender indulgence toward his folly she knew he might see.

He crossed over to her and drew her gently to her feet, clasping her in his arms and turning her chin up so that he could gaze into her eyes. What he saw there must have reassured him.

"Tonight I do not want recriminations or explanations. I need you so, Ariel. Do not deny me," he said roughly, a question in his voice.

Ariel had no intention of denying him, her blood racing at his touch, her senses afire. She did not reply, but did not repulse him when he led her toward the bed, which beckoned them enticingly. He removed her dressing gown and lowered her onto the smooth sheets, and then followed her down, abandoning his own robe in the process.

What followed was a far different experience from Ariel's initiation into the sensual delights she had previously endured. For long moments there were no words between them, their passion flaring into a white hot testimony to their desire. Ariel yearned for his possession and responded eagerly to the insistence of his mouth and hands. Although he put no restraint on the tumultuous demands of his body, he said little. Even at the ultimate climax of his passion he did not tell her he loved her, and she bit back the words of her own love. When their pulses had slowed and their violently beating hearts had quieted, he did not abandon her, but gathered her into his arms, his lips on her flowing hair, and held her against his strength.

"We will not be parted again. You will come to

331

Brussels with me?" he asked.

Although she hungered for a more fervent indication of his love and need, she thrilled to the idea that he could not do without her, that they would be together for the brief time allowed them.

"Oh, yes. I want that. But is it possible?" she murmured against his throat.

His hands tightened possessively and she felt his arousal. "Yes. Many officers are taking their wives with them. Whatever happens now in France, the final disposition of Napoleon will take some weeks. But our forces must be ready for him. Wellington is en route to Brussels and our regiment will join him there. Valentine will grant leave for me to return to the Dragoons. I would have gone anyway," he added fiercely, the force of his feeling evident in the tight grasp of his hands upon her. "But we will talk more of this in the morning. Try to sleep now. I will not leave you."

Long after his deep breathing signified that he had dropped immediately into an exhausted slumber, Ariel lay awake, trying to take some comfort from his protective arms. Their lovemaking had eased his frustrations—and she, too, had desired him, she could not deny that—but in reality she knew their physical response to each other only deepened their dilemma. With so many questions unanswered, Ariel ruminated a long while but then she finally drifted off to sleep.

For this night at least, her husband belonged to her.

Chapter Twenty-four

As Ian had warned Ariel, no sudden departure for Brussels could be brought about. There was still a faint hope that Louis XVIII's loyal troops might halt Napoleon, that Ney might make good his promise to capture the former emperor and put him in the infamous cage. But this latter possibility was soon dispelled. When Ney reached Napoleon beyond Lyons, he joined his former master with exuberance, and soon hundreds of veterans of the Grande Armée flocked to enroll under Napoleon's tricolor. Two weeks later the Corsican, supported by his enthusiastic battalions, was at the gates of Paris. The Bourbon King, Louis XVIII, placed on the throne of France by the victorious allies, had no recourse but to flee, and by March 19 he had slipped from the Tuileries bound for Ghent.

Paris greeted Napoleon with both enthusiasm and apprehension when he arrived the following day. The aristocrats, who remained, were cautious even if the general populace cheered. His chief support came from the army, although Marshal Ney, who had changed sides with such aclarity, was beginning to feel he might have made a mistake. Doubts intensified when Napoleon introduced a constitution which differed little from the charter under which the Bourbon had reigned, and the common folk feared conscription. It was obvious to every Frenchman that the Allies were determined to fight the usurper at the soonest possible moment. The Parisians were weary of war.

England itself teetered on the edge of revolt, spurred by the passage of the Corn Bill on March 20, the day Napoleon entered Paris. Protecting the price of local corn against foreign imports meant hunger and deprivation for the masses. The Dragoons and the militia were called out to prevent bloodshed from the angry crowds who would have attacked the Prince Regent's palace, Carlton House, if it had not been heavily guarded.

Ian, who had rejoined his regiment, after securing Valentine's leave, chafed at using his men to protect London when they could be bound for Brussels. His mood was testy and Ariel hesitated to make any move which would exacerbate the delicate relationship between them. Her only comfort was that he sought her bed every night although he made no avowals of love, his possession of her a silent, desperate hunger. Alistair had accompanied Ian to London, but he did not come to call, and she was appalled to learn he was now the center of a raging scandal. Ian came in one afternoon, furious, to relate the matter to her as she poured his tea in the drawing room. Fortunately both the earl and Arnold were not present and Harriet was hardly noticeable, shrinking from her brother-in-law's temper.

"Alistair is a damn fool," Ian raged as he took his teacup from his wife, stirring the brew so strongly Ariel feared for the china.

"What has he done?" Ariel asked calmly, trying to soothe her irate husband, hoping that his anger was not directed at her.

"Thrown his cap over the windmill and eloped with that damn Bletchford woman, I understand," Ian muttered. "He will be tossed out of the regiment, and his career blasted. Who knows what his father will do? How could he become embroiled in a first-class scandal on the eve of the greatest battle England must fight!" Ian growled, his irritation abating somewhat under Ariel's unruffled demeanor. She was finding his dismay at his friend's appalling conduct heartening, for it meant she had not been the cause of an irreparable breach.

Determined to cool Ian's temper, she bit back a shocked protest and tried to put as good a face as possible on the upset. "Perhaps he is truly in love with her, and felt he had no choice but to remove her from her unhappy situation with her husband."

"Nonsense. She is not some poor persecuted wife. She married Lord Bletchford of her own free will, wanting the prestige and money he could give her. I don't believe she cares a groat for

335

Alistair. She's a shallow jade," Ian fulminated.

Surprisingly Harriet entered the argument. "You cannot know her true feelings, Ian. She may have been driven to this desperate pass by the force of her unhappy state," she offered resolutely.

Ian looked quite taken aback, as if a mouse had reared up and roared at him. "You don't know what you're talking about, Harriet. If every bored wife decided to leave her husband, Parliament would be thronged with crimson cases and the business of government would grind to a halt. It's Alistair I am concerned with, not that silly fool. She has ruined him."

Harriet looked as if she would challenge Ian but subsided at a quelling glance from Ariel. Now was not the time for Harriet to air her own grievances as a betrayed wife.

"Perhaps the affair is not as grave as you fear. Where have they gone, and is there any chance matters may be retrieved?" Ariel asked, watching her husband as he put down his cup in disgust and paced around the room.

"Well, no one really knows. He certainly cannot take her down to Dorset to his family. And I doubt if her parents will receive them. And he has really dished his chances with the regiment. Wellington has not forgotten Paget's transgressions and he looks very hardly on an officer who puts his personal life before his duty," Ian explained, causing Ariel to wonder if his anger with Alistair reflected on his own frustrating condition. She did not want to contemplate the fact that perhaps he stayed with her for fear of blighting his career.

"I remember now the Earl of Uxbridge ran off with the Iron Duke's wife's sister. Naturally he would disapprove. And Alistair had hopes of a staff appointment," Ariel remembered, shaking her head in sorrow.

"Well, he can say good-bye to that," Ian remarked dryly.

Ariel suggested that they wait upon events before relegating Alistair to the devil, and was able to placate Ian somewhat. Later that evening his lovemaking again had that desperate quality which overset her. Before they drifted off to sleep, she asked him, in some fear of his reply, "This latest escapade of Alistair's, surely that persuades you he cared nothing for me, except as a friend, of course."

She felt Ian's body tense against hers and then relax. His hand roamed caressingly down the length of her body.

"Yes, I know, Ariel. I behaved stupidly, jumping to all sorts of unjustified conclusions," he said reluctantly, causing Ariel to smile. How he hated admitting he was in the wrong.

"Well, Alistair has paid a bitter price for his flirtatious ways," she conceded. "But I grieve for him. He will hate missing the fight." Really, men were like children, she thought, behaving in such nonsensical fashion, buffeted by every casual desire.

Ian raised her chin and looked searchingly at her in the dim light from the fire, which cast a slight glow on the room. "See what you have saved me from, Ariel. No sane man would leave a passionate wife and his comfortable marital couch, putting such pleasures at risk, just to dally with some silly chit who is no better than she should be." He grinned at her with a devilish expression, knowing she would not take his smug enjoyment without an argument.

To her chagrin, Ariel felt a blush spreading over her body. If he wanted an avowal of love from her, she would not oblige him. He might be able to stir her to the heights of rapture, but she would not admit her feelings as long as he made no attempt to tell her of his own.

"You are a rake and a cad, sir, to tease me so. Now I am almost dead with fatigue, so no more of your provocation." She turned on her side, showing him an uncompromising back, but he only chuckled and within minutes was breathing deeply. For Ariel, sleep proved strangely elusive. There was still much unresolved between them despite their passionate lovemaking. She had not told him about Arnold's deception, nor of the attempt at her own abduction. But Alistair's actions had driven it from her mind. She would tell him tomorrow.

However, on the following day, more news of Alistair and Lady Bletchford's ruinous behavior was explained, and by the culprit himself. Late that afternoon, while Ian was on guard duty at Carlton House, Alistair appeared at the Montague's home, a bit shamefaced but ready to brave out any criticism.

"You are kind to receive me, Ariel. I hoped Ian would be here so that you would both hear of my latest escapade. I am really up in the boughs now, and crave your indulgence. But I am not as black as I am painted, I insist. Too chivalrous by half, that is how I was forced into this coil," he told her, watching her with a rueful grin on his face.

"Oh, Alistair, what have you done? Ian told me yesterday, and I fear you have done irretreivable harm," Ariel reproved him, but could not resist his reckless charm.

"Yes, well, I know it looks bad, but really I am blameless. Olivia Bletchford called on me to rescue her from her husband. He had discovered our liaison, and others, for she was not especially prudent, and he beat her. She feared for her safety, for he threatened to lock her up in their country estate, and promised other punishment. All I did was take her down to her old aunt in Wiltshire. I had no intention of eloping with her, but Bletchford acted the cuckold and chased after us. He did not catch us and Olivia is now safely immured with her aunt. He will come round in time, if he does not act the fool and cite me in a divorce action. But I have no intention of shackling myself to such a ninny. Shameless, I know, but she is not the wife for me."

"Well, you might have thought of that before you cast out lures to her, and embroiled the poor woman in this scandal," Ariel said repressively, but relieved that he had not completely lost his senses.

339

He grinned unrepentantly. "I know, you are quite right to give me a set-down, but in all honesty, I must admit, she did a great deal of the luring. A prime piece she is, too, for casual dalliance," he added outrageously. "I just couldn't resist comforting her."

"Well, you should have resisted. What will happen to you now? Ian tells me your colonel won't have you back in the regiment."

"Don't fret. I have been to see Uxbridge and explained the matter to him. He needs staff, and since he understands my dilemma, having given in to temptation himself, he will take me on. I will miss the Dragoons, but the First Life Guards are a bonny group, and bound to see action first off," he responded cheerfully.

"You are fortunate to come out of this deplorable affair so comfortably. At least, unlike the Earl of Uxbridge, you have not left a wife and five children to suffer for your reckless ways," Ariel sighed. Really, Alistair was incorrigible. Still she could not help but smile at the way he had wriggled out of disaster. "Ian will be pleased you will not miss the fight."

"Yes, it will be capital to be in the field again," he agreed.

"And do take care, Alistair," Ariel warned. "You are so foolhardy, probably eager to commit some silly outrageous action just to redeem yourself."

"Ah, but the devil takes care of his own, you know." He smiled at her.

"You need a good sober wife, Alistair, who will

keep you in hand," she reproved, shaking her head in contemplation of the task. "But I doubt any worthwhile girl would risk taking you on."

"But I told you, Ariel, I would have been meek as a lamb, the very epitome of fidelity, if I had you by my side," he answered in his old careless manner. Then suddenly serious, he looked at her with a probing sincerity. "I hope all is well now with you and Ian. He and I settled his doubts in Sussex and he knows his fears were unfounded."

"All is well, Alistair. Ian is truly your friend, and has been concerned about you, but at bottom, he trusts you, as I do. See to it that you do not let us regret our confidence," Ariel concluded, hoping that she had heard the last of that affair.

"Are you brave enough to come riding in the park with me? I must show the flag, you know," he said, pleased by her championship and determined to take advantage of it.

"Yes, and begin those rumors all over again. I think I hear Ian coming in. Ask him if he wants his wife flaunting her association with one of London's most infamous rakes, if you please?" she challenged him as Ian entered the drawing room.

A little nervously she began to explain Alistair's presence, fearing a renewal of her husband's suspicions, but she need not have worried. Ian was delighted to see his friend and listened gravely to his explanations of the Bletchford elopement. When Alistair had finished his somewhat self-serving excuses, Ian laughed. He believed his friend but deplored his rash actions, although he agreed he was not one to prose on about virtues.

He had committed too many follies himself.

"I am happy Uxbridge will have you, Alistair, and that you will be with us when we face Napoleon, but don't press your luck. Eventually your sins will find you out," Ian concluded. Ariel was relieved he did not think it odd that Alistair had rushed around to confide his tale to her and seek her understanding.

Alistair took Ian's chafing in good heart. "You are quite right, Ian, I am sure to survive the battle and embroil myself in further troubles. Only the good die young, you know."

Ariel felt a shudder pass through her. Here were these two bravely, even cheerfully, preparing for yet another battle, chancing their lives with little thought. She could scarcely bear it, but she must not show her fears. As a soldier's daughter and wife, she must send them off with a smile and a quip. They would not appreciate tears and warnings.

Ian, unconcerned with Alistair's reputation, invited him to dine that evening, if he was brave enough to face the earl's tirades, and stalwart in the face of Arnold's obvious disapproval. Alistair thanked him and promised to be on his best behavior, then left on his own concerns.

"I am going to sport my number at White's now. Give all the old busybodies a chance to cut me, toss me out, whatever. Do me good, eh, Ariel, to be shunned by the members," Alistair suggested. If he doubted the reception he would receive, it did not seem to cause him any hesitation. So like him, to behave in this cavalier fashion, but Ariel would not rise to his teasing and she and Ian saw him on his way, hoping he would not have to suffer the ultimate rejection. Still, he would bluff his way through whatever fate offered. That was his style, and no matter how unhappy he felt beneath that reckless facade, few would guess at his misery.

On his departure, Ariel turned to Ian and requested his attention. "I have a grave matter to discuss with you, Ian, and I have hesitated long enough, but I did not want to add to your burdens," she said, as they entered the morning room, where they might be assured of some privacy.

Ariel noticed that Ian held himself stiffly, as if braced for some blow. What did he expect her to say? He did not sit down but stood, feet apart and hands clasped behind his back, and eyed her impassively. She felt too nervous to sit down herself although he politely indicated a chair. Instead she walked to the window and looked out on the watery day, not knowing how to begin. Then just as she took a deep breath and was about to confess, he said bleakly, "If you have requested my presence here to tell me you do not want our marriage to continue, I will not have it. We are married and will remain so." His voice was even, almost dispassionate, all emotion wiped from the tone.

Surprised by his introducing a topic which was far from her mind, she turned and faced him. "It was not about our marriage I wished to speak.

343

How can you think, after what has passed between us, I would wish such a thing."

"I know you believe you were forced into this situation but I had hoped, the last few days, you were coming to feel differently, even taking me in some affection. Conceited of me, perhaps," he finished cynically.

Ariel's eyes widened. How could he think she would welcome him into her bed as a mere expediency? "I am perfectly content with our marriage, Ian. I thought I had showed you that." She would willingly have admitted more if she had received some sign from him that he would welcome it, but his face remained schooled, impossible to read anything in those dark brooding eyes, which raked her.

"Content. Well, I suppose that's better than indifference or dislike. I had—" Then he broke off what he might have said and, shaking his head, resumed. "But pray continue, my dear, I am interrupting you with nonsense."

Not nonsense, thought Ariel, if he meant to ask her if her surrender implied what she kept so resolutely hidden. But no, this was no time to consider their personal affairs, even if she were willing to lower her pride and admit to her desire for his love. She shook off her yearning and determinedly launched into her discovery of Arnold's deception. "And all the while, Arnold is playing a role, pretending to despise your libertine ways while he is no better than he should be, keeping that woman, and castigating Harriet for

344

her inability to produce an heir," she finished in a gust of indignation.

Ian's reaction was unexpected. He laughed ruefully. "The clever dog, acting the puritan while indulging in all the delights of the flesh he pretends to find so disgusting. Who would have thought it? I bet he was furious that you caught him out. But what difference does it make?" he concluded cynically. "And you faced him with it, brave girl. Did he deny it?"

"No, he threatened me with all kinds of retribution if I told the earl. But I would not do that," Ariel said in some vexation.

"My sainted brother is apt to judge everyone by his own standards. He would rush to take advantage of such a coup. You are too charitable, Ariel," Ian demurred in that mocking voice which hid his real feelings, she knew.

"Well, I can't see that it would do any good, just upset your father and not resolve anything. It could not force Arnold to love Harriet or treat her with affection, although I have noticed he is much more forebearing with her," Ariel said with some satisfaction.

"You never cease to amaze me, Ariel. Here you have Arnold at your mercy and are willing to let him off the hook. Still, you are probably right. Why cause the governor such disappointment, only kick up his gout, and then we would all suffer from his temper," Ian agreed, but Ariel felt beneath his careless words was a deep regret that his father could not have viewed his own youthful

345

escapades with more charity. Didn't the earl realize that Ian was worth ten of his brother, and secretly craved a rapprochement with his father? They were both so proud and willful, Ariel mused, but then sobered thinking of the next budget of news she had to confide.

"That's not all, Ian. I hesitated to tell you, knowing you would fly into a pucker, but if you don't learn of my mishap from me, undoubtedly you will get a garbled account from John the coachman." Then she launched into an account of the attempted abduction, trying to minimize the danger. "Of course, it could just have been a chance encounter, two ruffians hoping for some jewelry or guineas. But I was fortunate that Sergeant Perkins came to my aid."

Ian's eyes flashed in anger. He took this news far more seriously than that of Arnold's mistress. Ariel might have come to real harm, and yet she had not wanted to alarm him. He crossed to her and took her in his arms, raising her head and looking at her with an expression she found difficult to deciper.

"You could have endured a far more disagreeable fate at the hands of those ruffians," he said, his anger barely in check. "You are such an innocent, Ariel. They might have inflicted dreadful indignities upon you. Even raped you, or sold you to some brothel. You were a fool to venture to that part of town unescorted, even on your errand of charity. And I do not think it was just a chance meeting. Someone is out to punish you, and I have

346

my own ideas as to who it could be. Francoise is perfectly capable of planning such a revenge, and even your dear cousin, Fiona, is not above consigning you to that particular hell."

Ariel, less disturbed, considered his words. "Francoise, perhaps, but surely not Fiona. At any rate, she has been banished to the country by Robert. He forced her to come here and apologize for her shocking manners in the drawing room, the day after the ball. And would she command the resources, or even the skill, to plan such a mean trick?" Ariel asked, feeling the comfort of Ian's arms around her banishing the fears of that dreadful attack.

Ian was not appeased and his arms tightened, his horror at the idea of her danger not alleviated by her assurances.

"If anything had happened to you . . ." His voice deepened and he kissed her with a desperate passion, almost convincing Ariel that he cared sincerely for her. But he said nothing more, just continued with those deep drugging caresses.

Finally he released her, bringing himself under control although she sensed he was still in the grip of some powerful emotion. "If this continues, I will take you here in the morning room, which would more than shock Lufton if he should interrupt us."

Trying to gauge his mood, Ariel challenged him bravely, "Surely not before tea, Ian."

"Before tea, before luncheon, and instead of breakfast. You have a veritable talent for arousing me, my dear, but come, I am a dolt to provoke

347

you so. However, be warned, I will not have you subject to danger. You are not to roam about London in this careless fashion. If you must visit your Sergeant Perkins, I will accompany you. Now promise me," he insisted.

"Of course, Ian, if you prefer," Ariel agreed demurely, quite warmed by his protective stance.

Chapter Twenty-five

While Ariel and Ian were completely absorbed by their personal and family concerns, they had temporarily shelved the investigation of the spy ring, which had brought them to their present pass. However, General Valentine, despite the preparations in the War Office for the inevitable confrontation with Napoleon, still pursued the traitors. He would accompany the army to Brussels as head of Intelligence but he would undertake his new duties with more confidence if he could apprehend the current nest of London-based agents. He had no illusions that they would not intensify their efforts now that their master had returned to lead France into more folly. He would have liked Ian and Alistair's cooperation but the latter had placed himself beyond his control by his heedless escapade and Ian thought only of preparing for the battle. Still he had other resources and he intended to use them. Chief among them was the gentleman who now faced him across his desk. The Marquis de Lisle had served his country in such a capacity before, and although now nearing middle age, he had lost none of his ingenuity or ruthlessness.

He greeted his visitor appreciatively. "Well, Theron, I see you and Melissa escaped from Paris just in advance of the Corsican. It is kind of you to call on me and give me a report, when I know you are eager to return to your estates."

"Well, it was a near thing," the marquis said. "And Melissa left a trunkful of new gowns behind, but you know how she enjoys an adventure. I think fleeing from a panting mob stirred her memories of more exciting days. She will never be a comfortable matron, content with her home and children, I fear." A striking man of saturnine cast, with hooded gray eyes and dark hair that was graying slightly at the brow, he looked, and indeed was, a formidably handsome figure. He was the image of the haughty aristocrat, no matter how relaxed and amiable at the moment.

"You are convinced that France will support Napoleon, then?" Valentine asked, now that the courtesies had been observed.

"Without a doubt. He has drawn them to his side with visions of glory, the restoration of poor little Belgium to France's fold. But he will not, must not succeed," the marquis said decisively. "We have suffered enough from that madman and his minions. And I have to say, along your lines of investigation, that Fouché, his secret police chief, has again been enrolled in his behalf," the marquis added, reminding Valentine of Napoleon's former wily and cruel agent. "He will use all his art and skill to further his master's project."

"He has been hard at work here for the past months. The peace did not signify any disruption in his plots, I can assure you. And we are again faced with a villain in our very midst, assuredly in the Foreign Office. I suppose now the traitor will redouble his efforts, giving aid and comfort to the enemy. How can any official of the government be so disloyal, plan the death and destruction of his country with such equanimity?" Valentine asked, shaking his head at the thought of the perfidy of one who should support and aid his country in this crisis.

"Greed is a great advocate, my dear Valentine," the marquis suggested suavely. "I fear we will always be burdened with those who would betray us. But come, what is the current menace?"

"Young Glendenning and Montague have discovered that the agent we are tracking is indubitably in the Foreign Office. At first we thought he might be here, in the War Department, but we now have proof he is a man high up in Castlereagh's confidence. Those two young rapscallions have flushed out the man's émigré confederates and we have settled them to our satisfaction, but alas, are no nearer unmasking the homegrown traitor. I have several suspects, among them Sir Robert Mackenzie, but Castlereagh will hear no word against him," Valentine explained.

"Mackenzie, that's a facer, I would have thought him most reliable, although that wife of his is a

351

temptress who is as grasping and ambitious as they come," the marquis mused.

"Well, I want you to try to flush out whoever it is," Valentine said. "Needless to say, it's a touchy assignment, but well within your powers, based on past performances." At one time the marquis had been instrumental in exposing a dangerous spy ring, but that was some years ago, and now that he had forsaken his former rakish ways under the yoke of a happy marriage, London saw little of him. "Perhaps I should be seeking Melissa's permission for such a venture?" he added quizzically.

The marquis's eyes rose in pretended horror. "For God's sake, don't enlist her in any ploys you have in mind. Domesticity has not subdued her, nor have I. And she has me completely under her thumb. Who would think I should become such an ardent benedict? The power of love is insidious," the marquis joked, but an underlying contentment spoke of his felicity.

"She's a handful, like my Sarah, but you are a lucky dog, Theron, and you know it," Valentine observed. "We both won wives who are beyond price. Be sure to give her my best. I admire her exceedingly."

The two men settled down to go over the evidence available to them, and had come to no conclusions when their conference was interrupted by a clerk who announced that Captain Montague claimed an audience with the general. Valentine frowned at the distraction but allowed that Ian might have some news relating to their discussion.

Ian greeted General Valentine politely and was

introduced to the marquis, who at first glance seemed to him a disdainful, idle aristocrat, a sort Ian did not particularly like. However, he doubted Valentine would be entertaining such a man for casual reasons and prepared to give the marquis the benefit of the doubt.

"An incident has occurred which gives me some disquiet in view of our recent business, General," Ian began formally, looking askance at the visitor. He was not prepared to say more before a stranger who should not be privy to their investigations.

"The marquis is an old friend and an accomplished agent," Valentine assured him, commending Ian's reluctance but dispelling it. "He has solved several of our most vexing problems in the past, Ian, so feel free to talk before him. We have no secrets from the marquis."

"A rather disturbing assault on my wife, General, has me wondering if we have flushed out our master spy," Ian began, and then related what Ariel had told him of the attack upon her.

"Good God, Ian, that could have had frightful consequences. I hope Ariel was not too shaken. She is all right?" Valentine asked in some agitation.

"Oh, yes, sir, quite unperturbed by the whole affair. I doubt she understands what it signifies. If I had been in town, the ruffians would not have chanced their luck, I think. But it does mean we are hard on the heels of the traitors, forcing them into the open," Ian answered, wondering what Valentine would make of his disclosures. He badly needed some assurances that Ariel would suffer no further danger.

Valentine explained to the marquis what the captain and his wife had undertaken for him, and the result, which had brought the Villefranches to brook. This news of Ian's meant they were within an ace of accomplishing their end, but neither Valentine nor the marquis could decide how to use this attempt on Ariel to further their plans. Finally, it was decided that they would put a couple of agents on the Montague house to see if anyone was watching Ariel and her movements. With that, Ian had to be content, although he promised that he would be on the alert himself, now that he knew what to expect. He parted from Valentine and the marquis with mutual hopes that their problems would soon be solved.

"I like your impetuous Scot, Lucien," the marquis remarked when Ian had departed. "I suppose he is eager to join in the fight, and spy chasing seems a tame endeavor in view of the coming action." The marquis felt a bit wistful and jealous of Ian's youth and opportunities.

"Oh, yes, I have had to allow him to rejoin his regiment, but he will not completely desert us in view of this recent exploit," Valentine assured him. "Before Wellington engages Napoleon, we will have captured our spy, I am convinced."

General Valentine's words proved to be too optimistic. The only suspicious characters seen entering the Montague Grosvenor Street home were an odd couple, recently met friends of Harriet's from one of Hannah More's salons. Ariel, pressed by her sister-in-law to lend her countenance at the tea party to which she had

354

invited her new friends, found the woman, a Miss Louisa Culpepper, a strange companion with her repressed features, her graying hair skewered tightly into a bun, and her dowdy dress. Her brother, Hubert, tall, lanky, and absentminded, appeared a mild-mannered man whose chief interest was Greco-Roman antiquities, although he endorsed his sister's views on education and feminine rights. Ariel failed to understand what Harriet found so entrancing in the pair, although she had to admit the elevated tone of the Culpeppers' conversation was a distinct change from the usual drawing room chatter of fashions and gossip. And Hubert Culpepper obviously admired Harriet, treated her with a gentle consideration which must have been soothing after Arnold's carping criticism. Ariel, who knew little of the classics, was astonished to hear her sister-in-law prose on about Greek architecture and the influence of the Greek tragedians on English drama. Obviously Harriet had been spending a good deal of her leisure reading up on these abstruse subjects. Under Hubert's careful handling, she glowed with confidence and pleasure.

The Culpeppers made their home in Oxford, where he was a don, and would soon depart for the university. While Louisa had been enrolling in Miss More's educational schemes, Hubert had been doing research in the British Museum on the poetry of Euripides. Ariel concluded, on bidding farewell to the couple, that Harriet had found solace in this intellectual challenge. Hubert neither patronized her sister-in-law nor scorned her few timid suggestions, which she must have found vastly appealing after Arnold's cold, indifferent scorn. The attraction of the pair remained a mystery to Ariel but she was pleased that Harriet had found a healthy distraction from her former pitiable condition.

"What did you think of the Culpeppers, Ariel?" Harriet asked eagerly after the couple had departed.

"Not in the usual style, certainly, Harriet, but very worthwhile companions for you. You will come to no harm with them," Ariel decided, giving her sister-in-law a warm, encouraging smile. "But are you really fascinated by the Greeks and all that scholarship?"

Harriet colored and looked at Ariel wistfully. "I don't quite understand all Hubert says, but he is so kind and patient with me."

"Valuable characteristics, I agree. His sister appears to be of a sterner stuff, but perhaps underneath that rather quelling facade she, too, is compassionate," Ariel teased gently, for she suspected that Harriet was much more intrigued by Hubert than his sister, and who could blame her. He treated her with such benevolent approval.

"Louisa is really quite nice once she relaxes, but you were very obliging to welcome them, Ariel. I wanted you to meet my new friends and see what a comfort they are to me. You, too, have been most kind and patient with my megrims," she added.

"If the Culpeppers have eased your unhappiness and given you a new interest, I thoroughly endorse them. Congratulations, Harriet, for coping so successfully with an uncomfortable situation." Ariel smiled at her sister-in-law. Lord knows the poor lady needed any respite she could find, for her marriage with Arnold offered cold comfort.

Comfort was not what Ariel sought from Ian, but strangely, since he had returned from Sussex, that was what he offered, his protective air toward her in great contrast to his previous attitude. Ariel sustained herself with the knowledge that if he did not love her, at least he held her in some affection.

Waiting to embark for Brussels made both of them impatient, suspended in a world where decisions and resolutions had no place. Even the spy investigations had ground to a halt although Ariel suspected that Ian continued to search for clues. He was occupied in gathering his kit and organizing his men for the journey across the Channel, a date which loomed ever closer as news of Napoleon's activities reached them. She dreaded the upcoming battle, but kept her own counsel about her fears. That was the least she could do for Ian, for he would have little patience with her worries as to his safety. She missed Alistair's cheerful company, for he had already left with the Life Guards for Belgium, promising they would meet before too long. He had come to make his farewells, bringing with him a callow young subaltern who was quite in awe of his commanding officer and said little, content to efface himself. He, too, hoped they would meet in Brussels and indifferently requested that Ariel might receive his sister, who would be accompanying him. All these young men, so avidly seeking glory on the ramparts, caused Ariel pangs of dread. How many of them would survive the carnage? She thought the earl shared her apprehension, for he behaved with gruff forbearance toward Ian now that the date for their departure approached. Ian informed her that his father's charity could be laid at her door. "Just one of the many things I have to be grateful to you for," he said enigmatically one evening as they prepared to retire.

"And what are the others?" Ariel asked lightly as she brushed her hair before the dressing table. Ian came over and stood behind her, their eyes meeting in the mirror. He placed his hands on her shoulders, his gaze warming to the delightful picture she made. "I don't think I will puff you up by telling you now. You would have a great conceit," he teased, but beneath his light badinage Ariel sensed a question. She rose and walked into his waiting arms, content to offer him the silent reassurance of her embrace. By mutual consent they did not talk of the future but beneath Ian's passion she sensed some deeper need. Soon, soon, she knew she would betray herself by admitting her love for him. Only the knowledge that he might reject such an avowal prevented her, and their relationship remained one circumscribed by the sensual pleasures of the bed, neither attempting to put their fears or hopes into words.

She had almost forgotten the reason for this marriage under the weight of the coming battle, when she was forced to a sudden realization of danger by a visitor she had never expected to see again.

Chapter Twenty-six

Some days after the Culpeppers' visit, Ariel was in her bedroom, ruefully contemplating the trunks which had been brought from the box room and which demanded a decision from her. What should she pack and did Ian expect her to superintend his own luggage? She and her maid, Nancy, were carefully putting away her winter wardrobe, for at last, spring showed some promise of banishing the gray clouds and gusty winds of March. Already the crocuses and daffodils had made a timid effort to brighten the Park, and April had rushed upon them. She was interrupted in her task by a maid who informed her she had a caller.

"Who is it, Evans?" Ariel asked the starchy parlor maid, who seemed very disapproving.

"Mr. Lufton would not say, except that it was a female person," Evans answered, disdain in every line. She indicated that the unnamed one was in the hall. It appeared that the caller had incurred both Evans's and Lufton's displeasure.

Ariel repressed a smile, careful not to show any reaction. Really, servants were such snobs. "I suppose this female person has a name?" she requested, waiting with some curiosity. Probably the visitor was Mrs. Perkins, who would not be received at the front entrance with any enthusiasm by the staff. She could not be a proper object of Mrs. Montague's attention. Ariel hoped that the homely Mrs. Perkins was not cowed by her reception, for it had taken courage to call at such an august address. She must be in real need of Ariel's assistance.

"I believe the name was Baines, madam," Evans finally admitted, barely concealing a sneer.

Flossie. What could she want? Had Arnold broken with her? Ariel then remembered she had required Flossie to apply to her if she found herself in trouble. "Thank you, Evans, I will be down directly. You might take Mrs. Baines into the morning room," Ariel directed the starchy maid, ignoring her sniff of indignation.

Requesting Nancy to get on with packing her woolens in lavender, Ariel prepared to see what Flossie wanted. Later, entering the morning room, she was amused to see the high-spirited woman much subdued, seated gingerly on the edge of an uncomfortable chair, clutching her beaded reticule and eyeing the decor with some trepidation.

"Good morning, Flossie. How nice to meet you again. Do relax and tell me what you have on your mind, for I doubt if this is a social call," Ariel said kindly, settling herself across from Mrs. Baines after shaking her hand warmly.

Flossie rushed into speech, her normally good-humored countenance drawn into lines of worry. "Oh, ma'am, I am that overset, I scarcely know whether I am on my head or my heels. I just could not manage any longer by myself."

"Is it about Arnold? Has he thrown you out?" Ariel asked, seeing that the poor woman was at her wit's end.

"No, no, it's nothing like that. I would not bother you about any such light thing. It's them papers," she replied, almost incoherent.

"The newspapers?" Ariel asked, puzzled. What could have thrown Flossie into such a pucker? She doubted that the woman read the gazettes, which were frightening the populace with threats of Napoleon. And certainly Flossie had too much good sense to heed the rumors flooding London. No, it must be a more personal matter.

"The papers Arnie is writing. He's up to some devilry with them, and making all kinds of wild statements about gold and estates, and all that rubbish. I can't abide mysteries, and he's so odd lately, muttering in his sleep. Oh, my, I shouldn't have said that, shock a nice lady like you." Flossie put her hand to her mouth as if to hold back the damning words.

But Ariel was not shocked, only concerned. She could not make head nor tail of Flossie's mutterings. But first she must calm the agitated woman.

"What are you talking about, Flossie? I suspect

Arnold has brought some documents to St. John's Wood which are giving you pause. Can you read enough to make out their import?" Ariel asked, a wild suspicion rising in her mind.

"No, ma'am. I can just make out sumpin' English, but this is all foreign words. Beyond me, but I just have a feeling Arnold is up to no good. The poor sod seems mighty upset over it all. Tetchy, he's been lately, and hasn't much time for me. I don't know really why he bothers comin' around," Flossie said, aggrieved, and Ariel thought she could understand the reason. Arnold, burdened with some problems of state, probably had not been enjoying Flossie's attributes and she would find that difficult to endure, her past experience based on men's more carnal appetites. But what was he plotting? Could the papers be in French, and if so, what did that signify? Ariel realized this latest turn of events needed a great deal of thought.

"Flossie, you were right to come to me. I will give the matter my best attention. Perhaps it might be possible for me to take a glimpse at the papers, and then we would be more apt to know where we stood." Ariel offered the suggestion brightly, as if there was nothing more natural that she should spy on her brother-in-law's private documents.

"Well, I don't know. He'd kill me if he thought I was prying into his concerns, but I just know there is somethin' rotten about the whole thing. I can't just sit still and let it all continue." Flossie seemed to be arguing with herself. Her loyalty, which Ariel found endearing, was warring with her practical nature, which told her there was something havey-cavey in Arnold's actions. Now anxious only to rid herself of this disturbing visitor, Ariel took pains to reassure Flossie that she would keep the matter secret and let her know shortly how to proceed.

"Are you all right for funds, Flossie, in case Arnold suddenly takes against you?" she asked.

"I've a bit put by. And I can always find a bed at my chum's, and go back to the Angel and Cow. I was a real good barmaid, you know, until I took up this line of work. A city gentleman had me in keeping before his lordship, not quite so nice in his habits but a jolly sort," Flossie confided artlessly. Ariel envied her her cheerful ability to take life as she found it. Flossie's current uneasiness must have been inspired by more than she had told her. Whatever happened, Flossie intended to land on her feet.

"I will try to come by tomorrow, and have a suggestion or two. Arnold is not often with you during the morning, is he?" she questioned in some abstraction, pondering how this disturbing news could be handled.

"Oh, no. He's off to his office all day, I guess. Usually comes to me after supper, no earlier than tea anyway. And I thank you, ma'am. You've made me easier in my mind. I knew a smart tonnish lady like you would have an answer. Nothing starched up about you, neither, like some I might come across. You'll tell me how to go on," Flossie answered, rising and settling down her quite glaring red skirts. Like most of her class, she was more than willing to leave thorny problems in the lap of her betters. Her own assessment, not Ariel's, who quite enjoyed Flossie's down-to-earth approach. She only hoped that poor Flossie would not find herself in trouble over her confidences. Reminding her to say nothing and wait until Ariel had decided upon a course of action, she bid good-bye to the grateful woman, her spirits now restored. Ariel only wished she was as sanguine.

Ian was late arriving back in Grosvenor Square that evening, which did not help Ariel in her dilemma. She had no time to talk to him about Flossie's visit, because they were promised to the Valentines for dinner and she hesitated to tell him about Arnold on the way to the Ravensham Park Street house. She needed time to deliberate, and somehow felt she must handle this on her own. How could she tell him about her suspicions of his brother without some evidence as to his chicanery, his treachery, if that was what it was? No, she must wait until she had looked at those papers.

It was a small party at the Valentines, the other guests being Sir Robert, Sarah's grandmother acting as hostess, and a rather worldly aristocrat who was introduced as the Marquis de Lisle with his much younger wife. Ariel was surprised to see that Ian had already met the marquis, who looked a formidable man, although with the most sophisticated manners. Lady de Lisle charmed Ariel immediately with her candid openness, and enthusiasm. She was dressed in the latest stare, her sun-streaked hair and elfin features set off by an azure blue and silver silk gown, and magnificent pearls.

Ariel had not seen Robert since he had brought Fiona to apologize, and since she was fond of her cousin and grateful for his past protection, she greeted him affectionately, although she was somewhat surprised to see him at the Valentines'. She did not suspect the dinner party had been arranged at the request of the marquis, who had now joined Valentine in the quest for the agent burrowing away in the Foreign Office. Neither gentleman showed anything but the most bland courtesy to Robert, nor had they confided their doubts of his loyalty to Castlereagh. Talk around the dinner table was easy and concerned suppositions about Wellington's strategies to repulse Napoleon, and the activity of the Allies. Robert spoke of the dispositions of the Congress, and the frustration of dealing with Metternich and the Tsar, whose visit to London the year before had set the whole town on its heels.

Ariel, sitting next to Robert, said little but she was able to make a cautious inquiry about Fiona.

"Is Fiona now in the country, Robert?" she asked, not wishing to disturb the tranquillity of the conversation but wondering if her former nemesis could have arranged her abduction before she departed.

"Yes, she has been gone some three days now. I regret exceedingly that she was the instigator of your problems, Ariel, when you were under my roof, and entitled to my protection and assistance after your tragedy," Robert said gravely. He had not forgiven his lovely wife, whom heretofore he had regarded as an angel. His disillusionment caused him great pain, and for that Ariel felt only compassion.

"I think she has learned a valuable lesson, Robert, and in time your marriage will resume its felicity, all the better for the honesty now between you," Ariel suggested kindly, toying with the roast pigeons which had been put before her. "Secrets between husband and wife can only lead to trouble. I know you have forgiven her, as I have, and will be able to eventually to put her transgressions from your mind."

"That is very generous of you, my dear. And I hope your own marriage has brought you happiness and a certain amount of comfort," Robert said, a bit of anxiety in his tone as he looked across at the shuttered face of Ian.

"Ian is all that is kind and thoughtful," Ariel replied, reluctant to discuss the state of her marriage. "My worries concern his ultimate fate when Wellington takes the field. I will accompany him to Brussels. Will you be going to Belgium, Robert?"

Before Robert could do more than nod his acquiescence, the marquis asked him smoothly, "Yes, Sir Robert. I understand several of you Foreign Office men will be following the army. Is this to see that the fruits of victory are properly garnered?"

"We expect to have our problems with the Allies, and a great deal of diplomacy must be exerted, Lord de Lisle," Robert replied, giving away little.

The marquis appeared to accept this tactful answer and did not refine further on the matter, although Ariel was puzzled by his speaking glance at General Valentine. After a luscious sweet of strawberries glacé, Lady Ravensham indicated the ladies must retire and leave the gentlemen to their port, and she guided her two guests and Sarah from the dining room. In the drawing room, Ariel at once was interrogated by Lady de Lisle, whose sprightly conversation was a tonic, keeping her own concerns at bay. She wondered for a moment what the gentlemen were discussing but had little time to brood under Melissa de Lisle's questioning.

It was obvious that Melissa and Sarah were bosom bows of long standing and, unlike many of the society women Ariel had met, did not confine their talk to children, fashion, and trivial gossip. Melissa had a great deal to say about conditions in Paris, whence she had so recently fled.

"Theron was in such a pucker," she said. "I would love to have remained longer to see Napoleon himself, but of course, Theron thought his first move would be to have us incarcerated in the Bastille. Sheer nonsense, and I missed all the fun, bundled into a carriage and rushed pell-mell across France to Calais!"

"Well, you might have been in some danger. I am sure Fouché had knowledge of your past efforts to foil his espionage attempts," Sarah countered, referring to some mystery in Melissa's past.

That young woman turned to Ariel and explained. "Some years ago, when I was shockingly disporting myself on the stage, I was fortunate to discover the ring leader of a group of spies, who operated from my theater. It was a great coup," Melissa explained merrily. Then she added, "I do hope you are not shocked to be in such close contact with a former actress, not at all de rigueur I admit, but I miss the stage occasionally, and can never regret being an actress."

"Don't be a ninny, Melissa," Sarah protested, "Ariel would not find your former antics shocking. And you were in considerable danger, which you faced bravely. I will tell you of Melissa's exploits someday, Ariel. She is much too modest to reveal them herself. And her adventures caught her an excellent husband," Sarah concluded roguishly, looking askance at Melissa.

"Theron was my partner in crime and so successful was the alliance that he decided to take me on for life, a decision no doubt he sometimes regrets. I am not a conformable matron ... but then he is far from a tame benedict," Melissa added with a small laugh.

"He is a very pattern card of respectability, Melissa, and I for one knew all along he would settle with you," Sarah argued. Both women laughed at the picture of the sardonic marquis who had accepted his fate with equanimity. Ariel had no doubt the union was a happy one, but she was entranced by this view of the marquis under his petite wife's thumb. She envied both women their happiness and only wished she could claim such domestic bliss. Of course, she was not so foolish as to believe they had not both encountered many obstacles before they had settled into tranquillity, for they were both strong-minded women with ideas of their own. Their situations proved that London marriages need not be the shallow unfaithful unions she had seen since her arrival here, and the two women cheered her with the hope that her own future would be resolved so happily. The gentlemen were some time at their after-dinner conversation and Ariel could not help but wonder what they were discussing. Perhaps Ian would tell her, but they had so many other matters to settle. She must take the first opportunity to tell him about Flossie's call and see what he made of it.

At last they were able to make their adieux and return to Grosvenor Street. In the carriage, Ian appeared distracted. "Your cousin Robert is a downy bird, gives little away. He has great power at the Foreign Office, privy to all kinds of secrets. He could do great damage if that was his intention."

"You do not think Robert would betray his trust. He is the soul of honor," Ariel insisted, appalled at Ian's suggestions.

"What I think is of little account, but I believe both the marquis and Valentine view him with some wariness. He was very skillful at parrying their questions about his work." Ian thrust his hands into his pockets and his brow furrowed as he worried about this latest turn of events. "I don't want to think badly of your cousin, but he is so reserved and uncommunicative, it is possible he could be leading a clever double life."

"I'll never believe that. I am sure it is someone else."

Ian grunted and then, shaking off his unease, turned to Ariel and said whimsically, "I did not have in mind a deep discussion of affairs of state when we are alone together like this, my dear. You are a certain and very pleasant distraction from all those nasty suspicions of traitors."

Ariel blushed, realizing what he intended, and then forgot Arnold, Robert, and the looming battle as Ian gathered her skillfully in his arms and began to kiss her with those languorous caresses which banished all thoughts from her mind, leaving her a helpless victim to their mutual passions.

Chapter Twenty-seven

Ariel awoke the next morning, stretching languorously, filled with a sensuous satisfaction. Turning her head, she noticed she was alone. Ian had evidently risen early despite their late night and ardent lovemaking. She had a hazy recollection of his kissing her good morning as he left, but she was appalled to find the morning so far advanced.

Ringing for her maid, she hurried into her clothes. She must catch Ian before he left the house and tell him of Flossie's visit and her suspicions of Arnold. Much as she might want to handle this disturbing turn of events herself, she knew Ian would be angry, and justifiably so, if she kept Flossie's visit to herself. And then, too, Lufton might mention her unusual caller and Ian would require some answers. Now that their marriage seemed to be entering a new phase of warmth and intimacy, she feared to endanger this growing closeness by secrecy and deception.

Still—she smiled reminiscently to herself as Nancy arranged her hair—if he had not been so pressing in his demands last night, driving all thoughts of Flossie, Arnold, the French conspiracy, and the coming battle from her mind, she would have told him. But he had overwhelmed her with his passion, and even if it was not the love she craved, it had wrung from her a response she could not deny, and she was helpless before her own desires, which he evoked so skillfully.

She was disappointed to learn when she arrived downstairs that Ian had left over an hour ago. Only Arnold still remained and he was just setting off for the Foreign Office when Ariel descended into the hall. He greeted her sourly and replied when she asked about Ian's whereabouts, "Your eager bridegroom obviously is not so enchanted that he neglects his duty."

Troubled and undecided upon her next action, Ariel nevertheless ordered the carriage to attend her shortly and determined to see Flossie without delay. Perhaps she should wait to confide in Ian, but how much more effective it would be to present him with some solid evidence. After all, he would not welcome the news that his brother had betrayed his country, nor did Ariel want to discover that Arnold was a traitor, realizing what the disgrace would mean to them all, especially the earl, who took such pride in his family name. Perhaps she was reading more into Flossie's disclosures than was justified by the fact that Arnold seemed to have removed a few documents from the Foreign Office. However, standing here in the hall dithering would solve nothing. She must investigate Flossie's fears and put them to rest, along with her own. Not for one moment did Ariel consider that she might be exposing herself to danger, although she should have hesitated, remembering her encounter with the two toughs outside the Perkinses' dwelling some days ago. Quickly she donned her bonnet and prepared to set forth.

If she had known of Ian's earlier interview with Arnold over the breakfast table, she would not have felt so capable of solving her dilemma unaided. The two brothers, who rarely had much to say to one another without acrimony, had been alone in the dining room, the earl having had his meal and departed to his club, when Arnold tendered his suggestion to Ian.

"I do not suppose you are foolish enough to think that your wife is a paragon of virtue, brother," Arnold said, eyeing Ian derisively as he ate his way steadily through a hefty beefsteak with unimpaired appetite. So accustomed to Arnold's jibes was Ian that at first he did not take in the slur upon Ariel.

Arnold, chagrined that he had not produced a rise from his brother, continued. "I happen to know what Castlereagh requested of the pair of you, as well as the reason for this extraordinary marriage. Come, admit it, Ian, you would never have become leg-shackled to such a one if there had not been an overriding reason which had nothing to do with a sudden passion. Fiona told me Sir Robert discovered you in Ariel's bedroom and insisted upon the vows and that suited Castlereagh well, too." Arnold spoke with such assurance that Ian realized it would be pointless to deny his reading of the affair, but he was not about to confide in his brother. Let him think what he pleased, but he would allow no criticism of Ariel. She deserved better than that, and Arnold had best hold his acid tongue.

Ian's expression was bland and none of the anger he felt showed in his silky tone when he replied to his brother's taunts. "I had no idea you listened to the idle gossip of silly women, Arnold. Haven't you learned you should not believe all you hear? I am completely satisfied with Ariel as my wife," he countered while calmly finishing his meal.

But Arnold was not to be put off by Ian's artless reply. He had prepared his campaign of distrust carefully and hurried to put it in play. "I always told you that your bedroom exploits would lead you into trouble. And you have been fairly caught, whatever you claim. What do you really know about your precious bride, anyway?"

"All I need to, Arnold, and a great deal more than you do. You have been misled by Fiona, a jealous and spiteful woman with her own ends to serve. Her own conduct deserves examination, loath as I am to gossip about any woman. Poor Fiona has received the ultimate punishment of her sins, banishment from the ton." Ian smiled a bit grimly. He was within an ace of losing his temper, and he knew how futile that would be in dealing with Arnold's innuendos. But he would entertain none of his brother's dirty suspicions against Ariel. He wondered what inspired Arnold's spite, but suspected that Ariel's discovery of his association with Flossie had overset him, and he was taking this opportunity to thwart any disclosures she intended making. How little he understood Ariel. She would never undertake to destroy the earl's faith in his eldest son nor cause Harriet further discomfort just to reveal Arnold's perfidy, but then his brother was apt to judge others by his own narrow circumscribed standards. To Arnold, exposure as an adulterous husband, the opposite of all he proclaimed, would be a horrifying event and he would do his best to diffuse the information before it could harm his consequence or, more important, his expectations from his father. The estate was entailed but the earl's considerable personal wealth, much of it a legacy from his wife, could be willed as he pleased.

"All you know is that Ariel is Sir Robert's cousin," Arnold persisted. "You do not know what she was up to during those years following her father about the Peninsula, a hardening experience for a gently bred woman, but she seemed to enjoy it. She speaks French very well, and has other talents. She could have been enlisted in the French cause for she certainly was left destitute on her father's death and probably at a desperate pass when Sir Robert fortuitously came upon her."

"Are you insinuating that Ariel became one of Fouché's agents or that she became a light-skirt?

By God, you deserve to be horsewhipped!" Ian rose, his temper thoroughly aroused by Arnold's insinuations. He was only prevented from giving Arnold the pasting he deserved by the entrance of the parlor maid to clear the table. He waited impatiently for her to leave, and then dragged his brother to his feet and shook him soundly.

"I will have no more of your nasty attempts to smear Ariel's reputation, and if this conversation is ever repeated outside this room, I will make you pay dearly for it." Ian turned from his brother in disgust. "There is nothing I would like better than to take you on in a fight, Arnold, but I doubt it would be much of a contest. You are adept at attacking women but a coward when your own safety is threatened. But I won't have you casting slurs upon my wife. You would be wise to heed my words." And before his brother could reply, Ian strode from the room, rage in every lineament. So frightening was his aspect that Lufton, hearing him shout for his phaeton, hurried silently to do his bidding. Lufton was no stranger to quarrels between the brothers and he believed that this time Master Arnold had nearly driven his younger brother's mercurial temper over the edge. Just as well that the captain would take out his anger on his horses, although he was a bang-up driver and not apt to use his cattle thus.

In the dining room, Arnold sat back, smiling craftily. Well, he had planted a seed of doubt in that arrogant devil's mind which would keep him thoroughly out of sorts for the day, and thus distracted from Arnold's own affairs.

But in this, as always, Arnold had misjudged his brother. While driving off to his regimental duties with the first flush of his rage cooling, Ian began to examine Arnold's insinuations with a more reasoned approach to the matter. Did Arnold really suspect Ariel of being a French agent or did he offer that merely to rouse his brother to such a state that he would overlook Arnold's own culpabilities? As for his intimation that Ariel had shared her favors with other men before Ian had arrived on the scene, he was certainly in a position to dispute that canard. He knew, only too well, her hesitation in consummating their marriage, her distrust of his own past libertine ways, and the virginity he had taken so roughly, before she finally complied with his demands. Not complied exactly, Ian admitted with a reminiscent chuckle, but enthusiastically joined him in the pleasures of the marriage bed. He had no regrets on that score. But satisfied as the memories of their mutual passion made him, he did not entirely forget Arnold's accusations. He trusted Ariel, but what disturbed him was Arnold's motivation for such lies. Here was a situation with overtones he could not decipher.

It was a troubled man who eventually wheeled his phaeton into the barracks and prepared to assume his military duties, hoping to banish the doubts and questions which that strange interview with Arnold had awakened.

While Ian was attempting to concentrate on the

training and the marshaling of his troops, Ariel prepared to fulfill her promise to Flossie. Completing her toilette and dismissing her maid, she looked at herself critically in the mirror. Yes, she had dressed with circumspection for this meeting, in a rather severe teal blue redingote faced in a darker blue with a matching poke bonnet which lacked any frivolous adornment. Taking up her reticule, she hesitated. Surely she would not require that protection! Then, remembering Arnold's face, she shook her head and crossed to her bureau, rummaging beneath a pile of kerchiefs for a small pistol. Her father had given it to her years ago when they were with the army in Spain. Not only had he insisted she carry it with her always—the threat of brigands, French troops, and other undesirables making it necessary—but he had taught her to use it. She was a skilled shot, and she concealed the gun in her reticule before embarking resolutely on her distasteful errand.

Arriving at Hookam's Lending Library, she dismissed the coachman, telling the man she would be meeting a friend who would drive her home. John, the coachman, reluctant to accede to these orders in view of what had happened previously to his mistress, grudgingly agreed. After all, the library was in a safe and unexceptional section of London, not prey to footpads or unsavory types who frequented the environs of the Perkinses' lodgings. She should come to no harm here, but Mrs. Montague was much too independent to suit his taste and he feared the captain would have his head if aught happened to

378

her. Still, he had no choice but to do as he was told. Shaking his grizzled head in disgust at the perversity of women, he returned to Grosvenor Street. Waiting until he was out of sight, Ariel walked to the end of the street and hailed a hackney, which brought her smartly to Flossie's rooms.

That dispirited woman greeted her less than enthusiastically. She had been having second thoughts about the situation which had impelled her to make that visit yesterday to Grosvenor Street. She enjoyed the comfort that Arnold supplied, and was too easygoing to bestir herself to find another protector, who might prove less generous and less accommodating in the boudoir. Flossie above all was practical, and it seemed now the height of folly to jeopardize her future by implying that Arnold was up to some chicanery, not that Flossie for one moment suspected how serious her suspicions could be. To give her her due, if she believed that her protector was betraying his duty, she would be appalled and disgusted, for she had a reverent view of King and country. All these thoughts muddled together in her mind made her reception of Ariel rather less warm than was her wont.

"I've been athinkin, Mrs. Montague, maybe I were a mite hasty in comin' to see you yesterday," Flossie said in some perplexity, fearing she had entered deep waters and not knowing how to extricate herself. "Arnie came round last night and seemed just as usual."

Ariel, understanding the woman's problem,

and with some knowledge of how her mind must be scurrying back and forth, hastened to reassure her. She removed her pelisse and gloves slowly, while marshaling her arguments. Then she turned and faced Flossie resolutely, hoping to impress upon her the seriousness of the matter, without driving her into a frenzy of apprehension.

"Listen closely, Flossie, to what I tell you. You did the proper thing in approaching me about your suspicions of these papers. Naturally, you are fond of Lord Montague and would hate to feel he was doing something against the law, but you cannot continue in this uncertainty. If you will trust me, we can unravel this coil and I promise, if our suspicions are unfounded, I will say nothing about them, and you can continue as you were before." Ariel wondered all the while if this was possible, for whatever the outcome, she doubted that Flossie would enjoy Arnold's protection for many more days.

Flossie frowned, her rouged cheeks creased in perplexity. She was not sure she understood all that Ariel was hinting, but she knew one thing— her life with Arnold was threatened and she might be forced back into the far more arduous situation of the pub, or even worse. Flossie had few illusions about the fate of an unprotected female, and knowledge that would shock this cosseted female. But she would never expose her fears about the rough fate awaiting her to Mrs. Montague, who had been all that was kind—not critical and disdainful as she could have been. She had kept her mouth buttoned, too, about Arnold and her, and for that she was grateful. After all, she needn't have gone to Grosvenor Street and asked for her help, a dangerous maneuver, for Arnie would have a fit if that ever came out. Reluctantly she conceded she would have to give Mrs. Montague whatever information she wanted, no matter that it was the ruin of her own hopes.

"Are the papers still here? Lord Montague has not removed them?" Ariel asked with some trepidation, for it had occurred to her that he might have done just that and then all her pains to make this secret visit would be for nothing.

"No, ma'am, they are still here in this desk, where he put them and warned me to leave them alone. I think the drawer is locked," Flossie added gloomily, half hoping this would put an end to the matter.

Ariel impatiently crossed to the indicated desk and tugged at the appropriate drawer. It was, indeed, locked. Now what could she do? Dare she break it open? She must see those papers.

"Have you any key which might fit this drawer, Flossie?"

"I might, ma'am, but perhaps we had best leave it," Flossie suggested with little hope of Ariel's agreeing.

"Now that we have embarked on this, we must see it to the end. Try and find some keys, and I will attempt to jiggle the lock with this hat pin," Ariel insisted, suiting her action to the words.

Sighing, Flossie turned to the mantel and, delving about, came up with a clutch of various-sized keys, which she offered reluctantly to Ariel.

Quickly trying several of the keys, Ariel muttered as each attempt was defeated, but finally the fifth key turned the lock gratingly. Ariel pulled out the drawer and extracted a bundle of heavy parchment leaves tied together with a red ribbon. Hurriedly unrolling the papers, she gasped at the title *A L'Empereur Napoleon Bonaparte*. Prepared as she was to find some damning evidence, she could still hardly believe what this signified. Turning to Flossie, she said, "You were right in your anxiety, Flossie, and as a loyal English subject you have acted bravely. Now I must study these papers, and make a true copy of some of the information. Can you find me pen and ink?" Ariel was driven by an uneasy feeling that time was pressing and she must accomplish her task and be away or find herself in an untenable, even dangerous position.

Chapter Twenty-eight

As Ariel, whose French was fluent, rapidly scanned the pages before her, she immediately grasped the diabolical cleverness of the strategy set out in the document. The author, who signed himself merely *Un Citoyen*, suggested that the outcome of the battle which would decide Napoleon's fate must turn on the support Marshal Blucher and his veteran troops might offer to Wellington. If Blucher's battalions could be subverted, or even delayed in the march to join Wellington, events would favor Napoleon. An observer did not need to be a spy to understand the importance of Blucher to Wellington's strategy. Without the Prussians, the Iron Duke would be vastly outnumbered and in danger of defeat, so any plan to thwart the juncture of the two armies would rebound in Napoleon's interest. If such a plan proved successful, the whole face of Europe could be changed. And the diagram for this treachery had been drawn in the British Foreign Office.

Marshal Blucher, an able if brutal commander, had never been popular with either his countrymen or his troops, although he was admired by fellow generals for his grasp of tactics and his courage. But he was vulnerable through his personal life, and here is where he would be rendered immobile, Ariel determined from the infamous design. He would be challenged to a duel in defense of a woman's honor on the eve of his scheduled march to join Wellington, and such were the demands of the code that he would answer the challenge or be disgraced. Thus either the battle would be fought without Blucher's troops or they would be commanded by a man who would undoubtedly lack Blucher's skill and determination. In either case it should prove a decisive blow to the Allies's cause.

The torturous mind which could conceive such a fell design shocked Ariel, but she had no difficulty in understanding the importance of the plan and what it might mean to the men who would fight that battle. And Ian would be among them, his life further endangered by treachery beyond the normal risks a soldier must expect. A storm of rage arose in Ariel, and she could barely restrain her shaking fingers to copy the evidence of this perfidy when Flossie brought her the writing materials. Who was the author of this plot? She could not believe that any Englishman could connive to bring about the deaths of his countrymen with such sangfroid. And who could he be? Only with the greatest difficulty did Ariel face the fact that the unknown *Citoyen* might be

Arnold himself. Perhaps he had discovered these papers and decided to track down the villain alone before unmasking him to his superiors, but somehow Ariel could not accept this explanation.

Knowing Arnold, she had little doubt that he would rush the news of such an infamous scheme to his chief, thereby earning plaudits for his cleverness and the gratitude of all concerned. That Arnold might be revealed as a master of deception, Ariel conceded, was the likelier explanation. On the evidence she had already unearthed, he had managed to act a role with great ingenuity. He had deceived his father with his spouting of Puritan morality while conducting a liaison for more than a year. Practicing an equal deception on his chiefs at the Foreign Office would not challenge his acting abilities. To her horror, Ariel found herself coming around to the view that Arnold was indeed the traitor she, Ian, Castlereagh, and many others had been searching for all this time. And now, within weeks of a great battle which would decide the fate of Europe, England's efforts to mount an effective attack were being undermined by one of the most privileged members of its society.

If Arnold had been a Luddite, one of those poor wretches thrown out of work by the rise of new machines, or a starving farm worker, or even a committed political radical, Ariel might have summoned some sympathy for his betrayal, but he had enjoyed all the perquisites of wealth and position. He, of all men, should never have been lured into treachery. What could impel him to such a pass? As she copied swiftly, Ariel kept reminding herself that she still had no proof that Arnold was the culprit. He might still be able to offer a credible story to explain the presence of these damning documents. So engrossed was she in her work, and the confused thoughts crowding her mind, that she paid little attention to Flossie, who was agitatedly pacing up and down the room, muttering to herself, urging Ariel to hurry with her task. Finally, Flossie's restless behavior disturbed Ariel's concentration. She looked up from her writing.

"Whatever is the matter, Flossie? Must you pace back and forth so? It is very distracting," Ariel complained.

"I don't like it, ma'am. I should never have got into this. It ain't right. And I have a fluttery feeling. I get that sometimes. It's a warning, you see. My ma had the second sight."

"Don't be ridiculous, Flossie. You have told me that Arnold never comes near you until at least teatime, and it is scarce gone noon now. And let me remind you that you have done your country a great service in this whole affair. Very important work."

Preening herself at the thought of her role, Flossie did appear conciliated for the moment. She stopped her restless pacing, trying to settle herself into a chair, but within minutes she was up again, crossing to the window and looking out into the street.

"Do hurry up, ma'am," Flossie urged. "I just have this idea that we might be surprised, get into all sorts of difficulty. Arnie can be quite nasty if he is annoyed."

"Well, I am more than annoyed, if what I suspect about him is true. He will have some very difficult questions to answer when I place this evidence before the proper authorities," Ariel replied with some asperity. She felt a certain compassion for Flossie, whose welfare would be affected by the outcome of this affair, but Flossie must simply be sacrificed to the greater good. Ariel had made up her mind to do what she could for the poor woman, but she had no intention of suppressing this information to protect Flossie when so many other lives were endangered.

Finally, she sighed, stood up, and carefully arranged the documents back into their original order, tied them with the red ribbon which had bound them, and looked at the bundle critically. She hoped it did not look as if it had been tampered with, but perhaps it didn't matter now. Arnold would be too busy explaining his role in this affair to wonder who had brought his treachery to the attention of those who would question him. Ariel frowned. The scandal would be painful, if what she believed turned out to be true, and there would be little any of them could do to minimize it. Not only Flossie, but the Earl, Harriet, Ian, all of them would suffer from the odium attached to a revealed traitor.

Ariel stood indecisively for a moment, the documents in her hand, hearing nothing, sunk in her disturbing thoughts, when she was aroused from her study by Flossie's sudden exclamation.

"Oh, my God, it's him. It's Arnie. He's just come through the door," she moaned. And before Ariel could rally her defenses, he strode into the room, his eyes drawn immediately to the documents in her hands.

"Just as I expected!" Arnold sneered. "You have been meddling in my affairs. Well, I have had enough of you, dear sister-in-law. Ever since your untimely marriage to my rake of a brother, you have been a problem. No doubt he will be glad to see the end of you, as I will."

"And what do you mean by that?" Ariel asked, determined not to be cowed by his pointed threats. He had abandoned all pretense now, because he realized that evasion and lies would no longer serve. She suspected he had no intention of letting her free to expose his double life, his treachery, but she refused to let him see how frightened she was. She realized that there was little chance of anyone coming to her aid, for no one knew where she was. But perhaps she might contrive to escape with Flossie's help.

Looking at that poor woman, Ariel could almost have laughed at her expression, if her situation had not been so grave. Flossie had backed away from Arnold in horror, wide-eyed and pale as the realization of what he implied toward Ariel had become apparent. Arnold ignored her, his whole concentration on Ariel.

She quickly decided she had little to lose by confronting him now. "Why have you betrayed your country, Arnold?" Ariel asked boldly.

"What do you care, dear sister-in-law? I had

good and sufficient reasons," Arnold replied, eyeing her complacently, knowing he had the upper hand.

"There is never a good and sufficient reason for treason. And you had a great deal to lose—your position, your father's regard, and a fortune," Ariel said, hoping to goad him into justifying himself. In turn, perhaps he would expose others who had been his co-conspirators. Although it seemed unlikely that she would ever be in a position to reveal her knowledge. Reading his character with some perspicacity, she felt he might be persuaded to boast of his achievements, and any way of delaying him from what he intended to do to her would give her some time to plan an escape. She must try to enlist Flossie's help, but that poor woman looked incapable of initiating any action, so overwhelmed was she by Arnold's changed demeanor, and Ariel suspected she had little idea of what was at stake.

Ariel was correct in her judgment of Arnold. He was only too eager to explain and excuse his perfidy, for he felt he had been persecuted and unappreciated. That was obvious.

"My wealth and prestige? My sainted father is a cheeseparing old fool. He has never given me my due, forcing me into marriage with that poor dowd and blaming me for not producing an heir. I tried to conform to his expectations, but whatever I did, it was never enough. Your gallant husband, despite his sins, was always held up to me as an example of a true Strathcairn. Laughable, isn't it?"

Ariel protested, "You know your father preferred you to Ian, Arnold, so that is not a fair assessment. The earl despised Ian's libertine ways and judged him hardly, which you did nothing to lessen, I might add. Ian is your brother but you seem to hate him."

"Yes, I do hate him. He has always gone his own way, paid no attention to the governor's admonitions, enjoyed all the vices, and never paid a farthing for his pleasures. While I was playing the dutiful son and husband, and what did I get for my obedience—contempt and a pitiful reward for my compliance," he ranted, thoroughly aroused by his fancied slights.

Ariel realized that Arnold was in the grip of an insidious jealousy that had festered and grown from childhood, and now in the relief of speaking his true feelings, he was abandoning all caution. If only she could keep him talking. She looked at Flossie, hoping Arnold's mistress might be so appalled by these revelations of her protector's true character that she would protest his intentions toward Ariel. She tried to gauge Flossie's reactions but the woman seemed stunned, a silent spectator to Arnold's surprising disclosures.

Once begun on his explanations, Arnold could not halt the spate of confession. "You want to know why I accepted Fouché's commission to supply Napoleon with information? Well, I will tell you, since you will never be able to reveal what you know. I will see to that," he promised, smiling evilly as Flossie gasped a protest. He turned to her, having paid little attention to his mistress since he had entered the room.

"And I want no nonsense from you, Flossie. You are hardly in a position to make trouble, eager as you were to accept my protection and the comforts I offered, for which I admit you paid in good coin. But do not rely on my good nature any longer, my dear. You will be silent about whatever takes place in this room, or I will see you pay as well as my dear sister-in-law. You were much too willing to confide in her, Flossie, and that could be the biggest mistake of your life." Arnold glowered at the woman, who had offered no demur to his previous behavior but, now that she found herself threatened, showed her true mettle.

"Don't talk so to me, Arnie. You are worse than the meanest beggar in Whitechapel, murderers and thieves they may be, but none of them would sell out their King to a monster like Napoleon, and to threaten a nice lady like Miss Ariel here. You must be crazy," she argued stoutly.

Arnold crossed the room to Flossie and hit her brutally across the cheek, sending her reeling. "Hold your tongue, and don't speak about what you cannot understand. You will do what I bid or it will be the worse for you. Now, leave us. I have some unfinished business with my dear sister-in-law, which need not concern you."

Massaging her bruised cheek, Flossie backed from the room, her eyes going in supplication to Ariel as if to beg her indulgence for abandoning the fight. Ariel would be forced to deal with Arnold as best she could, but she had no intention of appealing to him to spare her. She had too much

391

pride and self-respect to beg before such a traitor. Ariel straightened her back and stared forthrightly at her enemy.

"You are a fool as well as a knave, Arnold. You can murder me but that will not save you. Do you think that Ian or General Valentine, even Lord Castlereagh, are unaware of your treachery? This very moment they are preparing to unmask the renegade whose evil work they have at last discovered," she bravely bluffed, lying in the hope of oversetting his confidence.

"Don't try that flummery with me, madam. I have been much too clever for them all. And after I have disposed of you, I will be off to a secure place where I will receive the honors and appreciation I deserve!"

"And where will that be? At Napoleon's side in France? Don't be deceived, Arnold. Wellington will soon put the Corsican down, and you will be defeated with him. But perhaps that is not your plan, to put yourself in the way of that kind of danger," she jeered, hoping to shake him into more disclosures.

"I have no thought of joining that madman. I have perfected my schemes and will be lazing in the sun while Napoleon and Wellington fight it out in Belgium, and stupid glory-chasers like your Ian face shot and shell. I am too clever for them all." He shook off his temporary gratification at that picture of the future and turned to her, obviously no longer willing to postpone dealing with this trifling obstacle to his successful future. He found himself staring down the barrel of the formidable pistol Ariel was holding.

"I do not intend to allow you to dispose of me so tidily, Arnold. Surely you did not think I would come to such a meeting unprepared. I rather think your position is not as enviable as you believe," she said, looking at him levelly over the pistol. "I am no stranger to firearms, having had recourse to my own defense when I accompanied my father to Spain. I promise you I know how to use this if I have to," she finished grimly.

"And she will, depend on that, Arnold," said a familiar voice into the weighted silence. Ian had entered the room quietly behind Arnold's back. "Let me relieve you of that, my dear, and then we can all be comfortable while I hear what Arnold has to say about this unfortunate contretemps." Ian accepted the pistol, which Ariel thankfully surrendered, sending her a warning glance which reduced her to silence. For the moment she was too grateful to wonder how he had learned of her danger and come to her aid. Dealing with Arnold was of paramount importance. Her own questions could wait. She subsided exhaustedly into a chair by the fire, as Ian leaned negligently against the desk, his hand steady on the pistol as he waited to hear his brother's explanations.

Chapter Twenty-nine

For a few fraught moments no one spoke. Ian watched his brother passively, and Ariel could not tell what her husband was thinking. He did not exhibit shock or disgust or any expected emotion. Surely he was horrified to discover that not only was his brother a traitor but he had threatened his own wife. Perhaps the latter possibility did not disturb him as much, Ariel thought cynically.

Arnold considered his brother with a thoughtful stare, wondering just how much he knew. Ian said nothing, obviously waiting for Arnold to speak, and finally Arnold lost the duel of silence.

"There is no reason why I should explain my actions to you, Ian," he sneered, his eyes on the pistol as if judging its menace.

"Rather me than Valentine's interrogators or the Tower. They will not be very tolerant, I assure you." His voice was bland and emotionless, but he did not lower the gun, and continued to eye

Arnold with steely purpose.

"You misunderstood the situation. I lost my temper, because your dear wife drove me to excess with her persistent meddling in my affairs. I just wanted to frighten her off," Arnold blustered, wondering if he could bluff through this frightful coil. And, indeed, his chief anger was directed at Ariel for he firmly believed she was the source of all his troubles.

"I do not frighten easily," Ariel said, "and you cannot believe for one moment that Ian will accept that most specious of arguments."

"I am sure Arnold has learnt to his cost that you are a veritable tiger, my dear, in pursuit of justice," Ian said smoothly, without turning his head from his steady and unblinking view of his brother. Ariel decided she would be wise to make no further interruptions. Ian's cold, forbidding stance repelled any attempts on her part to enter the discussion. His whole attention was centered on Arnold and it was obvious he would not be fobbed off with anything but the truth. She waited, holding her breath, as not a muscle in Ian's taut body moved. Just so he must have looked before leading his men over the ramparts in Spain. He made a formidable enemy, and Arnold had best realize it.

"Ariel discovered my liaison with Flossie here," Arnold began, "and she has been making capital of it. Then she stuck her nose into my papers, for what reason God only knows, but I believe she had blackmail in mind. And now your sainted wife is willing to sell the information in those documents to the French!" So assured was Arnold in his statements that Ariel shuddered. What if Ian accepted his fictional version of her presence here? For a moment she was truly frightened, despite her boast, clenching her hands together and biting her lips to keep from shouting her denial of Arnold's canard.

"You must take me for a fool, Arnold. Try another tale, and I suggest it be the true one this time. I suspect you know very well that Castlereagh and Valentine have enlisted us in this effort to unmask the spy who has been exposing all our secrets to Napoleon. I have had suspicions of many, but it never occurred to me that my own brother was the culprit. Why, for God's sake, Arnold, did you stoop so low?" Ian demanded bitterly, his emotions at last rising to the surface.

Arnold flushed, but then turned on his brother in a veritable passion. "How easy for you, brother, to make a judgment, the noble, courageous and gallant officer content to risk all for King and country even unto giving up his vaunted freedom in a marriage of convenience on the orders of his superiors," he taunted.

If his barbs reached their target, Ian gave no sign of it. He continued his searching gaze at his brother, in no way discomposed by Arnold's assessment of his character and situation. If Ian remained unaffected, Ariel felt Arnold's poison, for his knowledge of their marriage was too near the actuality for comfort. But Ian did not intend to justify himself, recognizing Arnold's attempts to throw dissension between them and distract Ian from learning the truth.

"I may have indulged in a whole list of vices, Arnold, but I have never considered the ultimate infamy of betraying my country. And I cannot understand how you were tempted. Surely you put so much at risk for so little. What could the French offer you?" he asked, as if truly puzzled by this behavior of his brother.

"Money, lots of it, and respect, which I have never received from my family or my countrymen. I should be Foreign Minister, not that rigid popinjay, Castlereagh. My talents are far surpassing his, but Liverpool is besotted by the man. And what has he done in Vienna but antagonize our Allies, and treat the French and Talleyrand with arrogant stupidity? I would have handled matters far more diplomatically," he concluded, his rampant egotism and sense of ill-usage erupting with a sullen force which surprised Ariel. She had no idea that Arnold nurtured such a welter of disappointed hopes in his breast, and could he really think he rivaled Castlereagh in intelligence and experience? Obviously Arnold had hidden his true colors from the world and beguiled them all with his cloak of obedient propriety.

"So now that you know that I am the famous traitor you have been seeking so fruitlessly, what do you intend to do about it, brother?" Arnold said softly.

"I should turn you over to the authorities forthwith, but I am not sure that is the best solution. There is the disgrace, which neither Harriet nor the governor deserves, and other factors," Ian brooded, for the first time seeming uncertain. Then he shook off his unease, and turned to Ariel.

"I think it would be best, my dear, to allow Arnold and me to continue this discussion in private. Perhaps you might seek out the much-tried Flossie and see what assistance you can render," he said with some severity, his coldness disappointing Ariel, but she tried to make allowances, knowing how this news must have undone him. As if he followed her thoughts and realized the brusqueness of his words, he crossed to her side, carefully keeping his eye and his pistol on Arnold, and gave her a reassuring hug. "You have been a brave, clever girl, and I promise to make it up to you, all the unhappiness you have suffered from the Montagues, but please oblige me now and leave us." He smiled gently, realizing how much the revelation of Arnold's treachery and his accusations against her had alarmed her. "I trust you, Ariel, and you must return the compliment. I know it goes against your instincts to play the obedient wife, but I am afraid that is the role you must adopt in this." He tried to reassure her with a light touch but Ariel was not deceived, and only the warm and tender light in his eyes, an expression she had rarely seen in his usually shuttered face, persuaded her to accede to his request. When Ian looked at her thus, she could deny him nothing.

"All right, Ian, but I intend to have an explanation of your part in this—how you came to my rescue, and how you knew that Arnold might be our spy."

"I promise we will have a long heartfelt talk when this is over," he said as he bowed her out the door.

Ariel left in a welter of feeling, wondering about that last expression in his eyes. But she was a selfish dunce to be caviling about her own position when so much else was at risk. She resolutely banished all thoughts of the future and sought out Flossie, who was cowering in her bedroom, crying bitterly at the downfall of her world. Ariel did her best to offer comfort.

"I am so sorry, Flossie, that you have been caught in the middle of this dreadful situation. You deserve better of life. Your own generous spirit and true sense of patriotism led you to expose Arnold and it is not fair that you should have to suffer for it. I intend to see that you receive your due. We have cause to be grateful to you. Now come, let me bathe your face with this eau de cologne. That will take the sting from the bruise." Ariel soothed her sobbing companion while administering aid, for Arnold had truly given her a brutal blow and a livid bruise was rising on Flossie's plump reddened cheek, now considerably paler.

"The deceitful cad, behaving in such a way, and to think all this time he had me in keeping he was betraying us all. It doesn't bear thinking about," Flossie sniffed, somewhat comforted by Ariel's ministrations.

"Then don't think about it, Flossie, but try to have faith in a brighter day. Perhaps an income

400

will allow you to give up this life and become more respectable," Ariel suggested, trying to subdue all personal concerns in her efforts to bring Flossie about to a happier view, but her attention was distracted. She could not but worry about what was passing between the two brothers in the sitting room below.

"I would like to live in a country town, in Wiltshire, that's where I come from, you know. I have always dreamed of running a shop, but every time I get a bit put by, then hard times overtakes me, and I have to cough up the blunt," Flossie explained, drying her eyes and looking critically at herself in the glass. Despite her bruise and general dishevelment, which she was trying to correct, she appeared more cheerful at the thought that she might benefit from this whole dreadful affair, and in a way she could never have expected.

Ariel, envying Flossie's sangfroid and her ability to look at the more practical advantages of her dilemma, wished that she, too, could contemplate the future with such equanimity. She pushed the problems of what Ian wanted from her into the furthermost recesses of her mind. She would not begin to fret over them. She busied herself helping Flossie put herself to rights, and made an effort to chat cheerfully about Flossie's long-dreamed-of shop and the beauties of Wiltshire. Suddenly their conversation was interrupted by the unmistakable sound of a shot coming from beneath them.

"Oh, my God, what was that?" Flossie cried,

startled out of her reverie.

"I greatly fear it was a shot. I will go and see," Ariel offered. She could not put a name to her fears although Flossie sensed Ariel's unease and followed closely behind her down the stairs. As they approached the hall, the door to the sitting room opened and Ian appeared, shutting the door firmly behind him.

Ariel ran to him, her eyes wide with relief and questions tumbling from her lips. His answer was to take her in his arms with reassuring gentleness, holding her safely.

"It's all right, Ariel. There has been an accident, and I fear Arnold is dead. Now, be a good girl and wait upstairs with Mistress Baines. I have much business to clear up and will be occupied here for a time. I promise we will come about and all will be for the best," he explained gently, his arms sheltering her as she shuddered from the reaction to her terror.

"I thought it was you who was shot. I was so afraid," she stuttered.

"Now where is my valiant companion in arms? I am depending on your usual good sense, my dear, to help us solve this tragic situation. I know you won't disappoint me." Ariel noticed that beneath his calmness lurked strong emotions which he was barely controlling. How selfish of her to act the vaporish ninny, when he relied on her for good sense and courage. She would not fail him.

"Yes, of course, Ian. I will wait upstairs. Come along, Flossie. We are just adding to the confusion here." She turned toward the stairs and the waiting woman, comforted by the gleam of admiration and relief in Ian's eyes. She had a suspicion that Arnold's death was Ian's answer to the scandal which could affect them all. She must simply control her impatience until he could make all clear to her.

Several hours later, as the afternoon darkened into an early dusk, Ariel was still waiting, but this time in the privacy of her bedroom at Montague House. She had brought the tearful Flossie with her, to Lufton's dismay, and in other circumstances she could have enjoyed his confusion over the introduction of such a guest into a proper gentleman's household.

Under Ariel's orders, he had whisked her away to the housekeeper's wing, where Ariel hoped she was being kindly treated. She had advised Flossie to say nothing to the servants about her relationship with Arnold or the recent tragic events which had terminated it. She hoped the woman saw the wisdom of this advice and abided by it. But Flossie had a healthy ability to recover from disaster, and clinging to the promise of that dreamed-of shop, she promised that her lips were sealed. What explanation she would offer for her appearance in Grosvenor Street under Mrs. Montague's wing, Ariel could not imagine, but that did not concern her overmuch.

Ariel paced back and forth, shivering with cold although a bright fire blazed in the grate, throwing out substantial warmth into the room.

Several times she walked to the windows which overlooked the street, hoping to see some sign of Ian's arrival, although she knew she could not expect him soon. He had sent her home with Flossie in a hackney summoned by a mysterious man who guarded the entrance to the house in St. John's Wood, and she had passed the closed door of the sitting room on her way out with averted eyes. She could not bear to think of what had happened behind that door. Ian had kissed her passionately, seeking comfort and help from the embrace, which she had willingly given him, but then he had put her into the carriage and reentered the house to whatever dreadful matters confronted him there.

That had been more than four hours ago, and Ariel had heard nothing. She felt only relief that neither the earl nor Harriet had been home when she arrived with Flossie, because she could not have borne explaining her visitor and the past hours' events to either of them, although they would both have to learn of Arnold's treachery. Ariel suffered for these two innocent victims of Arnold's brutal and selfish greed, his egotism, and his complete indifference to the father and the wife who deserved his loyalty.

Finally, Ariel's patience was rewarded. A parlor maid entered her bedroom and requested that she join the family in the drawing room, as Captain Montague had just returned and had asked for her.

Ariel sighed with irritation. Would she never be alone with Ian to hear the real story? Then she chided herself for placing her own worries and doubts first. Naturally, he had to make some explanation to his father and to Harriet, and he needed her support in that painful duty. She hurried downstairs and met the trio, who turned at her entrance and viewed her gravely. For a moment Ariel felt like an intruder in the face of this common grief, but then Ian crossed to her side and, taking her hand, squeezed it gently.

"Come, Ariel, sit down. I have just told Father and Harriet of Arnold's accident. But they have many questions and I need your support to answer them." His voice was gentle, but his eyes flashed a warning and Ariel understood she must follow his lead. He would want to spare Harriet and the earl as much pain as possible and she girded herself for the inevitable shock and dismay.

She looked at Harriet, who was sitting quietly on the settee, her head bent, more composed than Ariel had expected. The earl was scowling fiercely, his bandaged foot stuck grotesquely at an angle, his head half turned from her as if ashamed to meet her gaze. How tragic for the old man, to hear such hideous facts about his elder son and heir. And had Ian told him the truth?

Chapter Thirty

"You see, Father, Ariel and I were not completely honest with you about our hurried marriage and return from Vienna. We had been requested by Castlereagh to discover if Ariel's connections by marriage, the Villefranches, were involved in a spy ring which had caused grave harm to our concerns, including the plotting of several attempts on Wellington's life," Ian explained, watching his father closely. He stood before the fireplace, his hands clasped behind his back in the challenging pose to which Ariel had become accustomed. Both the earl and Harriet regarded him somberly and did not interrupt. Ariel sensed that they both understood the gravity of his confidences and were loath to question him until he had completed his tale.

"Ariel did unmask the Villefranches but their conniving was not the main issue. The comte and comtesse were merely playing at espionage, although they did do considerable damage. They

407

have been thoroughly leashed now and sent back to France, where their fate will not be a happy one, punishment enough you might say. But the chief traitor still eluded us. We had some evidence that the man was high up in the Foreign Office, as, indeed, he proved to be, but I am not at liberty to tell you who he is. Valentine insists the whole affair be kept as secret as possible, and of course, I am under his orders," Ian insisted sternly, implying he would entertain no further inquiries on the man's identity.

Ariel approved of his protecting the earl and Harriet in this manner, but wondered how he would explain Arnold's death. She did not wonder for long, for Ian continued with his ingenious story.

"Arnold necessarily became involved in the investigation, and was present at the final unmasking of the traitor. Indeed, he arrived at the scene of the man's hidey-hole in St. John's Wood ahead of me, and in the ensuing struggle he was shot and killed before I could intervene. I deeply regret telling you this news, for I know what Arnold meant to you, Governor, and that he always behaved in a manner which won your approval, which I, alas, was far from doing," Ian concluded somewhat bitterly.

How kind and clever of Ian to hit upon such an explanation of Arnold's death, designed to spare his sister-in-law and father disgrace. Ariel remembered her father telling her that if one was forced to lie, it was best to adhere as closely as possible to the truth for elaborate fictions were usually exposed. Ian evidently agreed, for his story of Arnold's death was a masterly combination of truth and evasion. Ariel would never have expected him to contrive such a deception. But it had not been easy for him, she realized, noticing the drawn look on his face and the desperate appeal in his eyes as he turned to her as if seeking comfort. She answered his entreaty with silence, but she hoped he understood her approval and support.

The earl, responding with all the discipline and nobility which had been bred in him from generations of aristocrats, answered his son gruffly. "Thank you for telling us, Ian. I know you and your brother never loved each other, but this tragedy is a terrible blow. We can only accept it by the comfort of knowing that Arnold was true to his name and responsibilities, that he did his duty, and for that we must always honor him," the earl concluded, his eyes moist but his back straight as a lance. He embraced Ian in a somewhat shame-faced fashion and then turned to Harriet.

"We will care for you, Harriet, my dear. As Arnold's widow you have our utmost respect and support, you know," he offered, embarrassed at the show of emotion he had inadvertently been betrayed into exhibiting. Harriet, dry-eyed and sedate, did not appear to be as affected as the earl, but then she could not have regarded Arnold with any deep affection, considering his treatment of her.

But she surprised Ariel with the honesty and sincerity of her reaction. "I will not pretend that

Arnold and I were devoted, but I grieve for you, Father, in his passing, and I applaud his courage. You must not worry about me. I will come about and find comfort in the knowledge that he was a brave man."

Ariel was most impressed with her sister-in-law's calm demeanor and earnestness. Harriet had suffered much in her marriage but she did not intend to parade her relief, if that was what she felt, in view of the earl's unhappiness.

Harriet stood up. "Thank you for telling us of Arnold's end, Ian. If you will excuse me, I will go and lie down, for suddenly I feel most overcome," Harriet said with dignity.

"Let me accompany you, Harriet," Ariel offered, putting a comforting arm across her sister-in-law's shoulder and steering her toward the door.

"Thank you, Ariel, but I would prefer to be alone. Perhaps you can look in on me later, but right now I want no one," she answered, smiling slightly at Ariel but obviously determined to fight her problems out in solitude.

"Of course, my dear, if that is what you wish," Ariel agreed.

"The poor woman has more spine than I believed of her," the earl remarked as Ian closed the door behind her. Then turning to his son and Ariel, he frowned. "You understand, Ian, that Arnold's death has put new responsibilities on your shoulders. You are now the Viscount Montague, and as such my only heir. Do you not think you might resign from the army and take up your duty to the estate?" he asked somewhat hesitantly.

He paused and then continued under great stress, "I know in the past, my boy, I have not always been fair to you, and did not excuse your exploits as an excess of youthful spirits. I regret exceedingly our estrangement, and I hope now in the view of this tragedy we can mend our differences."

Ariel hoped that Ian would accept the olive branch the earl was extending. She felt for the old gentleman, so proud and stubborn an aristocrat, who was now realizing the fragility of life and trying to make amends for his mistakes. If only Ian would do the generous thing and let the past lie behind him with no recriminations. But he was equally stubborn and autocratic with the true Celt's inability to forget a slight.

However, Ian had either mellowed or conceded that his father was sincere in this effort at reconcilation. "I cannot resign from the army, Father, with the most important battle of our age looming before us in a matter of weeks. But I promise to take great care, mindful of my duty to the family," he said soberly, a cloud of emotion threatening to overset them all.

"Humph, well, I suppose I could expect no other answer, but remember, you have a duty to Ariel as well as your family, and take care, no rushing into foolhardy escapades or chasing glory in the cannon's mouth," the earl warned.

"Ariel will be going to Brussels with me next week, Governor, and you can be sure she is much more dangerous than any Frenchie. You can depend on her to keep me in line," he quipped, eager to avoid any more serious discussion. Then, realizing he could not leave his father without some expression of sympathy, he said, "I am sorry about Arnold, sir, and I will try to be a good son to you, not that I can make up for his loss."

"You'll do, my boy. You'll do. As for you, madam, see to it that you provide me with a clutch of grandchildren, and I will forgive you both any past transgressions." He took out his handkerchief from his sleeve, trumpeted a blast upon it, and turned away toward the door. Before leaving the room, he surprised Ariel by crossing to her and kissing her briefly on the cheek. "You are a good girl, you'll be the making of my scapegrace son," he growled, and made his departure before emotion could overwhelm him.

"That was kind of you, Ian, to tell your father that tale about Arnold's death, to spare him the shock and disgrace of the real story. But can you keep this whole affair a secret?" she asked.

Now that the excuse to keep up his defenses had passed, Ian sighed wearily, fatigue in every line of his body as he slumped down onto the settee next to her.

"I believe so. Valentine has agreed no good would come of revealing the truth. The government could not stand the scandal on the eve of meeting Napoleon. We will brush through right and tight, but it's been horrible, my own brother behaving in such a treacherous fashion. And even at the end so filled with invective and hatred toward me," Ian admitted, at a loss to understand this violent antipathy.

He then turned a ravaged face to Ariel and

blurted out, "But it was dreadful. I offered him the only honorable way out of his disgrace. And even so I had to persuade him to use the gun. Until the last he wanted, he begged me to let him go. And I could not trust him, could not leave him alone to do the deed in privacy, for he might have tried to escape. He was not only a traitor, but a coward, the shame of it!"

Ariel, deeply troubled by his sorrow and humiliation, laid a gentle hand on his arm, trying to get him to meet her compassionate gaze. "You did what you had to do, Ian, and you protected both your family and your country. Arnold was a sick man. Only a fatal flaw in his character could be responsible for his behavior, and you must not blame yourself for his evilness."

"Thank you, Ariel. That scene will haunt me always, I fear," he said somberly.

Hoping to take his mind off the horror he had experienced, Ariel asked, "What are your plans for Flossie? I have promised her an income to realize her shop in Wiltshire. Will this be possible, do you think?"

"Yes, we owe her a great deal. And will she keep silent about Arnold's real activities, do you think? How have you explained her presence here?" he asked, remembering that Mistress Baines was privy to the whole affair.

"I have just told Lufton she is a poor woman fallen on unfortunate times who needs our charity. And Flossie quite understands, and is as anxious as we are to keep the secret of Arnold's treachery. Without her we would possibly never have discovered the truth."

"Valentine will see to all the arrangements. And I believe that Father accepted my story and will come to grips with Arnold's death. Then there is Harriet." He sighed as if the burden of all these problems was too much.

"She will be fine. I believe she has already formed a tendre for an Oxford don, who has been much in her company. A much better man for her, and he seems to return her regard. In a year or so she will marry again, I am sure," Ariel offered brightly, hoping to lift Ian's spirits.

It seemed she was successful, for he roused himself from his dark mood to round upon her. "And let me tell you, Ariel, I am very angry with your total disregard of danger, rushing off to God knows where, trying to settle the whole business without any assistance. If it had not been for the men we had detailed to watch you, who knows what your fate would have been. Damn it, girl. Can you not leave these things to those who know how to manage them?" he railed at her, his unhappiness completely forgotten as he detailed his grievances.

For once Ariel did not flare in response to his accusations for she felt he had some right on his side. "It was stupid of me, Ian, but I had no time to tell you of Flossie's visit and the news of the documents, and I hesitated to accuse Arnold without proof. Then, too, Flossie assured me there was no danger of his arriving while I made my search. Normally he never came before teatime. Though it's true, I could not have managed without your timely rescue," she admitted, hoping to diffuse some of his anger.

"God, Ariel, when I learned you had walked heedlessly into danger, I almost lost my mind. I have been such a fool, jealous and unreasonable, but when I saw you facing Arnold with that pistol, I knew that if we came out of this affair, I would confess what I feel. I love you, girl, and although I know you have no reason to return my love, I hope you will give me the chance to prove what my love could mean." He looked down into her eyes with a wealth of passion.

"Oh, Ian, we have both been fools. I love you, too, and have been so afraid of telling you and—" But she could say no more for his lips came down on hers, shutting off any other remarks, and she surrendered to the fervency of his embrace, the drugging caresses which always robbed her of any ability to think but only to feel the overpowering emotion he evoked.

For long moments the only sound in the room were the contented murmurs of two lovers, united at last with misunderstandings and jealousies relegated to the past.

Finally, Ariel emerged from Ian's arms, smiling and trying to bring her pulses back to normal. "You must brood no longer about Arnold, Ian, and look to the future. As your father reminded you, my lord, you have heavy responsibilities." She spoke lightly, hoping to diffuse some of the emotion which threatened to overwhelm them.

"Chief among them, let me remind you, my lady, is getting an heir, if you remember," he agreed whimsically with a devilish gleam in his eye.

"You are indeed a scapegrace, sir, as your father warned me, but I fear I am an adventuress, so we are well matched." Ariel gave up any idea of subduing the outrageous actions of her husband, whose only answer to her feeble attempts to quell his roaming hands was to kiss her more thoroughly.

"If we are to fulfill father's wishes, we must put in a great deal of practice," he teased, and taking her by the hand, pushed her out of the room and toward the staircase.

"You have no consideration of the proprieties, sir," Ariel protested, but did not hang back.

"None at all. And neither have you. What else can you expect from an adventuress and a scapegrace," he said, determined to have the last word as they entered the bedroom and he locked the door behind them.